Also by Carlos Franqui
DIARY OF THE CUBAN REVOLUTION

Family Portrait with Fidel

FAMILY PORTRAIT *with* FIDEL

A Memoir

CARLOS FRANQUI

**Translated from the Spanish
by Alfred MacAdam**

RANDOM HOUSE **NEW YORK**

Library of Congress Cataloging in Publication Data
Franqui, Carlos, 1921–
Family portrait with Fidel.

Translation of: Retrato de familia con Fidel.
1. Cuba—History—1959–   . 2. Castro, Fidel,
1927–   —Personality. I. Title.
F1788.F686513   1984   972.91′064   83–42774
ISBN 0-394-53260-0

Manufactured in the United States of America
9 8 7 6 5 4 3 2

FOREWORD

PORTRAIT OF A TYRANT AS AN AGING TYRO
by G. Cabrera Infante

There are actually two portraits—or, rather, two versions of the same picture on the jacket * of *Family Portrait with Fidel*. Taken at the end of Batista's reign or just after the fall of that Cuban Humpty-Dumpty (he thought the Americans would pick him up again but not all his soldiers or all his policemen could keep him up there forever), the photo shows Carlos Franqui wearing a black, unkempt beard that instead of evoking the image of the Cuban *guerrillero* recalls what Robinson Crusoe must have looked like on his solitary island just after his rescue. But remember that if Robinson "was past running any more hazards," Crusoe "had a great mind to be upon the wing again."

In the second, *revised* print the photo has become a curious document: Fidel Castro is still, as usual, in the foreground, with the same, still anonymous man Friday with a mike facing him. But between the two men there is now a strange void, a blank space that is really the black hole of the totalitarian time: the eternal writing and rewriting the cloth of history on which a revisionist Penelope weaves the image of her constant (by night), inconstant (by day) Ulysses the crafty. But instead of taking the

* The original photograph showed Fidel Castro with Carlos Franqui and another man; Castro later had it doctored to eliminate Franqui. The book jacket juxtaposes these two versions with a third—to show Castro alone.

mick out of the group, they achieved just the opposite: the empty space in the photograph is Franqui who has disappeared from the picture but has left his shadow behind. By an unkind stroke he has been rubbed out from the history of revolutionary Cuba, from the revolution, from the future itself. Banished, one might say, from Marxist eternity. There's the rub. Such sleights of hand are not only possible but necessary in today's Cuban historiography. In other totalitarian countries in the past there were doctored photographs in which Trotsky appeared briefly alongside Lenin— from which Stalin had him banished forever, to Prinkipo and after. Goebbels had Ernst Roehm graphically purged from all photos with the Führer: had Hitler won the war he would have been standing (photographically) alone today like a solitary eagle where Roehm used to roam.

The first version of this curiously historic Cuban photograph (which would have been banal and therefore forgettable if it hadn't been turned into a true palimpsest: rubbed off for further use) was published in the too independent newspaper *Revolución*, more of a mouthpiece for rebels than a megaphone for the revolutionary government. It happened in 1962, when Carlos Franqui was editor in chief. The second, apparently definitive version, appeared in the official sheet *Granma*, a granny with big teeth under the shawl. It was 1973. In eleven years Franqui had gone from being a key man in the revolution, a leader who made and unmade ministers and one of the most widely known figures on the Cuban scene at home and abroad, to being a nonperson, a cipher, an invisible man in Castroite hagiography. Unquiet Franqui, a Peter made up to look like a small Judas, could not coexist with Fidel Castro, Maximum Messiah. Not even in an old photo. He was punished by erasure, not by firing squad, much in the way in science-fiction movies the hero's lieutenant (never, of course, Captain Quirt himself) is zapped into nothingness and beyond by a raygun. Whaam! *Sic transit rebellis*.

The same technique *Playboy* once used on excessively public pubic hair and too tender buttons, an airbrush with invisible ink, was used here. But why would anyone go to so much trouble to eliminate Franqui, quite frankly, when he just stays in the background taking nothing away from Castro's image? The English historian Hugh Thomas got to know Franqui personally rather well after he had shaved off his beard early in 1959 in Havana. Now in London, Thomas stared at the cover of this book for a good three minutes—and then asked me who the man was who had disappeared from the picture! I had to explain that it was Carlos Franqui with a beard. He had pulled a disappearing act that even the Great Houdini himself would have envied— and tried to copy. Lord Thomas did a historical double take. Both Fidel Castro and Franqui contributed to this successful revival (total in Cuba, partial abroad, like an eclipse) of *A Revolutionary Vanishes*. Franqui's book describes just how the *truco* was pulled off. As in many magic tricks, the explanation is better than the trick itself. (Ah, that's how it's done! Clever. I thought you always used mirrors.) If Fidel Castro is a Marxist Mandrake the Magician, Franqui is merely the man who lost his shadow in a picture. From an untouched Lothar, Mandrake's sidekick, he became for the love of Circe, the witch and bitch Revolution, a retouched Schlemihl, whose shadow was stolen by the red devil. But this invisible man, erased by totalitarian hands with a touch of the airbrush, has now produced a very visible book, a credible *wündersame Geschichte*. Like Chamisso, Franqui has been banished from his country. Unlike Chamisso, he is no aristocrat but a man of the humblest extraction.

Carlos Franqui is one of those rare cases of a revolutionary who decides (or is forced by political pressure) to become a writer. Franqui, a cunning man who was slow (or cautious) even about answering letters when he was in power, is now an author in his own write. The most eminent example of this metamorphosis of revolutionary into writer is, of course, Trotsky, and the comparison, if we set aside time, distance and Franqui's still untouched head, is not a bad one. But unlike Trotsky, Franqui joined the Cuban Communist Party without second thoughts when he was still very young. He was so young, in fact, that he must have been placed in the rank and file of the Communist Youth. He was so enthusiastic and eager and therefore useful to the cause that he was soon prompted to being a *cadre*. Poor from birth, a peasant who didn't even have the benefit of a nearby city or town, Franqui was what is called in Cuba a *guajiro macho*: a hick from the sticks. But as luck would have it, he was discovered when he was a mere boy by an extraordinary teacher, Melania Cobo, a well-educated black woman. With just one single stroke Franqui began his education and was spared the stupid prejudices that white peasants have against blacks in Cuba. Melania Cobo, who loved painting and music, stimulated Franqui's interest in the arts early in his life, nourishing alongside it his keen sense of social justice and his dabbling in politics. He was thus already highly developed politically when Fidel Castro was still an apprentice Jesuit in the most expensive religious schools in Santiago de Cuba and in Havana.

But if Franqui lived to become a Communist—or lived at all—it was because of his father's heroic tenacity. As a child Franqui almost died from a *cólico miserere*, as a ruptured appendix was called then. He survived only because his father, whom Franqui adored, carried him on horseback all the way to the nearest town and hospital, miles away from the family ranch. From that time on, with the same silent heroism as his father's, Franqui has continued to save his own spiritual self. He has put his life on the line time and time again because of his courage and his convictions. If he were to write about how he overcame all the obstacles he has had to face, in politics as in life, in and out of history, he would need yet another book—one his modesty forbids. In *Family Portrait with Fidel* he limits himself to his relationship with Castro, personal and political. But he never describes his last dangerous days on the island, his mind already made up to leave Cuba forever: how he managed to abandon ship with wife and family, closely watched by the sinister servicemen of the State Security, how he duped Raúl Castro and Ramiro Valdés, the Cuban Beria, and even Redbeard Piñeyro, head of the counterintelligence. Franqui says nothing of his ruses and his fear of never actually outwitting Castro or of his dramatic flight to Europe and his peripatetic exile in Italy, hounded by the same men he had named diplomatics in France and England.

As a matter of fact, Franqui doesn't even begin in the beginning: how he started out in Havana as a proofreader for the Communist newspaper *Hoy*, how he was soon promoted to copy reader and then elevated to the proofreader's heaven, the editorial board. But happiness is a word frequently misspelt. One day he had to stand in for a friend, a proofreader who was both a fanatical Communist and a movie fan. His former colleague wanted to attend a one-night stand of his favorite film. The time it takes to see a movie, those few precious hours of fun and fantasy colliding with ideological dogmatism became a clash of symbols that changed Franqui's life. A crucial typographical error appeared in an editorial which today is dogmatic nonsense prose but then seemed to state something borrowed, something true: the unthinkable such as "The triumph of Communism will never take place"—tautology in the place of ideology. The typo is the thing that will catch the tyrant with his political pants down. The truly funny thing is that this theological (or teleological) mistake was a clerical error: the fault of an elderly editor and not of an ill-intentioned or lazy proofreader. Franqui not only took the rap but he committed the crime of refusing to attend a self-criticism meeting: some sort of jam session by the party where they always promise jam not today but tomorrow. The fan who was a fanatic was fired from the newspaper but kept in the Party. As luck would have it, Franqui was fired from the paper and expelled from the Party and bitterly denounced everywhere for his contumacy or contumely or whatever. I happen to know all about it not only because I did know Franqui well then but also because my father wrote for the same newspaper. He, too, was an old Cuban Communist. Franqui was hunted then as he was to be later when he left Cuba in the late sixties. Aníbal Escalante (see under old Communists), the editor in chief of *Hoy* newspaper, told my father that Franqui, an enemy of the Party or of the people (whichever comes first), should not, I repeat, should not be given sanctuary in a Communist house. My mother, who could be a formidable fury, retorted: "Go tell Aníbal this is not a house but a room with no view. Or better still, tell him to come and tell *me*." Aníbal, who was no Hannibal, never dared cross my mother's Alps—or for short, cross her.

Left out in the ideological cold of the tropics and nowhere to live, Franqui sought refuge working on a magazine run by another journalist who had been expelled from *Hoy* and the Party. He was a man wounded in the Spanish Civil War (where he was sent by the Party when he was not yet eighteen) and now become a rabid anti-Communist. Franqui quickly realized that this Rolando Masferrer (who would be blown to bits in Miami years later, dying just as he had lived—dangerously) had devolved, almost without knowing it, from sworn anti-Communist to gangster to hired assassin: from Stalin to Prío to Batista. A double play and a double cross. Under Batista, Masferrer organized a gang of thugs called *tigres*, whose evil eyes burned holes in the body political day and night.

Franqui judiciously abandoned that precarious shelter and returned to indigence. Then he found work in another newspaper: a proofreader again, a galley slave. Soon thereafter, in the summer of 1947, he embarked on his first military venture—or was it adventure? He joined an action group whose purpose was to bring down General Trujillo, the dictator of the neighboring Dominican Republic. Two sworn enemies also participated in that military mission: Masferrer and Fidel Castro. At the time Castro was a prominent member of another Havana gang of daring shootists, the UIR, rivals of the MSR, run by Masferrer—all under cover of the word "revolution": that's what the twin Rs stood for. This wouldn't be the only time Franqui and Fidel Castro would be together in an antityrant battle. But it would be the last time Masferrer would accompany them. Soon Franqui and Castro would be in another group, the 26 July Movement, attacking yet another dictator who seemed to be forever in power in Cuba. Fulgencio Batista was back on his throne of blood again. Masferrer would eventually become one of Batista's cruelest *sbirri*. Once more, Cuba, the Pearl of the West Indies, was in for a dip in the deep gulf of extremes.

The only reason Franqui did not take part in the 26 July 1953 assault on the Moncada barracks in Santiago, led by Fidel Castro, was that he had no idea it was to take place. He didn't know because he was then a militant in a different anti-Batista group and they all operated like watertight compartments. However, on reading Castro's speech to his judges during his trial (*History Will Absolve Me*, a *samizdat* document we now know to have been written by somebody else: Castro's university professor Dr. Jorge Manach, then an undercover anti-Batistiano), Franqui realized that his political die had been tossed, although the cast of the die would not abolish the tyrant's fortune or men's ideas. Franqui and Fidel Castro frequently wrote to each other during the two years Castro was in jail. When Castro was paroled in 1955 there was Franqui waiting for him, apparently a journalist sent by the magazine *Carteles*, but in fact a supporter of Fidel, as Franqui always called him. During Castro's imprisonment, Franqui was appointed national head of propaganda for the 26 July Movement and was founder of the underground newspaper *Revolución*. Suddenly he was arrested by Batista's political police, tortured, threatened with murder and finally jailed. But his head wouldn't roll. Like Castro, he was freed very soon. Batista turned out to be only a part-time tyrant—the rest of the time he was too busy being a thief and a canasta player.

Franqui went directly into exile, first to Mexico, then to New York. Later he flew on to the Sierra Maestra, where Fidel Castro was learning how to be a guerrilla chief. In the Sierra (a geographic term that became then an almost theological definition: the Sierra was where the good guys went, the heaven of marksmen and Marxists) Franqui built Radio Rebelde from scratch. During the guerrilla war against Batista, Radio Rebelde had the same function as the BBC had during the war against Hitler: it broadcast not only the partisan truth but instructions for direct political action, such as sabotage and terrorism. Franqui permitted that the voice of Fidel Castro could be heard for the first time all over Cuba. Castro sounded truthful, modest and hopeful, not at all the herald of Armageddon he later became.

When Batista fled in the still of the morning on 1st January 1959 and his fearful followers scattered out of the country, Franqui returned to Havana for the first time since his imprisonment in 1957—quite ahead of Castro's chaotic stampede on the capital. Franqui immediately started publishing *Revolución* aboveground and it soon became a leviathan, both in Jonas's and Hobbes's sense. This was Franqui's heyday. Soon afterward his fortunes began slowly to decline: from those of a politician in Castro's grace to those of a man who fell from grace with God into a sea of troubles. Like all good ships, *Revolución* the newspaper sank with him.

Franqui, we must remember, is a journalist first and foremost, so his book is interspersed with scoops—some quite sensational. The most scandalous was picked up by the international press agencies and printed by *Time* magazine. But it's worth repeating. It goes like this. During the October crisis Fidel Castro, on a visit to a supposedly secret, Russian-manned missile base on the western end of the island, innocently asks a bilingual technician (all Russians speak with forked tongue) to show him the button that fires the rockets. The Russian complies. The Russian also shows Comrade Castro a radar screen which at that very moment is tracking an American reconnaissance plane on a routine flight over Cuba. "Is that an American spy plane?" asks Castro. *Da da*! Suddenly the Prime Minister presses the button. Swoosh! He didn't even have to aim: that was handled by computer. In any case, Castro has always had more faith in the trigger than in the bullet. The Russians, aghast, can only watch as their missile rises on the green, ghostly oscilloscope of the radar to collide with the moving spook. One second later the two shadows disappear from the screen with a flash.

American planes had been flying these Cuban routes with schedules as regular as those of commercial airlines since 1961—and not even the Russians were paying them any attention. But Fidel

Castro, wanting war, courting conflagration, and wishing apocalypse now or never, dared to shoot down an unarmed U-2. All this was very shocking to the Russians, veterans of the Cold War and old hands at escalation and de-escalation games. The result was that the only casualty of the undeclared missile war of October 1962, that poker for world powers, was caused by a chief of state posing as a trigger-happy gunner. More than a Marxian war was a Cuban Buzz Sawyer introducing his sidekick Roscoe Sweeney! But to accomplish his feat Fidel Castro had to use the sophisticated weaponry of the Soviet Union. For years Russian politicians (Brezhnev more seriously than Khrushchev) had considered this exotic and picturesque Third World leader a potentially dangerous man. Now they knew he was an actively dangerous man. That tardy conclusion cost Khrushchev his insolent office and his delightful dacha. Brezhnev inherited the hot air.

But more significant for the historians who know Cuba well is to find out in Franqui's book that the real strategist for the Cuban troops at the Bay of Pigs was not Fidel Castro, the commander in chief, as he was always called in Cuba and elsewhere, but an enigmatic general Ciutah. Like Lieutenant Kije, he was an invisible Russian soldier. Now we know that F. Ciutah was a true general in the Red Army, even though he was a Spaniard and a veteran of the Spanish Civil War as the last Loyalist commander in the Basque country. A tough military man, he ended up in Stalin's Russia, where he fought the Germans. General Ciutah was a confirmed Stalinist and loyal to the Russians even from his days as a general with the Spanish Republic. The Russian high command chose him to plot the strategy to defend Castro against the CIA landing. General Ciutah came secretly to Cuba under the alias of Angel Martínez—but he was no angel. The war plans were top secret, of course, but the KGB was in possession of the American landing maps months before the CIA invasion took place. It was a double cross for the doubly credulous.

The Cuban commander in chief, even before he had declared himself a socialist for life, was already just another pawn in the Soviet global strategy, a charade more than a chess game. From a literary point of view (the only view of things that interests me) it's like learning that Tolstoy's hero General Kutuzov never commanded the Russian army at Borodino. In fact, an unknown English marshal under a Muscovite pseudonym secretly gave all the orders! The historians—even Hugh Thomas, the European who knows most about Cuba—had to revise their thinking and correct their textbooks. The truth is that Fidel Castro's real genius lies in the arts of deception and while the world plays bridge by the book, he plays poker, bluffing and holding his cards close to his olive green chest. He has practiced and mastered the dealer's art from the beginning, actually even before the beginning. His true master is Machiavelli, in that he sees history as the manipulator who uses it as an instrument to control men, and politics as a way of masking truth and reaching power. Machiavelli was a playwright, Castro is an actor playing Macbeth every night. But he is Macbeth with a vengeance: he strives for a bigger kingdom, and the world is his stage. As a grand deceiver he is really extraordinary. But even more astonishing is the capacity of all concerned, both yesterday and today, close to him, as Franqui was, never really close, as I was, to let themselves be fooled willingly and cry out "Long live Fidel!"—at least part of the way.

In his book Franqui commits a sin all of us who worked on *Revolución* committed at the time. Whenever we learned of a new arbitrary decree or of another injustice in the name of justice or some other political crime (and even murder) committed by the regime, we would always say "Fidel probably doesn't even *know* about it," or "This is Raúl's doing," or "That's one of Che's Argentine tricks," or "It's Ramiro Valdés's fault—he is the Minister of the Interior, isn't he?" (Did any of us dare to think that Ramiro Valdés had been named head of the political police by Fidel Castro himself?) These were variations on a theme by Koestler titled "Refusal to Believe in Atrocities." Or our own unwillingness to think of our saints as sinners. Albert Speer repeats the pattern often in speaking about Hitler, and the same applies to Stalin's tales of horrors as told by Khrushchev. The guilty parties are always different, but the innocent is always one: Hitler, Stalin, Castro. Wolves in wool pulled over all eyes.

Franqui still finds himself in the same old ideological trap and almost shouts out now: "It cannot be possible that Fidel was like that!" He doesn't excuse that tyrant or put the blame only on his agents. Mephistopheles isn't the devil, Lucifer is. Satan, says the Book of Revelation, is the deceiver of the whole world. The devil's disciple is just one more damned soul: Raúl and the others are either stooges or stoolies. Franqui in the last analysis is a humanist: he believes in man. He refuses to reckon that others, Sartre's hell, are evil and that human beings, given the chance, will behave atrociously: man is intrinsically bad. This is of course heresy for both Communists and Christians. It is not that power corrupts historically and that absolute power corrupts absolutely, as Lord Acton decently warned us. It is that man is already corrupt the minute he is born, for all his associations are power relationships: in sex, the family, and society. Moreover, man is, in genetic rather than racial or social terms, a sick animal who knows he is going to die today, tomorrow, eventually anyway. He is avaricious, vain, and lusting for power always, everywhere. After such knowledge, what forfeiting? All that inner, innate perversity creates his thirst for posterity (and its instant form, success), for immortality and, in political terms, his hunger for history. Man is the only animal on the vast desert of eternity who believes that political mirages are for real, that history is an oasis, that true hell can somehow become imaginary heaven.

With this book Franqui sails in the stream of personal confessions as negotiated by Rousseau more than swam across by Saint Augustine. I'm thinking of the political vessels of Trotsky, Milovan Djilas, the early Koestler, and even Jorge Semprún now. But politics and journalism tend to fade: that's their fate. Despite Dante's feuds, poetry is what remains: Gobelins are more pertinent today than glib Ghibelines, and Guelphs are just a joke. History, too, is unimportant. Here it doesn't even count, because Franqui offers the opposite of a history book, which perforce describes change. The book is titled a *Portrait* and a portrait is the most obvious form of stasis. Nothing moves in a portrait, be it a photo or a painting: it doesn't even have a *discorso proprio*, as Leonardo saw five hundred years ago. "*Eppur si muove*," said the man who recanted: it is a written portrait and writing moves precisely because language *is* movement. Leonardo and Galileo are pertinent here because Franqui is an exile in Italy.

Lezama Lima in his Dantesque paradise would approve of Franqui's change of heart. "Cuba is frustrated in its political essence," was one of Lezama's favorite sentences and one that Franqui repeats again and again in his book: "Cuba is frustrated in what's politically essential." Or perhaps "Cuba is frustrated in what's essentially political." What Lezama implied in any case was that the poet's sole realm was that of poetry. The usurpers (usurper is one of the possible translations for tyrant) were the others, those political leaders who were (and are) merely bad jugglers whose oranges always end up on the floor. But Cuba is also frustrated in its historical essence, as Franqui lucidly dares to point out. Nevertheless, I think that Cuba has managed to express itself in a distinctive prose (as opposed to that of Spanish or South American writings) even *before* being a nation. Martí, Lezama, Virgilio Piñera, Lydia Cabrera, Carpentier (*et tu*, Alejo), Lino Novás Calvo, Severo Sarduy, Reinaldo Arenas, and now Franqui invent our literature with each new book from the nineteenth century to today. That Cuban invention tries to be a poetic perpetual motion of the first kind in prose. Finally, *Family Portrait with Fidel* is not a testimony: it is the testy matrimony of tender time and horrible history.

This necessary book will be attacked (it already has been in Spanish) with clamor or with silence: such are the forms of fanatical fury. It will be assaulted in concentric Cuban circles and in that central circle that is the Miami of all exiles: remember that Franqui is a revolutionary of the first water who never lets up. A brushing aside in writing can work as well as the retoucher's airbrush. Some people will try to dismiss Franqui because he writes as a poet and not as your run-of-the-mill political agent, or the embittered journalist, or a professional *exiliado*—but as a joyful peasant poet. One of those foreseeable attacks, one I have already heard, is directed against Franqui's style: against that form of writing of his which is an idiosyncratic way of speaking about whose originality I cannot say enough. It has been claimed, and not by a buffoon but by Buffon, that the style is the man. I could even go further to say that style in Franqui is history. History, as we all know, is nothing but a book called *History*. Historic justice, as in this book, should be called, then, poetic justice.

CONTENTS

2

3

4

5

6

APPENDIX

1

FROM PALMA TO SANTIAGO
(1959)

The Sierra fades in the darkness. A sudden glare reveals the city: Santiago de Cuba. Night falls as we, the barbudos, come down from the mountains looking like the saints of old. People rush out meet us. They are wild; they touch us, kiss our filthy beards. Batista fled at dawn on January 1. Nineteen fifty-nine was off to a good start. Rebel Santiago was free at last after seven years of tyranny. This was a real New Year's party, and a charge of collective joy ran through the rebels. One of them, though, felt nostalgic, as if he had left the one thing that mattered most to him back in the Sierra: Fidel Castro.

It may be that peace is more frightening to a fighting man than war. But at that moment we all had so many things on our minds: our dead, our families, the immediate future. But all serious thoughts went right out of our heads in Santiago. I watched as my comrades enjoyed their first plunge into the crowds, and when someone kissed my beard, I recoiled because it seemed like reverse profanation. I was being treated like a hero, although the only heroism I take seriously is collective heroism. In Santiago, thousands of young people had been tortured and murdered. The underground rebels fought Batista almost without weapons, putting their lives on the line every day. They had lost many more fighters than we did in the Sierra. Out there we did have arms, and we had the protection of nature as well. Those underground years in the city were a world of crime and horror, an anonymous struggle that swept Cubans into the anti-Batista resistance. The

Sierra gave us a sensation of freedom and victory no one could feel down in the city. Up there it was like a revolutionary vacation. But now we were the heroes instead of the city fighters. So, despite all the joy, I felt a shadow falling over us, a danger. Even my beard, which set me apart from everyone else, began to seem strange to me. I kept asking myself just what this revolution was. No matter: a new era had begun with the new year.

The 26 July Movement was a state of mind, amorphous and undefined. The people understood it in terms of entities and individuals: the Sierra, the cities, revolutionary unions, militia groups; sabotage, exile, the rebel army, Radio Rebelde, *Revolución*, the invading columns, Santiago, Havana; Che (Ernesto Guevara), Camilo Cienfuegos, Huber Matos, Juan Almeida, Efigenio Amejeiras, Celia Sánchez, Haydée Santamaría, Raúl Castro, Aníbal Escalante, Manuel Fajardo, Universo Sánchez, Faustino Pérez, Armando Hart, David Salvador Manso, Aldo Vera, Vilma Espín, Manuel Urrutia, Crescencio Pérez, Raúl Chibás, Enrique Oltuski, Manuel Ray, and the creator, comandante, and maximum hero, Fidel Castro.

But there had been another dimension to the struggle against Batista. The Directorio Revolucionario had played a decisive role in Havana after the Escambray Mountains front had been opened (1958) and after the war in central Cuba was started. The Directorio was alongside Che in the lightning campaign of Las Villas (autumn 1958). Led by Faure Chomón and Rolando Cubelas, it was the revolution's second force and derived its strength from the university students in Havana. The best men in the Directorio lost their lives in the struggle: José Antonio Echevarría, a magnetic anti-imperialist and Christian leader, died in the March 13, 1957, attack on Batista in the National Palace, and Frank País, yet another important Directorio leader, was shot down by Batista's police on July 30, 1958.

The 26 July Movement derived from an earlier political faction, the Ortodoxia (officially, the Partido del Pueblo Cubano), which was transformed under the leadership of Raúl Chibás, Fidel, and Abel Santamaría. The Communists, always well organized, had to pay for their historical short-sightedness, for having been pro-Batista and pro–Soviet Union. They had opposed the underground struggle, Moncada, and the Sierra. Their motto was "Unity and Class Struggle," but they were blind to the war the Cuban people were fighting right under their noses. So Carlos Rafael Rodríguez's short beard didn't bring much glory to the Communist party when he turned up in the Sierra at the very last minute. "Carlos Rafael appeared and Batista disappeared" was the joke you heard everywhere. In fact, Carlos Rafael hadn't been very popular since the day his picture appeared in the newspapers next to Batista's when he was one of Batista's ministers.

The old guard, the bourgeoisie, the politicos, the Church, the army, the honorable United States embassy, and the State Department—the whole pack—out of cynicism, blindness, and sheer bungling, eliminated themselves as factors in the new political situation. Out of pride and a totally unfounded superiority complex, they thought they could solve the Batista problem with a classic eleventh-hour coup—this one to be directed by General Cantillo. That blunder consolidated our victory.

The progressive elements of the bourgeoisie, the lower middle classes, always a powerful force in Cuba, saw in Fidel one of their own. They supported him. But what would the new politics be? We all had to look toward Fidel Castro and his rebel army, a combination of populism, liberating militarism, and old-fashioned caudillismo. I kept wondering what Fidel was thinking. No one knew, and all he ever said was, "We are going to make the revolution. The revolution that never came about in 1898 or 1933. This time we're going to make it come true." Revolution and Fidel Castro became one and the same thing in those words, his first public statement in Santiago. His style has never really changed. He never calls meetings to discuss what is to be done or even to find out what is being done. He improvises and never shares power. At most he would spare us a few words as he walked down a crowded hall or as he sat in his jeep. Fidel kept moving, only communicating with us when he was surrounded by crowds.

FIDEL PREPARES HIS MARCH ON HAVANA

For a week after Batista's departure, Fidel toured the island, from one end to the other—a nonstop round of speeches, press conferences, and crowds. Fidel retook in his own name the barracks attacked and seized by the 26 July Movement. His entrance into Havana was to be an apotheosis. But in the meantime there was the matter of the government. He never told us what he was thinking, but he didn't have to because he knew that he was the power and that any government was, therefore, meaningless. He would say to me, "You take care of this government business with Faustino Pérez and the others. Take it up with Urrutia. But keep it all quiet. I'll name ministers of education, agriculture, public works, and public affairs. Leave defense for one of Raúl's men. We'll get together before I leave." Then he would hop into his jeep for a spin around still-celebrating Santiago.

General Cantillo's famous coup never took place. The unanimous general strike of January 2 expressed the will of the people. The army capitulated, and the 26 July Movement took control of the streets and army barracks. General Cantillo was succeeded by Colonel Ramón Barquín, who flew from Havana to the Campamento Columbia military base just after his release from the Isla de Pinos prison. Barquín had prestige: he and his group of "incorruptibles" had been in jail since 1956. Before contacting us, however, he appointed new military and police commanders who obeyed only him. His background was a problem: a career officer, military attaché in Washington, educated in the United States. His arrival helped finish off Cantillo, but ensconced at the Columbia base, he himself became a threat.

Armando Hart of the 26 July Movement had also been a prisoner on Isla de Pinos, and he committed the error of flying to Columbia with Barquín. Later he justified his action by saying it was his right as a leader of the 26 July Movement. Barquín, Hart, and many others thought power was still in Havana, but Havana was no longer the head of the nation. Power was out in the streets in Oriente Province: Fidel was power.

In his first major speech on the night of January 1–2, Fidel made that quite clear by proclaiming Santiago the new capital of Cuba. Then he ordered rebel columns to occupy cities and barracks. The underground militia groups, wearing red-and-black armbands, had already taken over—with the support of the people—police stations and barracks, public buildings, the press, the Confederación de Trabajadores de Cuba (CTC; Confederation of Cuban Workers), banks, and other institutions. They had kept order by not allowing looting or revenge, but suddenly they were no longer recognized. The 26 July Movement disappeared as if by magic. Fidel, the rebel army, and its comandantes became the new power. The Directorio Revolucionario also disappeared, as did the splinter group the Second Front of the Escambray. And Che, who had finished off the brilliant campaign of Las Villas with the capture of Santa Clara, Che, the second most important man in the revolution, the man closest to Havana physically, was not ordered to seize the nearby Columbia base. Why?

Even though the Directorio had fought alongside Che in the interior, they were prohibited—by order of Fidel himself—from accompanying Che and Camilo. Why? Chomón and Cubelas, comandantes in the Directorio, were excluded from any further participation in military operations. All they could do was to occupy, as a symbolic gesture, the university and the National Palace. Later that occupation was declared illegal. Camilo Cienfuegos, Che's second-in-command in Las Villas, one hundred kilometers behind, was ordered to the Columbia base, while Che was sent to La Cabana, a place of no importance. Things were happening so fast there was no time to think about them.

I like to think things over on my feet, so despite the racket in Santiago I held a question-and-answer session with the sidewalks: Let's see. Fidel wants to take Havana by himself. Because things have happened so quickly, he hasn't had much success on the military side of things. His big finale, the battle for Santiago, which he had been preparing for months, never took place. There he was, sulking and silent, with Che the hero of the interior and Raúl taking the northern section of Oriente. Then came the general strike and the 26 July people were out in the streets. Fidel reacted quickly: Santiago was now the capital. Fidel marched on Havana. Power never eluded him, and he always managed not to share it.

At midnight, Fidel took the Columbia base by radio. Over CMKC, Fidel announced to the Columbia staff: "If Hart wants to talk to me, he'd better get out of there." Then he turned the microphone over to me, saying: "Barquín can talk to you." I told Barquín that the order was to hand Columbia over to the rebel columns under Camilo and Che as soon as they got there. The angry colonel said he would be happy to turn the base over to Hart right there and then. But Hart was upset at Fidel's tone and in no mood for jokes: he left the base on the run. There was lots of confusion: at Santiago University the students razzed Colonel Aza, appointed chief of police by Raúl Castro and shot three days later. Urrutia, ignorant of what was going on, protested. He was out of touch with reality and wanted to maintain two armies at the same time—the old, regular army and the rebel army. He also didn't want to name Fidel his delegate because Fidel, in a fit of legalistic punctiliousness, asked President Urrutia for a legal document that would allow him to name provisional ministers on the road to Havana.

Fidel began his career as a statesman by botching things up. He named a bunch of mayors who all promptly began to squabble. Raúl Chibás was right when he said that Fidel really wanted to appoint a president. But no one could be president with Fidel around. Or even minister, for that matter. Nothing. I had serious doubts, but no time to think. I was doing well with Radio Rebelde, the voice of the revolution. It was at Radio Rebelde that we first heard that Batista had run out; so, with Fidel still in the field, it fell to me to give the standing orders—general strike, advance of all rebel columns and militia groups, rejection of Cantillo's coup. All of which Fidel ratified in his proclamation. So naturally he told me *I* should become Minister of Labor—because *I* understood how *he* thought! Actually, he knew how I thought, but neither I nor anyone else knew Fidel's real ideas. I answered him with a joke, saying that if being Minister of Labor meant bringing socialism to the factories and putting the workers in charge, he could count on me. He looked me up and down and repeated the offer. I could see he was serious; I told him I had no labor-management credentials and couldn't take the job. So he offered me Finance, the job Raúl Chibás had turned down. He seemed to be trying to pull a fast one but got mad when I told him I knew nothing about finance. "Around here it looks like nobody knows anything." (He was right about that.) So he told me to do whatever I wanted and to figure things out with Urrutia, because he (Fidel) couldn't "stand around waiting for a new government to be named." Which meant that he didn't want either to be responsible for or to endorse a new government.

So I tried out my own game on him. I told him I wanted to start a revolution in Cuban culture. I had lots of friends and contacts in Europe and Latin America—artists, writers, scientists, philosophers, film makers—and I wanted to open up the island to them. We could get all kinds of support to help us launch our own cultural revival. We could change Cuban life through culture. Fidel's reaction: "No, no, no. Franqui, you're crazy. Anything but that." Totally disgusted, he jumped back into his jeep saying, "See you in Havana." So I started walking the streets in Santiago as I did when I went to meet Frank País to discuss programs Fidel never read. I knew I was screwed, but what could I do?

This was my second time around with the same problem: to fight Batista I had to accept Fidel. Or did I? What was I supposed to do now, pick up and leave? Did I fight just to lose? Maybe José Lezama Lima was right when he told me, "This is a nation whose political essence has miscarried." Shit. I was a rebel, and that was that.

Over the course of the struggle I had created two important institutions: Radio Rebelde and the newspaper *Revolución*. Even though logic told me it was time to quit, I just wouldn't give in. I had been fighting since I was a kid. My father, a worker, died in poverty and misery. My great uncle, a *mambí*, a nineteenth-century guerrilla fighter against the Spanish, was butchered by the rural police. I know how the blacks in my country have lived. I fought as a journalist against capitalists and Communists. It could be that I wanted to show myself that I really was worth something. I saw my own ambiguity and my own contradictions, but even today do I really know why I do things? No.

Off I went, then, to take part in naming the first radical government in Cuban history. I pushed for those I thought best in Urrutia's first government. I created a Ministry for the Recovery of Stolen Property and saw Faustino Pérez, the man who best represented the underground struggle, named minister. The city of Santiago greeted both minister and ministry with an ovation. I named Raúl Cepero Bonilla, a brilliant sugar economist and enemy of Julio Lobo, a sugar magnate, Minister of Domestic Commerce. I installed Regino Boti, coauthor of the 26 July Movement's economic program in Economy. The engineer Enrique Oltuski, who had been head of the 26 July Movement's Civic Resistance organization in Havana, went to Communications. Manuel Fernández, an old supporter of Antonio Guiteras, became Minister of Labor. I assumed Labor would be a crucial spot in the forthcoming union struggles with the Communists. A few days later I grabbed—right out of the hands of the U.S. journalist Jules Dubois—the text by Fidel in which he ended the general strike. I added the name of the union leader David Salvador to it; he had just gotten out of jail, and Fidel had somehow forgotten him.

As for me, I decided to be in and out at the same time. I accepted Fidel but kept my distance. I gave up Radio Rebelde and worked full time on *Revolución*. A newspaper is a good vehicle for fights, and since Fidel had looked askance at culture, I had to become a cultural guerrilla fighter. I said nothing but told Euclides Vásquez Candela to bring out the first number of *Revolución* in Santiago on January 2. That same night Raúl Castro seized the newspaper plant we were using and put his own man (Causse) in where I had put Euclides. The fight had begun, but the knockout punches would come later in Havana.

I flew to the Columbia base. At a stopover in Holguín, I ran
into Fidel's caravan, besieged as usual by photographers and reporters. The crowds were gigantic, and Fidel was bursting with
pure joy. Off to one side, waiting, were Raúl Chibás, symbol of
the Ortodoxia, which had lent its prestige to the 26 July Movement, and Herbert Matthews, the famous reporter of the New
York *Times*, the first man to interview Fidel in the Sierra, the
man who made the guerrilla war famous. Jules Dubois, the influen-
tial columnist of the *Chicago Tribune*, a powerful man in
Washington, so completely monopolized Fidel's time you would
have thought they were lifelong buddies. Chibás and Matthews
looked like wallflowers, so I went to keep them company. The
atmosphere around Fidel had begun to change: courtiers and ups-
tarts were pushing their way to the center of all power. Some
of my old press colleagues from Havana, lackeys of the old regime,
mocked me to my face. I had the last laugh when I told them
Revolución was going to publish the names of all the journalists
on Batista's secret payroll.

Columbia was a sight: there were thousands of regular army
officers who came to attention and saluted whenever a barbudo
like me came by—the same base, the same soldiers who had
punched and kicked us and shouted "Fresh meat!" when they
brought us in. They would set up a gauntlet line and make all
prisoners run through, hitting them from both sides. Arrogant
when they were on top, they were ludicrous in their humility in
defeat. Camilo was amused, but Che was worried. Chomón and
Cubelas had refused to surrender the palace. Che understood the
Directorio's mood; after all, it was they who had been with him
at Santa Clara. In fact, Cubelas was wounded there. Now Fidel
refused to let them enter Havana with the rebel forces. Camilo
laughed and suggested firing a couple of shells at the palace. I
said that the building was so ugly it would be better to keep
the government out in the streets. Che scolded us, saying that
these were serious matters, that we weren't in the Sierra any more,
and that the people were watching us. He was right. (It was
Che who later told me that Fidel had ordered the Directorio's

troops not to enter Havana with himself and Camilo. At the time I didn't know—just one more thing that happened in front of me without my knowing anything about it.)

From Columbia I went on to Carlos III. There, in the offices and plant of *Alerta*, we would bring out *Revolución*. Some people criticized me for absenting myself from Fidel's caravan, for not riding in the famous "jeep of the comandantes" on January 8 in Havana. Some naïve comrade was probably thinking that if I were near Fidel I could influence him and protect him from "bad influences." "Fidel listens to people." Sure, when he wants or has to. Other people would say that Fidel listened to me because of the way things worked out in Urrutia's government. I laughed, because they just didn't know Fidel. I told them Fidel was just not interested in the government and that he simply didn't want to take responsibility for it. He did, however, appoint some important ministers: in Agriculture, Humberto Sorí Marín, our enemy; in Finance, Luis Orlando; in Education, Armando Hart (by the process of elimination, because neither Celia Sánchez nor Haydée Santamaría accepted); in Public Works, Manuel Ray, because Fidel liked him and thought he could do the job. And his old teacher Miró Cardona he named prime minister.

Someone said he was neutralizing Urrutia by appointing a brilliant man. I was baffled. José Miró Cardona was the dean of lawyers, a State Department man, the secretary of the Civic Front, a conservative. And what a résumé! Defense lawyer for ex-President Ramón Grau when Grau was accused of stealing a fortune; defense lawyer for Colonel Casillas, murderer of the Communist sugar workers' leader Jesús Menéndez (Casillas, by the way, was shot at Santa Clara). Later on we saw that the Miró appointment was a masterpiece of intelligence and cynicism. Fidel once again managed to confuse the politicos, the bourgeoisie, and the Americans. The appointment was a fiction that lasted forty-five days. Here was Fidel's pragmatism in all its glory: to appoint this lawyer for thieves and murderers was nothing but an insult.

Fidel's entrance into Havana really was an apotheosis. From the balcony of the palace he asked the multitudes to open a path:

"The people are my bodyguard." And like Moses parting the waters, he crossed the sea of people that ran from Misiones Avenue to the bay, a hero out of Greek mythology and a collective orgasm. As for the sinister Columbia base, it would become a school and Fidel its first schoolmaster. In his first meeting in the Columbia barracks with Camilo—who looked like a combination of Christ and a rumba dancer—on his left and the Christian dove on his right, Fidel said great things. "Camilo, I'm on the right track." "Fidel, you are on the right track." Then came the "Who Needs Guns?" speech, disarming in more ways than one. Applause and delirium: FIDELFIDELFIDELFIDELFIDELFIDELFIDEL! The dove landed on Fidel's shoulder, and it was as if God himself had singled Fidel out as the man of the hour. Some jokers later said the dove was the first to see through Fidel and the first to shit on him.

BEARDS

Beards were the symbols of the revolution. How many barbudos were there? Perhaps two thousand. But Fidel was fond of biblical parables and always spoke of the Twelve. The mythic number he always used when he appeared on television does have something of the epic quality of the American Wild West to it and, of course, of the Bible. Twelve men and a Christ-Fidel who had gone out into the wilderness had freed us from the evil of tyranny. Twelve barbudos and the good hero, coming down from the Sierra, were offering us salvation. By magic, the clandestine forces, the 26 July Movement, the strikes, the taking of Cienfuegos, the assault on the National Palace, Frank País, José Antonio Echevarría, the guerrilla fronts, sabotage, the Santiago fighters—all of it disappears. The Directorio, unjustly accused of seizing arms in San

Antoní, is presented as an ambitious group attempting to divide the revolution. It is liquidated. The people, the true protagonists of the victory, are obliged to thank the heroes because they are now free.

I couldn't help thinking that the struggle and the war were carried on and won because of the truth. But power is made out of lies. Why when we were weak did we use the truth and now that we were strong did we lie? Was it a function of becoming gods on earth, of pride, of caudillismo, or was it something else? It was good old paternal power, over and against the power of the people. Fidel had become the Trinity in one person: the 26 July Movement, with its red-and-black colors, the olive-green of the rebel army, and, of course, himself. And like God he was everywhere. "In the beginning was the Word." So Fidel set out giving speeches and carrying on conversations that lasted six or seven hours. We lived on television, on words, and on hopes.

Razor sales plummeted and new beards sprouted everywhere. I just didn't like looking like the statue of a saint. Out in the Sierra I had made it clear that I would always be a civilian, a member of the directorate of the 26 July Movement. I'm just not a military man. Besides, even if I don't mind danger, I can't stand uniforms, discipline, and rank. And a magazine editor should be neither a military man nor a barbudo. So I cut off my beard and got a haircut. I wasn't the first—maybe the second—but there were few who shaved. Camilo made fun of me because he had to write me out a pass. I could no longer simply walk into places as I did wearing a beard.

I ran into Fidel in the National Palace, and when he saw me he exploded: "How could you cut off your beard?"

"The barber did it for me."

"You can't do it. It's the symbol of the revolution. It doesn't belong to you. It belongs to the revolution."

"It was so hot; besides, my kid didn't recognize me, and I don't like making love with a beard. Don't forget, I'm a civilian, not a military man."

"I just don't see how you could cut off your beard. What a mule you are! I just don't get it."

"Look, Fidel, the whiskers were mine, weren't they?"

"No. No. Nobody's allowed to shave around here."

"I'll tell the future for you: someday there will only be one set of whiskers around here—yours. Like to bet on it?"

Fidel cut me off by skulking into the presidential office. Faustino Pérez, Minister for the Recovery of Stolen Property, also cut off his blond beard. He didn't want to be confused with the man they called Barbaroja, Comandante Manuel Piñeyro, who was setting the foundation of his own legend (in Raúl Castro style) by executing people by his own command out in Oriente Province.

Very few shaved, so Fidel really had nothing to worry about. The problems began with the young beards in Havana. Beards were the fashion. And there were thousands of jokes about beards, like this one: One day a beardless man gets on a bus. The conductor comes to take his fare, but the man refuses to pay because he is a barbudo. (Barbudos didn't have to pay to get into movies or to ride buses because they had no salaries.) "So where's your beard?" asks the driver. "Secret service," answers the guy, giving the driver the finger, to the joy of the other passengers.

REVOLUCIÓN

It seemed to me that the only way to fight, to influence things, was through the newspaper. To be at a distance and yet to be inside. I knew that the paper would be the way to keep track of the phenomenon Fidel, who was a real phenomenon of popularity because he was the revolution. The hard thing would be to keep a certain balance, which would mean saying yes to Fidel and no to many other things. I wanted to keep the people informed because everything depended on the people. They thought I would continue with Radio Rebelde, which was just behind Fidel in popularity. But war is one thing and peace is another, and since nothing was ever discussed, I decided by myself to take on *Revolución*. When Fidel came to Havana he went to another publication, *Bohemia*, where he was photographed with his old friends Miguel Quevedo and Enrique de la Osa, but he stayed away from *Revolución*. He was not pleased that I was bringing it out, so he wouldn't give it his seal of approval. There were a few dirty tricks played on us by Raúl and the Communists, but no one had the nerve to cut me out of the newspaper I had created as a clandestine weapon of the revolution. So they mocked me, calling *Revolución* a worthless rag—which was okay with me, because it's always better to be underestimated.

I began to think about a different kind of journal. A front page with large photos and headlines—big news. It would be eye-catching, it would have impact, and it would be Cuban. I wanted to combine the modern poster and the huge posters people carry on our public holidays. Our colors would be the liberating red-and-black of the 26 July Movement, which was logical, because *Revolución* was the official publication of the movement. Our head of graphics was Ithiel León, who brought about a renovation in graphic design in art magazines. The head of the culture section was Guillermo Cabrera Infante. Jesse Fernández, the extraordinary Cuban photographer who worked on *Life*, came to help us in that field. There were also a few professional journalists, as well as young poets and writers just starting out—Severo Sarduy among them. Vicente Baez and Mateo took on the job of managing the financial side of things.

We had a general meeting of journalists, workers, and employees of the magazine *Alerta*, about a thousand people. We argued. Ten people were fired because they had collaborated with Batista. We established a principle: there would be collective discussion of all issues and equality among all. No seniority. The editorial staff, including the editor-in-chief and the other editors, would be paid a maximum of 500 pesos per month, which was less than what some of the machinists and typographers were making.

Revolución was a pleasant surprise for everyone. It set out to inform, to engage in polemics, to stimulate thought, and to criticize. The official Cuba kept silent. Che and Camilo paid us a visit or two, but Fidel kept away. The old underground groups had found their place. The official magazines and the organs of the parties were sterile, unread. And if *Revolución* was neither official nor the mouthpiece of any ideology, it was, it turned out, the newspaper of the revolution. It posed a challenge.

EXECUTIONS

In those January days, the topic on everyone's lips was the execution by firing squad of war criminals. In Santiago, Raúl Castro shot a group of hoodlums without granting them a trial. We protested against such methods. And Comandante René Rodríguez, an idiot, had the bright idea of shooting, out in Santa Clara, the criminal Colonel Alejandro García Olayón in front of TV and film cameras. The colonel's cephalic mass flew through the air with the greatest of ease. But the impact of the execution was huge, and it reached everyone. Fidel had said that there would be no vengeance, that justice would be done.

The crimes, the torturing committed by the Batista regime were myriad. But they included the experience of the frustrated revolution of 1930, which traumatized the nation. The criminals of the Machado regime had never been brought to trial: they were still murdering people, with Batista from 1934 to 1939, and again with Batista from 1952 to 1958. The fact that justice was never done produced a desire for vengeance, and this in turn created hit teams whose members had become gangsters. Then these gangs declared war on one another. There were hundreds of assassination attempts, which was one of the reasons why the army backed Batista's military coup.

Every day someone would discover a new unmarked cemetery.

The blood of those who were murdered seemed to run anew in every corner of Cuba. But there was no collective hysteria; rather, there was a collective desire for justice. What happened could be compared with the Nazi war-crime trials after World War II. I'm not saying Batista was another Hitler, but I would assert that crimes and torture, be they in thousands or millions, create the same feeling of repulsion, the same need for justice, in any time or place on earth. The Cuban national spirit, usually calm, remained so even in the face of all this rediscovered bloodshed, and demanded justice.

Fidel convoked the people at the National Palace. There he asked the multitude—inaugurating a style he would later call direct democracy—if they agreed that war criminals should be shot. "Put 'em up against the wall!" was shouted out by a few. Then a colossal "Yes!" resounded as the answer to Fidel's question. A national survey privately conducted registered that 93 percent of those polled agreed with the sentences and the executions. I also agreed. I had lived through the underground war, where the only value is life, and I had lived through a humanistic war out in the mountains. I had lived through the assassination and torture of my comrades and friends. I had been tortured. I felt no hatred and wanted no revenge. I simply thought that fewer lives would be lost in the long run if we could just execute the murderers and be done with it. We all agreed. Today I disagree and I take full responsibility for what happened then. Not out of compassion, not because I think Batista's or anyone else's goon squads are innocent or deserved to live. The problem is not who gets shot, it's who does the shooting. When you execute someone in cold blood, you are learning how to kill. That's how human beings are turned into murder-machines, and those machines are unstoppable. They need fuel, and when they don't get it, they go out to find it. So out of our decision to save blood by killing only criminals, there arose a new repressive power that would be implacable.

In January 1959 no one thought that way. And an international press campaign, which was started in the United States, complicated things still further. Where this campaign originated was a mystery, but it was backed by certain vested interests. Except for the liberal minority within the news system—the New York *Times*, CBS, *Newsweek*, the *Herald Tribune*—which had denounced Batista's crimes, the majority said nothing about them. Of course, they said nothing about Trujillo, Somoza, Pérez Jiménez, Castillo Armas, or Rojas Pinilla either. We just could not understand this U.S. policy with regard to Latin-American dictators. They seemed vaguely to be defending their old friends—in the name of justice. Things got worse and worse. Each newly discovered cemetery was matched by another new one. A vicious circle was created.

REVOLUCIÓN SPEAKS OUT

Revolución began to speak out on all issues, to start polemics. It published the monthly subventions Batista supplied to magazines and individual journalists. There was a general condemnation, with two exceptions, *Bohemia* and *Prensa Libre*. Fidel was not pleased by this demoralization of the press, because he was using it to his best advantage and wanted to be the only voice of authority in the nation. But *Revolución*'s circulation went up: it was the expression of the new Cuba.

The paper attacked the vested interests with great vigor. A lot of things were going through my mind. I was born in Sitio Grande, on a sugar plantation that was part of the Unidad mill system. My father was a cane-cutter. His buddies were the blacks who lived in the old slave shacks. My father died young because of the privations he endured. In the church at Cifuentes, the Spaniards who shot the *mambises* were blessed by the priest, and it was there that the mutilated body of my great-uncle was exposed to the public. He had suffered since childhood at the hands of both Cuban and foreign landowners and their rural police force.

I wanted to attack them, to show their relationship with Batista. I often imagined a farewell party for those rich despots in which they would ride their beautiful horses out of town to the accompaniment of the drums they despised. I thought often about seizing their libraries, their record collections—especially those belonging to the intellectuals who had played along with Batista. It wasn't that I craved vengeance; I just wanted to see some real changes, some collective changes.

Some rebels began to "requisition" cars that belonged to Batista supporters, to take over the houses of the rich. "Now there's a great idea," Raúl Castro said, "the barbudos living in the mansions of the rich." Great, I said, but dangerous, because men think in the way they live. And I wasn't wrong. Most of us agreed. Faustino Pérez, the stubborn Minister for the Recovery of Property, whose ministry took charge of the house-seizure problem, forbade the personal or unauthorized seizure of houses. Most of us, in fact, had gone to live in the same apartments we had had before the revolution. We also set our own salaries: Che's was the most austere, at 250 pesos per month.* A minister got 750 and a few others 1,000.

Fidel solved his own financial problems in true Solomonic form. He was famous for never paying his bills, but Celia Sánchez paid all of them with money left over from the taxes the rebel army had gathered at the end of the war. Fidel lived in Celia's small apartment on Once Street in the Vedado district. He also had a secret suite in the Habana-Libre-Hilton. He also rented for a symbolic dollar a month a house in Cojímar that belonged to his old friend from the Ortodoxo party Agustín Cruz.

I was living with my family in a small apartment in Carmen, on Santos Suárez, when one day a Chinese shopowner from my hometown turned up. He had helped out my father with credit when my father was out of work. For years he had tried to get

* Before the revolution one peso equaled one U.S. dollar.

his wife, who lived in Canton, to Cuba, but since Cuba had no relations with China, nothing ever happened. So as director of *Revolución*, I sent a telegram directly to Mao Tse-tung. One week later the woman was in Havana. The telegram tactic was a good one, one I used again later. In any case, Joaquín, the Chinese, was jubilant, and seeing how sparse my apartment was, he appeared with a refrigerator. I got mad and told him that things had changed and that we didn't do things like that to get refrigerators. Poor Joaquín almost died of shame, so I repented and told him he could buy me Bach's Brandenburg Concertos if he wanted to. Things like that happened to all of us. My, how austere we were in those days!

WHAT WAS FIDEL THINKING?

We all knew what Fidel was—the undisputed caudillo of the revolution. What Fidel was thinking no one knew. Our old disagreements, covered over during the time of fighting, never really disappeared. We went back to the old fight: we had to create institutions to neutralize his power, his popularity, his militaristic tendencies. But the terrible underground war had worn us down. The Directorio had lost its best cadres and its leader, José Antonio Echevarría, in the attack on the National Palace and was still in a rebuilding process when Batista fled. Che's legendary arrival and his lightning attack on Las Villas had annulled the importance of the Escambray Front group (a spinoff of the Directorio), and Fidel's order—which forbade the Directorio to share in the victory in Havana after it had fought at Placetas and Santa Clara—isolated the forces loyal to Chomón and Cubelas. In his first speech, Fidel accused those forces of having stolen arms, thus liquidating the Directorio as a political power.

Almost the same thing happened with the underground 26 July Movement. With Frank País and Daniel (René Ramos Latour), its best military men, dead, Santiago and Havana ceased to be centers of military action. The failure of the April strike called by the Directorio and the 26 July Movement allowed Fidel to take control of all clandestine forces through Comandante Delio Gómez Ochoa. Fidel's aim: to marginalize the movement and make it disappear. The man on the street had no notion of these internal struggles; for him there was only one 26 July Movement. For the people, the 26 July Movement was one thing, both in the cities and the mountains, and its symbol and creator was Fidel Castro. The *Granma* group, still intact after the military phase of the struggle, was the real new power in the nation. Che Guevara and Huber Matos were exceptions, albeit minimal ones, to that monolithic structure. The Moncada assault, the *Granma* landing, and the Sierra blend to become one thing: Fidel Castro, alone. The Sierra and the cities emerged from the struggle with deep scars, but the scars were different because they were two very different realities.

We found that there were now more things dividing us than the one thing that united us—a common enemy. The rebel from the Sierra knew only the victory of his struggle, while the urban rebel knew only failure. The city war was like a prizefight in which each round is made up of gains and losses; Fidel won his fight by a knockout. But as far as ideology was concerned, nothing was clear, and Fidel was the greatest enigma of all.

Raúl, on the other hand, was more easily deciphered; he was neither a hero nor popular. He was important because he controlled the army and Oriente Province. Then he married Vilma Espín, symbol of the Santiago group and a known antifidelista. This was Raúl's way of procuring the sympathy and support of Santiago. Raúl was an orthodox Communist, both by training and military temperament. Out in the Sierra he was nicknamed *El Casquito* (the little helmet). He was our declared enemy as well as the point of entry of the Cuban Communist party into the revolution. Che, the second most important figure in the revolution, was a Marxist but not a Party man, although he was certainly pro-Soviet and pro-PCC (Partido Comunista Cubano). His influence on Fidel and Raúl was not real but merely potential.

Camilo Cienfuegos was the real hero of the day. He was the youngest, the most handsome. He was loyal to Fidel, but he followed Che and other Marxists. Huber Matos was the hero of Santiago. Raúl Chibás was an extremely popular man and always discreetly on the sidelines. Juan Almeida, Celia Sánchez, and Haydée Santamaría were staunch fidelistas and contributed to Fidel's mystique. Almeida was the black associated with the Virgen del Cobre. Haydée and Melba Hernández were the women associated with the Moncada attack. Celia, the guerrilla heroine of the Sierra, was a mysterious woman who was with Fidel wherever he went. But it was Fidel who gave an identity to all, no matter what each one's ideological tendency might be.

The strongest, most powerful group was that of the pro-Soviet comandantes: Raúl, Che, and Ramiro Valdés. The most popular group was made up of people from the CTC, *Revolución*, and the 26 July Movement: David Salvador, Faustino Pérez, Marcelo Fernández, and myself. What divided these two groups was not their radical tendencies, their degree of anti-imperialist sentiment, or their anticapitalist beliefs; it was communism, pure and simple. The third important group comprised the democratic liberals: Almeida, Raúl Chibás, Huber Matos, Manuel Ray, and many comandantes from the urban struggle who had a background in the Ortodoxo party. The conservative group was made up of the heads of civic institutions, professional schools, and those of the upper middle classes were connected to the Civic Resistance group. It was a marginal but important force, on guard against us in an enormous network of newspapers, radio, and television stations.

The owners of sugar plantations and the large landowners were connected to U.S. politics, while the industrial bourgeoisie was rather more nationalistic; among these were Bacardí, Graví, Crusellas, and Trinidad (tobacco, food, and light industry). The foreign-owned industries we considered dangerous were electric, telephone, oil, mining, and banking. These companies had tremendous influence with the U.S. government, headed at the time by Eisenhower and Nixon. (Nixon, we might remember, was an enemy of Latin America and was treated accordingly when he visited.) So there were four major currents struggling for control of the nation. One was radically anti-imperialist, one was democratic-reformist, one was conservative and pro–United States, and one was Marxist and pro–Soviet Union. The first group also included organized labor, something in the neighborhood of a million people, both in the cities and in the country, as well as the youth of the nation, radicalized by both the war against Batista and the country's economic problems. The second group included a large petit bourgeois group and the better-off peasantry. The third was made up of the vested interests discussed above. And the fourth was made up of Raúl Castro, Che Guevara, a few comandantes, the old Communists, and some fellow travelers.

HORSE! HORSE!

Fidel went to Venezuela. This, his first overseas visit, deviated from New World protocol, whereby a new leader was expected first to visit Washington. Caracas welcomed Fidel with open arms. The two nations had both recently freed themselves from tyrants, we from Batista and the Venezuelans from Pérez Jiménez.

Now in Cuba power was concentrated in Fidel's hands. Urrutia was president of a government that didn't govern. Fifty days had passed, and the people began to grow restive. Miró Cardona, the prime minister, presented his resignation—and Fidel approved, because they had arranged things that way. So Fidel was named prime minister. He went into the government because, as they said then, there was no one else who could do the job. It also made him look innocent of ambition.

Revolución got into trouble by publishing the government's new program as front-page news. We stirred up a furor and earned Fidel's annoyance. You see, his notion of news was that papers should only tell the news he thought fit to print. On the other hand, we thought no one owned the news or the right to tell us what to say. Fidel then criticized *Revolución* and me personally. We countered with a criticism of his criticism.

One night, Beny Moré, the fantastic black singer who was nicknamed "Wild Man," heard some noise out in the street and broke up a party by shouting, "Here comes the Horse!" Everybody started shouting "Horse! Horse! Horse! Horse!" Fidel got mad and took off. From then on, the people stopped calling him Comandante and called him Horse. The Horse was the magic number one in the Cuban Chinese lottery. One in everything. That familiarity mortified Fidel at first, but finally he came to accept it for what it was, an expression of love. Then new laws were put through to right some of the country's social wrongs. Rents were lowered by 50 percent; then the price of meat, medicine, electricity, and telephone service was also lowered. Salaries were increased. The people were delirious with joy and went on a consumer binge. We were having a hell of a time.

Everybody thought that the state—that is, the economy—was a kind of God and that Fidel could do anything he wanted. The standard of living rose by 100 percent. The capitalists and their spokesmen began to worry out loud—but quietly. *Revolución,* of course, put itself in the forefront of those demanding that the rich give up something to the poor, but we really had no idea where we were heading. I personally had no interest in preserving the capitalist system, and even if I had thought we were heading toward socialism, it wouldn't have mattered. I thought the concepts of surplus value and the state were two infinite notions. We were out to ameliorate Cuba's social injustices.

At that time everything seemed to happen at night or at dawn. After hearing Fidel's marvelous television conversations, which lasted four or five hours, we were about to change the work hours in the sugar industry in order to abolish unemployment. The CTC was in agreement with us, as were Che and Raúl. At harvesttime, the sugar industry worked twenty-four hours a day in three shifts of eight hours. We planned to reduce the workday to six hours, have four shifts, and give work to one hundred thousand unemployed laborers. It could be done. Fidel publicly opposed the plan, thereby earning the applause of moderates and landowners. He was right. (Later on, Fidel would resolve the unemployment problem by adding so many supernumerary workers to the sugar mills that there was no way the system could work).

I was part of a Cuban tradition that had declared war on the sugar industry. Some people thought we were crazy, but we weren't. Ever since Columbus brought sugar cane to Cuba (it was not indigenous) it was a disaster. It ruined the cattle industry, tobacco, a more diversified agriculture, and our ability to feed ourselves. Sugar symbolized colonialism and slavery. Slaves were brought to Cuba for the sugar plantations, which needed a huge labor force for a backbreaking, nonproductive task. And it was the influence of the owners of sugar plantations that kept Cuba out of the wars of independence against Spain in the nineteenth century. They saw what had happened in Haiti and were scared to death. Their fear of a slave revolt paralyzed them: better Spain, slavery, and, of course, the plantations. When the enlightened *criollo* bourgeoisie and intelligentsia, whose thinking was influenced by French and U.S. revolutionary thought, decided in 1868 that the moment for freedom had come, they turned the slaves into soldiers. They lost after ten years, and the decimated bourgeoisie abandoned the fight for independence. In 1895, José Martí declared war. He united the veterans of the failed campaign and the new generation, which included intellectuals, peasants, tobacco growers, and generals. The plantation owners opposed the revolution, so the *mambí* army began to burn the sugar cane. Máximo Gómez, commander-in-chief of the *mambises*, exclaimed that Cuban blood was worth more than sugar. In 1898, with Spain sinking fast, the United States intervened—to protect America's sugar bowl.

The new republic was born deformed because it existed in order to produce sugar and wealth for U.S. investors. Sugar is Cuba's cancer. First, land: To grow the right amount of cane, one million five hundred thousand acres of land would be necessary. This meant that almost half of the best land in the nation was needed to produce between five and six million tons of sugar. Second, factories: A huge production system of one hundred and fifty huge factories was necessary for grinding the cane. These alone were worth approximately one billion dollars. These mills were to be supported by a national network of transportation, to get the cane from the plantation to the mill, from the mill to the refinery, from the refinery to the port. This meant roads, railway lines, warehouses, docks, ports. The most expensive element in sugar production is labor, so labor had to be kept cheap and plentiful. The number of agricultural workers involved in sugar production (which meant backbreaking labor in the tropical sun) was over six hundred thousand. The number involved in the rest of the industry, from milling to port, came to something like four hundred thousand. A million in total. Of course, the brown sugar that was produced was still not fine enough for consumption, so it had to be refined again—usually abroad.

The enormous quantity of sugar produced required a large market: Spain, the United States, the Soviet Union. And, as José Martí said (*Imperialism Revealed*, 1880): "The country that buys, controls; the country that sells, obeys." Sugar, like bananas, coffee, and cotton, is a typical product of the poor world. In the two centuries of Cuban sugar production, the price of sugar has been high in very few harvests, disastrously low in most. And the profits have been more than offset by the huge cost of the oil used in production and transportation: Cuba, we should remember, produces none. Similarly, the machinery used in the processing of the sugar also had to be imported.

There is no industry in the world that produces during four months of the year (the harvest period) and is idle the other eight. This absurd ratio creates misery and dead time. The actual period needed to grow sugar cane is six months, including the harvest, which means six months of nothing to do for the sugar workers. The result of this misuse of energy, labor, and arable land has been that Cuba must import almost all it consumes—material it could produce. This monoculture, despite its façade of industrialization, was inextricably bound to militarism, caudillismo, and the absence of genuine institutions. It produced both misery and tyranny.

Sugar shaped Cuban history. The slaveowners asserted that without sugar there would be no Cuba, and thus they justified the slave trade. Later on, the landowners would say the same thing when the Platt Amendment was passed and U.S. investors bought Cuban land and Cuban puppet governments for a pittance. The same refrain was heard right down to Batista and Canova, president of the landowners. And you still hear it, even though every Cuban revolution was against the sugar industry, because that industry requires a ruling class and dependence on foreign markets. If sugar and freedom are, therefore, contradictory terms, so are sugar and socialism. If the revolution was brought about because sugar cane was burned in 1895 and in 1958, how was it possible that it would be revolutionary under Fidel Castro?

Someone might ask how Cuba could survive without sugar, and if it could, why has it not done so? First, our agriculture could easily be diversified, so that we could be self-sufficient. Our cattle industry has already satisfied the needs of the nation—so why not expand it? Why should Cuba have to import cooking oils when it can produce corn, peanuts, and sunflowers? It could also develop its mining industry to export nickel and other minerals, exports that have a higher profit margin than sugar. We could develop our tourist industry, which was once in fact highly developed. This would not have to be an overnight operation: the number of acres dedicated to sugar cane could be progressively reduced and the workers redistributed, either in other branches of agriculture or in mining. There was a genuine antisugar element present in the early moments of the revolution, and it was clear that agrarian reform would be the major battleground in the economic transformation of the country. There was no revolutionary group not interested in some kind of radical reform of agriculture, but the reform that would take place was the one in Fidel Castro's mind. But time passed, and people began to get nervous. Che Guevara, Raúl Castro, and several peasant associations from Oriente Province—those controlled by the Communist José (Pepe) Ramírez—seized land spontaneously, but Fidel was outraged. He publicly ordered the restoration of the land, assuring everyone that the agrarian reform would be carried out well and in an orderly fashion.

A MEETING AT THE TREASURY

The war had been over for months, yet we still never met. It was incredibly hard to see Fidel. You could call Celia Sánchez again and again. If you were lucky and Fidel felt like talking to you, you talked. If not, nothing. If you ran into him in public, he was always surrounded by people, and it was only he who did the talking. We had lots of problems and no place to discuss them. And Fidel, like God, was everywhere and nowhere.

The 26 July Movement, with which 90 percent of the people identified, had disappeared. I was one of the six or seven nominal members of the 26 July's executive committee—named by Fidel himself—and even I never knew why it had ceased to exist. I was never called to any meeting of that committee. So we all went on insisting that we had to have a meeting. And after some months, Fidel convoked a national meeting, which he said would be the first in what would be a permanent contact between us.

One day we were all called to the Treasury, in Plaza de la Revolución: comandantes, ministers, administrators, important people of all sorts, high functionaries. It was a public meeting on a large scale, which meant that nothing serious could be done there. It didn't bode well, but we all thought that something was something. The meeting began with Fidel speaking about some ordinary administrative problems. Julio Duarte, president of the Exchequer, was secretary, and, along with Humberto Sorí Marín, auditor of the army and Minister of Agriculture, and Camilo Cienfuegos, chief of the army, served on the judicial commission. The slow trial and the illegality of certain sentences passed on Batista's war criminals were the subjects under discussion. The majority favored putting an end to the executions and providing some minimal sort of trial for the accused to guarantee their legal rights. This was approved, and the commission (Duarte, Sorí Marín, Cienfuegos) were to send an official telegram to the entire army formally ending the executions.

Raúl Castro was furious. Fidel spoke on about the problems we had proposed to him. Raúl was in a bad humor in those days because he felt abandoned by Fidel. He often spoke about going to Santo Domingo to begin a guerrilla war there. Suddenly, Raúl stood up, and without asking permission to speak, shouted to Fidel, "This is a lot of shit!" Everyone froze. Fidel, with a threatening look, turned to his brother and said, "Tell the assembly you are sorry and take back what you said." To this Raúl responded in a way no less surprising than his first outburst. He burst into tears. From tragedy we went to melodrama. No one uttered a word. There seemed to be a serious rift between the Castro brothers. I tried to pull the fat out of the fire by saying that Raúl had simply used an expression that was just a bit strong, more in tone than in intention. Raúl begged our pardon.

The meeting went on but never got to the main issues. And of course the presence of outsiders meant it was impossible to discuss the real problem: the lack of any collective intention in the leadership, the lack of contact between Fidel and the rest of us. The problem was fidelismo. That was the first and the last meeting. I do have two memories of that meeting—Raúl's expletive and his answer to the official telegram about sentences and executions: "It came too late. Last night we shot the last prisoners."

A TRIP TO THE UNITED STATES

Fidel's first trip to the United States [on April 15, 1959] demonstrated his intelligence. He neither requested nor accepted the
classical official invitation; rather, he had himself invited by the
press, the Press Club, through the good offices of a man of irre-
proachable credentials for the American establishment, Jules
Dubois. Dubois at the time was president of SIP and an opponent
of Batista and of the censorship imposed by Latin-American dictators. He was the Chicago *Tribune*'s correspondent in Cuba, a
retired colonel, and a person to whom the State Department listened.

For his part, Fidel, through OPLA, hired one of the best public
relations firms in the United States, and it took charge of all
his public appearances during the trip. "Smiles, lots of smiles,"
was its constant counsel. Afterward the public relations people
admitted they had never handled such a consummate actor—even
his "fidelenglish" was an asset. He evinced no personality problems
and answered the most impertinent questions calmly. He never
lost his temper, always kept his good humor. And he visited progressive universities, liberal organizations, the zoo, Yankee
Stadium; he ate hot dogs and hamburgers, and tried to make a
media splash.

Fidel's appearance also helped. He was always in olive-green
fatigues—these were never starched or pressed. He wore his hair
and beard shaggy so he would seem older and more mature than
his thirty-three years. The publicity people said he looked like
an ancient Roman hero. Of course, he was backed by a most
respectable delegation, José (Pepín) Bosch and Daniel Bacardí—
both of them symbols of international and industrial Cuba. Fidel
didn't try to pass himself off as a folk hero and never asked for
a cent; instead, he tried to look like a calm, serious statesman
people would take seriously. Jules Dubois, himself a guarantee
of anti-Communist sentiment, introduced the delegation at the
Press Club to a thunderous ovation. The only person suspected
by the naïve Americans of being tainted by Marxism was your

humble servant. I had to laugh, knowing tht Raúl and the Communists had their sights on me all the time. Fidel was a hit.

ZOO OR PICASSO

Once again I lost my cultural battles with Fidel. I tried to bring him to the Museum of Modern Art to see Picasso's *Guernica* and Wifredo Lam's *Jungle.* What I wanted was to get Picasso's support for the revolution, but Fidel wasn't buying. Neither in New York nor in Washington. He did go to the zoo, and he did go to Texas and Canada. On other levels the trip was less successful; the efforts Rufo López Fresquet, Minister of Finance and president of the National Bank, made to secure credits and contracts came to nothing. Fidel didn't really care, and in this he was just like Eisenhower and Nixon. Fidel would agree *in principle* with anything but would never do anything concrete. The meeting between Fidel and Nixon was an out-and-out disaster; their mutual dislike would be long-lived. Fidel's strategy was to seem a friend to all; he would offer his hand and let the others not shake it. And in Washington the prevailing atmosphere was pure disdain. One incident typifies the entire scene. Someone came into the room where the delegation was waiting and was announced as "Mister So-and-so, in charge of Cuban affairs." To this Fidel could only reply, "And I thought I was in charge of Cuban affairs."

BLUESHIRTS

On May Day, 1959, the militia paraded through all the streets of Cuba. A new instrument of the revolution made its debut: the blue shirts and trousers of the militia, whose uniform—once that of common laborers—became the symbol of the new revolutionaries. They were volunteers, they were hard workers, and they were somewhere between soldiers and civilians. They represented spontaneity and organization. The militiaman was the third hero of 1959. He was the collective hero, the true "Party of the Revolution." Men, women, young, old, black, mulatto, workers, peasants, students, professional people, intellectuals, middle-class people, the poor. The militia was the new revolution that gave an identity to all, without prejudice. It asked only for volunteers; it gave military training, it provided care for factories, and it endowed all with political and human awareness. It was armed democracy and came to have a million members.

Who created it? It was in the air, but it was the unions and the 26 July Movement that provided the impetus. But it was rapidly taken over by those who were in just the right place to do so: the army, with Raúl and the Communists right behind it. But there were conflicts from the outset, because the militia represented egalitarian freedom, and the army demanded obedience to higher authority. An armed people is not an army. And this populist spirit showed just what it could do in the sugarcane campaigns, in the literacy campaign, and in the fighting that took place in the Escambray Mountains against the anti-Castro rebels. The militia never had the repressive character of the Security Police or the Defense Committees; nor, logically, did it ever have the regime's political and technical confidence, as did Security, the Defense Committees, and the army. The militia was an instrument of revolutionary democracy, the libertarian phase of the Cuban Revolution.

The militia was used, but no one had any confidence in it. That would have required those in power to share power with a revolutionary institution at the popular level. This would be the second time the Cuban Revolution would lose an opportunity to have a people's organization. First the 26 July Movement was discarded, later it would be the militia. The Russo-Castroite concept that began to take shape and control created an elitist power structure: the people were organized into cadres, watched over and administered by Security, the army, and the bureaucracy. There was only one chief who held all power. His motto was

"Work and Fight," not "Think, Work, and Fight." The people immediately took to the militia's combination of instruction and discussion that united all in a common task. The red-and-black of the 26 July Movement was replaced by militia blue. But those in power refused to accept this participation of the people in the government.

AGRARIAN REFORM

The plantation system has always been one of Cuba's greatest plagues. Specifically in the case of sugar, because cattle ranching always had a different aspect: milk and meat were cheap and relatively abundant, given the economic level of the nation. Milk cost twenty centavos a liter, and first-quality meat half a peso per pound. The human cost for production was lower because the work was less backbreaking and the steers required very few of our home-grown cowboys. This is in comparison with sugar cane, whose cultivation really demands slave labor. The sugar workers and their unions were, in fact, the vanguard of Cuban social struggle. In 1959, city people felt guilty about the condition of their country cousins.

This was a recognition of the existence of two Cubas: the peasant, traditionally a symbol of disorder to be disdained, and the city dweller, whose ideals are those of the United States—money, power, conspicuous consumption, skyscrapers, air conditioning. The purely Cuban was eclipsed by all that imported grandeur. The revolution of 1895 was drowned in a sea of sugar, Yankees, autonomists, and Spanish merchants, all enemies of Cuban popular culture. That culture existed on a kind of no man's land between the plantations, where Cubans without land, called for that reason *precaristas*, lived illegally.

The life of the *precaristas*—poverty, debt, and the threat of being turned off the land by the rural police—was the life of my childhood. The "royal road," which was in no way regal, passed right by the shack my father had made out of palm branches and *guano* (royal palm bud shields), and on it you could always see families of peasants moving out on foot carrying their belongings. The Acosta-Domínguez family, neighbors of ours, one year could not pay their bill at the local general store, owned by the *gallego* Pereiras. They were literally yanked out of the ground, their ground, and put out on the road, with Corporal Felipe and his squad escorting them on their way. That image is burned into my memory.

So you can understand that agrarian reform is an idea that was never far out of my mind. And in the first months of 1959, the revolution again made it a fashionable notion. The barbudos seemed an emanation of the land because of their having lived in the Sierra. The Comandante and his Twelve Followers were the revolution, not the city, the clandestine war, the 26 July Movement, the strikes, the sabotage, the people's boycott of Batista's elections. The revolution was the hero, not the people. When Fidel came down from the mountain, the urban revolution became a peasant revolution. The problem was that it was never a peasant revolution. Out in the Sierra we were with mountain people—a persecuted, poor group, to be sure, but not peasants. But by fidelista magic the Sierra and the peasantry became one.

Fidel, like Moses, came down from the mountain and gave us liberty. Now, the mountains of Cuba are not extensive and are sparsely populated, but the flatland, the farmland, is another matter. The Cuban Revolution is not the Chinese Revolution. The revolutionaries in the Sierra were city people who fled to the mountains, as can be seen in a quick review of the lives of the comandantes. The 26 July Movement was urban, and the revolution in which it participated had the people as its protagonist. Six months before the victory, there were only three hundred of us out in the Sierra. If you added to that those fighting in the Escambray and the *Segundo Frente* we wouldn't have reached one thousand. Three months after the victory there were two thousand of us. Batista's army had fifty thousand when it gave up. The mountain war was important, no doubt about that, but it was not the decisive factor in the victory. What beat Batista was the Cuban people's total opposition to him.

The hero of 1959 was the guerrilla-barbudo, and right behind him was the peasant. Havana felt guilty about the treatment the peasants had had and wanted to make amends. The 26 July Movement, the Directorio, *Revolución*, the comandantes, and Fidel took advantage of this guilt to make the city sympathize with the country and to make everyone aware of the situation of agriculture. So everyone, especially the rich, who were trying to save their own skins, began screaming about agrarian reform. Time passed, and Fidel neither said nor did a thing.

We at *Revolución* never shut up. We wanted to create an awareness in the people about the situation of agriculture, of the workers, and of Cuban culture. So we attacked the powerful voices of conservatism, of the status quo: the navy, the radio station CMQ, the magazine *Hoy*. At the same time we opposed the pro-Communist, pro-Soviet left, supported by Raúl and his group. We wanted to create awareness and institutions; we couldn't get involved with politics because it was simply impossible. Fidel's popularity bordered on madness, and it would have been madness to oppose him politically. Our only chance, it seemed to me, was to inform, convince, radicalize the people. When I supported the plan for creating four shifts of six hours to replace the traditional three shifts of eight hours in the sugar industry, Fidel accused me of wanting to destroy the sugar industry. I was, am, and always will be in favor of destroying it, whether it belongs to capitalists or to the state, or even if it belongs to the workers themselves. It has never brought Cuba anything but misery, and it will certainly never bring it true independence.

Fidel preached patience. We had to gain time. He was right. Che and Raúl were wrong, because it was premature to oppose the United States and to provide all our enemies (internal and foreign) with a reason for uniting against us. So Fidel gained time by traveling: to the United States, to Canada, to Argentina, to Brazil, to Uruguay. And it was there he produced slogans that captured everybody's imagination: "Freedom with bread. Bread without terror." "Neither dictatorship from the right nor dictatorship from the left." "Neither capitalism nor socialism. Revolutionary humanism." Some were both biblical and nationalist: "A revolution of the poor and for the poor. A revolution as Cuban as our palms. Not a red revolution but an olive-green revolution." In his speech at the meeting of the twenty-one Latin-American nations, a calm, moderate Fidel demanded thirty billion dollars—no strings attached—for Latin America, a precursor of Kennedy's Alliance for Progress. He knew he was earning the respect of the middle classes with his slogans and was perfectly aware that the United States would never pay a cent. Raúl and the Communists began to get restless and allowed properties to be expropriated without any recourse to law. Fidel put an end to this when in a televised speech he declared that there would be a "profound, organized, and legal" land reform and that spontaneous occupations of private property would not be countenanced.

Two land reform plans were elaborated at the same time. One was created by Sorí Marín, Minister of Agriculture, and was moderate; the other, created by Che Guevara and his group, with the participation of Osvaldo Dorticós, Minister of Revolutionary Laws, was much more radical. Fidel took part in the deliberations of both groups. Sorí Marín's plan helped him gain time and to calm down the vested interests; Che's plan, which was more to Fidel's liking, would satisfy even the most impatient and could be used when the right moment came. Sorí Marín's plan would provide lands, but it accentuated individual and collective grants, leaving the average-size holdings intact and maintaining the plantations as a means of protecting agriculture in general. Che's plan would destroy the plantations and seek to start a class struggle, a fight with the United States and with Cuban capitalists. It eliminated individual land grants and tended toward state ownership. Both plans were secret.

My only contribution was to suggest that the plan be signed

into law on May 17, the day Niceto Pérez, a peasant martyr, died fighting against peasant evictions. Raúl wanted the plan to be associated with the name of a Communist martyr from Oriente Province. Fidel chose his best stage for the signing of the historic law that ended the plantation system, the camp at La Plata in the Sierra Maestra. It was there that a council of ministers (not all of them in shape for mountain climbing) signed the law. There was one person missing: Sorí Marín. After a row with Fidel, the night Fidel's son, Fidelito, was injured in an accident, he resigned. His protest was secret, but it was his first step toward disgrace. He later tried to form an opposition group, and in 1961, after a secret trip to the United States, he was captured and shot. After all the secret plans, it was Fidel's own plan that was put into practice. The plan created the Institute of Agrarian Reform (INRA; Instituto National de Reforma Agraria), whose nominal head would be the geographer who joined Che's column in the last week of the war, Captain Antonio Núñez Jiménez.

Fidel maintained the suspense about the limitations on the size of plantations right up until the end—Fidel the Mysterious. In the meantime, I was preparing a special edition of *Revolución* with Pino Santos, our economics editor, about the law and Cuba's agrarian problems. We were soon to lose Santos; Fidel brought him over to INRA, which was a shame, because he was a good economics journalist and not so hot either as a plain economist or an agrarian expert. In any case, Fidel just wouldn't tell us the magic number; he wanted to surprise us. When I badgered him about it, he invited me out to La Plata so we could make a "historic broadcast" as we had done over Radio Rebelde during the war. And then he reminded me—he never forgets anything— about the first agrarian reform program we promulgated in the *Sierra*, and how I protested because the plantations were not touched. "You had no confidence in me then. Now you're going to see that the plantation system is finished. You never had to worry, after all." I told him I was never a prophet and that it was hard to know what was going on because there was no communication. Fidel put his arm around me and told me to set things up with Radio Rebelde and *Revolución*. It was then I told him I would stay with the newspaper instead of going out to La Plata. He was shocked and disgusted when I told him I wanted to oversee the publication of the newspaper, which would reproduce the new law in its entirety. Fidel went on his way, certain that I was going to miss a historic moment.

It was true. I really can't stand those photographs of the "great moments" of Western culture. In any case, tension and expectations about the new law were mounting. The telephone down at *Revolución* never stopped ringing, and strange new faces kept turning up. I refused to let the cat out of the bag. I had the presses start up—after closing the pressrooms to all outsiders and posting guards so no one could get in.

Just then an old comrade from the 26 July Movement, a hero of the underground war, Aldo Vera, now chief of a police group, called: "Which one of the *Revolución* people wrote the story about the torture of Felo, the cartoonist?" Felo was an old friend, a serious guy. The day before he had come to the editorial offices to tell us that he had been held for a few hours down at the old Bureau of Investigations (which now had a different name), and that he had been made to "play horse." The inventor of this torture was Mario Gil, an underground fighter, who was in the Camagüey campaign. He had been chief of Fidel's personal guard, but Fidel had sent him on to the police force, where he was second in command at interrogation. What they would do was to make the prisoner get down on all fours and walk like a horse. Then they would make him carry one or two policemen up and down the stairs. It was intended more as a humiliation than anything else, but I thought it was a bad precedent to set. So I published a protest note, saying that the revolution should not mistreat anyone.

I could only answer Aldo's question with another question: "Aldo, is this 'playing horse' stuff true or not?"

"You just tell me the reporter's name so I can arrest him."

"Calm down, Aldo. The person responsible for what's printed here is me. And anyway, I don't see what you want with us.

You should arrest anyone who mistreats a prisoner. Don't forget, we were both tortured down at the Bureau by Faget."

"Riding some son of a bitch around a little is a game. You can't compare it with what they used to do around here."

"No, it isn't the same—yet—but that's how you begin."

"Tell me the reporter's name."

"The man you want is me, Aldo."

"Okay, I'm coming to get you, then."

"Now listen, Aldo, can you imagine the feast tomorrow's newspapers are going to have with this: 'Editor of *Revolución* jailed for denouncing torture'? And on the day the agrarian reform law is to be signed. Come on, Aldo, we're old buddies."

"We used to be."

"This could cost you your job."

"Who cares? I'm coming for you."

"Listen, Aldo, it may not matter to you, but it matters to me. You can meet me at my apartment over on Carmen Street."

I went home to wait for Aldo, not thinking about being arrested but about the brouhaha to come. Fidel would never forgive the marring of the glory of the agrarian reform by such an incident. I suspected that Raúl, who hated both *Revolución* and Aldo, was behind all of this. Then Aldo came and arrested me.

So for the second time in my life I was a prisoner in the Bureau of Investigations. There at the desk was Sergeant Bocanegra, who was from my hometown and had been a sergeant there under Piedra and Faget. He wasn't bad then and he was with the good guys now. Surprised, he said, "You here again?" To which I could only answer: "You still here?" Aldo threatened to send me to La Cabaña jail; he was berserk. I had told my wife, Margot, to telephone our friends in a quiet way—the important thing was to avoid a scandal.

I told Aldo to calm down, that if Faget hadn't been able to upset me, there was no way he could. Aldo figured that the article about torture was a plant, part of a plot to get him out of the police force. I hadn't even known he was the head of that particular branch, because each division had a new name no one could figure out. Then Aldo's phone rang. He said nothing, but I knew it was friends of mine from Havana. Two hours later my friend Efigenio Amejeiras, chief of police, turned up with a shocked look on his face. He was followed by Raúl himself, wearing an ironic expression. He resolved everything with a laugh, saying that such things really shouldn't happen among comrades from the underground days. Aldo was still irate about the article. I tried to explain that the only thing I hadn't known about Felo's torture was the fact that Aldo was the head of this particular police division. I added that the building we were in was a terrible place and that I was going to suggest to Fidel that it be demolished. But I smelled a rat—named Raúl—because he seemed to know too much about the whole thing.

Fidel wasn't in Havana, and if our enemies in the conservative press had found out about my arrest, they could have had a field day and deflated the impact of Fidel's agrarian reform law. Raúl could have gotten rid of me and Aldo in one shot; let's not forget that Aldo was a man of considerable prestige in underground circles and that *Revolución* was a dangerous adversary for Raúl. Well, that wasn't the first time Raúl had pulled a fast one, and it wasn't his last.

Later, Fidel berated me for not being at La Plata when the broadcast took place and for making a mistake with some of the figures related to the new law. I told him I couldn't be in two places at once and described the incident with Aldo Vera. He thanked me for avoiding a scandal, said he would not allow torture and that he would turn the Bureau into a park (which he later did).

The next day, May 18, was a Cuban party—a tragedy for some of the rich, but who cared? The people went wild over their first revolutionary law, singing songs like this one: "With a steer / or without a steer / we busted open their heads so dear."

Havana opened its arms to the peasants. The middle classes supported the land reform law, and the motto of the day was: "The 26th of July and Fidel Say: 'People of Havana, Invite a Peasant Home.'"

But it wasn't all sweetness and light. Production plummeted, and the rebel army began to seize farms, to imprison landowners, and to kill off breeding bulls just for fun. A class war had begun all through the countryside. On one side, the owners began to sabotage production, and on the other, the rebels disrupted what production there was. Every group hated every other group: it was as if a cyclone were picking everything up to blow it all away.

URRUTIA: A TRAITOR OR NOT?

One afternoon in June, Celia Sánchez called me up. Fidel wanted to see me at the house he was renting over in Cojímar. I found him strolling around the neighborhood. He asked permission to go into a house, asked me to stand by, and began to write. When he finished, he passed me the manuscript and told me to read it. It was his resignation from the post of prime minister. I told him it would shock the nation and asked him what his reasons were for resigning. "Problems with the President. I'm not going to resort to the usual Latin-American–style coup. I'm going directly to the people, because the people will know what to do. You are the only one who knows anything about this, and I want you to publish a special edition of the newspaper announcing it. Seal the place off and don't leak a word. You might as well print a million copies—you know, with those big headlines you like so much." I told him I'd do it, but that the message was incomplete because he didn't include his reasons. "I'll give the reasons when I go on TV."

I told him he ought to tell Che, Camilo, Raúl, and the others what he was doing because if they thought I was printing lies they'd burn down the newspaper. "Don't you worry, Franqui, those are my problems." Of course, when the first edition hit the morning streets, there almost was a riot. The entire nation shut down, and there were demonstrations everywhere. Raúl wanted to take over the paper and accused me of counterrevolutionary activities. Camilo Cienfuegos telephoned me from Las Villas just to curse me out for not telling him. I calmed him down and told him exactly what I had discussed with Fidel in Cojímar. I told him he should have a talk with Celia and Raúl and to tell Raúl that he ought to seize Fidel's house instead of *Revolución*. "This Fidel really likes to fuck around" was Camilo's summary of the day's events.

But this was typical of Fidel. He never told anyone anything because his notion of power demanded everyone's unconditional confidence. And since he could never share power, he could never share the idea of making big news. The country was in an uproar. The people instinctively supported Fidel, who went on television a few days later and accused President Urrutia of being "on the point of committing treason" by denouncing the Communist presence in Fidel's government. This is exactly the thing Comandante Pedro Díaz Lanz, commander of the air force, had done some days before, when he deserted and appeared before a committee of the United States Congress to accuse Fidel of being a Communist and of nurturing Communist infiltration in the army.

Urrutia, naïve to the end, was sitting in front of his television set fully expecting to see Fidel accuse his brother Raúl of being a Communist. He listened to Fidel, called station CMQ, and resigned. Fidel then ordered Dorticós to summon Miró Cardona so he could be named president. Raúl, Che, Ramiro, and other comandantes asked him to reconsider, because it was well known that Miró Cardona was a conservative and pro-U.S. Fidel told them that to be president, Miró would do anything, even turn Communist. His mind had to be changed. Carlos Rafael Rodríguez, Joaquín Ordoquí, Edith García Buchaca, representing the Party, got together with Raúl and Che and proposed Dorticós. This was an astute move by the Party: Dorticós was an old fellow traveler. But at the same time he had been a lawyer for the sugar plantation owners of Las Villas, so he had a few old debts to pay. Che had met him during the Escambray fighting (Dorticós, along with Ray, had been involved in Civic Resistance before taking refuge in Mexico) and admired him for the way he had written out the agrarian reform law. Dorticós was Minister of Revolutionary Laws, and a good lawyer. His relations with all groups were good.

Fidel offered poor Miró Cardona the post of ambassador to the United States, but Miró chose Spain instead, possibly because his father was a *catalán* and a *mambí* general. Soon after, we would all see a photo of Miró along with Franco and his Moorish guards. The real result of the fall of Urrutia was to make some of us realize that there was a conflict between majority rule and individual justice. Urrutia had always been in an untenable situation. He was never president, simply because Fidel always held all the power. He had to lose because there was no way Fidel was going to let him do anything. The idea that he was ever "on the point of committing treason" was absurd, an injustice. A dangerous precedent had been set, and we did nothing about it. Fidel arranged things with a *fait accompli.* Urrutia never had a chance to defend himself and had to flee, dressed up as a milkman. The only "evidence" ever presented against him came in the form of a statement by his secretary Olivares, who said he had heard Urrutia say certain things. Total hearsay. Well, that might have been the first big lie we swallowed, but it sure wasn't the last.

ON THE ROAD

From the coasts of Cuba you can both see and hear nearby lands: Jamaica, Haiti, Santo Domingo, Yucatán. Mexico has always had a fascination for Cubans, while South America has somehow been cut off from us. The Caribbean is not only a sea, but a world unto itself. Brazil constitutes the unknown, a kind of "dark continent" that speaks directly to us because we, too, have Africa within us. Repressed and unknown, it is, nevertheless, there.

I think the Cuban consciousness will come into its own when it rediscovers its African origins. The Spanish element in our society is a kind of "given," but it has only been since independence that we have begun to see another Cuba. We are a tropical society and have only just begun to assimilate that part of us into our culture. Writers and artists such as Martí, Ortíz, Lam, Lezama Lima, Porro, Caturla, Cabrera Infante, Piñera, Reinaldo Arenas, Cardenas, Camacho, Lydia Cabrera, and others are opening up the frontier of this total Cuban world. But there is still a *machista*, anticultural strain in our society that effectively blocks the flowering of our culture.

But the fact that Cuba is an island makes it into a closed world. Even though it is open to outside influences, it is something of a prison. In 1947, I took part in the Cayo Confites expedition to Santo Domingo against Trujillo, in part because I had always been poor and unable to travel. I wanted to get out, so I joined the Party. Later I found that the Party is an island you can't escape from. I tried, and they made me a pariah. The owners of newspapers, on the other side, made you sell out to them if you wanted to work. So, at the age of twenty-five, I found all doors closed to me. The only people who would take me in were the Cabrera Infantes, the parents of Guillermo Cabrera Infante.

For me the Cayo Confites adventure was the solution to my problems. I could travel and fight in a just cause. I would learn what war was and get to know myself. I might survive this horrible period of my life, maybe even get to Europe. I ended up like the others, in a Colombian jail. My first article on the disaster—of course—caused me to lose my job on the newspaper *Luz*. The sea was my enemy.

In 1954, by pure chance, I got to travel. Someone had to carry a short color film to the laboratories to be developed; the laboratories were in New York. I flew to Miami and took a bus that went through the southeastern states to Washington and then to New York. What I saw of the South was depressing: a desolate countryside, the blacks standing on buses because they couldn't sit in the seats reserved for whites. That overt racism made a greater impression on me than Washington, with all its buildings and cherry trees in bloom. New York was something else; it was like a pyramid reaching for the sky. I saw all the paintings I had wanted to see for my entire life: Picasso, Calder, Miró, Matisse, black and Oceanic art, pre-Columbian, Renaissance—you name it, I saw it. Best of all, Wifredo Lam's *Jungle* directly opposite Picasso's *Les Demoiselles d'Avignon.* Two years later I would get to Mexico and Central America.

In 1959, with Fidel, I discovered the liberal United States, its universities, Harlem. Europe finally came, in the same year, when my wife, Margot, and I got to make our "grand tour." I was still intent on carrying out my cultural guerrilla war. *Revolución* would invite Picasso, Sartre, Breton, Le Corbusier, and other Europeans to Cuba. Neruda would be the first Latin American. I went personally to ask people if they would help us out. I ran into Sartre in Paris, at a rehearsal of one of his plays. He first granted me a few minutes, which soon turned into hours of discussion about Cuba, revolution, socialism, Marxism. . . . The result was the visit of Jean-Paul Sartre and Simone de Beauvoir to Cuba. I think I must have been a kind of Cuban nightmare for Sartre, the return of one of his forgotten errors. To me he seemed a kind of monument, a synthesis of Marx, Freud, existentialism—something I myself had dreamed.

I next met André Breton. Breton, the poet of revolution and surrealism, had predicted a revolution in Cuba when he was there in 1947. He intuited our world, understood it, and showed his love for it in his collection of tropical art. We became friends, but because of his health he was forced to limit himself to publishing in *Lunes.* I was also introduced to Le Corbusier. I wanted him to design *Revolución*'s new offices because I was sick of the Americanized architecture of Havana. I wanted Le Corbusier because he symbolized a dramatic break, which is just what I hoped to bring about. We discussed materials, the tropics, and the idea of a tropical architecture that would be alive and sensual. I wanted to change Havana into a human city where people could find a place to sit down, where indoors and outdoors would merge, an open city. Le Corbusier agreed and said he would accept his fee in Cuban pesos at the going rate for a Cuban architect. The only demand he made was that there be no murals by Picasso in his building because, as he said, "I'm a painter myself."

I began to meet more and more people. Henri Lefebvre, a leader in progressive thought in France, who promised his collaboration. The staff of *Express*, which gave me a warm welcome. Giselle Halimi, Claude Faux, Michel Leiris, Eduard Pignon, Hélène Parmelin. Things were going great until a certain evening when I caused no small embarrassment to myself and my French hosts by overindulging—you can take the boy out of the country, but you can't take the country out of the boy (at least not overnight). But I did make friends: Jean Daniel, Siné, François Giroud, Juan Goytisolo, and K. S. Karol.

Then I went looking for Picasso. When I met him, he asked me where my beard was. I remembered the joke made by the beardless man on the Havana bus and told him I was on a secret mission—namely to kidnap him and bring him to Havana. The meeting was a great success. Picasso talked about the Cuban exiles he had met as a young man, and about his Cuban grandmother. (It figures that if every Cuban has a black grandfather, every Spaniard ought to have a Cuban grandmother.) But Picasso really did know about Cuba—its dances, its food, all kinds of customs we knew little about. I asked him for help, for a project I had been brewing for a long time. It involved the monument to the American battleship *Maine*, the sinking of which gave the Americans a pretext for intervening in our war of independence. At a meeting of ministers I had managed to get official sanctioning of the destruction of the *Maine* monument and the construction of a work by Picasso—an aggressive dove. Picasso liked the idea, asked for photos of the site, and proposed a gigantic cubist structure, a kind of beast of freedom that would face all directions at once. Margot and I had lunch with Picasso and Jacqueline: it wasn't a day I can reconstruct detail by detail because it went by in a flash, but it was a day I'll never forget.

BOITEL

Pedro Luis Boitel was one of the 26 July Movement's student leaders and earned as much prestige because of his struggle against Batista as he had in 1959 fighting for a genuine university reform, one that would include autonomy and free elections. His importance at the university was growing daily. Fidel and Raúl tried to use him against Comandante Cubelas, a Directorio hero (a man, by the way, they had used against Faure Chomón at the beginning of 1959): they "resigned" him from his post as vice-president of Governance so he could preside over the university. But the majority of the students rejected the maneuver and backed up Boitel, Heredia, and the directors of the National Student Front.

The university was a key spot because it was the birthplace and the home of the revolution. It supported the radical social and political changes the revolution brought, but it demanded the autonomy and free elections that had traditionally been its rights. At that point they ran afoul of Fidel, who wanted no elections, and no autonomy for anyone, especially the students. The students (like the unions) swallowed Fidel's Montevideo statement ("A new, humanist, Latin-American revolution. Freedom with bread, bread without terror") hook, line, and sinker. But April isn't September, and now Fidel was demanding "unity" and obedience from students, unions, and the people. Neither the university nor the unions could remain independent, and neither did. Boitel resigned and won a moral victory. Then he began an opposition campaign. Before the end of 1960 he was in jail. He was the only 26 July Movement leader who died in the hunger strike that took place in 1974 in Fidel's jails.

FREEDOM WITH BREAD, BREAD WITHOUT TERROR

We got back to Havana at the end of October. *Revolución*'s polemic with the Communists was red-hot, and Raúl was beginning to take action. Fidel's attitude was still unclear. The internal situation was tense because of the agrarian reform that had wiped out the plantation system in three areas: sugar, cattle, and rice. Coffee and tobacco were not cultivated on large-scale plantations, so they remained untouched. The conservative *Diario de la Marina* kept screaming that we were watermelons—green outside and red inside. The right wing, supported by the United States and the landowners, was attacking; at the same time, so were the Communists, led by Raúl. So we were between two enemies. The poet Baragano, one of *Revolución*'s editors, was attacked for a lecture he had given years before. I answered by publishing on the front page of *Revolución* a facsimile of a dedication Juan Marinello, president of the Communist party, had written in a book given to Santiago Ray. Ray had been one of Batista's ministers, one the Directorio had tried to shoot at the time when Batista's repression had been hardest.

Public opinion was with us. The Party was livid and lost every single union election to choose representatives for the first free congress of the CTC. The 26 July Movement's worker contingent won 95 percent of the votes, the Communists 5 percent. It had been a referendum. Raúl, Ramiro Valdés, and their group were violent and aggressive. They were preparing some action, but no one knew what it would be. Every day the chant "Unity, unity!" rang out louder and louder, as did the no less threatening "Up against the wall." Our crowd answered with "*Revolución!* 26 July, bread without terror, freedom with bread!" And the people echoed our cheers.

One day I was called down to the CTC for a discussion. Almost everyone was there: comandantes, ministers, labor leaders, representatives of the 26 July Movement, the old underground groups. Missing were the comandantes from the Sierra, Raúl, Che, and Ramiro Valdés. The subject of the meeting was a discussion of Communist infiltration and how to stop it. Now there were two distinct groups on the Communist side. Che was not the same as Raúl, who was Moscow's man. In the same way, Cienfuegos, Almeida, and Amejeiras weren't Ramiro Valdés or Guillermo Garciá. But we, too, were split. People like Manuel Ray, Eloy Gutiérrez Manoyo, the *Segundo Frente* people, and a few ministers were in favor of democratic reforms, negotiation with the United States, and private property, while most of us were in favor of a radical revolution of an anti-imperialist, anticapitalist, socialist nature.

We rejected the Russian model and the rather pitiful Communist party of Cuba, which was its Trojan Horse, and we rejected the police-state militarism of Raúl and Ramiro. The real struggle was not going to be between neocolonial capitalism and socialism but between Russian and Cuban socialism. The meeting then moved on from an exchange of opinions to a plan of action. It was proposed that a delegation speak directly with Fidel and tell him that he could no longer allow Raúl to go on stuffing the army and the revolution with Communists. The majority favored this idea. But I'm a rather distrustful peasant (and I knew Fidel better than most), so I began to have doubts. I wondered if we were somehow being manipulated, but I repressed my doubts. What was clear was our total faith in Fidel. But it was clear to me that if we all went down as a body to see Fidel—which was what was proposed—he was going to view us as an opposition group. And sharing power was something Fidel Castro would never do.

I argued that Fidel had to know about Communist infiltration, and that the business about Urrutia's being "about to commit treason" was a symbol we ought to try to understand. I suggested a different tactic. We would win the Workers' Congress by a huge majority. We should just try to go on as we were and let our good work speak for itself. To go against the Communists would create allies for them. *Revolución* would continue its attacks on the Party, showing just how antirevolutionary it had been in its cozy relationship with Batista. We would all fight, but not as a high-profile group. Then someone suggested we all resign our positions. I argued that to resign would be like confessing to treason. Well, I won the day, but not resoundingly. My comrades understood that they could not approach Fidel directly, but I understood just how naïve they were.

As fighters they were terrific—they had resisted torture, prison, any number of fights—but they had no idea what power was, what politics was. They thought they could speak man to man with Fidel now, when even during the underground days it had been impossible. They couldn't understand that Fidel had to be fought with his own weapons—institutions and public opinion, acts instead of words. We couldn't hope to beat Fidel, but we could at least try to create a counterbalance to him. I think I kept my friends from doing something rash, and later events were to prove me correct. Years later, I was handed a document written by State Security about that meeting, which they called a conspiracy. I was identified as the intellectual chief of the group and Huber Matos as its political leader. We were all marked men.

HUBER MATOS

Before leaving for Europe, Comandante Huber Matos came to see me. He, too, was concerned about Communist infiltration in the army and the situation of the 26 July Movement. At the time, Matos ran Camagüey, where he had accomplished great things through his own efficiency and where, accordingly, he was held in great esteem. During the war against Batista, he had also done great things. He flew the first planeload of men and arms in from Costa Rica. During the siege of Santiago, it was he, with only about one hundred men, who kept Batista's army from entering and leaving the city. For rebel Santiago, Huber Matos was a legend. He was a teacher at the Manzanillo institute, like Fidel a member of the Ortodoxo party, and the owner of a small rice plantation. He followed the ideas of Antonio Guiteras; he was anti-imperialist and a believer in democracy.

Camagüey was the most seignorial province in Cuba, the whitest and the most Castilian. Its economy was based on cattle, sugar, and fruit production, particularly oranges. It was almost devoid of black laborers and had only a sparse peasant population. It brought in sugar workers from other provinces of Cuba as well as from Haiti and Jamaica. From its cattle ranches came most of the nation's meat, from huge ranches like the famous King Ranch. It was a province of large estates and gentlemen on horseback, the Agramontes, the Cisneros and other patriots of the independence movement. For all that, Huber Matos had made one and all toe the line. The agrarian reform worked there, and production did not fall off, because Huber ran the show, not Fidel.

But jealousy makes friends into enemies. Huber was not a veteran of the Moncada attack or of the *Granma* landing, but his popularity was as great as that of any hero of the revolution. So intrigues began to be set in motion to undermine him, intrigues fomented by Raúl and even by Fidel. Huber told me that he couldn't go on much longer without being able to resolve administrative problems and to deal with the army (Raúl) and political forces (Fidel). He had decided that if he couldn't talk things out face to face with Fidel, he'd resign. I tried to convince him not to and told him his situation was like that of many of us. Then I brought up the matter of Urrutia, and how when he and his secretary Olivares had discussed Communist infiltration and Urrutia's intention to resign, Olivares had gone straight to Fidel with the news. I told Huber that Fidel didn't accept resignations, not even in the Sierra. It was useless.

Huber probably felt his moral strength was enough to keep Fidel at bay and that his own prestige was great enough to guarantee his safety. He had misjudged his enemies, very badly. Even today I disagree with his self-martyrdom, although I admire his bravery. Some days later, Huber called me to say he had spoken with other friends about the situation. This in itself was foolish, because all our telephones were tapped. *Revolución* was under constant surveillance, and we had even caught one of Raúl's personal bodyguards in the printing shop (Raúl later came by to apologize to the workers about the "mistake"). So when I answered Huber, I knew I was speaking to more than one person, and so I said that I realized he was trying to resolve a personal situation but that I feared his private motives would be taken as political acts.

One afternoon my office phone rang. It was Fidel, asking me what I thought about Huber Matos's resignation. I had to be careful, so I laughed. Fidel, not at all amused, asked me what was so funny. I told him I was so surprised to hear his voice that I thought it was someone imitating him. Then I took the initiative and asked him what he thought. "I think I'll accept his resignation, and besides, he's left a letter—" I interrupted him to say that I thought it was a good idea to accept Huber's resignation, and then Fidel hung up. Within a few hours, no one was talking about Huber's resignation because the word "plot" had been substituted. Camilo Cienfuegos went to Camagüey to arrest Huber and the officers of his column who had resigned with him. Huber remained calm throughout, even when Camilo went on radio and television in Camagüey to accuse Huber of serious crimes. And as in the Urrutia case, the accusations were simultaneously violent and vague. Additional problems arose when a radio announcer from Camagüey, Jorge Enrique Mendoza, who had joined Radio Rebelde at the end of the war and who had become popular because of his melodious voice, began to gather "evidence." He talked a lot about whether or not Huber's officers were part of this conspiratory resignation, about some kind of manifesto (which never appeared), about declarations Huber *was going to make* (and never did), about whether the coordinator of the 26 July Movement's activities in Camagüey, Joaquín Agramonte, was involved in the conspiracy, about whether *Revolución* was trying to exalt Huber. Of course, Huber could have done lots of things, such as starting a revolt, but he did absolutely nothing. Huber was never involved in counterrevolutionary activities of any kind, but Fidel viewed him as a rival.

There was a meeting of the Council of Ministers, and Faustino Pérez spoke out: "I think Comandante Huber Matos is innocent and should be set free instantly." To which Raúl Castro replied: "Huber Matos is a traitor to the revolution and should be shot." Ministers Manuel Ray and Enrique Oltuski agreed with Faustino. Che remarked, with acid Argentine irony, "I guess we'll have to shoot the lot of them." He laughed, but no one knew if he was joking or not. Fidel ended the discussion by saying, "Either Huber Matos is a traitor or I'm a liar." Faustino told him that was Batista-style terrorism. "No," said Fidel, "revolutionary terrorism." All I could say was that the revolution could ill afford to shoot Huber Matos or any other comrade in arms. I reminded Fidel of his own words: "This revolution will not devour its own children." Then Che spoke out, this time seriously: "People who have the courage to stick to their opinions, people like Faustino, Ray, and Oltuski, who are risking their lives by doing so, should not only not be shot, but should go on being ministers." Fidel, as usual, had the last word: "No, we won't shoot him. And we won't make him a martyr. We shall remand him to the courts of the revolution. As for Faustino and the others, well, they cannot go on as ministers because they have lost the confidence of the revolution."

Faustino, who had been doing a terrific job in property recovery, was replaced by an opportunist named Rolando Díaz Astarain. Ray was replaced by Camilo Cienfuegos's brother Osmaní, the

Party's candidate. Manuel Fernández was replaced by Augusto Martínez Sánchez, Raúl's secretary. This meant that four key ministers were Raúl's men. The most important was Labor, because now Raúl and the Party could attack the free trade unions.

Huber Matos, in a trial in which Fidel refused to allow him to speak, was sentenced, along with his comrades from the Antonio Guiteras column, to twenty years in jail. Our problem, my problem, was Huber's: should I do what he did or try to keep going? I kept going, and I think I would do the same thing again. I can say that *Revolución* did accomplish things over the following two years in a losing struggle against the Cuban Communists and the Soviet Union, and that we were loyal to the ideas of Huber, Daniel, Frank País, and Echevarría even if we didn't resign. Many years later, when I was working in the archives of the revolution, during a permanent "socialist disgrace," I received from Fidel Castro himself a series of documents: angry letters Fidel and Huber had sent each other in the Sierra, Huber's resignation, a Security report signed by Comandante Manuel Piñeyro about Huber's "conspiracy." Aside from Huber's name, the names of Faustino Pérez, David Salvador, various labor leaders, and 26 July Movement leaders were also included. I was supposed to be the intellectual leader of the conspiracy. Fidel told me I could "take a good look" at everything, but I already knew what was there.

CAMILO

Camilo Cienfuegos was the toast of Havana. He was the nicest and the most Cuban of all the barbudos, the youthful hero. What his ideas were would be difficult to say, even for me, who was his friend. His intellectual master was Che Guevara. At least he was during the war when Camilo, because of his incredible bravery, made himself conspicuous. Efigenio Amejeiras, one of Fidel's Twelve, himself a terrific fighter of legendary proportion, used to say that Camilo didn't know what fear was, that he had no notion of death. And that he never bragged. The only anecdote he liked to tell concerned the battle of Las Mercedes. Che and Camilo were chasing a hundred or so soldiers who were running along the road at Vegas in Jibacoa. The mountains of the Sierra turn into foothills out there, and the river creates a crisscross effect that makes the whole area ideal for ambushes. It was a race, and no one could tell who was running faster, Che and Camilo or the troops. In one fire fight, Camilo set up an ambush, but as it turned out, it was Che and his people who fell into it. Che saw some soldiers and told them he would set them free if they gave up. The soldiers answered that they would rather be prisoners than dead. You see, they were protected by the river bank but hemmed in by Camilo's machine gun. Then Che came up with one of his tricks. He tore up a white shirt, put it on a stick, and waved it. When he came out, he found Camilo laughing his head off, shouting: "I've captured Che! You gave up, you Argentine asshole!"

Che's sense of humor was just as good as Camilo's. And because he was brave, he never minded telling about running away and being afraid—in fact, he told those stories more often than he told about his victories. I never heard more than bits and pieces about the Santa Clara battle, and that was the key to the downfall of Batista. He also knew who was giving the orders, so he never said a word about being sent to La Cabana instead of being sent to take the Columbia base on January 2: it was Fidel who ordered Camilo to come from Yaguajay, one hundred kilometers away. Camilo shared the glory with Che when he negotiated the surrender of the base. Fidel's plan was simple: to leave Raúl out in the cold, to downplay Che's importance, and to exalt Camilo as a symbol of Cuba. It didn't quite work, but only because Camilo was such a naturally generous person.

What were his ideas? He was really a helter-skelter thinker. He sympathized with socialism and tended to follow Che, but

at the same time he was not limited to a program. He disliked
the underground fighters, as did all the fighters from the Sierra.
Like Che, he was in favor of allowing the Communists in at the
moment of victory and backed the promotion of Félix Torres, a
shotgun man from Yaguajay, perhaps the least authentic and the
most sinister of all the Communists in Cuba, to the rank of comandante. (It was Félix Torres who provoked half the province of
Las Villas into revolt with his abuses.) Camilo brought his brother
Osmaní, a militant Communist, into the army. Osmaní, along
with Alfredo Guevara and the "Mexican" group (Ordoquí, Edith
García Buchaca, and Dorticós) were (with Raúl, of course) the
Party's (and the Soviet Union's) Trojan Horse for entering the
revolution and detroying both the 26 July Movement and the
underground forces. But for all that, Camilo, like Che, was a
mild person. He also thought he wouldn't live long; in August
1958, as he was leaving the Sierra, he left all his manuscripts
with me, those he wrote and those written by other *guerrilleros*.
As he handed them to me, he said: "Your responsibility is to
publish the true history of the revolution."

He had no real respect for rank. One day in Cienaga de Zapatas,
as he was walking with Fidel and Celia, he began to tease Fidel.
"Fidel, someone's got to write our history." Fidel said nothing.
Camilo went on: "Someday you'll be an old geezer and you'll
lie like hell. And I won't be here to correct you." Camilo was
no fan of Raúl Castro. When Huber Matos resigned, Camilo arrested Huber (who didn't put up a fight in any case). He then
spoke at a press conference and accused Huber of treason. Because
it was he who spoke, the accusation was believed. It's possible
he was following orders. The official accounts of the affair record
no protests, but there were protests. We realized that Fidel would
allow no legal opposition to his leadership, because we realized
that we weren't living in a time of legality but of FIDELity. I
think Raúl, Ramiro Valdés, and Piñeyro, following Fidel's lead,
invented Huber's conspiracy, and that Che, Camilo, Almeida,
Amejeiras, and the rest believed it. They were fresh from the
war, when Fidel never lied. Now we were at peace.

One night Camilo Cienfuegos took off from Camagüey in a small Cessna with an inexperienced pilot. He disappeared, and not a single trace of him was ever found. Ever since, the theories have proliferated about his supposed assassins. I think it was simply his destiny to die young. It was Camilo who had endorsed the arrest of Huber Matos by bringing Huber in himself. He seemed, therefore, to be a part of Fidel's party. So why would Fidel have him murdered? The search for Camilo lasted a week and left Cuba in mourning. Everyone forgot Huber Matos, except Fidel, who later blamed Huber—indirectly, of course—for Camilo's disappearance. But Camilo was gone forever.

CHANGES OF MINISTERS AND POLICIES

In November there was an official change in policy. Che Guevara took Felipe Pazos's place as president of the National Bank, the radical Marxist in place of the moderate expert. The Minister of Labor was also changed, and this, as we shall see, was a key development. One by one, the Communists were losing all the unions in the country in the first free elections called by the revolution. The 26 July Movement and its labor leaders got 90 percent of the votes, the Communists 5 percent, and the Auténtico party the other 5 percent. Raúl was furious. We were on the eve of the first great workers' congress, the creation of the new, revolutionary CTC.

The Communists used one of their old tactics. By controlling the Ministry of Labor they could change the course of the labor movement. That's what they did in 1939–40, when they made a deal with Batista. They bureaucratized the union movement, established control from above, and began the union gangsterism and coercion that Eusebio Mujal would later use against the Communists themselves as well as anyone else who got in his way. Now, through Raúl, they were able to get their handpicked man, Augusto Martínez Sánchez, in. He took the place of Manuel Fernández, who, unlike Felipe Pazos, was no moderate. He was, in fact, a Guiterista and a radical anti-imperialist. He had been, as well, the teacher of Armando Hart and Faustino Pérez. Manuel Fernández's would be the hand that would slay the free and democratic workers' movement, the hand that would close the curtain on the union movement. He was a lawyer, and like Dorticós, he had some skeletons in his closet. He had been the secretary of one of Batista's men and had taken refuge with the Second Front. Raúl took him up, made him into a comandante and his personal hit man. He had been Minister of Defense, standing in for Fidel as prime minister when Fidel was abroad in April and May. Now he was in charge of labor.

Raúl Castro was the new Minister of Defense. Faustino and Ray were removed and their substitutes were Rolando Díaz Astarain and Osmaní Cienfuegos, in Recovery of Stolen Property and Public Works, respectively—a ninety-degree turnaround, according to some. It wasn't really. It was simply a matter of making official what had already been a fact since June, when Dorticós took over. Because of Raúl, Che, and Ramiro, the Communists were able to infilitrate wherever they desired—the army, State Security, INRA, the government itself. These were, by the way, the very men Fidel had publicly criticized in violent terms a short time before. Now he made their power official. The game was quite obvious to us, but not to the people. They took the comandantes for 26 July Movement leaders, not for old-line Communists. The old conservative jeer—calling them melons (green, or olive-green, on the outside, but red inside)—never rang truer.

THE FREE LABOR CONGRESS

On November 18, 1959, the new national workers' congress met in the old palace of the Confederation of Cuban Workers (CTC). By direct, secret, and free ballot—in the first and last free elections held under Fidel Castro—3,200 delegates were chosen from among all the unions and union groups in the country. Three thousand were from the 26 July Movement and two hundred came from the Communists and other groups. The Cuban proletariat had a long tradition of socialist struggle and was being reborn after opposing the Batista dictatorship, contributing its own martyrs, and fomenting its own key strikes—the sugar strike of 1956; the bank and electric strike of 1957; the general strike that was a response to the murder of Frank País; the frustrated, repressed strike of 1958; and the decisive, triumphant strike of 1959 that quashed the efforts of General Cantillo, the army, the United States embassy, and the Cuban conservatives. The Cuban labor movement had always been characterized by being independent, anti-imperialist, and free right from the start. It was socialist, antimilitarist, anti-Batista, and, like the majority of the people, at one with the 26 July Movement.

During the Batista years, labor had begun to reject the Communists because the Party had played along with the dictator and was out of touch with the people. The workers themselves felt they were part of something new, something Cuban, a new kind of revolution. That spirit had been created in the slave cabins on the sugar plantations. Later, in the tobacco factories, the workers would listen to paid readers recite all sorts of books as they worked; the owners would pay the readers, who were chosen by the workers (by vote). The texts were discussed and chosen by the workers. It was among those workers that Martí found money and men. During the long, frustrated republican period, the unions had many causes to fight for, among them the right of Cubans to be apprentices, the right to be paid in money (they were usually paid in coupons redeemable at the company store). During the

Machado years, in the thirties, socialist ideology displaced the earlier anarchist influence.

The workers made their strikes radical in August 1933. Gerardo Machado was about to fall, and the Communists, who were directing the Confederation's strike, tried to stop it because of instructions from the International. They changed tactics, had talks with Machado, and were promised higher wages. Then the dictator fell, but it was the army that had power. In 1933 the revolutionary government of Guiteras had accomplished great things, but it was all drowned in blood in 1935, when Fulgencio Batista came to power. The Confederation was reorganized and made legal in 1939, when the Communists made their deal with Batista. Its upper echelons were dependent, but the grass-roots development was independent. The movement was well organized throughout Cuba and obtained economic advantages: an eight-hour day, a minimum wage, the right to strike, compensation, protection from being fired. The rights promulgated by the revolution of 1933 and the constitution of 1940 had become facts. Between 1944 and 1952, the Confederation was divided by Mujal and his henchmen, who took advantage of special-interest groups and the support the Communists were giving to Batista. After 1952 it was again reorganized and was one of the protagonists in the struggle that became a triumph in 1959.

The workers loved Fidel; whatever he asked, they gave. But they never gave up their independent unions. When Che, Raúl, and Fidel himself pressured them with their call for unity, they answered with a clear yes in favor of the revolution and of humanistic socialism. But they voted no to the Communists. The Congress and the unions rejected outside influence absolutely. The two hundred Communist delegates abstained from all votes, while the three thousand who did vote chose a CTC that was pure 26 July Movement. The executive was totally 26 July: David Salvador, Conrado Bécquer, José María de Aguilera, Jesús Soto, José Pellón, Cabrera. Then the Congress tumultuously applauded Fidel, pledged its support to the revolutionary government, and swore to attack the enemies of the revolution.

The Congress also voted its enthusiastic support of *Revolución*, at the time involved in rough polemics. The Congress felt *Revolución* to be its voice, a voice that spoke out against vested interests, conservatives, Communists, and Soviet sympathizers that were attempting to usurp the revolution. Those enemies, meanwhile, were not asleep. The conservatives were looking toward Washington, the Party faithful toward Moscow. Raúl was busy in the background, along with Carlos Rafael Rodríguez and Aríbal Escalante. Their plan was simple: have the new Minister of Labor "take care" of the upstart unions and the CTC. When Fidel saw he could not bring the workers around to his point of view, he decided to let nature take its course. He was right; he had more important problems for the moment—the economy and the United States. In the future, he would have plenty of time for this little matter.

2

1960: NEW YEAR'S EVE IN THE HABANA-LIBRE HOTEL

To bid farewell to 1959 and to greet the new and, as we would soon see, decisive 1960, we had an official dinner in the Habana-Libre. The mix at our table was a bit odd: Fidel, Celia, my wife, Margot, and I. Then two guests of *Revolución*, Giselle Halimi and Claude Faux, French writers and lawyers, friends of Sartre and Simone de Beauvoir, who would themselves soon visit the island. And Joe Louis, the American mulatto who had knocked out the Aryan great white hope, Max Schmeling, was Fidel Castro's personal guest. Louis wasn't scarred or physically smashed up; he was mentally beaten, punchy. I was a fan of his and remembered the party we had in my hometown with the blacks when he beat Schmeling. But what Louis meant as a symbol wasn't lost on me: Fidel was warning me again. For him, sports were more important than culture. Back in the Sierra, Fidel had wanted us to broadcast scenes from the war on Radio Rebelde while Che and I insisted on reading poetry. I remembered that on our trips to New York and Washington Fidel had refused to go to art museums, preferring to have his picture taken in the zoo. I remembered when he refused to support our petition to have the Cintas painting collection sent to Cuba. But, for all that, we still had room to maneuver, and *Revolución* still retained some autonomy. *Lunes*, the Monday literary supplement edited by Guillermo Cabrera Infante, annoyed some but impressed everyone.

We were preparing for important visits: Jean-Paul Sartre, Simone de Beauvoir, Pablo Neruda, and others. We wanted to bring culture to the people. Fidel didn't see things that way, but he took advantage of the propaganda. Nineteen fifty-nine had been a year of experiments, discoveries, and conflicts, a strange mixture of the old and the new, of collective justice mixed with individual injustice. Nineteen sixty would be the final test. It didn't look bad. There was a balance of power. On one side, *Revolución*, *Lunes*, the intellectuals, television, the students, the unions, and the old underground groups. On the other, Raúl, Ramiro Valdés, the army, the Communists, the government, Che. And Fidel above us all. The United States seemed to be setting up an attack, and the bourgeoisie, the landowners, the Catholic Church, and the politicos were emigrating. The bourgeoisie still had control of the press and the economy in cities, but the revolution held the country. Still, nothing was clear either for them or for us. The future, reform or revolution, would be determined by the position the United States would adopt, not by Fidel's desires. I personally wasn't concerned about the U.S. reaction because I already knew it would be one of outrage, but I was worried about the pro-Soviet backlash that would take place in Cuba and the possibility that Fidel would ally himself totally with the Soviet Union if there was a break with the United States. Many of us saw the perils built into the Soviet bureaucratic structure, which blends so easily with the militarism and caudillismo of a man like Fidel Castro. At the moment, however, the people were still armed as militia, so anything was possible, even a humanistic revolution that could be profound, democratic, respectful of civil rights, and where the people would be the actors instead of the spectators.

MIKOYAN: A KEY VISIT

In the early days of February, Anastas Mikoyan, vice-prime minister of the Soviet Union, came to Cuba. Fidel Castro, Raúl, Che Guevara, and President Dorticós met him at the Havana airport.

He was given a huge reception and an extended tour of the island—with Fidel at his side—which lasted for weeks. A major topic was the Soviet Union's purchase of Cuban sugar and our purchase of Russian oil. All of these arrangements were supposed to signify our open relationship with the entire world instead of "just a part of the world." We all thought it was a good thing, an assertion and affirmation of our independence as well as a gesture of good will. While the contracts were important, they did not, at the time, seem so absolutely important. Again, things happened so fast I couldn't grasp the meaning of major events.

There were, of course, many people in Cuba who were resisting any kind of change. Their blind criticism confused the valid critics who saw exactly which way the regime was tending. Some individuals, Boitel and Valladares among them, organized protests; they would soon be jailed. The journalist José Luis Massó went so far as to remind Mikoyan on television of the Soviet invasion of Hungary. As 1960 began to pass, we realized just how important Mikoyan's visit was, how it marked the moment in which Fidel Castro changed his strategy, which was now to seek the support of the Soviet Union in order to counter the United States. The invitation to bring the Soviet exposition from Mexico to Cuba and Mikoyan's visit were timed perfectly by Alexander Alexayev (Russia's representative in Cuba), Fidel, and Raúl's henchmen in Havana, Mexico, and Moscow. The result was, as we have already seen, that the Soviets would buy our sugar and we would buy their crude oil. Now, you wouldn't have to be a prophet to figure that Esso and Shell would refuse to refine Russian oil. This was how Fidel's trap was going to work. Later we saw the far-reaching results of Mikoyan's trip: the Soviet Union and the "socialist group" became the buyers of our sugar and our oil suppliers. At the time this seemed a reasonable response to the U.S. economic blockade. So imperialist pride worked in Fidel Castro's favor: if Esso and Shell wouldn't refine Russian crude, Cuba would nationalize the refineries.

SARTRE-BEAUVOIR

Jean-Paul Sartre and Simone de Beauvoir arrived in 1960, during one of the best moments of the Cuban Revolution and one of the best moments we had at *Revolución*. There was a party atmosphere throughout the island, a collective joy that manifested itself in singing and playing bongo drums. It was a Cuban way of changing life: voluntary labor, militia duty, rumba, all at the same time. *Revolución* was a new-style paper: huge photos, a front page that blended the poster with modern graphics. Our intention was to create a visual impact, because we wanted to capture our audience in order to educate it. Education through information. Our colors were red and black—the 26 July Movement and (why not?) Stendhal. We had a great staff. The literary people included Cabrera Infante, Pablo A. Fernández, Heberto Padilla, Arenas, Calvert Casey, Baragano, Severo Sarduy, Maso. The reporters and journalists were the best in Cuba: Barbeito, Hernández, Constantín, Benítez, Vazquez Candela, Arcocha. Photography was in the hands of Jesse Fernández, who left *Life* to work for us, along with Corrales, Korda, Salas, and Mayito. We were in the polemic business: with *La Marina*, a paper with one hundred years' worth of conservative tradition; with *Prensa Libre*, which waged a great war of words with us; with *Hoy*, the Communist party organ, directed by Carlos Rafael Rodríguez.

Sartre came into town like an *enfant terrible* in the true French tradition, and within a week both he and Simone de Beauvoir were incredibly popular, in large measure because the people got to see both of them—Sartre, ugly but *simpático*, and Simone, more reserved but interested in everything Cuban. They were everywhere: at meetings, on the street, in the carnival, out in the country, on television. In the recently established National Theater, Miriam Acevedo put on an extraordinary *Putain Respetueuse*. That was the only time we managed to drag Fidel to a cultural event. We photographed him flanked by Miriam Acevedo ("My best *putain*," as Sartre said) and Simone and surrounded by the other actors. The fact was that Sartre was fascinated by that wonderful 1960 and saw a living, spontaneous revolution that was not yet dominated by the Communist party. He was fascinated by the absence of a bureaucratic structure. He saw Fidel in dialogue with the people. But, of course, Sartre could only see what was on the surface.

We told him how worried we were about the caudillo, about the disappearance of the 26 July Movement, about how the guerrilla forces were being incorporated into Raúl's military structure and how the Communist party's bureaucratic mechanism was slowly but surely taking over. At the end of his visit, Sartre had a long talk with Fidel in which he spoke about the revolution as something unique, something socialist as well. This put Fidel on his guard, and he told Sartre that he was afraid to tell the world that the Cuban revolution would be socialist. He added that he hoped Sartre would understand the danger Cuba would be in if the revolution were called socialist and that Sartre should not describe it in that way. Which Sartre agreed not to do. Then Sartre said he could easily arrange to have friends—scientists, philosophers, writers—come to Cuba to teach without salary. To which Fidel said nothing, an answer I understood perfectly well. Once again Cuba would be deprived of a chance at cultural stimulation and revitalization. This negative attitude of Fidel's was disturbing, especially because of the man making the offer. How could we create a socialist society without rebuilding our cultural life, without having cultural freedom?

LA COUBRE

It was carnival time in Havana. The streets were filled with people dancing to conga rhythms, and Sartre and Simone de Beauvoir were right there with them. To the extent that the people included their names when calling dance steps (remember, Sartre's name is quite a mouthful for a *habanero* at carnival time): "Saltre, Simona: one-two-three / Saltre, Simona: take a step. / Look out now 'cause here I come." That beginning of 1960 was fantastic, because it brought us our second independence.

At the time, a French freighter, *La Coubre*, was being emptied of its cargo of arms and dynamite. These had been sold to us by Belgium, because although we had lost our traditional arms supplier, the United States, we didn't want to turn automatically to the USSR. Suddenly a huge explosion down at the docks shook all of Havana and a colossal mushroom cloud formed in the sky. The air was filled with wailing sirens, and the streets and hospitals were crowded with the dead and wounded. The joy of the carnival fell off the faces of the people like so many masks.

The next day there was a state funeral for the innocent victims. From the Malecón to Doce y Vientitrés the streets were solid with people, all moving to the presidential platform at the entrance to Colón cemetery. The people waited in silence, tense. Fidel began to speak: "We shall answer counterrevolutionary terror with revolutionary terror." The other face of Cuban reality had begun to show itself. Just what did happen to *La Coubre*? Fidel scoffed at the idea of an accident. He said he had no doubt that the explosion was an act of sabotage: first they refuse to sell us arms, now they blow up the arms we buy elsewhere. After all, hadn't the counterrevolutionaries and the imperialists tried to sabotage us before, in 1959? They certainly did. It is probably a fact that someone deliberately blew up *La Coubre*, but who? Now a new terror was being born, the Red terror. You could see it on Fidel's face as he spoke.

ATTACKS AND COUNTERATTACKS

Cuba acquired some Russian crude oil at a very low price, but the oil companies refused to refine it. It was a clear conflict between the nation and the foreign companies. Were the companies to give in, they would be conceding that the government had legitimate control over them. So they declared the refineries to be their own, private property. Besides, they could afford to be arrogant: they had the support of the Eisenhower-Nixon regime and the old imperialist belief that they spoke for the United States. It was a rough situation, with little room in it for maneuvering. Whether or not the oil was refined was a small issue, of no importance next to the matter of national sovereignty. There was no going back: the Cuban government took over Esso and Shell—but it did not nationalize them. The companies went wild, and the U.S. government threatened to suspend the sugar quota.

Now, the fact was that we sold sugar to the United States and bought practically everything from them. The entire industrial and mechanical structure of the nation was imported from the United States: there was no factory, shop, motor, nut, bolt, automobile, refrigerator, television—nothing manufactured— that didn't come from up north. And if somehow something was not "Made in U.S.A.," it came from Europe. In reality, Cuba was simultaneously a real and an artificial country. It was an extension of the U.S. market, the U.S. world. To break with that world would mean going back to square one; to accommodate ourselves to it would mean giving up any chance for reform.

Our relations with the United States brought prosperity to a majority of Cuban citizens, but an important minority, almost a third of the population, was excluded from the economy. This group was made up of unemployed workers, marginal groups, and young people. The economy was extremely limited because of our dependence on sugar and the United States, and our job market was stagnant. At the same time, the population continued to grow. Clearly this situation could not continue indefinitely. Of course, the Cuban standard of living, in comparison with the rest of Latin America, was high: we had good salaries, we were consumers, we exported, and we imported. But Cuban life was paralyzed: we were crucified on the twin crosses of sugar and economic dependence. And the sugar industry was itself stagnant, fixed by quotas set elsewhere. So industrial development and agricultural diversification were kept to a minimum.

The student population, in and out of universities, was the logical place where the pressure to change things would build up. The students would in the end provide the shock troops for the revolution. It was they who recognized that Cuba was in effect a fiction, that every attempt the nation made to establish democratic institutions was subverted by the army, the sugar industry (both native and foreign-owned), and the United States. The Cuban people had throughout their history called for a more just distribution of the nation's wealth, in the same way that they had demanded the freedom and independence they loved and longed for.

The life of the nation was stifled by a triple alliance: the power of Yankee money, the Spanish world that could never tolerate Cuban culture, and the home-grown oligarchy of the Platt era, which had deprived us of independence, the republic, and freedom. The black element in our culture and the peasant element were both suppressed. The struggle against Batista brought back to life precisely those elements lost in 1899 and 1933. With the triumph of the revolution, the people openly questioned the validity of all the dominant structures in the nation, beginning with the army. The people felt themselves to be the protagonists in this struggle. It was a great moment, a time for action, for not turning back. So each attack provoked a counterattack. They wouldn't refine Russian crude, so we took over the refineries. They suspended the sugar quota, so we nationalized the mills. They ordered the economic blockade, so we nationalized U.S. property. The counterattack was always sharper than the attack that had provoked it. They thought they had us on the ropes, but they didn't. We were a small nation, unarmed, without Soviet support, but we were united and we just said no to them.

In the past, lesser actions had brought the marines into other Latin-American nations. But times change. We got moral support from Europe, Africa, and Asia. Which is not to say that there was no hesitation on our part—even the pro-Soviet Communists and their followers advised Fidel to keep calm, while the Soviets themselves recommended moderation. The revolutionary "left" became right, while the "right" became left. All except Che Guevara. The effect of Soviet pressure on Fidel was to radicalize him further, because what he wanted to do was compromise the Soviets by drawing them into our conflict with the United States. The 26 July Movement remained radically anti-imperialist and antimilitarist: it never accepted either the old Communists or the new ones (Raúl, Ramiro, etc.). As a matter of fact, the existence of independent trade unions and an uncensored press began to be of some concern to the pro-Soviet bloc, because they saw a popular revolution taking place that was not under their control. Especially worrisome for them was the national militia: everybody joined, more than a million men and women. This was a truly armed democracy—rifles for all and the chance to do volunteer work. It was all very Cuban, in the tradition that included Varela, Martí, Guiteras, Chibás, Echevarría, and Frank País. The revolution became anti-imperialism and freedom, the overthrow of the monoculture-militarist-dictatorship-dependence structure. When we nationalized sugar, we all felt a U.S. invasion was imminent, all but Fidel, who insisted that we had caught the Yankees off guard and that they were too slow to act to do anything right away. He was right. Nixon spouted off, but nothing happened. He probably counted on the economic blockade, keeping the CIA and its Guatemalan connection as an ace in the hole. They could always arm an expeditionary force to liquidate the Cuban Revolution.

NATIONALIZATION

The ceremony in the Cerro stadium was a tropical madness, a party complete with shots in the air, rumba, and chanting: "Hey, Fidel, go ahead, hit the Yankees on the head! / Bang bang, bam bam, score a knockout on Uncle Sam!" A throng moved out onto the old baseball fields. Then silence: it was time to hear Fidel.

With the historic decree in his hand, he began his microphone game. It seems he was hoarse: who wouldn't be if he, like Fidel, had been speaking for two years in a row for twelve or fourteen hours a day? Cuba may be an oral country, and its politicians certainly have been ever since Martí, but Fidel was the national champion. Usually he improvised, but this time he began to read the decree—and his voice gave out. Then he stopped, waited, then announced that his voice was coming back. It came and it went, again and again, and Fidel put on a mime act, opening his cavernous mouth and stretching out his huge arms. Some people said Fidel was just dramatizing the situation, but the fact was that he had lost his voice at a moment when he would have given anything to be able to talk. Then he just sat down.

First, tremendous silence. Then the people burst into a collective conga, and tensions evaporated. But Fidel, never a fan of the conga, realized that he was losing control of the event and made signs to the people to stop. No one paid the slightest attention, and time began to pass. Fidel signed to Raúl to do something. Now, Raúl is an aggressive sort, personally brave, but lacking historical worth. He has a complex, not Oedipus but Fidel. His vitriolic humor disappears the minute he approaches the speaker's platform, and his face turns into an exact replica of Chaplin's dictator. He's an operetta-class Hitler. The people instinctively rejected him, and Fidel augmented that negative image by saying that Raúl was the bad guy, the tough guy. They complemented each other perfectly, like Laurel and Hardy. But Laurel in this case had no self-confidence: he relied on the party machinery.

Finally the conga stopped, and Raúl read the decree with a tremor in his voice: the sugar industry was nationalized. The party started all over again, and even the next day Cuba was whirling around in a rumba cyclone.

NATIONALIZATION OR SOCIALIZATION?

The nationalization of the sugar industry was a death blow for private property. Some said that to nationalize was not necessarily to socialize. If we study the Russian Revolution and the application of its model in other countries, we see that state-controlled nationalization does nothing more than create and support a gigantic, nonproductive, and repressive bureaucratic superstate, a party that is the state, that is the father, that is the owner. Was another sort of state possible? Was our small island, dependent as it was on the United States, capable of becoming self-sufficient and independent? The pro-Soviet crowd said no, that our only hope was the Soviet Union. My crowd said yes, that we could count on the people, who had made a new, autonomous revolution. But what about Fidel?

The moment had come for the nation to break out of its ancient prison: sugar. Cuban conservatives had always asserted that without sugar there would be no Cuba, but revolutionaries had always asserted that with sugar there was no country, no liberty, and no independence. Power tends to be conservative, and again we must note the difference between power as such and the revolution, which was the people. The problem was that Fidel was power. A choice existed: the people or sugar? Are the people the principal capital of the revolution or is industry? For the Soviets and their satellites, industrialization is the answer to every problem, but we Cubans believed that the answer resided in the people themselves. We wondered if it would be possible to feed Cuba without sugar and without the United States. And if it was not possible, people would say, then why have a revolution? We were convinced we could survive, that we could challenge an economic blockade and even stand up to a physical blockade.

After all, Cuba is a tropical country, capable of sustaining a varied agriculture. We could feed ourselves. We could even survive a cutoff of our energy supplies, in part because the alcohol that sugar cane produces can be substituted for oil. Sugar would have to be a transitional product. We would have to develop our nickel production—Cuba possesses one of the world's largest deposits of ore. We would have to expend our energy supplies on developing that industry. Second, we would have to reorient our agriculture so that we would be self-sufficient with regard to food. Third, we would have to develop our tourism, an industry for which Cuba is ideal. We could then have relations with the entire world and not just a single part—the United States or the Soviet Union. Martí preached a policy of unity with the Spanish-speaking world: we could go beyond that and have relations with Africa, a motherland for so many of us, with Asia, and with the Third World. We could have relations with the socialist world.

Sure, sure, people said, economic resistance is possible, but what about military resistance? Without the Soviet Union, Cuba wouldn't exist. Which is a replay of: without the United States, Cuba wouldn't exist. People forget that Cuba stood alone in its conflict with the United States and its own capitalist class. We were a united people, ready to die, and with world opinion on our side. I know that in a short while people will say that Blas Roca* himself was on the *Granma*, that Laika, the canine cosmonaut, actually landed in the Sierra and that the Russian generals turned her into a hot dog at the Bay of Pigs, and that the one and only Mikoyan saved us in the missile crisis. But the fact of

* Francisco Calderio, a prominent Communist.

the matter is that we had the possibility of establishing our own Cuban socialism because the working class, the peasants, the youth of the nation, and a goodly sector of the middle classes were with us. The nation was coming into its own because it had taken back its wealth, had recovered its dignity, and was both free and independent.

This was the moment to have confidence in the people and to create new ways of life. To socialize our major industries would have been easy. The sugar workers were already politicized, and it would have been relatively simple to show them that they could work just as hard for their own interests as they had worked for the boss. The same applied to the cattle industry, which was in fact already supplying the nation with cheap milk and meat. Other industries, like tobacco, would also fall in line. We could stimulate the fishing industry and stop importing cooking oils—an absurdity in a country producing peanuts, corn, and sunflowers. We could turn to the people, to their long experience with the land. And land reform itself would be no problem because only a small minority of the peasants were freeholders, and most of these because the revolution gave them land. We possessed a sound transportation system, so distribution was no problem. Even the professional classes—including ten thousand physicians—supported the revolution. The counterrevolutionary bourgeoisie was already in the United States; good riddance to them. There was no real opposition to the revolution anywhere in Cuba. (Abroad, of course, opposition existed, but it could not, without U.S. assistance, topple the revolution.)

All we needed was to give power to the people—not to a military dictator. We did not need the Russian model, or any Soviet influence. Our thesis, as Comandante Daniel* put it in his polemic with Che Guevara, was, "We want to be free of Yankee imperialism, but we don't want to run into Russian imperialism in getting away from the United States." We also thought, and history has proven us right, that the Soviet Union was incapable of substituting

---

* René Ramos Latour's code name.

for the United States in its economic relations with Cuba. For one thing, it was too far away. For another, it had a totally different industrial structure. Russian spare parts were useless for U.S.-made machines. Russia didn't make the things we needed. And its ecomony, state-run instead of socialist, had already shown in Eastern Europe and China just how inefficient the Russians were. Besides, great powers like to control small ones.

In conversations with Fidel, we expressed our concerns about the Soviet Union and the models it offered, particularly its tendency to state monopoly instead of real socialism. Some of Fidel's decisions bothered us: state-owned farms instead of self-regulating cooperative farms. A tendency to gigantism: where there had been one huge plantation, Fidel combined ten and made a superplantation. We wanted small-scale agriculture so that we would not be substituting for the old boss a new administrator, for the old owner a new, state owner. But Fidel had an innate distrust of the people; he preferred militarization to organization. He also thought that in peacetime and in economics the same rules applied as in wartime and guerrilla fighting—that a group of leaders could change everything. It just wasn't so.

Fidel's strategy was to compromise the Soviet Union by rapidly deploying the structures of the Soviet state—the Communist party and a State Security agency. But even the Soviet government was unwilling to comply. The Soviets advised patience and constantly warned us, before and after the fact, about turning Cuba into a socialist state. All Soviet emissaries, ambassadors—even Khrushchev and Mikoyan—recommended calm and patience. As did China and the Eastern bloc nations. They were all shocked at the accelerated and artificial process of nationalization they saw us engaged in. The more they worried, the faster Fidel went. He envisioned a new kind of government—a Russian structure, but with himself at the top—that would be perfect for Third World nations. In that social structure, the role of the people was to work and to obey unquestioningly.

Fidel thought that those of us who had taken part in the revolution were not really ready for socialism. This was not true: we were not ready to accept Russian nonsocialism, not ready to accept a new caudillo. In a discussion with me, Fidel said that the only people in Cuba who knew anything about socialism were the old Communists and that I ought to set aside my prejudices against them and the Soviet Union. He believed, as he said, that the people were not yet ready for socialism, and that Stalinism had been the only way the revolutionary minority in the Soviet Union had been able to impose the revolution on a nonrevolutionary majority. I must point out that, at that particular moment, there existed no political apparatus in Cuba. Fidel had caused the 26 July Movement to vanish and had liquidated the Directorio in his two speeches of January 1959. The free trade unions, the popular militia, the revolutionary press, and their adherents were struggling against the reactionaries, the old Communists, and Soviet influence. Raúl, Ramiro, Che, and even Fidel himself had begun to attack us. The government had begun its war against the people. The people resisted, but Fidel possessed the power that turned them from protagonists into obedient servants.

THE PRESS

The press wars were ferocious. *La Marina* spewed out its rage against us every day, as did the other papers that served vested interests. Genuine criticism became confused with name-calling, and the air was charged with shrill cries about falling production, economic pitfalls, and the growing Communist presence in the revolution.

Bohemia was the most popular, most widely read magazine in Cuba. It had stood fast against Batista and praised Fidel even in the most difficult times. One day, its editor in chief, Miguel Quevedo, a friend of Fidel's, went out fishing and sent Fidel an enormous fish as a gift. That was, it turned out, Quevedo's farewell present: he headed north and never returned. Celia Sánchez froze the fish in the Once Street apartment, and seventeen years later it was still there. That deep-sea mummy stands as a monument to the moment when the minimal independence left to newspapers and magazines disappeared. Editors like Quevedo were replaced by groups or committees—but these were not even made up of workers. *Bohemia* and *Prensa Libre* were not like *La Marina*— the mouthpiece of privileged groups; they were simply independent. There was no time to think, only to fight.

Prensa Libre was scrupulous in its editorial policy, but its staff made mistakes because they just did not understand the situation. Nor did we. *Revolución* wanted to argue the issues, but we certainly did not want our opposite numbers to vanish—with the exception of *La Marina*. We wanted to see a clear distance between power and the press, between information and distortion. The problem in the case of *Diario de la Marina* (The Navy Newspaper) was clear, and a crisis was inevitable. Now, *La Marina* was a well-run paper that had been around for almost one hundred and fifty years. In its early numbers you could find advertisements for slaves; during the wars of independence, it fought against free Cuba. When it announced the deaths of José Martí and Antonio Maceo, it also announced banquets to celebrate the great events. I always hated *La Marina*: it had defended Franco and fascism in general. It was the mouthpiece of the sugar interests, of foreign interests, and of the Church hierarchy—always pro-Spain and anti-Cuba. It accepted Batista's bribes and presented his version of the news, unlike *Bohemia*, *Prensa Libre*, and the radio, which revealed (when they could) the crimes of the tyrant and the actions being taken by rebel groups. It was actually the Americans who had saved *La Marina* in 1898. I was all ready to seize it when Batista fell. We at *Revolución* were prepared to take it over, but Fidel vetoed the move, saying it would be seen as a negative step. When the editorial staff of *La Marina* finally fled, I ran over to close the paper down with a final headline: "140 Years Reactionary and One Day with the People."

Then we organized a wild party in the streets of Havana to celebrate the burial of the now dead *La Marina*. It was the people themselves who invented this tradition of comic funerals. The most memorable was held in 1975, in honor of Generalissimo Francisco Franco. *Revolución* wrote it up in a special edition that pointed out the hatred Franco's bureaucrats had for us. Mind you, I would gladly bury both Franco and *La Marina* all over again, but not *Bohemia* or *Prensa Libre*. I never imagined the Spanish tyrant would die peacefully in his bed, much less that the government of my country would decree a week of official mourning for General Francisco Franco—and would be unaware of the death of Mao in 1976. The offices of *La Marina*, the famous Prado and Teniente Rey building, exuded centuries of rancid colonialism.

The press itself, on the other hand, was fantastic. I wanted to make it into a national press and print as our first book a huge edition of *Don Quixote*. I had even convinced Fidel to write a preface. Once again, I was mistaken. As everyone said in Havana in those days, whatever we created fell right into Communist hands. Our good buddies from *Hoy*, together with Blas Roca, Carlos Rafael Rodríguez, and Raúl Valdés Vivo, got the Prado and Teniente Rey mansion. As Marx said, no one really knows for whom he is working. The *Hoy* crowd just loved the building because they thought it meant power. I think they really found their true niche: where you live tells a great deal about who you are. *Revolución* moved from the historic Carlos III building, the *Alerta* works, to the modern offices and shop of *Prensa Libre*, in Plaza de la Revolución. The building is in Walter Gropius's style—all windows and central air conditioning. (If the air conditioning broke down, the building turned into an oven; if you opened the window, your desk turned into a leaflet barrage.) The print shop was magnificent.

The disappearance of *Prensa Libre* didn't affect me in any way—at least not in the way I rejoiced when *La Marina* fell. *Prensa Libre* for us was an intelligent antagonist against whom we could measure our own abilities, strengths, and weaknesses. What we at *Revolución* really wanted, as far as location was concerned, was a new building that was to be designed by Le Corbusier and a German press like *Prensa Libre*'s that some of us had seen near Munich. But we all had the sensation that a whole world was vanishing before our eyes and that there was nothing we could do about it. I tried to look ahead, toward the new world that was being born, and I thought the role of the press, of the world of culture, and of the free unions would be critical. *Revolución*'s job had been to fight the old Cuba, and now it would be to fight against the pseudosocialism of the Soviet world. It was too big a job, but all in all, I think we fought a good fight until 1962, when everything hit bottom.

FIDEL VISITS NEW YORK: 1960

One day in September, strolling along Doce y Veintitrés, eating oysters as he did when he was a student (oysters had not yet disappeared, the Caribbean was still revolutionary, and that popular criollo aphrodisiac had not yet been replaced by Rumanian chemicals), Fidel stopped to chat with a black shoeshine-boy, a man famous as the best source of gossip in Havana. "What do you say I go up to New York and speak at the UN?" "*Caballo*, get on up there and put it to those damn Yankees." That was Fidel's amusing way of announcing his imminent departure to the rest of us.*

The trip had been a long time in preparation. Celia Sánchez had secretly rented a house in New York, and Ramiro Valdés had sent a detachment of Security rats up to check the food stocked there for poison. The health of the rats continued excellent—

---

* Fidel Castro first visited New York on April 15, 1959. This visit to the United Nations took place in September 1960.

which was only natural: we found out later that they had been infiltrated by the CIA, which was under orders to protect both the house and Fidel Castro. Fidel was no doubt an enemy, but nothing was going to happen to him on American soil.

The trip was a platform for denunciations, for making contacts, and for creating an international reputation for Cuba. It was a way for us to meet, without unduly compromising ourselves, the heads of state who would speak that year at the UN: Krushchev, Nasser, Nehru, Sékou Touré, Tito, and Gomulka. The situation was red-hot. The Americans restricted Fidel and his delegation, journalists included, to New York City. Fidel responded by confining the U.S. ambassador, Philip Bonsal, to the Vedado district of Havana.

A few days before leaving for New York, at a huge meeting in the Plaza de la Revolución, Fidel had publicly torn up the military treaty that had "united Cuba to the United States." I wanted to photograph the torn treaty for the front page of *Revolución*, so I grabbed it out of Fidel's hands the moment he tore it, much to the astonishment of Carlos Rafael Rodríguez, then editor of the Communist paper *Hoy*. Fidel warned me to take good care of the document because he would need it at the UN. Well, we brought out our special edition, but we took such good care of the treaty that it disappeared. Pití Fajardo, Fidel's secretary at the time (he would die soon after in the Escambray) started calling me every day to tell me Fidel wanted both the treaty and the photos. I couldn't find the treaty, and I knew Fidel intended to rip it again in his UN show. The day before Fidel's scheduled departure, the document turned up in *Revolución*'s safe. That night I slept with the treaty. The next morning I got up early, tucked the treaty under my arm, and headed for the airport feeling like a real left-wing intellectual. There they were: Fidel, the delegation, Raúl Roa, Regino Boti, Ramiro Valdés, Security, the journalists—*tutti*.

As soon as he saw me, Fidel asked for the treaty. I handed it over and breathed a sigh of relief. Fidel opened the cylinder and took out—to my shock and horror—half a treaty! How could I have lost it, I, who had carried all kinds of papers during the underground days and the war? Fidel, who usually swore like a drill sergeant, kept calm but told me we wouldn't leave until I turned up the other half. I was hysterical but tried to reassure him (and myself) by saying the other half had to be in my house. It was—on the floor next to the bed.

We took off and headed north. Fidel turned to Ramiro Valdés and asked if we would have an escort plane with us. Valdés stuttered out a no. "We're in danger. If I were running the CIA, I'd shoot down the plane at sea and report the whole thing as an accident." Silence reigned. Fidel went on, "At least we should have had an escort. What a mistake." Everybody started to look around. Suddenly we heard a huge roar: a squadron of planes heading toward us from the north. Yankee fighters. Everybody panicked. Except me: I had been so scared about the lost treaty that I had no more fright left; besides, I had taken a few motion sickness pills and drunk a couple of daiquiris. I enjoyed watching the warriors turn pale. The fighters came closer, and we could make out U.S. territory ahead. Fidel was calm. I think he said all those things just to see how we would react. I realized there were too many planes for an attack. They were our honorary escort. We entered U.S. territory literally under the CIA's wing.

We landed in New York and stepped out into a crowd of cops and cameras. When our own photographer, Raúl Corrales, tried to take the first photo of Fidel, he was passed through the air like a ball from one "Jiménez" to another. (Cuban military intelligence had been modeled on that of the U.S. Army, so it was called G-2. A G-2 agent in Cuba was automatically translated into our slang as a "Jiménez.") We found we couldn't go to Celia Sánchez's place because by then it was neither secret nor safe. Fidel wanted to hang his hammock in the UN gardens, but regulations forbade it. Then Fidel suggested we camp out in Central Park, maybe set up guerrilla operations there. Finally we were offered lodging in the Hotel Teresa in Harlem. We were delighted, especially Fidel, because he knew that being in the black ghetto had enormous political value. The Teresa, as it turned out, was something of a bordello, but at least we had enough space.

Ramiro Valdés was livid, especially when the female inhabitants of the Teresa showed up. Ramiro was upset because he figured, policeman that he was, the U.S. press would try to get some defamatory photos of us, but he finally resigned himself to whatever would come. Besides, black Harlem was all around us, protecting us. We could hear the chant: "Fidel-Lumumba, Fidel-Lumumba" all the time. There were anti-Fidel demonstrations by Cuban exiles and pro-Fidel demonstrations by Cuban sympathizers. The police were constantly breaking up increasingly violent demonstrations with Western-style cavalry charges. Harlem took us in, and Fidel, to show his gratitude, had Juan Almeida, the comandante, the black associated with the Virgin of Charity, flown up. The rest of us were white men. So Almeida and Celia became the symbols of negritude and the female world.

FIDEL ADDRESSES THE GENERAL ASSEMBLY

The young Fidel Castro, with his beard, his military bearing, his Roman profile, his olive-green uniform, created a stir. He was thirty-four years old, the symbol of a young revolution. He approached the lectern without a prepared speech: where all heads of state read, he would improvise. The media of the entire world closely followed every word. During the first hour, Fidel captivated everyone with the speech he had memorized. Even during the second he kept everyone's attention. In the third hour, people began to get bored. By the fourth, the delegates began to squint at their watches, wondering if he would ever finish.

Of course, even in Cuba people fell asleep during Fidel's harangues. And this despite their affection for Fidel and their interest in what he had to say. He would go on for hours and hours, so that more than one fell into disgrace by nodding off and being caught in the act. Now, in the UN the only person who had already allowed himself the luxury of a nap during a speech was Nehru, who had succumbed during speeches by Khrushchev and Kennedy. This time, impassive and hermitic, he stayed awake.

When Khrushchev saw that people were no longer paying attention, he took off his shoe and pounded on the table, an allusion to those famous, symbolic missiles. So Fidel went on for more than four hours. That was Fidel in a nutshell, a man with no sense of limits. Once he gets started, he doesn't know how to stop. At the end he was cheered. A left-wing Italian journalist, an old hand and a friend, observed that Fidel had said all he had to say in the first hour, that it was a shame he had gone on so long, but that the performance reminded him of Mussolini. We made our excuses by chalking it up to tropical exuberance.

VODKA WITH PEPPER, KHRUSHCHEV-STYLE

Nikita Khrushchev invited Fidel Castro and the Cuban delegation to a dinner at the Russian consulate in New York. Khrushchev seemed *simpático*: a certain Ukrainian vivacity, his report to the Twentieth Congress on de-Stalinization, his peasant aspect, his wisecracks, his vodka-and-pepper disguised as water. His thesis on peace and coexistence was also interesting. He was not grandiloquent or melodramatic like other Russians, who conceal their hideous melancholy and arrogance in a costume of false humility. Khrushchev was the hope, if not the reality, of a less Stalinist, more humane Soviet Union.

I had begun to observe Khrushchev as if he were some rare animal; José Pardo Llada, a Cuban colleague, and I watched him as we strolled through the General Assembly. We both were and were not delegates, because the same U.S. bureaucrats who had confined us all to New York had also demanded that we be included in the official delegation. We were there as journalists, although, to be sure, Ramiro Valdés, Raúl Roa, and Emilio Aragonés were not sympathetic either to us or to our task. Fidel was involved in his own work and had no time for anything else. The "brain trust" Fidel included in the delegation had to spend its time gathering information on everything from economics to politics, so they never had a free evening. Naturally, they were furious when I slipped out at night to take in what I could of New York. Besides, I knew very well Fidel would never really rely on the information they could provide. He was always "too busy" to meet with them.

Just before leaving Havana, I had a run-in with Ramiro Valdés. I had appointed Cabrera Infante, Benites, Corrales, and Salas as reporters to cover the trip. Valdés objected, saying that the reporters would be chosen by Security, from a list provided by Zamorita, their press chief. Zamorita was yet another ex-Batista man, "reconstructed," of course, by Escalante and Valdés to work in Security. I told Ramiro Valdés I wouldn't accept his offer, and Valdés told Fidel. I told Fidel that all he had to do was to name Ramiro director of *Revolución* and make Zamorita his second in command. He could do that, but no one could make me accept Security flunkies as my reporters. Fidel told Ramiro to leave me alone. As a result, there we were, Pardo and I, with less real work to do. So we went out to meet people from other delegations, to get interviews, and to observe characters.

We were in the act of studying that paunchy, inelegant gentleman Khrushchev when he suddenly asked us who we were. When we told him we were Cubans, he threw his arms around us and asked for Fidel. Khrushchev may have surprised us, but the reporters who covered the Assembly were ready. We told him where Fidel was (on the other side of the Assembly), and Nikita, still hugging us close, went on to meet him. TV cameras, photographers, journalists, and delegates all ran along with us. It was a tremendous gesture on Khrushchev's part—the Russian going to the barbudo. Pardo—the best radio journalist Cuba has ever had—was beside himself with joy. "Tomorrow we'll be on every front page in the world!" As we got closer to Fidel, the crush got greater and greater. Pardo stuck it out, and in the picture he's right between Khrushchev and Fidel. Of me all you can see is my head in a corner. What did Khrushchev's meeting with Fidel mean? Moral (at least) support for Cuba and a "hands off" warning to the Yankees.

Later on, I thought: Who can ever break loose from a Russian bear hug? The photograph had a curiously socialist beginning and end. It was published all over the world. I found it in Berlin, Moscow, Warsaw, Prague, Budapest. A few years later, Pardo discovered true socialism and left Cuba. His face was erased from the picture. My head became a black spot in 1961. I guess the photo was jinxed because even Nikita Khrushchev fell into disgrace, and with him the picture. Only Fidel is left. And even he has had to discard a lot of photos—this one with Khrushchev, records of his visits to the Soviet Union in 1963 and 1964, and others.

We were late for the official banquet with Khrushchev, Honorio Muñoz, an old Cuban Communist, got paler and paler as time went by; after all, to dine with Khrushchev represented heaven to him. He would peek at his watch, then at Fidel; then he'd point out to Ramiro Valdés that we would be late. Ramiro knew Fidel perfectly well and said nothing. Fidel liked to keep people waiting and had also forgotten about New York traffic. Of course, Cuban experience in these matters of protocol was zero. Meanwhile, it was already nightfall, and at the Russian consulate, both Khrushchev and Gromyko had descended the main stairway in order to receive Fidel at the door. The cameramen began to take pictures—but no Fidel. The reporters started to make wisecracks. Maybe Mr. K. is being stood up by this handsome devil? Was Fidel a Communist? To which Khrushchev astutely answered, "I don't know if he is a Communist, but I am certainly a fidelista." A Ukrainian refugee shouted something, Khrushchev went out to the street to shout back, and the incident ended with a laugh. A half-hour late, we finally arrived.

After the official greetings, we went upstairs, where Russian humor disappeared. Gromyko's face was longer and sadder than ever. Even Khrushchev was solemn. We sat down, and Khrushchev invited us to make ourselves at home and take off our jackets.

Then he made the first of a long line of toasts. Fidel, fearful of so much alcohol, immediately reached for his cigars. The Russians went pale as they passed around the cigars. Then Khrushchev began to make jokes, almost as a contrast to the Comandante's dour figure. The vodka took its toll: Boti, our Minister of Economy, interrupted Fidel (it was possible in those days) and began to discourse on world problems. Muñoz was really in paradise and began to imagine himself with Khrushchev taking over Wall Street. Nikita told counterrevolutionary jokes from the Lenin era. I asked him if he knew any Khrushchev jokes. He said he could do better than that. He pointed to Gromyko and said, "Cubans, form your revolutionary tribunal and sentence Gromyko here. He was the one who recognized Batista." You could hear a pin drop. Too bad Carlos Rafael Rodríguez, the Soviets' man in Havana, wasn't there. In any case, Gromyko never moved a muscle. He just drank and smoked—he was the only Russian who knew how to handle cigars. The evening ended without any more problems.

I asked Khrushchev for an interview. He said he would see me in the Soviet Union, because he wanted me to have firsthand experience of Soviet society and its triumph over capitalism. The honeymoon between Fidel and the Russians had begun.

RECEPTION AT THE HOTEL TERESA

The Fair Treatment for Cuba Committee, a New York group, offered us a reception at the Hotel Teresa. All of progressive, intellectual New York turned out for the occasion, including representatives of the future Black Power movement and the beat-generation poets. Allen Ginsburg astonished Ramiro Valdés with this question: "Marijuana is revolutionary, but the imperialists have invented all kinds of stories about it just so no one will smoke it and rebel. What does the Cuban Revolution think about marijuana?" I confess that even I—no smoker of marijuana; indifferent to it, if anything—was surprised by the question. It was a fact that lots of peasants out in the Sierra grew marijuana secretly because it was second only to coffee as a cash crop. As with so many other things, Fidel turned a blind eye to the clandestine marijuana farmers, and it was only at the end of the war that he began a crackdown on marijuana. I would agree with Malcolm X, who pointed out that all drugs are traps set by the dominating groups in a society, especially nowadays, when one can see that the drug industry is a multinational business. Cartier-Bresson was at the Teresa that night. His photographs may still be seen.

A TRIP TO MOSCOW

My request for an interview with Khrushchev turned into an invitation, not only for me but for a delegation of journalists. I had wanted to make a trip on my own, but that was impossible. We flew first to Madrid, then on to Paris. In Paris we changed to Aeroflot for the flight to Moscow. We were surprised that the Russian plane had first- and second-class seats and that the décor was in a hideous neo-Empire style. Someone asked who it was who got to go first-class in a socialist plane. And then came the great beef puzzle, posed by Guillermo Cabrera Infante: in an egalitarian division of a steer, who gets the filet mignon?

We landed at Moscow and strolled out of the plane Cuban-style: every man for himself, no order, no protocol—we still hadn't learned. For the Soviet officials this was a real problem. Finally they led me to a microphone and a battery of television cameras: a live interview, without prepared texts, a rare event indeed. Then came a volley of kisses, which almost constituted a profanation of our Latin-American machismo. There were Central Committee members there, as well as people from the government and the press corps (Ylichov from *Izvestia* and Adzubei from *Pravda,* and people from Tass and Radio Moscow). Our official guide would be Commander Chernichev (we called him the Red Terror when we got close enough to him to detect his personal fragrance). Fortunately, we had along with us a young, very pro-Soviet woman who managed to take up Chernichev's time and free us.

The interview went something like this: (Interviewer:) "How would you define the Cuban revolution?" (Me:) "It is the *pachanga* revolution!" I saw horror pass over the face of the translator. I don't know why I used that Cuban expression, so I quickly added: "The revolution of joy." The surprise was mutual. They thought of Cuba as the "heroic island," nothing more. (Besides, you'd have to be straight from Mars to talk about revolution and joy to these Muscovites, veterans of forty years of Russian-style socialism.) I continued my explanation: "Look, we Cubans try to have fun with everything, cyclones, demonstrations, hunger, even war." I told them that in the Sierra we once had a three-hour truce so we could have a dance. I explained that these things made life more bearable. Then, in a more serious vein, one my interviewers would understand, I stated that the Cuban people were ready to make any sacrifice, even to die, in order to defend their revolution of freedom and joy. All of which sounded like Chinese to the Russians.

From the airport we went to the Hotel Ukraina, an ugly, bureaucratic pile near the Moscow River. Here and there we saw photographic murals of the Khrushchev-Fidel meeting, with Pepe Pardo Llada right in the middle and my head melting into the crowd. We were ushered into the dining room for the inevitable toasts, the waves of vodka downed at incredible speed. There we found our ambassador, Commandante Faure Chomón, who, following Russian tradition, was made to chugalug an enormous glass of vodka. Pale, but holding his own, Faure drank it down and was applauded. We toasted Lenin, Fidel, Khrushchev, the Soviet Union, Cuba—toasts, toasts, toasts. We couldn't last much longer, so I tried to hold things up by asking if it were true that the Party was launching an antialchoholism campaign. The chief of protocol said that indeed it was and asked us to drink to its success!

We went in to eat, and our interpreter, a young woman named Zoia, brought out paper and pencil, began to read me the menu, and asked me what we would want to eat. I was surprised, because we had already ordered dinner. I was even more surprised when I realized she wanted to know what we would eat that night, at tomorrow's lunch and supper, and the next day, and the day after as well—a whole week's meals. I had never thought about what I would eat the next day, and I felt silly ordering everybody else's meals. I couldn't get over the meticulous planning of the Russians, so I answered Zoia in true Cuban style—I said nothing at all. This didn't bother her; she just wrote some things down and handed her notes and some forms (in triplicate) to the maître d'.

Although the food was good, the meal lasted longer than a rich man's wake. Two unbearable hours, with all that vodka sloshing around in our guts; the only reason we survived was because of the constant jokes made by Cabrera Infante and José Viñas. First, always in Cuban slang, they suggested that Comrade Chernichev hadn't played fireman recently, at least not since the last world war; then they said Universo's boots were nothing compared with Chernichev's—this was an allusion to Comandante Universo, who was caught with his boots off in a fire fight, went barefoot for a month, and then refused to take his boots off ever again. As a matter of fact, none of us out in the Sierra was particularly aquatic; it was too much trouble to strip and bathe. Che always said that the bark protected the tree. To which Camilo always answered, "And your bark is certainly worse than your bite— the soldiers run away when they're downwind of you."

Our guests immediately presented us with a tour that would leave us absolutely no free time. We would visit Moscow, Leningrad, Stalingrad, Kiev, and see factories, schools, newspapers, et cetera. There was no reasoning with them. They told me that Khrushchev would receive me, that I shouldn't worry, and that I should enjoy my visit to the USSR. Cabrera Infante wanted to see Chekhov's house and the Pushkin museum, and he wanted to meet Ilya Ehrenburg—all of which embarrassed our hosts. So we toured Moscow. It is an impressive city; not the West at all, certainly not the tropics either. The new Palace of the Congresses was not as ugly and depressing as the Stalin-era architecture, but it was out of place and destroyed the atmosphere of the square. The Moscow subway was a marvel, clean and well designed, although the decoration is a horror. Outside Lenin's tomb there was always a long line, always the changing of the honor guard. After creating a great revolution, Lenin ended up mummified like one of the Pharaohs. What I didn't know then was that the whole Soviet Union is mummified. Later I learned why so many people turned out to adore Lenin—you need a reason to go to Moscow and unless you live there, you have to get a visa to visit it. So Lenin is the great pretext, the way you get your papers stamped.

When I saw Stalin there next to Lenin, I involuntarily uttered a Cuban-Cervantine expression: *"Hideputa!"* ("Whoreson!"). Our interpreter went pale and skipped that word. Later I found out that in her family (all of whom had been revolutionaries), as in virtually all other families, Stalin had claimed one of his victims. Mine wasn't the only incident regarding Stalin. Our ambassador had a fight when he ripped Stalin's name off a wreath offered by a high-ranking delegation from Cuba. He was lucky, because that day Stalin's mummy was removed from the mausoleum. I did notice that the bureaucrats got mad if they heard you speak ill of Stalin.

We found Khrushchev in the stadium, reading. But he was another man, not the fat Communist peasant who had absolutely dominated the New York press corps with his wit, not the man who managed to give a human image to socialism, who had impressed the United States and the rest of the world. Someone said he must be sick, because no one could change so totally in three weeks. But no, he wasn't sick; he was dead, killed by bureaucratitis. In New York he was interesting; here he was a bore. Not even he could free himself of the bureaucratic malaise of his nation.

After Khrushchev, we went on to meet Yekaterina Furtseva, the Soviet Minister of Culture, and her second-in-command. Right off the bat they launched into an attack on degenerate, bourgeois modern art, which ended with high praise for socialist realism, which, they said, was both popular and revolutionary. Someone in Havana believed them, because at that very moment *Lunes* and *Revolución* were fighting tooth and nail against the devotees of socialist realism. I should have kept quiet, because, although there were no official Communists among us, there were some informers who would repeat anything we said to wash away a few of their own sins. I asked Furtseva and her lackey if they thought the same of Picasso, which they did. I suggested that it was therefore immoral that he was known as one of the most famous Communists in the world. They stuck to his painting, saying that he was nothing but a humorist who managed to fool everyone. I asked if they thought *Guernica* was a joke. They did, and said Picasso himself had said it was. I couldn't believe it; they were repeating as the truth what Giovanni Papini (a fascist) had written in a book of imaginary interviews. Someone changed the subject.

Our problem was that we admired more than the revolution: we also admired the Russian avant-garde of the twenties and the anticzarist culture that had preceded it. This drew a laugh from the Minister, who reminded us, as we left, that socialist realism was the art of the people. As the lackey was showing us out, someone asked if it was true that Le Corbusier had once drawn up plans for a new Moscow. The lackey told us to talk to an old man who was closing a window. The old boy said it was true, that Le Corbusier had said that since so many things had to be changed, it was better to change Moscow itself. Then he added that Le Corbusier need not have troubled himself, because the Russians already had Tatlin, Lissitzky, Mayakovsky, Kandinsky, and Malevich. When we asked him who he was, he told us he was one of the constructivists, then went on with his work. "He's getting a little old" was all our solicitous lackey could say.

All the buildings we saw seemed good, and all the people to whom we spoke answered our questions in a positive way. They seemed to have resolved a number of problems: work, sanitation, and education. The officials all declared that the Soviet Union was about to catch up to and surpass the United States in all areas. Even the most incredulous among us (Cabrera Infante, Juan Arcocha, myself) could not find fault with the "reality" we had seen. We did see one or two of the dachas used by the bureaucrats, and we were aware of the privileges of the high-ranking, but all in all our impression was positive. Khrushchev's Russia worked, and many Cuban delegations declared the Soviet Union an earthly paradise.

PRAGUE

Some of us wanted to go to China. First, *Revolución* had had some direct communications (telegrams to Mao, which had been answered immediately); second, we knew that in China the Cuban Revolution had caused a sensation; third, the Chinese had not copied the commercial techniques the Soviets and the Eastern-bloc nations had themselves lifted from the capitalist countries (concessions for credit "given"). Fourth—and most important— was the fact that a significant part of the Cuban world is Chinese— principally Cantonese. Havana had an extraordinary Chinatown, with extensions all over the country. The Peking Opera, which had been invited by *Revolución*, was a fantastic synthesis of theater, dance, poetry, and music. So there were many reasons why we might want to visit China. But throughout our trip through the Soviet Union, the highest-level officials—in the Party, in the press, and especially Chernichev—spoke ill of the Chinese, of their chauvinism, their terrorism, their cult of personality, their ingratitude toward the Soviet Union. At the time, we didn't understand what was going on.

We also didn't understand that the Russians were going to make sure we would never get to China. They detoured us to the Eastern-bloc countries, to Prague and East Berlin, to other invitations. We were lucky when we landed in Prague, because no one turned out to greet us. We went directly to the Hotel Yalta, on Wenceslaus Square. On our own. There was a dance in progress and we saw lots of good-looking Czech girls. The dreary atmosphere that prevailed in Moscow suddenly disappeared, and the kind of night life we had in Havana came back to us. Now, Cubans (except me) are good dancers—so off we went, kicking up our heels. I went for a stroll around the city and stopped for a Pilsner beer in a beer garden founded before America had been discovered. I can't say I felt at home in Prague, but I sympathized with the life I felt all around me, which had something in common with Cuba in its liveliness. You could feel that bureacracy up above, but you could also feel the people in the streets.

When I got back to the hotel, I was surrounded by my colleagues, each of whom wanted twenty dollars. When I asked why each one wanted the same amount, they told me that that was how much the girls charged. I was flabbergasted that there could be prostitution under socialism. But there was; the guys who had the twenty dollars (I was in no position to use public money for public women) told me all about it the next day. The girls had government-owned—and bugged—apartments and would only accept dollars or coupons. These coupons they later turned in at the State Bank, where they were given vouchers, a small part of which was redeemable in money. The vouchers they used at a special store. We visited it and found, to our surprise, that it was crammed with the best consumer goods from the West—all the things no ordinary Czech could buy, available to anyone with foreign money. But it wasn't only for foreigners; we saw lots of high-ranking Czechs there, including interpreters and hotel personnel who did a little black-market money-changing on the side. We had discovered a side of socialism we didn't like.

Later on we would find out that the same corruption existed in Moscow—and that Khrushchev was trying to root it out. The difference was that in Prague it was all out in the open, while in Moscow it was undercover. It was apropos of this corruption that I had a run-in with Che Guevara when I got back to Havana. I told the story of the socialist prostitutes in Prague and the special stores, and Che called me a liar. I told him he just had not seen the same city we had seen because he was kept in official circles. He wouldn't believe me. Two years later, at an identical Council of Ministers' meeting, Che stood up and said that he had to apologize to me because he had finally seen the things I had seen. That moreover he had been duped by the same socialist government into buying Czech machinery and factories, all of which had turned out to be junk—worn-out stuff the Czechs (and other socialist countries) couldn't use. Prague was our first window into socialism.

BEACHES TO THE PEOPLE

The best beaches in Cuba belonged to the rich, and the rich, of course, were lily-white. In Havana, it was chic to belong to a club—the Miramar Yacht Club, the Country Club, the Havana Yacht Club, the Vedado Tennis Club. It cost a fortune to get in, if in fact you could—someone could blackball you—and the monthly fees were the equivalent of half a year's salary for an ordinary worker. One guy who had avoided (without having to avoid) being blackballed was the Yankee millionaire Irénée du Pont, who bought the peninsula of Hicacos (about thirty kilometers long, on the north coast) and made it into his private beach. He even had his own customs office, so that his guests from the United States were really visiting du Pont–land, not Cuba. The only beaches the people had possessed little sand and no shade. Most *habaneros* made do with a sunbath or sweated their way out to public beaches on crowded buses.

Revolución launched a huge campaign against these snobby clubs; our intention was to open them to the people by breaking down the massive walls that surrounded them—a kind of tropical storming of the Bastille. When I saw the poor, blacks and whites, enjoying those privileged spots, I felt we had done something necessary, something fine that somehow compensated for a few less honorable acts.

The tearing down of the walls led to some mischief. When the last walls had fallen, someone suggested we move on to the houses of the rich, which were also surrounded by walls. Lots of mansions had been abandoned and were subsequently seized by the revolution. In one of these lived Emilio Aragonés—excuse me, Captain Aragonés (who never fired a shot)—a school chum of Fidel's at the Belén Jesuit school, and, like President Dorticós, a bourgeois from Cienfuegos. When the mob came to his house, he asked who had given the order for this operation, to which the crowd shouted, "El Caballo." "If El Caballo gave the order, proceed." One hundred meters from Aragonés lived Luis Buch and his wife, Conchita, in a house they owned, where Faustino, Hart, Haydée, and I had been hidden by Conchita. Conchita is from Santiago and breathes fire. When the crowd started to knock down her wall, she came out and began to swear like a trooper. The crowd called her a snob, to which she answered: "You bastards. You're brave now, but what did you ever do against Batista? Bastards, I'll bet half of you were Batista's stooges. I'm a revolutionary and certainly no snob." Then someone said that the order had come from Fidel, and that if Conchita were really a revolutionary she'd follow orders. Conchita was ready for that one: "El Caballo never gave me this house. But if the revolution needs it, my husband and I will give it gladly. But no one's going to knock it down, especially no son of a bitch playing revolutionary. Not even Fidel would dare touch this wall. All this looks queer to me, so I'll call Fidel and find out about it. Don't think I'm an asshole like fatso Aragonés over there. You all just wait." Down at the National Palace, laughing their heads off, they told Conchita it was a mistake, that the order only applied to beach clubs. Well, that was the end of Bastille Day in Havana. Except for the black shoeshine boy from Doce y Veintitrés, who shouted out: "Sir, sir, please let me take a swing at the walls of these white bastards. I want to have some fun with my pick, and this here white lady won't let me." Conchita picked up on his lead, "Com'ere, brutha. Take a good swing at that wall over there. The house belonged to Martínez Sáenz, a pal of Batista's." That was that.

PABLO NERUDA

Revolución's last guest of 1960 was Pablo Neruda, who sailed to Havana with his wife, Matilde. We all went down to the dock to meet him—all of us except the poet Nicolás Guillén, a Communist like Neruda himself. Carlos Rafael Rodríguez and the other Party faithful were also conspicuously absent. Don Pablo was a giant who still had the air of a child about him. He knew that we had read his poems out in the Sierra over Radio Rebelde, and he appreciated the sympathy that Che, *Lunes*, and *Revolución* had for him. A curious event that took place in Caracas in January of 1959 clouded Neruda's relationship with revolutionary Cuba: when Neruda went to greet Fidel, Fidel tried to smash the camera that had recorded the event. Neruda describes the event in his *Memoirs.*

We had prepared a beautiful wooden house for Neruda, a house recently nationalized by Urban Reform, which we thought would remind him of his own Isla Negra. But Neruda, like Sartre and Simone de Beauvoir, preferred the Hotel Nacional. The Nacional and the Hilton (now the Habana-Libre) are two contradictory symbols of Havana: the Hilton is a U.S.-style skyscraper rising high above Havana, cold, antiseptic, a vertical axis of power. The Nacional, on the other hand, is a marvelous hotel in *criollo* style, right on the beach, with its own tranquil gardens. It stretched out horizontally. Fidel, the comandantes, and the ministers did not like the Nacional, preferring, instead, the Hilton, which they took over. Radically anti-imperialist in politics, they nevertheless identified with the grandeur of the United States, its power and its force.

There was a certain amount of sabotage against Neruda, perpetrated by the Communists, by Guillén (who couldn't abide Neruda's superiority as a poet) and by some frustrated intellectuals who all signed a shameful letter of denunciation of Neruda. Raúl Castro, oddly enough, was also involved. Somehow Neruda was caught up in the cultural battle raging around *Lunes* and *Revolución*, and his recent book, *Estravagario*, was a cause of ideological concern because in it Neruda, self-critical, spoke out in favor of the freedom of poets, of all men, to write, to love, and to live. It was a clear departure from the Stalinist dictum about not writing any but committed poetry. There was also the problem that Fidel never did like poetry. It almost seemed to bother him that José Martí was a great poet as well as the liberator of Cuba. But Neruda was too big to sweep under the rug, and *Revolución* made him, as it had already done with Sartre and Simone de Beauvoir, into front-page news, complete with huge photos.

In those turbulent days toward the end of 1960, the people were called to the Plaza de la Revolución, where Fidel was going to read them a declaration. I told Fidel that at the reading of the declaration Pablo Neruda should also be asked to read some of his poetry. Fidel agreed and told me to have Neruda prepare a poem. Meanwhile, the pro-Soviets, the Communists, and Raúl Castro worked things out so that Nicolás Guillén, our "national poet" would also speak. We had tried to get rid of Guillén by proposing that he be sent, with the rank of ambassador, as cultural attaché to the Soviet Union. He was chosen for the job and got the salary, but he never really went. "You bastards think you're smart, sending me to Moscow, which is a dreary dump, as you well know." We all feigned shock that he would say such a thing about the Workers' Paradise. "I wouldn't be caught dead in Moscow. Even when I was exiled for being a Communist I lived in Paris."

The day of the reading of the declaration came, and the people flooded the plaza, singing and dancing. It was one of the greatest, most moving demonstrations I had ever seen in Havana. It really was the Revolution of Joy. The people marched, chanting: "Fidel, go ahead / Hit the Yankees on the head." Up on the presidential tribunal the great ones gathered, including Neruda and Guillén. Guillén made jokes about the crowd's really being there to cheer for him, but when the time came for the poems, disaster struck. Guillén said that he, as a Cuban, should read first. A million people waiting and Guillén making demands. Fidel started making jokes—that Guillén should read Neruda's poem and vice versa. Neruda turned to Fidel and said, "You have honored me by inviting me to read a poem to the marvelous people gathered here today. You decide who reads first—it doesn't matter at all to me." Guillén read in his fine, professional poetry-reciter's voice and was courteously applauded. But Neruda, who read in a thin voice, moved the crowd and received an ovation.

Fidel read the declaration, which was written in high style and yet contained a moving element of a liberating, truly American spirit. It was confirmed by the people in a flood of joy. It seemed that day as if the Americas, poetry, and revolution all met in one theme: freedom.

FREE-SPENDING YEARS

As the revolution turned its thoughts into practice, the buying power of the people doubled. The revolution cut in half rents and the price of medicine, telephone service, and food. Gambling was outlawed, and many public works projects were begun. The consumption of meat soared, and the rhythm of production changed. Cuban and U.S. capitalism had left us a good supply of goods, as had agricultural and industrial production. So the supply of luxury items, mainly from the United States, was huge. Cars, television sets, radios, and appliances were suddenly available to all. But who benefited most? When rents were lowered by fifty percent, no one thought about the difference in income of those paying rent, with the result that it was the middle class that really made money. This was Fidel's utopian side. No one gave a thought to increasing production, or to the changes taking place in the production structure. Not even to the fact that we were living on what the old society had left, not on what we ourselves had made.

Another major problem of the 1959–60 period was agricultural production. We were passing from private property to state ownership and creating panic among the smaller landowners. The administrators sent out to run the huge plantations were incompetent, and Fidel did not believe in cooperative farms (which would therefore be short-lived). Because of earlier overproduction, we had a sugar surplus, but the actual plantations were not in good condition because no new cane had been planted during the unstable end of the Batista era. In 1959 we were still importing a large portion of our food. Nothing had changed, and the shift to state ownership of agriculture merely meant a change of bosses for the workers, whose situation remained the same. Where decentralization and cooperative ventures might have altered the relationship between the farm worker and production for the good, we ended up with a perpetuation of the old structure.

The effects of centralization and bureaucratization began to be felt. The Institute of Agrarian Reform (Instituto de Reforma

Agraria; INRA) was directed by Fidel himself. Below him were people like Antonio Núñez Jiménez (a geographer) and Oscar Pino Santos (a journalist), who knew nothing about agriculture or administration. In the cattle industry, the situation was terrible. Breeding stock was indiscriminately slaughtered and cattle were sold to Venezuela. The Marquis of Cuevitas himself handed the checks over to Fidel. It was a crime, but any protest was met with laughter. The agronomist René Dumont, in his first visit, sounded the alarm. He was furious with *Revolución* because we paid attention to celebrities like Sartre, Neruda, and Picasso, but he didn't know that agriculture was Fidel's private affair and that we just couldn't stick our noses in whenever we wanted.

Dumont fascinated Fidel, but at the time Dumont didn't know how dangerous that could be. But he fought a good fight, and when Fidel realized things were sinking fast, he called Dumont a savior. Of course, he carefully pointed out to Dumont that although Dumont was the expert, he, Fidel, was the politician, the last word. Finally the Frenchman was expelled, accused of being an enemy agent. I think that I could have been helpful if I had met Dumont, but I was unable to contact people Fidel had invited to Cuba. It wouldn't have changed anything in any case. Fidel became the new agricultural czar of Cuba. The result was a decline in production, one that saw the best sugar land in the world become the worst.

PARTY POLITICS

The Ministry of Labor's persecution of the labor movement became implacable. Unions were taken over, and the duly elected leadership was replaced by Communists. This effectively undid the free elections held one year earlier, in which 90 percent of the unions chose non-Communist leaders. Fidel Castro had made his decision. Instead of a new society created from below by the workers, Cuba would be a society in which the workers were a productive force obedient to the dictates of those in power. The prime movers of this new society would be Fidel, ten comandantes, and the members of the old Communist party.

A fusion of the Russian model and the new dictatorial militarism of Fidel Castro was taking place. In a casual conversation with him, one in which I expressed my concern with the course of events, he made a statement that shook me to the core: "Only the old Communists and the Soviets know anything about communism. We must be patient and learn from them." I said I knew the Cuban Communists better than he, and that they knew nothing at all about communism. I told him they were unpopular, that the people did not consider them revolutionary, and that they had joined forces with Batista. They fought against the revolution of 1930, had ruined the labor movement, had denounced Moncada, had rejected the Sierra campaign and the clandestine war, and had thrown their lot in with tyranny. Fidel agreed with what I said but insisted that Cuba needed the Communists and would learn from them. I told him to watch out for the second-line Communists, the younger ones of the Prague-Mexico group, including Aníbal Escalante and Isidoro Malmierca, because they were Stalinists with strong ties to Moscow. Fidel insisted that in a revolutionary situation it often turned out that the people were not ready and that a revolutionary minority had to take it upon itself to impose socialism on the people. This was an apology for Stalinism. I could see it coming, and there was no way out.

But what could the people see? They saw the revolution nationalizing property, expropriating foreign-owned industries. They saw the old order disappearing and Cuba recovering national independence and dignity. They could also see the heavy hand of the CIA and the capitalists organizing expeditions outside the country. The workers supported as best they could their own unions and knew the charges brought against the union leadership were false. The only thing the unions were guilty of was not being militant Communists, which was a fact, since the unions derived from the Auténtico and Ortodoxo parties, themselves the result of the 1930 revolution that Batista had destroyed. Why the revolution had begun to devour its own children, the working class, was a mystery.

Out of this persecution, resistance groups were born. David Salvador's group went underground, as did many persecuted workers from the interior, who headed for the mountains. David Salvador and Manuel Ray met, but they could not agree on a common program because Ray believed in democracy and Salvador in a humanist socialism. Which meant that Ray wanted to conserve the middle classes, while Salvador was concerned only with the workers. But even Ray was too much for the Americans, who at the time were organizing the Playa Girón attack with a highly controlled, obedient force. Meanwhile Cuba had its own CIA, Soviet-style, thanks to Ramiro Valdés, Manuel Piñeyro, Raúl Castro, Malmierca, Osvaldo Sánchez and others.

Others, including myself, took another stance. We would fight passively, holding out as best we could. We would let the counter-revolutionary opposition, supported by the CIA, be liquidated, but we would inform the people of everything that was happening: the economic crisis especially. But hanging on was not easy, because in the confusion of the moment the Party was eliminating any and all opposition. *Revolución* was the only symbol that remained of a revolutionary opposition, and even its red-and-black colors had begun to fade. Our strategy was to attack everyone, everyone except Fidel Castro. So we tried to tell the Cuban people that Soviet socialism (Raúl Castro and the old Communists) was against their interests. To a limited extent, we succeeded, partly because our enemies always tried to get rid of us in the same way—through Fidel. But you just can't push Fidel. He does things when he wants to. So we survived. Meanwhile, the country was kept in a state of agitation because of the United States, which would unwittingly provide the ideal excuse for wholesale destruction.

PAPER AND INK

We wanted to unite high and low culture, to remove the stigma from the black, clandestine religious rites that had survived throughout Cuba. That religion, whose ceremonies resembled ancient Greek theater (chorus, solo voice, divine possession), had either been persecuted or marginalized, defined as a superstition. Well, we wanted to confer on it the dignity it deserved as a central element in Cuban culture. In effect, we wanted to break down the notion that the white, dominant culture was best, and to do so we exalted rumba, conga, carnival—Cuba's other, black culture. Of course this didn't sit well with Fidel or with Raúl (who preferred waltzes and boleros). And when the Castro brothers and the hard-line Communists heard the Internationale played in congo rhythm, they raised the roof. "High" dance then was still Alicia Alonso—Yankeephile then and Russophile now.

When the blockade went into effect, we stopped receiving records (made in USA) and many of our best bands went north. We tried to get records of our music made in Europe, but the project failed. We didn't want Cuba to turn into what we had seen in Moscow or even Prague, so we invented Paper and Ink, festivals of popular culture, awarding silver palms to the best performers of popular music. We wanted our first Paper and Ink to take place in the Capitol building. We wanted to profane that august, grotesque building with the great Beny Moré, but Núñez Jiménez wouldn't let us. So we went to the Centro Gallego, which is right on that miserable central park, right near the newspaper *Hoy*. They were having some kind of congress of journalists from the socialist world when the racket from our festival blew their ears out. Some thought it was a counterrevolutionary coup, but Carlos Rafael Rodríguez calmed them down by announcing, "It's one of *Revolución*'s parties." That ended the congress, because the participants all came over to dance.

These festivals were a wild success. Not without problems, but we took care of that with a patrol system. Then we started costume balls. Ithiel León, subdirector of *Revolución*, brought down the house when he came to a party disguised as Groucho Marx and carrying *Das Kapital* under his arm. Things worked so well that people started getting mad, especially Fidel and Escalante. So they launched a program of expositions of Russian painting, which coincided with the Russification of Cuba. Fidel even sent Leovigildo González, a mediocre realist painter, to paint some hideous billboards for the Valley of Viñales. The place is one of the most beautiful spots in Cuba, but they tried to sacrifice it to socialist realism. The realism of nature eventually won out, unlike Paper and Ink, which succumbed.

3

1961: A HOT YEAR

Nineteen sixty-one began with a political heat wave. The United States severed relations with Cuba. At any other time it would have been a catastrophe, but we were wild and simply did not worry about the long-term consequences. When you're in a fight, with your blood boiling, you don't really know when you've been hit. No one thought about it seriously, and, if we had thought about it at all, we would have rejoiced at the break. We had finally thrown an enormous load off our backs.

Nineteen sixty-one was the year of the literacy campaign. The city was going to teach the country how to read and write. One hundred thousand young volunteers were going to teach five hundred thousand illiterates their ABC's. It was one of those incredible things a revolution can do. The university students were the vanguard of the campaign, and even the lower middle classes, usually so concerned about the virginity of their daughters, willingly agreed to send them—unchaperoned—out to the far corners of the island. It was all a bit helter-skelter, but what could you expect? The year had begun well.

And badly. The Escambray Mountains were full of rebels, at least a thousand. How was it possible? We knew who they were: peasants, workers, the common people. They weren't Batista supporters—those had all gone north. The middle classes had also pretty much flown the coop. And it wasn't the CIA or any counter-revolutionary movement. They were too busy setting up an invasion brigade outside of Cuba, recruiting in the United States, and training under the benevolent eyes of several Caribbean tyrants.

The reports about what was going on came in from the Escambray, but Fidel refused to take action. Usually he was quick to react, but this time he was slow, as if he refused to believe that what he had done could be accomplished by anyone else. Some suspected his tardiness was a tactic, that he wanted to let the rebels grow in number and then swoop down on all of them at once. Dorticós, the president, who was from Cienfuegos and knew the region well, was worried. It was true that there were no large-scale battles, and this led Fidel to remark that they were merely imitating us. It was in part that, but there was more.

The rebels were almost all individuals who had been unjustly persecuted by the revolution. Comandante Raúl Menéndez Tomasevich, who later directed the antiguerrilla operations, would say, "Félix Torres stirs 'em up and I string 'em up." The peasants not only didn't reject the rebels but actually helped them. Why? Some said it was fear, but that was just not true. The revolution had simply forgotten about the Trinidad region, one of the most traditionalist and Catholic in Cuba. There were lots of promises, but no results. The revolution had used the mountains, and now, because it needed them no longer, it paid them no attention— not only in the Escambray, but in the Sierra Maestra as well. The fact is that during the anti-Batista years there had been clashes and rivalries between rebel groups. Those problems were never resolved, and, after 1959, the zone was administered by incompetents.

The famous Communist comandante Félix Torres was the biggest problem. Nicknamed Comandante Whitelies, he was made a comandante at the end of the war, at Yaguajay. He can only be discussed in the context of Party politics, the ultimate reason why there were uprisings in the Escambray and elsewhere. The rebels were former revolutionaries who had fled to the mountains and fought just to stay out of prison. Félix Torres had the dubious virtue of being a visible Communist, but there were others, in the highest places, who were invisible: Ramiro Valdés, head of Security, Raúl Castro, Aníbal Escalante, and, of course, Fidel himself.

In the Escambray, Félix Torres persecuted, shot, and jailed anyone he pleased. He became the local boss and went way beyond all the old capitalists in exploiting workers and peasants. He revived one of the most odious exploitation rackets, the so-called payment by job, which had been the cause of huge labor riots. Under that system, the worker was not paid a minimum wage over an eight-hour day; the boss paid according to the quantity of work done. In practice, it meant more work and less pay. Torres and other administrators took away the peasants' land, the very land they had received through agrarian reform. From others they stole their right to work; in many factories, the workers who had fought against Batista were thrown out by the Communist overseers.

Comandante Torres also developed a Lolita complex and set up a harem of peasant girls. With his power he could buy or acquire anything he wanted. Persecution increased throughout the country, and rebels began to appear who were not from the Escambray zone. Once again, the CIA and the U.S.-based counter-revolutionaries misread the situation. This kind of uncontrolled opposition was not to their liking, so they urged the rebel leaders to stop fighting. They were to wait for the invasion that was about to take place. By doing that, the CIA paralyzed an ongoing guerrilla campaign and caused the rebels' defeat. A guerrilla fighter who is inactive—who is not fighting, learning, and extending his territory—is a dead man. And that's just what happened. A small group of rebels with experience in the war against Batista rejected U.S. advice and did fight. They resisted under incredibly bad conditions against wave after wave of well-armed regular army and militia units for seven years. Those who waited, the majority, didn't last three months.

The event that turned the Cuban people against the rebels was the murder of Conrado Benítez, a black student, by the rebels. He was a poor boy working in the literacy campaign, and it was his death, not Fidel's speeches, that moved the people to demand action. When Fidel finally took the Escambray action seriously, he mobilized the militias, the army, the comandantes, and the best guerrilla fighters from the Sierra and the *Segundo Frente.* Sixty thousand volunteer militiamen swept the mountains in massive search-and-destroy missions. Then Fidel ordered the deportation en masse of the peasant population.

General Valeriano Wyler's sadly famous concentration camps of the War of Independence (1896) forced the peasants into towns and cities. Batista tried expulsion in 1957. Secretly, with tremendous speed, and using Stalin's mass deportation tactics, Fidel Castro ordered all peasant families, no matter what their politics might be, to be deported. The men went to prison, and any suspected rebel supporters were shot. The women and children were sent to houses the rich owners had abandoned, in the most aristocratic neighborhoods in Havana.

The zone that included the Escambray, Isla de Pinos, and Camagüey was sealed off. As incredible as it may seem, it was a long time before anyone was aware of what had happened. All we could see was a vague problem with peasant families living in the mansions the revolution had given them. Executions became the order of the day, and the red terror began to bubble up to the surface. The Escambray campaign did not take long. Eight hundred men were taken prisoner, not counting the dead, the wounded, and the executed. Then Fidel, in an important news statement, announced the end of the Escambray action. This was his first use of a highly effective ploy that became standard operating procedure. He would announce the end of a military operation before it was actually over. In that way the operation was psychologically sealed off, both within the nation and abroad. The Escambray became taboo, a secret. But six or seven years later there were still rebels out there carrying out raids. In my opinion, the Escambray was doomed from the start. Its main support was revolutionary opposition, which was spontaneous and disorganized, the expression of a confused historical moment.

Outwardly, the great struggle of the day was between the revolution and the USA, with its Cuban bourgeois allies. The people supported Fidel because they saw him as the undisputed leader of the revolution. The Escambray and the other persecutions were a puzzle because there seemed to be no reason for harassing people who had fought for the revolution. And at the same time no one could understand why the government was treating the old Communist party and its militants with such respect, why it was incorporating them into the government. No one saw the effects of partisan politics: the creation of a bureaucracy, the disorganization of the means of production, the strengthening of the state structure, the rise of militarism, and the exclusion of the people from the creation of a new society.

In this milieu, a revolutionary opposition was unthinkable. Curiously enough, the spontaneous opposition that did spring up did not seek aid from the United States. Even if they did, they never got it, because the CIA, which is overtly Fidel's enemy, has always been his potential ally. The CIA has its own way of doing business. It wanted to control the counterrevolution and to retake Cuba on its own terms, using former Batista supporters or recruits from the bourgeoisie. The result was that, for the Cuban people, opposition and counterrevolution became synonyms.

TORTURE

One day, one of *Revolución*'s reporters, a comrade in arms from the underground days who had been with Che during the Escambray campaign, and who was our logical choice to cover the operation, came to Havana and told me people were being tortured. He explained that Comandante Dermitio Escalona and some others were using the old "apple bobbing" technique, whereby you immerse the prisoner's head in a barrel of water until he almost drowns. Just when he's about to die, you pull him out. A breath of air and then back into the barrel, again and again, until he either talks or drowns. I asked the reporter if he would risk taking some pictures, and to my surprise he pulled out a roll of film, which he promptly developed. The photos clearly showed Comandante Escalona and his thugs beating and torturing prisoners.

I grabbed the photos and ran right to the Palacio, where a meeting of ministers was taking place. I handed Fidel the photos thinking I was giving him some terrible evidence of which he was ignorant. To my shock, Fidel showed not the slightest surprise. "Look, Franqui, you know that Juan Almeida is a real human being, right? Well, one day, Almeida caught a bunch of people out there who told him they were innocent. Almeida had no proof, so he let them go. A little later, the same people ran into Escalona. He grabbed them and put the fear of God into them. Want to know what happened? They all talked, and we uncovered a whole network. We've taken hundreds of prisoners, broken a nationwide organization, and saved the lives of who knows how many revolutionaries. A little pressure, and they talked." "But Fidel, that's exactly what they told me in the Bureau of Investigations when Batista's men were torturing me. Torture is efficient: it annihilates the enemy. But what about the moral degradation it entails? Suppose it becomes the norm in the police and the army? Who could stop it then?" Fidel agreed, saying that the revolution would execute its enemies, but it wouldn't torture them.

Security became so secret and powerful that you couldn't talk about it. But things leaked out concerning imprisonments, injustices, deportations, and executions. We didn't hear much about physical torture in the jails run by Raúl, Ramiro Valdés, and Sergio del Valle, but we did hear about psychological torture: darkness, heat, cold, solitary confinement, death threats. That day I left the palace totally confused. How could Fidel condone Escalona's methods? Assuming he did, would he keep his word and stop it? I felt half clean and half dirty, with a sick feeling in my guts.

I GO TO BRAZIL

It was Friday, April 7, 1961. President Dorticós summoned me to the palace and informed me that in the coming week the General Assembly of the United Nations would meet and vote on a resolution in favor of Cuba. We needed a yes vote from Brazil, but neither the ambassador nor his ministry could give us any guarantees. Someone would have to speak directly with Janio Quadros—not in an official way. He meant, to my surprise, me. He said I could get in to see him and that I would be able to convince him that his vote would be vital to the Cuban people. Then he added that Fidel said I was the right man for the job. I agreed, but I think they chose me because no one else wanted to get into any trouble. Well, that was Friday, and I had to be in Quadros's office on Monday.

Quadros had visited Cuba and had shown himself sympathetic to our cause. We had good relations with Brazil, and our chargé d'affaires there was Raulito Roa, the son of our Minister of Foreign Affairs. He was a chip off the old block. During the war against Batista, he was sent to the United States while his father went to Mexico. They sat out the war and waited, until Batista fell, to return, confident that with all their connections they would get government positions. Both father and son were affable types, skillful, obedient, and able to speak two or three languages. Perfect bureaucrats.

Dorticós told me I would leave that afternoon and go via Mexico, Bogotá, Rio, and then Brasilia. He also said that Ramiro Valdés wanted to send two "comrades" from Security with me. I declined the offer, saying I would take Antonio Manuel Castellanos, a man I knew very well. Which was exactly what Dorticós knew I would say. We shook hands and off I went.

At that time, Security was moving comandantes, ministers, and anyone of any importance into new houses. Some of us tried to stay where we were—Che, Faustino, Celia, Haydée, Chomón, Orlando Blanco, and I among them. The new houses were those that had been abandoned by the Havana middle class. This reopened a polemic that had been simmering since 1959. Many of us went right back to our old apartments after the war, while others wanted to "profane" (as they said) the houses of the rich. It was they who were "profaned." These houses came equipped with twenty-four-hour, round-the-clock guards—because of the counterrevolutionary threat, but it was also a good way to keep an eye on you in the Soviet style. Celia, Haydée, and I had eluded the new-house situation simply because we were civilians. All military personnel, however, had to move into these. I had been living in my own flat all this time with no problem. Castellanos was my cousin and worked at *Revolución*. He and I were the only two who fired back when, a few months earlier, *Revolución* was mysteriously attacked with hand grenades. Security had infiltrated the terrorists, but curiously enough had not managed to capture any. Then my friend Amejeiras told me my apartment in Santos Suárez had been attacked—fortunately for me, while I was on vacation. This was all related to my protest about the torture and my having been thrown in jail, a matter I'll get to later. I believed Amejeiras and feared Ramiro and his thugs more than I feared the counterrevolutionaries. Since I wouldn't obey the order to move, Fidel stepped in, told me I was in danger and that I would simply have to follow orders. The next day the Urban Reform people handed me the keys to my new house. I'd be a hypocrite if I were to say I didn't like what I found— swimming pool, books, nice furniture, garden, air conditioning— but at the same time I felt guilty.

Fidel himself never had those problems, since he was accustomed to living in houses like that. Besides, he had a real security problem. But he would change his houses, make them his own, by bringing in cows and farm equipment. What was really happening was that we were creating a new elite, despite all the rhetoric about the need to protect us, the need for upper-echelon people to be able to relax. This new elite would one day be dangerous.

RIO

On Sunday Castellanos and I landed in Rio. The Cuban embassy was in Copacabana, a rich neighborhood. Castellanos and I did a little touring and saw how the city and the *favelas* (slums) were separated by a kind of no man's land, a huge hole in the ground. The background was impressive because of the huge quantity of shit on it; you see, the poor people lived up on the mountains and emptied their chamber pots down the hillsides. Sometimes you could see a line of backsides using that huge void as a collective outhouse. Despite all the misery, there was something powerful in that slum world—the black rhythm, the people who could sing and laugh despite centuries of privation.

On Monday we took the plane to Brasilia. In the middle of a wilderness, a forest of skyscrapers, as if New York had landed there like some misguided airplane. Niemeyer's cold, dehumanized architecture seemed like some kind of madness, an island of reinforced concrete surrounded by forests. One had to wonder about how all that money could have been better spent in a nation with so many problems, and the idea of installing the government there made it all seem like a prison. A sort of Latin-American military man's idea of utopia. I simply walked into the presidential offices and stated that I had an interview with President Quadros. Cuba was a kind of magic word at the time, so I "bumped" a long line of military types and several U.S. diplomats and found myself face to face with Janio Quadros. He had a simple office, and I found the office reflected the man.

After a few jokes about my abrupt, unannounced entrance, he asked me what brought me to Brazil. I told him we had proof that an invasion of Cuba was being launched from various Caribbean bases and that the invaders had support from some very powerful sources. I went on to say that Mexico and other friendly nations would present in the UN a motion supporting Cuba's right to self-determination and that we considered Brazil's vote vital to our interests. I told him we could defeat the invasion, but that we had to stop the foreign powers who might support the invasion militarily. The support of Brazil, Mexico, and Venezuela would tip the balance in our favor. Without a moment's hesitation, Quadros said that Cuba's cause was that of Brazil and the rest of Latin America, and that Cuba would have Brazil's vote. He promised to call Brazil's UN delegation immediately. Then we had a chat about conditions in Cuba, both of us fully aware of the bigwigs cooling their heels in the waiting rooms.

I passed a gallery of very long faces when I left Quadros's office and then walked right into a pack of U.S. journalists, all eager to find out what the President and the editor in chief of *Revolución* had discussed. I dodged all questions and headed for the airport. Janio Quadros kept his word, and I am inclined to think that Kennedy had Brazil, Mexico, and Venezuela in the back of his mind during the Bay of Pigs operation. Of course, Quadros ended up paying the piper; a military coup eliminated his government. Now, Che and I had a philosophical discussion about Quadros. The same year I spoke with him, Che also had a long talk with him. Who had brought him the bad luck, Che or I? On the way back to Cuba I had to stop over in Panama, where red tape held us up for hours and hours. I saw the famous canal and was struck by the resemblance of the people of Panama to us Cubans. In any case, I wanted to get back to Havana because I felt something in the air. I arrived on Friday, the eve of the Playa Girón war.

AIR RAIDS

On Saturday morning, April 15, 1961, the airports of Santiago and Havana were bombed. It was a clear signal. As in the invasion of Egypt, the first objective was the destruction of the few military planes we had. We were put on alert, but nothing more happened either on Saturday or Sunday. The funeral of the victims of the air raid was a highly emotional event, and Fidel chose that moment to proclaim the socialist nature of the revolution. This was a sign to both the Soviet Union and the United States, but to Cuba itself the declaration was Fidel's way of taking advantage of a critical moment to make something seem the result of Cuba's having outside enemies, as if Cuba had in that instant to become socialist because of the invasion.

Why the invasion and the air raids weren't simultaneous is still a mystery. Fidel had already said that with three thousand five hundred kilometers of coastline, Cuba was an easy island to invade, but that because of its shape its communications were rapid and so we could quickly locate any invading force. He was right. At the time, our real strength lay in the militia units and in our support among the people. Our people were even more important than our weapons, although I still cannot understand why, when we all knew an invasion was imminent and when our relations with the Soviet Union were so cordial, we were so lacking in planes, artillery, and transport—everything.

At dawn on Monday, the seventeenth, just after 3:00 A.M., a call came through to *Revolución* from New York. It was the New York *Times* calling to ask if we had any news about an invasion of the island. Elio Constantín, an editor, rather confusedly asked the *Times* for information. The *Times* man said that the word was out that the island had been invaded and that he had called the foreign ministry and the presidential palace but that there was no answer in either place. He said he'd call back later. I telephoned the apartment on Once Street. Celia answered, and I told her what I had just heard. Fidel took the phone, and after I told him, he said he had just had a report from a militia group that said they had seen enemy troops landing at Playa Larga. What Fidel was concerned about was the number of landings. Would the enemy concentrate in one place or make several simultaneous attacks? By 10:00 A.M. Fidel was convinced that the enemy force was concentrated in the Zapata swamps. From a strategic point of view, the Zapata swamps was a good place for a landing:

it was close to Havana and still isolated. It had a port and an airport. The swamp itself covers the southern coast of three provinces: Las Villas, Matanzas, and Havana. The problem is that the swamp is virtually impassable, even on foot. The only road consists of two highways that cross the swamp, and on each side, quagmire. The invaders had taken the two highways. They controlled the air and the sea. On land, their heavy machine guns and tanks were creating havoc, and their paratroopers were defending the rear guard in the Covadonga area. Under these conditions it was very difficult to counterattack; the quagmire protected the invaders. Another problem was Fidel's general staff, which was composed almost entirely of Party men, military bureaucrats who had never fired a shot in their lives: Fatty Aragonés, Osmaní Cienfuegos, Flavio Bravo, Augusto Martínez, and others. In reality, Fidel never had a general staff, either in peace or war; he would simply consult with each person individually. And this staff of advisers couldn't last. Their only plan was to propose a withdrawal to the interior of Matanzas that supposedly would lure the invaders out to where they could be attacked. Only idiots could have devised a strategy like that.

The volume of enemy fire was tremendous, and there were many wounded among the militiamen during the first hours of fighting. Fortunately, while brave Augusto Martínez hid under a table and the others pondered the situation with their chins in their hands, Amejeiras and the old rebel outfits from the Sierra reached the front. The first counterattacks were turned back; the well-equipped enemy fought well and established their beachheads. What we didn't know was whether the invasion force would be only Cubans or if U.S. troops and planes would support them. The standard ploy was to stage a landing, set up a "government," and call for help. Fidel's only hope was to liquidate the invasion force before they could call in aid. We had five planes left and we had to use them wisely.

PLAYA GIRÓN AND THE ESCAMBRAY

The five planes were ordered to sink the ships the invasion force was using. The objective was to deprive the troops on shore of supplies and to show them they were going to be caught like rats in a trap. Fidel Castro's motto in this case was that saving time meant saving lives. But the counterattacks had to move along those well-defended highways, so Fidel's economy drive had no real validity. We lost a lot of men. This frontal attack of men against machines (the enemy tanks) had nothing to do with guerrilla war; in fact, it was a Russian tactic, probably the idea of the two Soviet generals, both of Spanish origin (they fought for the Republic in the Spanish Civil War and fled to the Soviet Union to fight later in World War II). One of them was a veteran, a fox named Ciutah.* He was sent by the Red Army and the Party as an adviser and was the father of the new Cuban army. He was the only person who could have taken charge of the Girón campaign. The other Hispano-Russian general was an expert in antiguerrilla war who ran the Escambray cleanup. But the real factor in our favor at Girón was the militias: Amejeiras's column embarked on a suicide mission. They were massacred, but they reached the beach.

Both the Escambray and Girón campaigns made me wonder about Fidel. Why had he delayed so long in going after the rebels in the Escambray? Why were we so poorly equipped at Girón when everyone knew it was just a matter of time before the invasion took place? Why had Fidel sent Pití Fajardo, a doctor and chief of Fidel's own bodyguard, out to "take care" of the Escambray rebels when he had less military experience than many other comandantes? Pití, of course, was killed very soon. Apparently, Fidel had two distinct strategies: he knew the Escambray groups

---

* See page 182.

were disorganized, unprotected, and unsupported by the CIA. What little did come from the United States to the Escambray was picked up by the militiamen and thus even that uprising was identified with the Yankees. The other strategy was the counterattack at Girón. Where the sweep of the Escambray was deliberately slow, the Girón campaign was deliberately swift. Fidel won on both counts; his enemies were totally discredited and he became the incarnation of the revolution.

The people saw the enemy, but—despite the real criticism of Communist abuses that they made—they gave their vote of confidence to Fidel. The enemy, and now the Escambray rebels, too, were tarred with the CIA brush. Any opposition was automatically considered counterrevolutionary, automatically seen as fomented by the CIA, automatically dismissed as Yankee. This pattern clearly emerged after Playa Girón, but it is visible throughout the supposedly socialist world, from the Soviet Union to China, from Vietnam to Cuba. In the world where the state is supposed to disappear, a monolithic party emerges to oppress, to suffocate all liberty, to repress the people, and to create a privileged bureaucracy to enjoy wealth and power.

PLAYA GIRÓN: THE FIGHTING

The beachhead occupied by the invaders was retaken within seventy-two hours, but the fighting was furious. Abandoned by the United States, without air support or supplies, with no escape route, and with the entire Cuban people attacking them (the very people they had been sure would rise up to support them), the brigade felt betrayed and lost. On the third day of fighting, I was in a jeep with Fidel and his escort. We had stopped somewhere along the front. Suddenly a group of invaders sprang out of a thicket in the swamp. They threw down their weapons and put their hands up. Fidel and the rest of us were shocked. One burst of machine-gun fire would have sent the lot of us to the next world. Those men had fought as best they could, but it was all over. Fidel reacted by saying he would announce the wholesale surrender of the brigade as a way of gaining time and short-circuiting any U.S. reaction. He also ordered that the prisoners not be mistreated.

His next idea was to put the prisoners on television. I reminded him of the ill effects of showing a prisoner on TV who was forced to talk. I brought up the televised trial of the criminal Major Jesús Sosa Blanco.* Cubans don't like either cruelty or Roman circuses. "We'll convince them, Franqui. Talk it over with these guys, and I'll bet they accept." Some of the prisoners said they would, so I added that if we were to guarantee that no one would be shot, that there would be a free and open discussion of things, we would have a program without precedent on television. Fidel told the prisoners they wouldn't be shot—and told us he would exchange them for American tractors.

The discussions were really something. The invaders lost not only the battle but the debate as well. Mind you, they won some rounds. Felipe Rivero, José Andreu, and others jolted Carlos Rafael Rodríguez, and in doing so earned the admiration of the people for their bravery. But the majority of the prisoners, even after they said some rather rough things to Fidel himself, ended up applauding him—on television in a broadcast seen around the world.

There were atrocities committed by both sides during the course of the fighting, but these were really the exception and not the rule. If you consider that the invaders lost far fewer men than we did, if you consider that the prisoners spent so little time in jail, you can see that Fidel Castro managed the whole business

---

* He was accused of killing a number of people in cold blood during the 1957–58 campaigns and was executed after a disorderly public trial in January 1959.

with much greater presence of mind than he managed the control of the rest of the island's population. For crimes of no importance you could be jailed, and these invaders were going to be released. It was a propaganda move, and it worked.

THE VICTORY AT PLAYA GIRÓN: AN ASSESSMENT

The victory at Girón was an extraordinary triumph for Cuba and a defeat for the United States and the CIA. All counterrevolutionary potential was henceforth liquidated. The possibility of a long, dangerous local war, a puppet government that would request and be granted aid from (read: intervention by) the United States had ceased to exist. The "unity" imposed from above by the CIA just fell apart. Miró Cardona, the so-called president-designate, was nothing more than a prisoner on a closely guarded U.S. military base; he would later write an open letter in which he explained that the aid of the powerful has its price—you must become a puppet. Kennedy had inherited the operation from the Republicans Eisenhower and Nixon, but he took complete responsibility. It was he who gave the green light to the landing and the red light to any U.S. air cover. The failure was his; and it was then that the war between him and the CIA began.

Cuba's prestige soared. But internally, the victory was a disaster. The counterrevolutionaries, we must remember, fought to overthrow the revolution; the Escambray rebels fought only against Communist influence, militarism, and repression. The victory at Girón could have been the beginning of a setting to rights of internal errors, of a cessation of Party politics, of a recovery of the disaffected, of understanding that within Cuba there was no counterrevolution. Just the opposite took place.

The indiscriminate, mass jailings all over the island were hideous. The jails soon overflowed, so prisons had to be improvised. Out in the country, they used stables and corrals; in cities, the prisoners were put into sports arenas, the stadium-prisons so popular in Latin America. Remember Chile? The stadium prisons were not as cruel in Cuba, you say; yes, but they were no less stadiums for that. And no less illegal. The jailings were not really intended to nip future revolts in the bud but were directed at revolutionaries, hated by the Communists, who had not even participated in the revolution. The most heavily attacked groups were the old underground fighters, the independent unionists, the Directorio, the independent students, Catholics, members of the Ortodoxos, professional people, technicians, and peasants. The Communist vendetta was accompanied by a vendetta carried out by the local Comités de Defensa de la Revolución, who still hate anyone with a job.

The Communists hated my crowd even more than they hated the capitalists we had overcome, because they could not stand the idea of a radical revolution that was not inspired, directed, and organized by the Soviet Union. Now, with the new powers Fidel had graciously granted them, they were destroying the revolution with all their hate and fury. Fidel gave the green light. Raúl organized the persecution with Ramiro Valdés and Security, which was headed up by Isidoro Malmierca, who had been trained in Moscow by the KGB. Malmierca was a friend of Shelepin, Khrushchev's enemy. The long, expert Soviet repressive arm was now joined to the Castroite military body, which meant total repression. There was collective hysteria, because a denunciation could send anyone to jail—even some Latin-American exiles living in Cuba being trained for guerrilla fighting ended up in the Príncipe jail. Sometimes people were picked up merely because they were present when another suspect was nabbed. There was a grotesque story about a Chinese peanut vendor who got on a bus full of prisoners to sell his peanuts. When he tried to get off, the police, laughing their heads off, told him he had just won a free trip to jail. Anyone considered dangerous before the operation was automatically executed—Humberto Sorí Marín and Eufemio Fernández were two such victims.

The roundup of suspects was as fast as lightning, but so was their release. A week or two after the arrests about 80 percent of all the prisoners were free, which meant that some twenty thousand still remained behind bars. Those set free were, of course, completely terrorized. The mood was one of uncertainty, so everyone tried to leave the country. Originally, only the Batista supporters had fled, then the middle classes went; now people of every class who had sympathized with the revolution were emigrating. We who were part of the revolution protested the injustice of the jailings, but it was no use. We were all suspects, and Fidel was invisible. If you did reach him, he would tell you to see Aníbal Escalante, and few people were dumb enough to go to the heart of the repression machine to talk to the head man.

Fidel would tell us we were going to build a socialist society and then quickly add that only the Communists understood socialism, only they were politically faithful and trustworthy. He set the example. His secretary, the ever-faithful Celia Sánchez, was removed and replaced by an old-line Communist. His personal bodyguard, Valle, who had protected him in both war and peace, was transferred, and an old-line Communist was put in his place. Comandante Amejeiras, a hero at Playa Girón, the man whose column, despite tremendous losses, had beaten the enemy, was demoted from being chief of the national police force (which at the time was still independent of Security, Valdés, and Malmierca). That entire police force, by the way, including its guerrilla leaders, either disappeared or became part of Security. Fear, the mortal enemy of our revolution, grew like a weed.

LUNES IN HOT WATER

Edith García Buchaca, the government's director of cultural affairs (a Communist, married to Joaquín Ordoquí and previously married to Carlos Rafael Rodríguez) casually mentioned to me one day that Fidel wanted to have a meeting with the writers. At the time, the *Lunes* team was working around the clock to publish four volumes of eyewitness accounts of the Playa Girón action as well as two special supplements, also on Playa Girón. We realized that militiamen and volunteers of all kinds had flocked to Girón out of a sense of duty, and we wanted to preserve their vision of what had happened. Besides, it was the moment in which the greatest number of writers and artists felt united with the revolution. This was not a propaganda campaign. The writers wrote as Cubans in order to share their experiences at Girón with other Cubans. At the same time, they maintained their identity as artists. The whole enterprise was an attempt to record what we believed were important documents in our national consciousness.

From its inception *Lunes* had been very polemical. Our thesis was that we had to break down the barriers that separated elite culture from mass culture. We wanted to bring the highest quality of culture to hundreds of thousands of readers. We were motivated by a motto we got directly from José Martí: "Culture brings freedom." So we published huge editions with pictures and texts by Marx, Borges, Sartre, Neruda, Faulkner, Lezama Lima, Martí, Breton, Picasso, Miró, Virginia Woolf, Trotsky, Bernanos, and Brecht. We also published protest issues on cultural colonialism in Puerto Rico, Latin America, and Asia. We called into question all the commonplaces of Cuban history and literature. Even *Lunes*'s typography was a scandal for left- and right-wing prudes. We played with letters in the same way that Apollinaire, the futurists, the Dadaists, and the surrealists had done. And we included black and Cuban folk traditions as well. We tried to translate Cuban culture into visual symbols.

But now a general crackdown was taking place. The old-line Communists, supported by the Castro brothers and headed by Aníbal Escalante, were making a clean sweep of things. *Revolución* and its supplement, *Lunes*, were going against the tide of events, in part because we believed that as an integral part of the literacy campaign, cultural literacy was something that should be totally free of controls. Edith García Buchaca and her Council of Culture were in the vanguard of the attack on *Lunes*. Guillermo Cabrera Infante and I went to the Council to protest. There we were met by the guilty silence of Alejo Carpentier: *Bohemia* had attacked him on his return to Cuba because of his neutrality and self-imposed exile during the Batista years. We had defended him as an important novelist. Now, seeing which way the wind was blowing, he set sail east, remarking that the best policy in times of danger is to take cover. He went to Paris as cultural attaché, where he insulated himself from the kind of attacks we would continue to receive.

The first meeting with Fidel took place one Sunday in the National Library. There was a huge turnout. Fidel and his general staff were seated on one side, and almost all of Cuba's best-known writers and artists were on the other. Fidel, in his usual dramatic style, opened the meeting by saying, "Whoever is most afraid should speak first." It was a dare no one would take at first. Then Virgilio Piñera, skinny, badly dressed, with his ironic little voice, stepped forward. Virgilio was a timorous soul, the author of a Greek tragedy set on a Cuban plantation, *Electra Garrigó*, and of fantastic stories that had caught the eye of Jorge Luis Borges during the forties. He stepped forward and answered Fidel: "Doctor Castro, have you ever asked youself why any writer should be afraid of the revolution? And since it seems I'm the one who is most afraid, let me ask why the revolution is so afraid of writers?"

Such was the tone of the first meeting. When Fidel called a second meeting for the following Sunday, he alluded to me indirectly when he referred to "certain arrogant people who should be here and aren't." I had meant my absence to be a protest, but now I had to defend my point of view, even if I knew I would lose anyway. The library was like a courtroom: above, the presidential tribunal, with Fidel, Ordoquí, Carlos Rafael Rodríguez, Edith Buchaca, Dorticós, Hart, Alfredo Guevara, and a few comandantes and lawyers; below, the artists and writers. Someone up above suggested I join them, but I said I liked it fine where I was. We were a mixed bag—the *Lunes* team, Lezama Lima, some Catholic writers sympathetic to the revolution, some old, some young.

Alfredo Guevara took the floor: "I accuse *Lunes* and *Revolución* of trying to split the revolution from within; of being enemies of the Soviet Union; of revisionism; of sowing ideological confusion; of having introduced Polish and Yugoslavian ideas; of having praised Czech and Polish films; of being the spokesmen for existentialism, surrealism, U.S. literature, bourgeois decadence, elitism; of refusing to see the accomplishments of the revolution; of not praising the armed forces." We were, it seemed, a big internal threat, the Trojan Horse of the counterrevolution. Guevara went on to say that *P.M.*, the film seized and censored by ICAIC (Cuban Film Institute, directed by Guevara) and defended by us, was counterrevolutionary, showed decadence instead of the armed forces and their struggle, that Sabá Cabrera (brother of Guillermo Cabrera Infante) and Orlando Jiménez, who made the film, embodied the antirevolutionary ideology of *Lunes* and *Revolución*. We might recall that Alfredo Guevara had been Raúl's buddy since their Prague days, that he had been Fidel's personal friend since their days at the university and later in Mexico and Bogotá. He was always sent where the Party needed him. His specialties were espionage and dirty tricks.

During the fifties he had infiltrated a cultural society, Nuestro Tiempo, some friends of mine and I had founded as a means of reviving our sleeping Cuban culture and to give our generation a forum. Nuestro Tiempo was avant-garde in art, theater, and music—its interests were cultural, not ideological. But Guevara and the Party divided and paralyzed it by offering free trips to Communist countries. In that way, they also emasculated the group's political activities. Through another Party man, Marcos Rodríguez, they managed to keep Nuestro Tiempo from demonstrating against Batista. When the struggle against Batista really got hot, Guevara took off for Mexico. A few hard-liners wanted to expel him from the Party, but Carlos Rafael Rodríguez, Ordoquí, and Edith Buchaca kept him in. Later he went through the motions of a public self-criticism and joined the 26 July Movement in Mexico.

I could barely keep my temper as Guevara went on accusing *Revolución* and *Lunes*. When he finished, I went up to Fidel and said, "You have reproached me in the past because I have never asked you for anything. Well, now I'm asking you to correct an injustice being committed here right in front of you—this charge that *Revolución* is trying to divide the revolution from within. Your silence is like an endorsement of the charge." Fidel nodded but said nothing. He never said anything. Then I understood that Alfredito wasn't the one accusing *Revolución*: it was Fidel.

DEFENSE OF *REVOLUCIÓN* AND *LUNES*

I spoke out firmly but dispassionately in defense of *Revolución* and *Lunes*. I declared that almost everyone present knew the history of the newspaper and its martyrs, its anti-imperialist struggle, its impassioned defense of great social transformations. I reminded those present that *Lunes*—when the timid were afraid to do it, and the right attacked us for doing it—had published fundamental texts by Marx and other revolutionaries. I added that the *Lunes* team had gone out to the Girón battleground, while others, like Guevara and the film crowd, had either stayed home or remained out of range. I declared the proceedings to be a maneuver by the Party, a bureaucratic act of censorship. I went on to discuss *Revolución*'s campaign in favor of Cuba throughout the Americas and Europe as well as the visits by foreign intellectuals we had sponsored. I pointed out, with regard to *P.M.*, that for Cubans party-going, dancing, *pachanga*, and love were a way of life, that there was an African element in us, but that the accusers were lily-white, orthodox, and inquisitorial. I also quoted Martí's dictum about culture bringing freedom.

People got fired up and almost unanimously came out in favor of *Lunes*, the new literature, the new art, and freedom of expression. The poet Pablo Armando Fernández publicly ridiculed the Party men, while Roberto Fernández Retamar and Lisandro Otero, as yet not cultural policemen, stated that if the politicians knew nothing about literature they shouldn't try to run it. Alejo Carpentier and Cintio Vitier kept their mouths shut. Some of the Party faithful paid their dues and were rewarded: Amado Blanco, the dentist-writer who was the voice of *Información*, got his ambassadorial post by attacking us. The ICAIC group went with their chief, Guevara, because he promised them films if they did. Of the three hundred persons present, no more than twenty accepted the official charges.

Carlos Rafael Rodríguez, more subtle than Guevara, and more dangerous, did not attack us directly. He wanted to destroy *Lunes*, and his thesis was that, yes, modern, new, hermetic texts should be published, but slowly, in small editions, so the people could be educated to appreciate them, and so we wouldn't waste precious paper. Elite art and literature just weren't meant to be mass-marketed. We countered by saying it was he, Carlos Rafael Rodríguez, who wanted to maintain the notion of an elite culture, while we wanted the people to have all literature at their disposal, to read or not as they saw fit.

Three people backed me up in those difficult moments: Haydée Santamaría, who spoke out sharply, indignant at Guevara's attack; Yevgeny Yevtushenko, who viewed the proceedings with all the horror his own Moscow experiences had taught him and who was astounded at our courage and our unanimous protest. Fidel never forgave him, even after his later public self-criticism. The third was José Lezama Lima. I had already paid homage to him as a great, pure poet who had stimulated Cuban literature. I stated at the proceedings that the revolution should recognize this great artist and respect both his independence and his ethics. Lezama was applauded, and not only by those below. I went on to defend the painter Wifredo Lam, who was despised despite his being a great painter. He hadn't rejected his own art then as he has now. Indeed, even if his painting continues to be great—which it does— his person can only inspire pity. This is in contrast to Lezama, who, as writer, Cuban, and human being gets greater and greater.

Well, we won that round against the Party: Fidel, Carlos Rafael Rodríguez, and the others. But the bureaucracy and the power structure never lose in the long run. They invented a paper shortage to suppress *Lunes.* Then came a Writers' Congress and a Union of Writers (Moscow style). I decided not to participate in any more meetings or to legitimize them with my presence. I also chose not to hear Fidel's words—ambiguous outside of Cuba, all too clear inside—"With the revolution, everything; against the revolution, nothing." The problem was that the revolution was Fidel and his personal tastes in art, literature, and politics.

Even out in the Sierra, Fidel didn't like our reading poems by Vallejo, Lorca, or Neruda over Radio Rebelde. He wanted us to read episodes from a book entitled *The Mambi War.* He became infuriated when he saw the famous scene in the Russian film *Ballad of a Soldier* where the soldier, confronted by the monstrous German tank, feels fear and hesitates before destroying it. Fidel was a man who knew what war was, but he had begun to think in terms of American westerns, in which the heroes can tear up tanks with their bare hands and have no natural fears to overcome. I realized that culture and power cannot coexist. There are in art, literature, and philosophy at least two things Fidel Castro cannot accept: all of them oblige the individual to think for himself, and all of them take the individual out of the present moment and insert him in a living and permanent tradition. Politics creates a tradition of ashes. The victory at Playa Girón unleashed Fidel's repressed hatred of anything that wasn't obedience, work, official communism, and military strength based on the cult of one man. The unions were eliminated, the militiamen were made into regular army troops, and an elite Communist party came into being. How could a living culture exist in such a society? The historical death of a new and free revolution had already taken place.

VUELTAS PRISON AND OTHER CRIMES

One day an old friend, a revolutionary from the province of Las Villas, came to see me. I was shocked to learn he had just spent some months in prison, that he had been picked up one night by Security in a raid aimed at finding out who had been burning cane fields. The arrest order was given by an old Communist prosecutor, Sixto.

That's right, Sixto, the lawyer. I ended up in the Vueltas prison along with hundreds of other guys. I didn't know most of them, but I saw lots of our buddies there from the Batista days. Like me, they didn't know why they had been arrested. The guards wouldn't tell us anything. Funny, they didn't question us, either. And if we tried to talk to them, they told us to shut up and threatened us. Time passed, and we lost hope. Our families had no idea where we were. Then came a strange sort of trial. They accused a peasant of burning sugar cane in the Vueltas district, of being an enemy of the revolution. Security told him either to confess or to suffer the consequences. Sixto ran the show: he wouldn't allow the peasant a lawyer or permit any witnesses to testify in his defense. The peasant refused to confess. His family and his friends were there, but they weren't allowed to speak. Well, they condemned him to be put up against the wall and shot. The family screamed, but the guards shut them up. In the middle of the night, they handcuffed us and marched us outside. We marched to the outskirts of the town, to the cemetery. They took the peasant, blindfolded him, and put him up against the wall. His ten-year-old son tried to run over and hug him, but the guards grabbed him. The firing squad opened fire, and the peasant's head went flying through the air. Then they tossed the body on an oxcart and took him away. When we got to the cemetery gates they rounded up all of us prisoners between two lines of guards. As the oxcart passed, Sixto made us a little speech: "For each burned cane field one of you gets shot. Now you're free. Don't let me catch you around here when the sun comes up." I was free. I lost my job. When I tried to find out why, they gave me a runaround—from one office to another, from the Party to Security. I've come to see if you can help me get out of the country because there's nothing left for me to do here.

I promised to do what I could, thinking all the time that I, too, would like to get out. Something inside me broke down. It was impossible to pardon crimes like that in the name of the revolution, and every day more stories like my friend's came in. I went to see Juan Almeida, a comandante and an old friend from the Sierra, the head of the province. I told my friend's story. Almeida, almost in sign language, told me his command no longer existed, that Security had made him into a joke, and that in fact he was being watched, as were so many other comandantes. Faustino Pérez, the number two man in the revolution, had lost all rank and was reduced to nothing because of his protest over Huber Matos's imprisonment. Now he was out in the Escambray fighting against the rebels, but he had been accused of being a leader of the counterrevolutionaries by Fidel's military secretary. Amejeiras and the other comandantes were desperate, because they saw their men falling one by one.

At one routine inspection, Malmierca ordered several captains from the Sierra to clean up the floor where he had just spit— with their bare hands. One of them punched him, and they were all thrown in jail for conspiracy. Fidel refused to see them, so in desperation they went on a hunger strike. Fidel had them released, but they were not allowed to resume their old commands.

We managed to save one old comrade condemned to death out in the swamp: we proved that at the time he was supposed to have committed a crime he was actually having dinner with Fidel Castro and President Dorticós in his own house. Oddly enough, he was *Revolución*'s distributor out in Zapatas. And these were the goings on of everyday life. I seemed to be living some kind of tragic dream in some other world.

So we began to protest this Party terrorism, to bring a halt to the fear that dominated us. I went to the palace, and before Fidel and the Council of Ministers I denounced Escalante. I brought proof of his activities, including his purloining a list of *Revolución*'s subscribers, which the Party ordered given to *Hoy*, the Party newspaper. I listed persecutions, arbitrary imprisonments, other outrages. My statements were met with silence and with countercharges against *Revolución*'s Moscow correspondent, Juan Arcocha. Fidel said that Carlos Rafael Rodríguez, who was due to leave for the Red Mecca, would investigate and get the facts. But the things I talked about did not merit any investigation because, of course, I was known to have anti-Party prejudices. On the way out, Fidel put his arm around me to calm me down, so I took the opportunity to stir him up: "Fidel, you keep an eye on Escalante, because he's the Party's man and he's dangerous. Now he's after me and my friends; tomorrow he's going to want real power." At least I left him thinking about a possible threat.

Everything was totally confused. You could see the old Cuba fading away. You could see the U.S. threat, the threat of the counterrevolutionaries. You could see just how popular Fidel still was with the people despite the obvious injustices. I could see how any opposition would be branded counterrevolutionary: the case of David Salvador proved it. And in exile, if you weren't a Batista man or pro-Yankee, you were nothing. This I saw clearly in Raúl Chibás, Manuel Ray, Menoyo, and others. They were accused of practicing fidelismo without Fidel. But none of these things could justify my accepting the deformation and degeneration that was taking place within the revolution and that threatened to destroy it.

This would not prove to be a passing situation. Rather, it looked to me as though things were growing according to their nature. A monster had been born. Its father was tripartite—militarism, caudillismo, and the total power of Fidel Castro. Its mother was the Soviet model, the amalgam of state, Party, and state ownership. I would have left then, because, as Cabrera Infante often remarked, no one can stop historical erosion. Cuba, following the thinking of yet another writer, José Lezama Lima, seemed frustrated in its political essence. I, as director of *Revolución*, felt responsible for what would happen to a lot of people, so I could not just run out on them. I thought then as I do now: my job is to fight, to make people aware of things, to say no when it seems necessary. But we were falling into the abyss and we knew it.

OPERATION P

One memorable night, Fidel Castro, Raúl Castro, and Ramiro Valdés ordered squad cars to seal off the bohemian sections of Havana and other cities. They were trying out a new police technique—mass arrests. Anyone caught in the enclosed area who could not produce the proper identification documents (it was not the rule yet for everyone to carry papers) was arrested. Several thousand prisoners were taken to police stations, detention centers, and the Príncipe prison. There were two sweeps. One was quick and generalized. The other was selective, with lists provided by the local Defense Committees, and included homosexuals, vagrants, suspicious types, intellectuals, artists, Catholics, Protestants, practitioners of voodoo. In red-light zones, they picked up prostitutes and pimps. Once down at the Príncipe—or in any other prison—those arrested were made to undress and put on a uniform, a striped suit with a huge P across the backside. Capital P: pederast, prostitute, pimp. Even the men who happened to be with prostitutes at that moment were imprisoned; even those walking down the street. It was a real police party.

In the Colón neighborhood, certain streets were shared by families and houses of prostitution. I knew the place well because I had worked on newspapers printed there, and I certainly will not deny having visited houses of prostitution there—I don't know any man who hasn't. That was where we corrected the proofs of the newspaper *Luz* in 1947; it was a place where nonconformists and activists of all sorts met. At dawn, Eddy Chibás would come to see the director of the magazine *Brana* with his fiery articles. When the paper closed at 3:00 A.M., we all met—the whole staff, from linotypers to street vendors, to have a drink. In true Cuban style, the café contained a mixture of journalists, prostitutes, homosexuals, passers-by—everything. As the cops picked people up, the same jokes would ring out every time: "Don't get mixed up with the wrong bunch, now!" The cops would size you up, and take you in if you looked a little too refined, or delicate, or just plain guilty.

That was Colón, and Zanja, where the newspaper *La Calle* was published, was the same. On Sundays they published a sports newspaper, one of whose reporters was Fidel Castro. That was where the famous Shanghai theater was located, which was a place right out of Fellini, with fat whores who would do collective stripteases. That was where Havana's Chinatown began. Now, that community was almost totally Maoist at the time and ran into tremendous problems during the pro-Soviet period. All of these neighborhoods coexisted. Their business was sex, and the only real victims were the women who worked there.

Operation P was the first massive socialist raid of the Cuban revolution. If you look at it from the point of view of neighboring countries, the operation had a peculiarly Cuban flavor: the letter P is a taboo letter among us; now it was emblazoned on the prisoner's back, like a Cubist phallic symbol. The letter symbolized police prudery—no Cuban says "prostitutes," "pimps," or "pederasts" because we have more vivid, if less refined, terms. But the roundup included more than the people caught where they shouldn't have been. The police invaded private homes, because they had lists of people they wanted. And all this with no warning, without even the pretense of legality.

Virgilio Piñera, who had spoken out at the first of Fidel's "conversations with writers," lived in Guanabo, which is a few kilometers outside of Havana. He was arrested in his house at midnight, dragged down to the Príncipe, and dressed in his uniform—a scene right out of one of his own absurdist stories. Soon the Príncipe, an old castle-prison left us by Spanish military architects, was overflowing with prisoners. Someone spotted Virgilio and accused him of being a spy for *Revolución* trying to gather information for a story. No one would believe he was just one more prisoner. He was surrounded and threatened, and only survived because he fainted.

The operation managed to annoy the whole country, and there was a general protest. It went too far. Cuban cruelty allows you to make fun of a homosexual, but not to imprison or harass him. Lots of people inquired about Virgilio and other artists, even some of the Communists. Carlos Rafael Rodríguez, Blas Roca, and many of the "comrade" intellectuals in the party (whose names I won't mention now, just as I refused to in a discussion I had with Escalante) were troubled by this antihomosexual movement. I went to the palace to vent my anger to Fidel, Raúl, and the others. There they were with Ramiro Valdés, Isidoro Malmierca, Barbaroja (Manuel Piñeyro), and José Abrahantes. Valdés is an ugly, unpopular, taciturn neurotic who is corrupt, as are almost all moralists. He was bragging about the success of the operation while the others laughed. He said that all the socialist Security forces he had consulted (Soviet, Chinese, Vietnamese, Czech, and German) had reported what they had in store for such people: execution, twenty years at hard labor, reeducation camps. He had even brought in a Czech homosexual-detection machine. This drew a real laugh from the Castro brothers.

My remarks to Valdés were brief and violent. He thought I was protesting about Virgilio Piñera, and said that so many people had complained, that Piñera would be released. But I said I was protesting the way in which the police had carried out the operation, their violence. I told him I protested the persecution of people who, according to the Marxists themselves, were nothing more than the victims of the old society. Valdés said the revolution wanted to end all that homosexuality and degeneration, but when I pointed out that none of the great tyrants, Hitler and Stalin among them, had managed such a thing, he accused me of defending homosexuality, of being against "revolutionary morality." He really flew off the handle when I told him that historically the greatest persecutors of homosexuals had themselves been homosexuals. Fidel and Dorticós intervened at that point and said the prostitutes would be sent to reeducation camps and be made into new women, with new jobs. Pimps would be prosecuted to the full extent of the law. Homosexuals would not be prosecuted, but they would be allowed no influence in art, culture, or education. They said the operation was important as an anticounterrevolutionary step.

They assured me that these were the best methods for cleaning up Cuban society, although I noted that I failed to see how removing the effects of a problem could be the same as removing the causes. Then they said that was the last time they would resort to such action. Operation P was one of the terrible moments of a terrible year, 1961. We were now in a Reign of Terror. I saw no way out but to protest as best I could: I would defend the homosexuals against these power-mad *machistas*. I would defend anyone against the Party's power.

THE CÁRDENAS UPRISING

Cárdenas is a city on the north coast of Matanzas, next to Varadero, one hundred kilometers from Havana. Varadero, with its wonderful beach, was like paradise, and it was there that the first Stakhanovite workers came to enjoy the fruits of their labor: beaches, the houses of the wealthy, and luxury hotels. Foreign journalists, revolutionary tourists, and friendly visitors were all lodged there in a carnival atmosphere of music and joy. A foreigner could clearly see the people happily enjoying the property they had recovered through the revolution.

Three or four kilometers from Varadero there were other incredible things to be seen: persecuted people, peasants whose land had been given them and then taken away, jailed revolutionaries, and fishermen who refused to change their lives. They were used to fishing alone, in the style Hemingway describes in *The Old Man and the Sea*, but the revolution had other ideas. First it gave the fishermen new houses, which were gratefully received; then it took away the fishermen's boats and tried to make the men work in teams—they would stop being fishermen and become sea workers. This the fishermen refused to do, so Security stepped in to harass them and to stop any mass migrations to the north. Even so, many risked the currents of the Gulf and fled.

One day the people of Cárdenas could stand this Red terror no longer and took to the streets. They demanded freedom and food, an end to terrorism and persecution. There were demonstrations everywhere, mostly carried out by poor black women. That is, it was a revolt of the poorest of the poor. Cárdenas is itself a poor zone: aside from tourism, it produces sisal, sugar, some fruit, and seafood. The symbol the women of Cárdenas chose for their revolt was an empty pot, which was almost bizarre when you think that the women (neither black nor poor) who had demonstrated against Allende in Chile had chosen the same symbol. Compared to Varadero, Cárdenas was misery itself. Where in one all was pleasure and luxury, in the other there was want, privation. Whereas the comandantes and tourists had everything and anything, the poor of Cárdenas had nothing.

The military chief of the province, Comandante Jorge (Papito) Serguera, a follower of Raúl Castro, immediately consulted the Castro brothers. The order was to stifle the demonstrations immediately, to attack the people demonstrating, and to charge them with being counterrevolutionaries. Many people were jailed, and the poor black women were magically transformed into middle-class ladies, enemies of the revolution. But the revolt was a symptom of popular discontent. The Party had disrupted life with its rationing and its disorganization of the economy. The excuse was the old Stalin line that if the people were not ready for socialism, a revolutionary minority would have to impose it on them. So Cuba invaded Cárdenas with troops, tanks, and air patrols. The troops, of course, came from other parts of the island and were told they were suppressing a counterrevolutionary uprising.

I went to Cárdenas to see things for myself. When I got there I found Dorticós about to deliver a victory speech. He invited me to sit on the platform with him, but I told him I wanted to see things from another point of view. They made a party of the occasion, distributing rum and beer to the people, allowing free rides on buses—the same tactic corrupt politicos had used before the revolution. I was struck by the display of socialist weaponry against the defenseless counterrevolutionary people. I was reminded of Budapest. Behind it all was Fidel, who very discreetly remained invisible. I tried to get the facts—knowing full well that the official version would be lies—so I looked up some old friends.

I found some old guerrilla fighters and asked them point-blank if they would shoot civilians. They said they would never do it, but they said it in hushed tones because the place was crawling with G-2 men and Communists. All it would take was a simple denunciation and you'd be up against the wall. They told me to keep on fighting, as we had in the old days. Then I listened to Dorticós and his threats. I decided, after talking to some friends, that the only thing to do was to try to organize some resistance within the revolution, to denounce injustice, to appeal to Fidel, to keep a channel open to Che (who was changing his mind about things), and to watch out for Ramiro, Raúl, Escalante, and Malmierca.

On the way back to Havana I passed through Varadero and wondered what sort of Cuba the visitors were seeing while ten minutes away there was a carnival of persecution in full swing. These people saw a stage-set Cuba, not the reality we had to live in every day, and they took the part for the whole. Mind you, I'm not talking about those cynics who would stroll through Havana exclaiming about how wonderful things were, but how they, of course, could never live without their books, their personal freedom, their record collections. Or that Venezuelan who said that he would support Cuban communism but would fight against it in Venezuela. They never saw the other Cuba, just as people never saw the other Russia during the Stalin era. They also think that any crime committed in the name of socialism is no crime at all.

This, too, is a problem of seeing the obvious and missing what is not before one's eyes. For progressive people it is easy to see oppression in the capitalist world. It was against that oppression that we rebelled in Cuba—the same sort that filled jails in Franco's Spain, that makes the black ghettos of New York a hell, that hides Rio's misery at carnival time. But people should also open their eyes to the crimes that make socialism as it is practiced in the world into the negation of the ideal of socialism. My advice to travelers is not to confuse what you see with what actually exists. Try to look beyond.

RATIONING

One day we woke up and, wonder of wonders, there was nothing to eat—no coffee, no rice, no sugar, no meat, no beans, no milk, no fruit—yes, we had no bananas. Fidel had the answer: "If there's nothing else to eat, we'll eat malanga." (Malanga is the farinaceous root that kept the guerrillas alive in the Sierra.) Then malanga disappeared. Cuba, it turns out, is not the Sierra. You just couldn't plant malanga anywhere and expect it to grow—which is something you can do with sweet potatoes, corn, bananas, avocados, and mangoes. We had plenty of nothing, but we did have long lines, rationing, price increases, a black market, and a crisis that affected both the economy and the means of production.

But how was it that everything ran out all of a sudden? The disappearance of manufactured goods, screws, spare parts, luxury items was understandable. It all came from the north, and the blockade existed. But what about the agricultural products that a tropical country can produce? Che spelled it out: we couldn't blame imperialism for a decline in national output. Fidel had given power to the old Communists, who, he said, were the only ones who knew about socialism—Escalante and the others. These were the results; they had Sovietized everything, from top to bottom. They tried to fix machines with lectures on Marxism, and if a worker said that the International was useless for machine maintenance, he was accused of being a counterrevolutionary.

What had really happened? First, there was an extraordinary increase in the buying power of the individual citizen, by at least 100 percent. Second, all food reserves were used up, as were supplies of luxury goods. Third, there was a slump in agricultural production because large landowners and cattle ranchers simply abandoned the land left them after expropriation. This amounted to something like two hundred acres, which they didn't see fit to cultivate. Most of the grazing and farmland in Cuba had been nationalized, but the problem was that the administrators sent out to run things by the Party were all city men, who just botched up everything. The fourth factor was that we had eaten all our cattle. This meant we had neither milk nor meat. The transportation system was also allowed to collapse, so that what was produced never made it to market.

Here's an example of what happened. The old Havana market had been famous for its fruits, fish, and other seafood, Chinese shark-fin soup, and tropical delicacies. It was a special place, not necessarily cheap, but the place to find—even if you remained a window-shopper—all the great products of the tropics arrayed as in a painting. The market had its own life, its own peculiarly Cuban mix of white, black, Chinese, music, color. Well and good.

The government appointed Tomás García, an old-line Communist, to take over the market. He would make a socialist market, carefully planned and arranged. "Here we shall make a great Red market, just like the one in Moscow." They expropriated everything—pushcarts, stalls, everything. They stopped the sale of fried foods. They eradicated private property, which meant that orange sellers and peelers were put out of business. Where there was capitalist anarchy, Tomás would create order—the kind they had in Moscow. So now every stand had to sell just one thing, which meant that there were lines everywhere, whereas before there hadn't been any.

Tomás García was confident that things would work out for the best, that future proletarian and socialist mothers would not have to stand on line. By the way, a new supply of mothers was more or less guaranteed when a shipment of socialist condoms never arrived. The Chinese did send some, but—this may have been Cuban machismo—people claimed they were too small. This was the origin of what would later be called the Fidel generation. There were lines of pregnant mulattas, dancing and chanting: "Fidel, Fidel, watch me swell. Here you see the revolution; now please give a smart solution." And if one of the administrators saw a woman who didn't look particularly pregnant and asked her how far along she was, she would usually say, without missing a beat, "Twenty-four hours."

Dorticós broke all records for cynicism when he announced with a straight face that oranges were bourgeois fruit. This bothered me very much, because I had always consumed oranges in great quantities, since they were so cheap. Now I would get calls in which jokers would call me a "bourgeois orange-eater." When people asked where the most common foods were, the answer would come right back: "They're in the future, brother, in the future." The joke that summed up everything went like this. In the new Cuban family the mother is the nation; the father, the comrade; the child, the future. One night the child starts crying and wakes up his older brother, who in turn wakes up his father saying, "Comrade, the future is covered with shit."

$$\overline{\mathbf{4}}$$

WAS FIDEL A COMMUNIST?

The questions people were always asking and continued to ask were: Was Fidel a Communist? Had he become a Communist? Is he a Communist? What was his plan? Was it really the Cuban situation—Cuba's economic dependence and the U.S. blockade— that threw Cuba into the clutches of the Soviet Union? No one thought Fidel was a Communist. I mean no one. We knew that Raúl Castro was a Communist, that Che Guevara was also, and that Camilo, Ramiro, Celia, Haydée, and some comandantes and other collaborators were Communists, too. But no one knew about Fidel, including me—who saw him at quite close range—and even his most intelligent enemies.

FIDEL: ORIGINS AND EDUCATION

Fidel's father, Angel, was an adventurer from Galicia who came to the island as a cavalry quartermaster in the Spanish army in the war against the *mambises* at the end of the last century. When the war was over, Angel got together a gang of laborers and began to make money. Then he acquired a huge plantation, Manacas, of about ten thousand acres in Oriente Province.

Fidel, who was born on August 13, 1926, was taken, at the age of six, to Santiago and enrolled in the La Salle school of the Colegio La Salle, run by Marist brothers. From there he went to the Colegio Dolores, in Santiago, and then to Belén, a Jesuit school in Havana. In October 1945 he enrolled in the University of Havana. He then went through a brief period of university gangsterism, trying to make a name for himself. There were two groups active in university politics: the MSR (Movimiento Socialista Revolucionaria) and the UIR (Unión Insurreccional Revolucionaria). Fidel joined the UIR, which had fewer ideological pretensions and which was composed of less corrupt individuals.

This was gang warfare disguised as revolutionary politics. Actually, it was a collective exercise in machismo, which is its own ideology. Machismo creates its own way of life, one in which everything negative is feminine. As our Mexican friends Octavio Paz and Carlos Fuentes point out, the feminine is screwed beforehand. Latin-American machismo derives from its amalgam of Indian, Spanish, and black cultures. Its negative hero is the dictator (one of Batista's mottoes was "Batista is the Man"), and its positive hero is the rebel. They are at odds in politics, but they both love power. And both despise homosexuality, as if every macho had his hidden gay side. The result was that the macho came to despise art, music, and culture in general: these are perceived as feminine or (worse yet) homosexual.

The macho idealizes the country because the city, for him, is the scene of degeneration and homosexuality. "In the country there are no homosexuals," Fidel would say to me. I had to point out that this was true only because the country fags all came to the city. Then I pointed out that even among his breeding bulls there were some bulls that allowed themselves to be mounted by the others. He refused to believe me. The fact is that while Fidel was born out in the wilds of Oriente, he never really lived there. By the same token, he hated the city because he never really lived in it, only in the religious schools in which he lived as a boarding student for some fourteen years. It's true that the two brands of machismo, conservative and rebel, are quite different. The conservatives (generals, soldiers, police) always defend the establishment, while the rebels attack it. Nevertheless, both groups share the same views about morality and culture. They hate popular culture and all the Indian and black elements in it. Anything that isn't white is no good.

And by the way, the macho's favorite *objet d'art* is the pistol. Not for nothing is the pistol Fidel's principal fascination, the gift he gives to those he esteems—he gave a fancy pistol with an inscription on its butt to Ben Bella in 1962. What this all has to do with communism will soon be made clear.

By 1947, Fidel was tired of gangsterism and joined the Cayo Confites expedition against Trujillo, which is where I met him. Unfortunately for Fidel, he found more enemies than friends on that expedition: Manolo Castro, president of the FEU (Federación de Estudiantes Universitarios), who was later murdered (Fidel was implicated, but it was said he never fired); Rolando Masferrer and Eufemio Fernández, who were commanding fire teams. Fidel had to team up with Juan Bosch and the Dominicans. But the fact is that he did become a leader and was one of those who really tried to get to Santo Domingo.

Another decisive event in this period of Fidel's life was the uprising that took place in Bogotá, Colombia, on April 9, 1948. There Fidel learned what a tragedy a popular uprising can be when it lacks organization and leadership. The "bogotazo," as it was called, was a crime committed by Colombian conservatives. They murdered Jorge Gaitán, the liberal leader, and branded any other opposition politician a Communist, including Romulo Betancourt and José Figueres. Even Fidel, who at the time sympathized with Perón's anti-imperialist stance, was accused of being a Communist at the time of the "bogotazo." But the event was important, because it helped Fidel discover his own leadership abilities. From then on, he viewed himself as one born to lead, not to follow.

When he returned to Cuba, he joined Eddy Chibás's Ortodoxo party. The Ortodoxos were the best of what was left from the revolution of 1930. It was a reform party, and its moral position and honesty turned it into the most important political party in Cuba. But Fidel discovered that traditional politics did not fit in well with his impatient, domineering personality. Within the Ortodoxos, Fidel could only be another member, when in fact he was a man of action. Batista's coup on March 10, 1952, gave Fidel the opportunity he needed in life, because the struggle against

Batista led to the July 26, 1953, attack on the barracks at Moncada and Bayamo. Now, it is important to note that the thousand young people who backed up the one hundred and fifty or so troops who assaulted the barracks were all members of the Ortodoxo party. There was not a single Communist among them. Except Raúl Castro.

We know that Raúl was invited to a Communist festival in Vienna, and that he was arrested and set free when he returned to Havana, but very few knew then that Raúl was a member of the Communist Youth. Fidel knew—of course. Fidel invited Raúl to take part in the Moncada assault just when it was about to take place. Raúl knew nothing of the plans for the operation, but he was one of its leaders, commanding ten men.

The Moncada operation suprised everyone, especially the Communists. On July 25, Aníbal Escalante was rendering homage in a theater in Santiago to Blas Roca, the secretary-general of the Cuban Communist Party. After the raid, the army jailed many politicians, including two Communist leaders, Joaquín Ordoquí and Lázaro Peña. At his trial, Ordoquí condemned the attack, branded it a *Putsch*, and called Fidel and company terrorists. The Communist press severely attacked the raid, calling it "a service to the dictatorship and contrary to the interests of the people." Raúl Castro was ejected from the Communist Youth. Later he would justify the Party's action, saying that even though the Moncada raid was ultimately the progenitor of a Communist revolution, the Party was still right in having thrown him out. Walterio Carbonell, a black student leader, was expelled from the Communist party for having sent a telegram to his old friend Fidel Castro to express his solidarity with his friend's action.

At the trial of the Moncada group, one of Lenin's books appeared among the evidence. It's curious how history changes with time. At the trial, the allegations of Batista's prosecutor about Communist influence were denied. Years later, the same book would be a badge of honor—the first appearance of Lenin in the context of the Cuban revolution. *History Will Absolve Me* would be Fidel's first political statement, but neither its ideas nor its language reveals a clandestine communism. There is a consistency of thought in all of Fidel's writing and manifestoes between 1953 and 1958. He talks about reestablishing the constitution of 1940, about democratic elections, and about reforms. He violently rejects the Batista regime's charges of being a Communist, and, as if that were not enough, he forms the 26 July Movement, when the Communists were condemning insurrection, guerrilla warfare, and sabotage.

In July 1958, out in the Sierra, Fidel made some startling statements to Jules Dubois, an American correspondent with State Department connections. Some of the young radicals from Santiago—Nilsa Espín, Rivero, and the president of the student body, Jorge Ibarra, dropped out of the 26 July Movement because of the conservatism of those remarks. In fact, Fidel's statements were so reactionary they were suspicious. But until the end of the war and the beginning of 1959, no one believed Fidel was a Communist. Now, in 1959, when the agrarian reform had yet to take place and Fidel was more or less incommunicado, Raúl and Che began to take certain matters into their own hands—especially regarding the takeover of plantations by means of Communist peasant leaders. In a public address, Fidel severely criticized those methods, ordered the restitution of the lands, and said that the agrarian reform would be strictly legal. In his visits to the university and to the offices of *Bohemia* and *Revolución*, he would say in a loud voice: "I believe only in the revolution. I will shoot anyone who opposes the revolution—including Raúl and Che." These remarks have turned out to be as suspect as his statements to Dubois.

But how effective they were at the time! Fidel wasn't playing some game with Raúl and Che. They didn't know what he was up to. Raúl was so fed up that he said to me one day that if things didn't start changing soon, he was going to fight in Santo Domingo. Again, was Fidel a Communist or not? Let's begin by trying to be objective, which means not taking Fidel seriously when he says, "I am not now nor have I ever been a Communist.

I am and shall forever be a Marxist-Leninist." Let's begin with Fidel in jail for a year and a half on the Isla de Pinos after the raid on Moncada. He seems to have spent his time reading, carrying out a serious study of Marx, Engels, Lenin, and Trotsky. Lenin fascinated him, but not only Lenin—Robespierre, too. This we see in his letters to Nati Revueltas, with whom he apparently had a rather lovely affair at the time. In those letters we see Fidel thinking out loud with a person who has no political affiliations.

Other letters from prison written by Fidel to Melba Hernández and Haydée Santamaría, Moncada associates, are also significant. They reveal Fidel's Machiavellian side. Of course, most politicians are Machiavellian, but here we see that Fidel was creating a public image (in favor of the constitution of 1940, etc.) that was at odds with the image he projected for his close associates. He talks about having to use people. For example, Armando Hart criticized Justo Carrillo, whom Fidel had just seen and praised to the skies. Fidel retorted that he knew what Carrillo was all about, but that he had to use him because Carrillo had important military connections. He did the same thing with Rafael García Barcenas and ex-President Carlos Prío Socorrás. Seen in this context, the copy of Lenin that Fidel had with him at Moncada takes on a certain importance. You just don't carry a book you don't care about in a life-and-death situation. Why wouldn't he leave Lenin behind when he had so many other things to worry about? Someone might say that lots of people study Marx and Lenin without becoming Communists, and that's a fact. But the real fact is that Fidel studied Marxism with a dedication he did not exercise in his other readings.

FIDEL IN MEXICO, 1955–56

In Mexico, while the future *Granma* team was preparing for guerrilla warfare in different places, they all quietly organized study groups. This provided yet another dose of Marxism and Leninism, and even of some Stalinism. I remember in this context my discussion in Miguel Schultz Prison with Che and Fidel about Stalin's *Principles of Leninism.* It is interesting, by the way, to note the confidence Fidel had in the Moncada veterans, in exile, during the *Granma* expedition, and after victory. They all remained, along with a few new trustworthy additions, such as Armando Hart and Vilma Espín. But it is important to study Raúl Castro's role in all this. Without Fidel, Raúl wouldn't have existed as a force in the group. He would have been a strict party-line Communist who would never have participated in the revolution. It was Fidel who included him in the Moncada assault, knowing full well that he had been in Bucharest, that he was a member of the Party, that he was part of a clique, known as the Prague group, which included Alfredo Guevara, Leonel Soto, Flavio Bravo, Raúl Valdés Vivo, and Osvaldo Sánchez—all leaders of the Communist Youth and all trained in Moscow and Prague.

Now why did Fidel want Raúl around? Partly for family reasons, no doubt. But Fidel also knew how Raúl thought, how his mind worked. (Raúl is not like Ramón; at the time, Ramón was a plantation owner, but now he is a full member of the Trinity.) In the Moncada attack, Raúl was merely present, but at the time of the *Granma* expedition he was a full-fledged leader, out in the vanguard. He would be one of the famous Twelve. During 1957, Raúl showed what he could do. He was a good organizer of military actions and well-disciplined. But, always a Communist, he was therefore an enemy of the urban guerrilla groups. Raúl was not the first man to be promoted to comandante in the Sierra. That was Che, who, although wounded and with broken weapons, managed to create, after Uvero,* and with the help of the Santiago underground forces, the second guerrilla front. During 1957, however, many other guerrilla fighters distinguished themselves in the Sierra: Juan Almeida, Camilo Cienfuegos, Efigenio Amejeiras, Manuel Fajardo, Lalo Sardiñas, Víctor Mora, Pinares, Andrés

---

* On May 28, 1957, the guerrillas seized El Uvero, a military post, confiscating ammunition and supplies.

Cuevas, and Ramón Paz Ferro, for example. Raúl was one of them, but he was not greater than they.

So why did Fidel choose him to be chief of the column that went to the second Oriente front in March 1958, a few days before the April strike? It was a key moment for Fidel in all his various roles—Fidel the military man, the leader, the self-promoter, and the future Communist. Frank País, the other 26 July Movement leader, had been thinking about the duration of the war since the outset, because the history of the events during the wars of 1868 and 1895 was utterly convincing. Our thesis was that the war could not be won with the Sierra alone, without the cities and without the workers and students. The guerrilla war was important, but the 26 July Movement was more important, because we had to be fighting everywhere at once—in Havana, Santiago, the Sierra, everywhere. We had few weapons, little money, little experience, and few real leaders. Frank País was the man of the hour, because, simply put, the *Granma* expedition was a disaster that weakened the movement. It was absurd and expensive to train a hundred men in Mexico and then risk everything on a dangerous sea voyage. When they landed, they lost all the best weapons, and when they tried to regroup, they left tracks for the army to follow. At Alegría de Pío they were thoroughly routed.

The cause of the disaster was inexperience, not a lack of ability. They should have trained the body of the troops inside Cuba, in the interior, and brought Fidel alone in from the outside. After the *Granma*, Fidel was opposed to any more operations in the same style, just as earlier he opposed, after the Moncada attack, any more assaults on large military barracks. But Fidel's military-caudillo image demanded two great moments that would surround him with the mythic aura of a hero. With fewer than half the men, money, and arms Fidel had, Frank País attacked all of Santiago. He took the navy station, burned the police station, and held the city for a number of hours. Three of his men were killed, but he lost no weapons. The attack caused a sensation in Santiago and throughout the rest of Cuba. Of the eighty-two participants in the *Granma* landing, seventy—killed, wounded, or taken prisoner—were lost, along with most of the arms and supplies.

The Twelve were saved because of the efficient organization of the 26 July Movement among the peasants under the control of Crescencio Pérez. To compensate for the *Granma* disaster, we had to show that we were still fighting, so the militia groups of the 26 July Movement carried out sabatoge actions all over Cuba. The Directorio won the sympathy of Havana, but Batista's reprisals were violent. There were hundreds of people murdered in the Christmas crackdown. After this countermove by Batista, the 26 July Movement leadership met in the Sierra with Fidel and suggested the interview with Herbert Matthews of the New York *Times*. They also sent him men, arms, ammunition, money, and medicine. At the same time, Frank País and René Ramos Latour ("Daniel") began to lay the groundwork for a second guerrilla front in the north of Oriente Province, where many people on the run from Batista had organized small groups to harass army outposts. País and Ramos Latour had no choice. They had to reinforce the Sierra, which they did on four separate occasions in 1957. If Fidel's front had fallen, the revolution would have been in danger.

Of course, to drain resources from the urban movement would accomplish the same thing. Frank País preferred to die in Santiago rather than abandon the 26 July Movement, which had by then reorganized throughout the island. When Frank País was killed (July 30, 1957), there was a general strike throughout the country that shook the nation to its roots. After the strike (August), Fidel changed his mind about the second Oriente front and demanded that all arms and men be sent to the Sierra. Ramos Latour, País's successor, not only made a tremendous effort to supply the Sierra, but also fought against the furious repression that raged throughout the island. The small guerrilla units operating in the second Oriente front zone had by now acquired considerable experience and were harassing the enemy. At the beginning of 1958, action would pick up on the second front because in March, just before the April strike, Fidel sent Raúl with a column of one hundred men out to the second front.

Why did he run the risk of weakening the Sierra, where there were only two hundred men left? To take over the second front, so that Santiago wouldn't have its own army. But why send Raúl, the number two man in the revolution? Fidel never dissimulated his distrust of Santiago, so it was logical that he wouldn't send Ramos Latour, Escalante, Menéndez Tomasevich, Paz, or any other guerrilla leader from Oriente. But he could have sent Cienfuegos, Almeida, or Amejeiras instead of Raúl, who was in no way superior to any of them. Let's begin by saying that he sent Raúl knowing full well that Raúl was a Communist, because for Fidel ideology is more important than family ties. He knew that Raúl, unlike Che, who was a sort of free-lance Communist, was an orthodox, Stalinist, well-disciplined Party man. The emergence of a Castro-Communist configuration begins at this moment.

Fidel knew every side of Raúl: the Communist, the obedient follower, the disagreeable man, the man who was against the masses, the violent and repressive man, the neurotic suffering from a little-brother complex. The legend of the good Fidel and the bad Raúl was being born, a legend both brothers fomented. "If something happens to Fidel, the Almendares River will be called the Red River because it will run with blood instead of water." "If something happens to me, watch out, 'cause Raúl will be on his way." So Fidel, through Raúl, controlled the huge second front. The Sierra was in danger because of Batista's offensive, but things improved somewhat after the April strike because one hundred new men were brought in along with two planeloads of supplies flown in from the 26 July Movement's foreign bases. One load was Huber Matos's, the other was Pedro Díaz Lanz's and mine. They came in during March and May.

In August 1958, after our victory over Batista's offensive, the rebel columns began their invasion of the island. It was the beginning of the end. Fidel knew that whoever took Havana and Santa Clara would win huge political popularity, and he sent Che Guevara and Camilo Cienfuegos. Anyway you look at it, Che made himself into a guerrilla leader through force of will, talent, and sheer audacity. He made sick men with broken weapons into the second guerrilla force in the Sierra. He carried out the first raids into the lowlands. He created the first free zone in Hombrito and changed the war into one of positions instead of the nomadic guerrilla fighting of the earlier phase. Within the free zone he set up factories, bakeries, hospitals, arms-repair shops, and Radio Rebelde—all with supplies sent by the urban underground. He raised the level of the war, even if it was all a bit premature.

Fidel, ever the pragmatist, later used Che's innovations. Che had always declared himself to be a Communist, but his brand of communism never convinced Fidel, who recognized Che's independence of character and his sense of morality. Che and I had many arguments during that period. He would defend the Soviet Union and the Cuban Communist Party, while I attacked them. For him, they were synonymous with socialism. I defended a free socialism and a humanist revolution. Fidel would say that soon enough I would see Che arguing with and fighting against the Communists in the same way he disagreed with me. (And that was a fact, but Che's enlightenment is another story.) Fidel's problems with Che had nothing to do with communism; rather, they were related to Che's independence of spirit. He was ungovernable. Fidel sent him to Las Villas, which was exactly the right thing, but he sent along Ramiro Valdés as his second in command. Ramiro was yet another pro-Communist.

The other column was commanded by Camilo Cienfuegos, another brave fighter but also a man sympathetic to the Communists. His father and his brother were militant Communists. Because of their relationship with Camilo, Félix Torres and his Communist shotgun men had a very special position in the Yaguajay attack. In the early months of 1959, Fidel made yet another democratic profession of faith, talking about the "olive-green revolution, as Cuban as the palm trees." During his trip to Uruguay, he ended a speech heard by thousands with the motto: "Bread without terror. Freedom with bread. Neither a dictatorship of the right nor a dictatorship of the left—a humanist revolution." The Communists protested. But while Fidel was saying all that, Raúl, Ramiro Valdés, Osmaní Cienfuegos, Alfredo Guevara, and other Communists were quietly taking control of the army. It is clear now that all Fidel was doing was buying time. There are, in sum, three aspects of Fidel Castro that we must bear in mind:

1. The Cuban people wanted profound changes with regard to freedom and democracy.
2. Within the trade unions, the 26 July Movement obtained 95 percent of the delegate votes in the first free union elections. The Communists, 5 percent. (Fidel, Raúl, and Che pressured the executive of the CTC to include Communists, but the congress refused.)
3. The U.S. position was as yet undefined, but the United States was clearly unhappy with what was going on in Cuba. The Cuban middle class, sympathetic to the United States, was also unhappy.

FIDEL'S HUMANITARIANISM

One of the things that surprised me when I got to the Sierra was the human dimension of the war. The rebel army seemed quixotic, with Fidel playing the part of the don. He ordered us to give medical treatment to the enemy wounded as if they were our own comrades in arms. We were not to murder anyone. We were not to kill, torture, or in any way offend prisoners. We were to explain what we were doing to them and why, in order to educate them to our cause. We were to respect the peasants, their traditions, their wives, and their goods—we had to pay them for anything we took. There was an egalitarianism as well between comandantes and soldiers. Rank had no privileges. We were family, and we worked together out of respect instead of mere obedience. There were very few comandantes, so they did not constitute a class.

In the urban underground we struggled to keep our men from becoming common murderers because we knew just how dangerous it was to give anyone a license to kill. We believed that life was a genuine revolutionary value, and that you don't change the world simply by killing people. We realized that even killing in self-defense dehumanizes a person, so we required that all innocent parties be respected. We rejected terrorism because Batista represented terrorism. We used a minimum of violence against the absolute violence of the regime, sabotaging its strategic areas (power stations, gas lines, telephone lines, transportation, factories, and sugar production). We carefully planned each act of sabotage in order that no innocent people be killed. We even went so far as to warn passers-by.

A good example is what we did at 222 Suárez Street, in Havana. We had dug a tunnel from the house to a main meter center for gas and electricity. We blew it up, and the capital was paralyzed for three days. Not one casualty. Tremendous political effect. That was how we gained the sympathy of the people. I still remember the arguments that raged in the Príncipe prison, where they had me and other 26 July Movement members as prisoners. The Communists, who were required by the Party to be against sabotage, applauded. Then they realized what they were doing and embarrassingly added that sabotage was not a "correct method." Thousands of acts of sabotage all over the island cost us thousands of lives, but the ratio of our dead to innocent victims was one thousand to one.

To find in open war the same nonviolent attitude that we had shown toward the cities was quite a shock. The battle of Jigüe was in this sense a masterpiece. We took two hundred and fifty prisoners, officers and men, after a furious battle that cost us the lives of a brave fighter, Cuevas, and of many more. Then we patched up their wounded, fed everyone, and set them free. We even let the officers keep their sidearms. Three of us, Faustino Pérez, Horacio Rodríguez, and I—unarmed—led the prisoners to an enemy camp and turned them over to the International Red Cross. While we were there, signing some forms, in Vegas de Jibacoa in the Sierra Maestra, who should appear but Che Guevara riding a mule! He chatted with the captured officers in a cordial way, and then had to give his autograph to our other prisoners. After events like that, Batista's days were numbered, because the troops could see that the barbudos were not their enemy, that they were men fighting for freedom. That humanitarianism was no façade; it was the real thing.

But was it for Fidel? Was it humanitarianism, or merely a tactic for winning the war? Cubans in general detest violence, although it certainly has been a part of Cuban reality since the Spaniards massacred the Indians in the era of the Conquest. And our history since colonial times right on into the twentieth century has been spattered with blood. We thought things were going to change, but as soon as victory was ours, we began to see executions right and left. Humanism was eradicated in Red terror, and Fidel the humane became Fidel the implacable. Why the harshness, the mistreatment, the omnipotence of Security? Why were prisoners denied visiting privileges? Why was habeas corpus suspended—which not even Batista had dared to do? Do people change when they get power?

What is the difference between a man when he is part of an opposition group and when he has absolute power? Our revolution was never in danger because of counterrevolutionaries, but Fidel is a calculating man who believes in terror as a means of government. He responded to a critical letter of mine once by saying: "All criticism is opposition. All opposition is counterrevolutionary." Then he repeated his definition of Stalinism as the dictatorship of a revolutionary minority during difficult times, a minority that functions like a father who must deny his children something he has promised them. Of course, Fidel always thought of himself as the revolution, so the paternal image is doubly important. I tried to argue that he was wrong to mix up opinion with criticism, that he was wrong to make conscience and obedience the same thing, because that was a military notion that didn't have any validity in normal society. I added that the war against Batista wasn't won by those on top telling those below what to do but by everyone working together. I said that during the war he was a real leader and not a caudillo in the Latin-American tradition, that we revolutionaries were not yes men, and that criticism and discussion were not revolutionary acts.

Fidel was not interested in my ideas about the individual's need to have opinions of his own and called me a stubborn fool. I told him that he must know, being the king of stubborn fools. Ultimately I saw that there is no one more dangerous than a repressive leader, that nothing could stand in his way, not even the people. The only question was whether we were just now seeing the real Fidel or if he had actually undergone a metamorphosis. Che Guevara never forgot the first man he shot using a rifle with a telescopic lens, precisely because Che never forgot that the enemy is a man, a human being. Fidel was different; he had to kill, and he did it in a cold way, without emotion. I found among the old papers I carried through the war one document that provides a precedent for Fidel's postvictory cruelty. This was the use of symbolic executions, in which a man was told he would be executed, put up against a wall, and then not shot. Such a man becomes sick because of mental torture. The false executioner becomes a danger to society. We carried out all kinds of executions—real, moral, and symbolic.

SUGAR CANE

Ain't gonna cut no cane no mo'.
De win' kin cut it down.
Lola kin cut it down
De way she cuts me down.

Revolution in Cuba means burning sugar cane—it did in 1868, 1895, and 1930–33, and it did for us. When a plantation owner came to see Máximo Gómez, leader of the *mambí* army, to protest that the war was destroying the wealth of the nation, Máximo Gómez answered that with so much of the nation's blood running everywhere there was no time to worry about the damned sugar cane. This was the same argument *Revolución* used to respond to attacks on the 26 July Movement because sugar cane was being burned. According to the plantation owners, "without sugar, Cuba couldn't exist." We answered that without freedom Cuba couldn't exist. All this business of sugar and Cuba's existence was a variation on what Cubans had been hearing since the nineteenth century, only then the refrain was: "Sugar and slaves are the lifeblood of Cuba." That kind of thinking kept Cuba under Spanish rule for an extra fifty years, and then, during the time of the republic, under U.S. domination until our revolution.

In 1952, the year of Batista's coup, Cuba produced 7.2 million tons of sugar. The sugar cane was new stock that had been planted during the democratic reign of Carlos Prío Socorrás, and it inaugurated a period of large harvests. Batista's coup came right in the middle of the harvest, so he couldn't limit production in 1952. Afterward there materialized a conflict between a correct economic program and pure speculation. For Cuba, it was better to produce more sugar at a lower price than less sugar at a higher price, because in a competitive market Cuba could keep its lead in the world market, and by keeping prices low, it discouraged the development of competition in the rest of the world. High production meant more sugar to export.

Conversely, if the harvest were diminished, the diminished quantity of sugar produced would bring about a price increase and stimulate foreign production—which would then be able to compete. The country received the same in foreign exchange for a high-quantity export at low prices as it did for a smaller quantity exported at higher prices. The owners preferred to control the market and to earn more in the long run rather than go for quick profits. The workers went along and accepted the harder work in order to keep their jobs secure. In fact, they earned about the same, whether it was a short harvest of three months (with a higher daily wage) or a long one of four months (with a lower daily wage). The difference was the amount of work—more, naturally, in the long harvest. The restrictions Batista imposed in 1953 (the London Accord) favored foreign economic interests, and speculation on the sugar reserves of the previous year made Batista and his pals millions of dollars. The Cuban sugar harvest was reduced to five million tons, and Cuba itself lost markets to other sugar producers.

Many newly planted cane plants were left uncut, and the owners neither planted new ones nor thinned out their fields, because they were fearful of the war, of Batista, and of the economic uncertainty of the times. There were protests, burned cane fields, and strikes. In December 1955 there was a huge strike in the sugar industry that shook the entire nation. It was both a political and an economic strike that united university students and sugar workers against Batista. A student leader, José Antonio Echevarría, Faure Chomón, and almost the entire Directorio took part in the strike action out in Las Villas, while the 26 July Movement did the same in Camagüey. When the revolution was victorious in 1959, many sugar plantations were in full operation, and the harvests of 1959 and 1960 were large. The problem was that many cane fields were old. While the actual plant lasts for several years, how much it yields depends largely on the fertilizers and care given it.

At a Council of Ministers' meeting at the end of 1961, Fidel Castro announced that the next day he was going on television to tell the people to destroy part of their cane fields in order to plant vegetables and fruit. Che Guevara, Raúl Cepero Bonilla (Minister of Commerce and an expert on sugar), and I criticized Fidel's plan. All three of us were against sugar. Che, Minister of Industry, wanted to develop nickel production and other industries; Cepero was famous for his attacks in *Prensa Libre* on the plantation owners; and I wanted to see the gradual phasing out of sugar (and the dependence it entailed) in favor of diversification in agriculture and development of nickel and light industry. We had to feed ourselves and to be independent. The three of us unanimously disagreed with the idea of Fidel's giving such a speech at the time the agrarian reform was still an ongoing process, because of the disorder it would produce among the landowners and the potentially disastrous results that would ensue since the new administrators knew nothing about sugar and its cultivation. The people would not destroy only the small amount of cane Fidel wanted them to destroy; they would destroy a lot.

If this happened, sugar production would fall and so would our foreign exchange. We would have to import less, especially foodstuffs. With all the economic problems we were experiencing, the idea of destroying cane fields seemed just plain crazy. If Fidel were to say on TV, "Destroy cane fields and plant vegetables," the harvest would be lost. Fidel did not want to eliminate the sugar industry, but he did want to limit production. Unfortunately, a television speech wasn't the way to do it. Despite our suggestions, Fidel wanted to proceed. I repeated that the cane plants had to be renewed, that there hadn't been new plantings for ten years. Cepero Bonilla pointed out that the land left to the plantation owners was not being cultivated and that we therefore could not count on all that land as far as the harvest was concerned. In fact, we had no idea about production because the cane inspectors who used to make these calculations no longer existed. The people themselves had not taken care of the fields, so we had no idea what we would get from nationalized fields. Che then warned Fidel that the people would take Fidel's suggestion too far and avenge themselves on the cane for all their years of suffering.

But Fidel knew better. "I'll bet you a banquet, to which the entire Council of Ministers will be invited, that I'm right. If I win, you pay; if I lose, I pay." Fidel gave his speech, as did Raúl and the administrators. The people began to plow the cane under. The harvests were reduced by a full 50 percent, from six million tons to three. The famous bet never came up in polite conversation. As a result of Fidel's speech half the cane fields were destroyed, ruining the work of years and of hundreds of thousands of workers. We calculated the losses in hundreds of thousands of pesos. Other sugar producers had a field day, and it took years to replant those fields. But the error actually increased our foreign exchange. The price of sugar went so high that we could sell what we had at extremely good prices.

Be that as it may, the sugar speech was Fidel's first huge economic error. Not his last. In another speech, he told farmers to stop planting mountain coffee. We consumed a huge amount of coffee in Cuba and even managed to export some. Coffee had a special meaning for the guerrilla fighters because their war in the Sierra Maestra, Oriente, and Escambray was fought in the shade of coffee trees. Fidel figured he could make up for the sugar disaster (which meant shifting large numbers of workers back into sugar production) by negotiating a sugar treaty with the Soviets. His idea was to sell the sugar high and buy cheap coffee. Thus the labor generally used in planting mountain coffee could be used otherwise. First coffee prices went up, then coffee became scarce, then there was no more, then it was rationed. There was a popular song sung by Bola de Nieve (Snowball) that went:

> Oh, Mama Inés,
> all us blacks
> jus' luvs ah' coffee.

One day, a Colombian tourist, a Communist and a coffee grower, told the Comandante that in Mexico they cultivate coffee on the bottomland. The Comandante liked that idea and ordered Cubans to go into Mexican-style production. This became the famous Havana green belt—half a million *habaneros* and an equal number in Las Villas were ordered out to plant coffee. Millions of dollars were spent in seeds and plants. Lots of European artists and intellectuals took time out to plant their own coffee bushes. The peasants told the Comandante that the land they wanted to use wouldn't produce coffee because it wasn't well tilled and that they should experiment first. But Fidel was sure the earth would pour forth his famous trinity: coffee, fruit, and luscious beans. The peasants protested that even if the coffee were to take root (which it didn't) the other plants would kill it. "Your problem is that you're all a bunch of conservatives. You're backward, pessimists. I'm going to prove it to you here the way I did at Moncada when they told me no one could start a revolution here.

Well, we made the revolution, and now we'll win this one, too. You'll come to me and say I was right." Tongue in cheek, the peasants all nodded in agreement. Well, first the tractors we bought never showed up. Then we tried planting coffee Indian-style—digging a hole in the hard ground and sticking in a seedling. All the plants died, and if anyone was heard singing Bola de Nieve's song, he was hauled off to jail as a counterrevolutionary. Similar disasters happened with our attempts to raise rice and cattle. So we had no coffee, no milk, no meat, no rice, no corn, no beans—and even our tomato plants got blight. The joke that summed it all up was, "Now we're going to send Fidel to the United States. If he does there what he did here, the United States is done for."

How did it all happen? It happened because all power was concentrated in one man. Socialism became dictatorship; socialism became Stalin, Mao, Kim Il Sung, Brezhnev, Husak, Fidel Castro. The old-style dictators, from Hitler to Pinochet, always tried to turn back the tide of history, and some succeeded for a while. The new-style dictators, with their cult of personality, don't try to stop history or turn it back; they send it forward, they change everything, and they paralyze it totally. Fidel became the revolution, and the state became the owner of everything within it. Power became vertical, with absolute power located above. Marx thought that the state would eventually disappear, but how can it, when every day it gets stronger and stronger? The state becomes a colossal monopoly that devours everything, that becomes totalitarian in its inability to tolerate deviations of any kind. Fidel's variety is typical of the Third World—the caudillo, monoculture, militarism, an adaptation of local conditions based on the Soviet model. It's the same all over—in Islam, in China, in Vietnam, in the Eastern-bloc countries. Only Tito's Yugoslavia seemed an exception, a moderate capitalism combined with a moderate Sovietization.

A FEW CHANGES

Fidel changed everything, every day—ministers, offices, plans, streets. These were not structural changes, or changes in the nature of things, but mere cosmetic changes. Cuba would be his self-portrait, his mirror. He abolished several Cuban holidays: Easter, Christmas, New Year's Eve, the Epiphany, the carnival. All these combined Christian and pagan, Spanish and black customs.

For example, Christmas Eve was a holiday that was thoroughly Cuban in its combination of the Spanish and the black traditions. It was always celebrated with music—guitar or bongo drums—and eating, especially of roast pig covered with green guava leaves and cooked over coals. Sometimes the pig would be roasted in a pit, or it would be roasted on a spit over a fire until the skin burst and the melted fat poured out. Among the dishes served on Christmas Eve were pork cooked with rice and black beans, corn, turkey fricassee, and avocado salad. We also ate lots of Spanish *turrón* (almond candy) and generally drank a bottle of good Spanish wine, followed by Cuban beer or rum. And always there was lots of music. Even the poorest families found a way to celebrate Christmas Eve.

New Year's Eve was spent in the street, with dancing and a rite of cleansing. Water was poured everywhere and everything was swept clean. Carnival was a special holiday in Santiago, with conga dancing all over town. In Havana there was less participation and more spectacle. And of course the black neighborhoods celebrated their own holidays, with special rites and rituals. Cubans were always fond of their holidays and of having a good time in general. Well, socialism eradicated all that and turned both Havana and Santiago into tropical Moscows. All celebrations were prohibited, by order of Fidel.

There was another legend related to Cuban partying, the idea that Havana was a kind of colossal bordello, the Sodom and Gomorrah of the Americas. Now, it is true that there were a few thousand prostitutes in Havana, primarily in three districts—Colón, Zanja, and Ayestarán—but there is no city of almost two million people in the world, capitalist or socialist, that does not have its prostitutes. We found them in Prague and even in Moscow, but in the socialist world they "officially" do not exist. (A Cuban diplomat in Moscow was sent to ask our big brothers how to eliminate prostitution and was told that under socialism there is none. But while living in Moscow he was approached again and again by prostitutes, so he went to the protocol section to ask how to handle them. They sent him to a special branch of the police force that dealt with prostitutes, which of course obliged him to ask why they had that special force if they did not have prostitutes.)

The myth of Havana filled with hordes of depraved tourists is nothing more than a myth, one that tries to associate what prostitution there was with another world, the black world with its particular music and culture. Not even the U.S. Marines on leave were able to get in there, and more than one ended up bleeding for trying to do so. Even today no foreigner is allowed in: where Yankees couldn't go, neither can the Russians. The pleasures of that world have nothing to do with pornography; it concerns popular music and dancing. That was far from the world of the Spanish Royal Academy, but we had our own academies of dancing—Mars and Bellona, where all our popular dances were taught as art.

What Fidel has done is to impose on Cuba all the punishments he suffered as a boy in his Jesuit school: censure, separation of the sexes, discipline, thought control, a Spartan mentality. He hates culture, liberty, and any kind of literary or scientific brilliance. All sensuality, of course, is anathema to him. We used to have one main prison, Isla de Pinos; now we have many. We used to have a few barracks; now we have many. We used to have many plantations; now we have only one, and it belongs to Fidel. Who enjoys the fruits of the revolution, the houses of the rich, the luxuries of the rich? The Comandante and his court.

EL SOCIOLISMO

The new system abolished all contradictions: first those of the bourgeoisie and its notion of private property; then norms, laws, and old institutions; then the division of powers among the executive, the legislative, and the judicial; then the free press; then independent schools; then independent unions. It abolished the middle classes and the peasantry. It abolished regional autonomy, including neighborhoods, properties held in common, municipalities, and provinces. It also abolished individual autonomy—not by law, but by deed. It abolished religion, ideas, political parties. And when there was nothing left to abolish, it abolished the proletariat. It went even further: it abolished the people, the market system, and often even the means of production. But it never abolished the Communist party, the state, the police, the army, money, and salaries.

Actually, the Party took over the state—or perhaps the state was grafted onto the Party. The new union was the Party-state. With nationalization, everything passed into the state to form a total state. Now we had a state-Party owner that possessed all. Where before there were thousands of private properties, large or small, now there was only one, which belonged to the state. Where before there was anarchy in production, which led to inequalities and injustice, now there was a tyranny in production that paralyzed the economy and life itself, freezing existing differences into their specific positions. The Leninist law of unequal development was suppressed from above, not from below. The system inherited not only class differences but also natural differences—rich and poor lands, developed and undeveloped areas.

In effect, did the revolution change anything? Yes, everything in the highest echelons of Cuban society changed: the Party-state was the new ruling class. But nothing changed below. Those of us—almost two million—who have suffered through this process know that the monster is not socialism. The word just has no meaning any more. Each side has its buzzwords. Pinochet and

Videla always talk about the "free world," while Kim Il Sung, Teng Siao-ping, Husak, Pan Van-don, and Brezhnev talk about the "proletariat," "popular democracy," "communism," "internationalism," and "free territory." No one believes these words any more because everyday reality gives them the lie. The socialist world is not socialist; it's a world where the people are forced to work and to endure permanent rationing and scarcity, where they have neither rights nor freedoms. If they are taught to read— an essential prerogative if the wall of ignorance is to be destroyed once and for all—they are deprived of the freedom to read what they like. The increase in literacy is more than offset by the increase in the new elite above. There is no equality in education, because the new elite gives special attention to the children of Party members and state officials. The same applies to labor. There is no unemployment, because people are made to work at forced labor, in reeducation camps, and in military service. Salaries are not equal and are insufficient. This goes as well for housing, medical attention, transportation, and food.

Those above enjoy privileges. So there are no more old bourgeois around, so what? There are plenty of bureaucrats who administer, control, and enjoy wealth. Above, everything is different, while below it's the same old thing. In Cuba, we call this system *sociolismo.* *

---

* This is a pun in which the word *socio*, meaning "partner" or "buddy," is blended with *socialismo*, or "socialism."

5

1962

It was in the first days of January of that uncertain 1962. I had just barely returned, but I knew I ought to be on my way. Nazim Hikmet, the Turkish poet, friend of Lenin and Trotsky, was seriously concerned about my future and told me he could get me a place in Moscow to study Marxism-Leninism. He said it was my only way out. The idea horrified me. I was desperate, when suddenly the African god Shango came to my rescue: an invitation to visit Egypt and interview Nasser. Then on to India to see Nehru. From there I would travel to Oceania and Africa. Was I running away? Yes and no. Besides, I had learned the hard way about exile. I had been a saboteur in the city, had been sent into exile, and had returned to fight in the Sierra. In 1961, I had lived through my first socialist exile, and now in 1962 I would begin my second.

I flew from Prague to Cairo, and when I saw Egyptian art for the first time, I felt I was in a dream. I had lived in Mérida in 1957 and had seen the Mayan ruins of Chichen Itzá. That had been my first experience of the North American world, one that moved me to the core, me, a man from the Caribbean, where that remote past just did not exist. For me, Egypt was a lesson in the possibilities of the human imagination.

But the experience of Nasser's Egypt was not so moving. It was the same old thing—a touch of social transformation, the visible evidence of the terrible burdens of the past, and the glaring privileges of a nascent bureaucracy. Nasser was a kind of god among the people. Our interview was a success. He declared his support of the Cuban people's right to change their lives, his support of our self-determination, of our neutrality, and of the principle of nonintervention. I thought about Che Guevara, our first visitor to Egypt, who had used all the time he could spare to establish contacts with the rest of the Third World. If only I could have stayed longer in Egypt . . . but I had to go on to New Delhi and Nehru.

INDIA

No sooner had I stepped out of the plane, than I noticed a strange line of people and flowers. I began to wonder about the flowers when suddenly I was almost drowned in them. They turned my head into a garden. There was my friend the Cuban ambassador Armando Flores—whose name, meaning "flowers," completed the joke. Flores understood my desire to see the city, but he looked me over with a certain skepticism that I would comprehend only later. After the *de rigueur* meeting with a "Friends of Cuba" committee, I went out for a walk through the town. It was yet another marvel—that sea barrier I had lived with all my life was finally coming down. The world was turning into one big trip for me. I strolled through a large park through which flowed one of the tributaries of the Ganges. I saw someone putting a snake to sleep by talking to it (that guy should have been a politician), others delousing each other—not killing the lice, but letting them go in the grass—and the inevitable, touristic sacred cows. As yet, I didn't know that in India all animals are gods, and that therefore they had to be respected, left unharmed. I saw families taking water from the river for cooking, others bathing in it. I saw funeral processions, with the mourners all dressed in white. I saw cadavers being burned and ashes being thrown into the river where children were playing.

I saw so much I could no longer see anything. I thought about nonviolence, about Gandhi, and about this sensual, sweet, and miserable land. I saw very little prostitution, but I did see the remains of British colonialism in Delhi's architecture. And, of course, the castes. Delhi, for all I know, is probably the least Indian city of India, but it was all I had time for. I went on to the interview with Nehru as well prepared as I could be. He would answer my quite difficult questions with long silences. He was simply dressed in dark olive-green and wore a rose. His office was sober as well. I tried to talk a bit about Tagore, and Nehru's look seemed to say, "Look, you fool, do you think I imagine you came all the way from Havana to talk about poetry?" He was on guard, and for an hour I could get nothing out of him. I would quote one of his statements on self-determination, and he would answer with another statement that canceled the first one. I was getting desperate, because the nonaligned nations would be meeting soon and a statement of support for Cuba by Nehru would be extremely important.

When I was a journalist, I never made up an interview, but that day I was sorely tempted. I figured I could get away with it, what with the translation and the time it would take for news to get back to Nehru. I started to calm down, while Flores (who was translating what I said into English) began to get nervous. As we got up to leave, I shook Nehru's hand and reminded him of his meeting with Fidel in New York, of the applause and shouts of the people. Then and only then—because he thought he was speaking off the record—did Nehru open up. He said a lot of things about Cuba and Cuban rights. I published only what he said at the end and never got into trouble. It was my most difficult interview, because I was too smart for my own good, too well prepared. Again I hated to leave the country I was in. I had seen so little. I sensed its spirituality, but its problems seemed to me so overwhelming that I could not imagine any future for it.

RETURN TO HAVANA

When I got back to Havana from Algeria, I found a quite breatha-
ble atmosphere. Aníbal Escalante had been shipped off to Moscow,
and Isidoro Malmierca, number two man in the police repression
business, had been substituted. The people were also breathing
more easily. They were happy despite the terrorism, the executions,
the economic disaster, and the rationing the Party boys had provoked. Nothing had changed—there were no amnesties, no
prisoners let out of jail—but a few 26 July Movement people
began to show signs of life. Celia Sánchez was back with Fidel,
and the famous Prague Communists (Leonel Soto, Raúl Valdés
Vivo, Flavio Bravo, Alfredo Guevara) had been somewhat scattered.

I ran into Fidel as he was leaving a television station, and he
invited me into his car for a chat. There I noticed the first change.
Fidel was no longer surrounded by Communists; some of his old
personal guard from the Sierra days were with him. Fidel was a
new man. He reminded me that I had warned him about how
dangerous Escalante was (I had forgotten), and that I had been
right. He went on to describe how Escalante had screwed up
the Cuban economy, how he had persecuted revolutionaries,
caused revolt, and created discontent all over the place. "Escalante,
all by himself?" I asked. "No, that bastard the Soviet ambassador.
A real son of a bitch, worse than the American Bonsal."* He
told me how the Soviet embassy, which had gotten into trouble,
tried to weasel out by telling him that Varela, an old Communist
working in Foreign Relations, had said some bad things about
him (Fidel) in the presence of a Russian official. It turned out
that Malmierca and others got out of trouble by using the same
scapegoat tricks.

I told him that scapegoats weren't the difficulty; the problem
was that the bureaucratic, centralized system held all power and

* Philip Bonsal, American ambassador to Cuba, 1959–61.

excluded the people from any governmental participation. He tried to tell me that everything was okay, that he had changed the administrators, and that from then on it would be clear sailing. I asked what would be done about the injustices committed. Nothing. Then he asked me about Ahmed Ben Bella and Algeria, because he had liked my articles in *Revolución*. (That had been yet another polemic with the Cuban Communists, the pro-Soviet crowd, and the French Communists.) I dropped a bomb on him when I said that the only weapons the Algerians had been given free had come from China; the Czechs had demanded cash on the barrelhead. I told him that Cuba, China, and the Congo were very popular among the people and that Ben Bella seemed to me a real revolutionary—one who wanted to know all about our agricultural reform, since he was going to carry one out himself.

I described the man I thought most dangerous to Ben Bella's plans, Colonel Houari Boumédienne. It was he who controlled the army, the only really organized force in Algeria; while Ben Bella had the people, Boumédienne had the power. Fidel said that he wanted to help Ben Bella organize his own military force, that Che and Masetti were going to supply military aid, and that he wanted me to go back—perhaps as ambassador. I knew this was his way of offering me a chance to get back into his good graces—and I wanted to go back to Algeria, but not as ambassador—but I kept quiet. Fidel had a way of offering you things in order to find out what you really wanted. If you took his offer, he had you. If not, he could easily find out what was on your mind. A clever routine. But I'm a peasant, and I learned in the underground how to act innocent and believe it myself. I just kept quiet. I wanted to leave *Revolución*, but I did not want to work in the government because I couldn't fight the Party and be part of the power structure at the same time.

Fidel went on and on about Algeria and finally left me at the door of *Revolución*. I began to think it all over and finally concluded that Guillermo Cabrera Infante was right when he said that Escalante was nothing but Fidel's cat's-paw, that Raúl Castro had learned all the Marxism he would ever know from Escalante and Ordoquí. Raúl had supported the Party from the beginning and would continue to do so. Che was the only one who had seen the light: "I was the first Party supporter and later became one of the toughest anti-Party men." What we had then was a temporary truce. We had won a historic battle because we had managed to associate in the minds of the people the Communists, the Soviet Union, the economic disaster, the injustices, the crimes, and the persecutions that plagued Cuba. For the moment, the Stalinization process had halted.

But it wasn't dead. Up above the old Communists were the new ones: Raúl, Ramiro, Security, the army, and Fidel, the father of Party politics. Once again he had managed to make a ninety-degree turnabout and convince people someone else was guilty of sins he had committed. Fidel created the monster so it would eat up other people, but when he saw that it might eat him, too, he eliminated it. Escalante then made a mistake. When one of his daughters got married, he ordered that one of the houses the Comandante had set aside for himself be given to his daughter. He thought he was powerful, but he didn't know Fidel. Only three days before, Fidel had named Escalante secretary-organizer of the Party's central committee. Three days later, Escalante was liquidated. Fidel delivered a public address about Escalante in which he denounced the Communists and presented himself as their victim.

But the Fidel-Stalinization process went on. Everything was under central control. No institution was free of central control. *Lunes* was gone, as were movies and television. Everything was in one pair of hands. Maybe we had had only the illusion of a victory, but that was better than nothing.

ANOTHER TRIP TO ALGERIA

Among the people invited to Havana for the July 26, 1962, celebrations was our old friend Siné, the French cartoonist, and his girl friend, Anita. They had given aid to the Algerian resistance in Paris and were friends of Ben Bella. When Siné was in Algiers, he spoke with Ben Bella about Cuba and the visit he was going to make. Ben Bella wrote a letter to Fidel, gave it to Siné, and told him he would be able to see Fidel through me. When Siné got to Cuba, I immediately called Celia Sánchez and told her about the letter. Days went by, then weeks. Fidel was unavailable. Siné began to get worried, because he had to leave, and so I tried to pressure Celia, but Fidel kept us all waiting.

Siné became a humorless humorist. The night before he was to leave, we threw a going-away party for him. A Cuban colleague interpreted his situation for him: Siné had published in *Revolución* a cartoon in which Khrushchev appeared with a little Chinaman behind him. The cartoon enfuriated the Soviets and their friends, who all accused us of being pro-China. Now it was Siné who had the Chinaman behind him, although the Chinaman was in fact a Russian; in Cuban popular humor, to have a Chinaman behind one's back means to have bad luck. Another bit of black humor: a voice from beyond, Fidel's, materialized for Siné at the airport. After midnight we brought Siné back to the Presidente Hotel, when suddenly Fidel appeared. He started talking as if nothing were wrong, discussing projects, concocting marvelous plans. The skeptical Siné enjoyed Fidel's audacity, his outrageous cleverness. Fidel said he would answer Ben Bella's letter right away, and then (it was now after three in the morning), he told me, as he left, to get ready to go back to Algeria. I would represent Cuba in Ben Bella's formal inauguration. I was to bring Fidel's presents and, of course, his answer to Ben Bella's letter. I was also to tell Ben Bella to watch out for Boumédienne.

The plane was to leave at eight in the morning. Fidel's letter to Boumédienne is interesting. Fidel suggested that he negotiate with France, that he not rush into nationalizing oil or anything else, that he be firm but moderate. Fidel reminded Ben Bella that De Gaulle was not like the Americans. Then he offered both his personal friendship and that of Cuba. Later on, at the airport, there were some more surprises. I would be accompanied by two comandantes. The first was Dermitio Escalona, the man from the Escambray I had denounced to Fidel for torturing prisoners. He was no friend of mine, to say the least. The other wasn't really a comandante, but a major general, the Hispano-Soviet general named Ciutah, a.k.a. Angel Martínez. Maybe he wasn't a Cuban or a comandante, but he sure was a Soviet major general. He was a Communist higher-up, the man who directed and shaped Soviet ideology and technique for the Cuban army and bureaucracy.

Angel Martínez looked like your average grandfather, a nice guy; he was a history professor and an art lover, intelligent and astute. But he was Raúl's cat's-paw, and Raúl was Moscow's cat's-paw. Another was Fidel, of course. Fidel, speaking in his elegant style, designated me, in this, my only official mission, president of the delegation. Not a big deal, but still mysterious. He told me to invite Ben Bella to Cuba, anytime he wished— perhaps at the time of his imminent visit to the United Nations. On the plane, Escalona kept quiet, but Angel and I chatted about many things. He told me about how his love for art almost cost him his life during the Spanish Civil War. He was out for a walk when he saw some men burning artworks. He impulsively ordered them to stop, whereupon they grabbed him, called him a Francoist and set about to hang him. He wouldn't tell me who the other group was, probably because relations between the Communists and the other revolutionary groups were so bad at the time. On the way to the noose, Angel pointed to a palace filled with artworks and dared his captors to burn it. He figured he would either buy time or, better, that he would be spotted by his own men. Fortunately, his men did see him, and they hanged the captors in Angel's place.

I asked him why Stalin had executed so many Russian, Czech,

Polish, Yugoslav, and Hungarian Communists who had fought in Spain. His explanation-rationalization was this: Russian artillery was very good, but their tanks and other weapons were of very poor quality. The Communists in Spain wanted to reveal all that, so that the weaponry could be upgraded, but Beria and Security were worried they might be called to account, so they shot everyone before any of them could speak with Stalin. The Spanish generals told him anyway, and the weapons were improved. This was a logical, but insufficient explanation as far as I was concerned, and I told him so. I tried to draw him out on the question of Stalin and the terror he brought to the Soviet Union, but Martínez ducked my questions. When we got to Algeria we barely saw each other. I saw a lot of Ben Bella, while Martínez and Escalona saw a lot of the army. And that was how the Soviets used Cuba to insinuate themselves into Algeria.

I told Ben Bella about what Fidel had said concerning Boumédienne, mentioning that I myself had probably exaggerated things because of the repugnance I feel around hermetic military men. Ben Bella said he was aware of the danger, but that he preferred to wait until a crime was committed before harming an innocent man. He said he thought things would work out. Then I mentioned Ciutah, and gave Ben Bella a capsule biography of the man, adding that Fidel told me that the Soviets had sent him to be director of the Cuban Military Academy. Ben Bella noted ironically that we were certainly being well looked after.

After the inauguration, I went to Milan to see Valerio Riva, the editor at Feltrinelli. We had worked out a project to publish Cuban literature all over Europe in an attempt to break down the cultural blockade. We both wanted as well to publish a history of the Cuban Revolution narrated by Fidel. At the time I was writing *The Book of the Twelve*, which would be an introduction to the history and personalities of the revolution. Among the authors Riva and I wanted to publish were José Lezama Lima, Guillermo Cabrera Infante, and Heberto Padilla. I was trying to extricate myself from *Revolución* without bringing the house down on everyone else. But of this, more anon.

THE CUBAN MISSILE CRISIS

There are many, many versions of this famous event. Fidel Castro has two (almost three); Khrushchev, in his memoirs, another; and the Kennedys, yet one more. Fidel's first version (hot off the presses) was that "the missiles were installed in Cuba because the Soviet Union asked permission to do so." His second contradicts that one: "The Cuban government asked the Soviets for the missiles." The third said that both parties had agreed on the installation of the missiles. All three versions may be found by anyone who cares to look for them in the magazines of the period. Which is the correct version?

The first person to talk about missiles in connection with Cuba was Nikita Khrushchev, in Moscow, in 1960. Cuba as yet had not declared itself socialist. The Soviet Union was very interested in what it called "the heroic island," a revolutionary people, fighting against imperialism, only ninety miles away from the United States. The Soviets attempted to exploit the situation, but without compromising themselves too much. At the beginning of 1960, Mikoyan made his first visit to Havana, while many high-level delegations from Cuba, one led by Che Guevara, went to Moscow. There were other, less noticed, delegations, one in particular that was headed by Aníbal Escalante and represented the Cuban Communist Party. It went with Fidel's blessing. There were still others that were quite secret.

Khrushchev's celebrated boutade about Cuba and missiles went like this: "Speaking in a figurative sense, now, if there were U.S. aggression against Cuba, such missiles could land right on the head of the aggressor—always thinking of things figuratively, of course." That's how the Russian side of the missile story began. The New York *Times* downplayed Khrushchev's ambiguous threat, and Khrushchev himself went no further with it. Then, in September 1960, Fidel spoke at the United Nations, with Khrushchev and other heads of state present. He alluded to a threatening statement directed at Cuba by Admiral Byrne, commander of the U.S. naval base at Guantánamo, and pointed out the danger of nuclear war if such a threat were to turn into direct action.

Fidel clearly wanted to compromise Khrushchev. But the Americans still did not take Khrushchev's remarks literally. On the other hand, Khrushchev's pounding his shoe on the desk at the General Assembly was an ambiguous sort of statement of support for Fidel. That September I went to Moscow to interview Khrushchev. I wanted to find out how we could get from figurative language to direct statements. I spent hours in the Kremlin going over the subject with him, and we finally arrived at a Solomonic decision, which was interpreted in contradictory fashion by the press services of the United States and the rest of the world.

An elementary lesson we have to take into account in this missile business is that no great power, neither the Soviet Union nor the United States, is going to give missiles to anyone who asks for them. The USSR installs missiles where it chooses and nowhere else. Mao asked the Russians for missiles and they turned him down flat—which is why Sino-Soviet relations became so frigid. Imagine now that if the Russians deny missiles to eight hundred million Chinese Communists, are they cheerfully going to give them to eight million Cubans just ninety miles off the U.S. coast? The real story is the one that Fidel told in the hottest moments of the crisis, and it was Jean Daniel, now director of the *Nouvelle Observateur,* who first broke the story in *L'Express* on December 14, 1963.

In 1962, Aleksei Adzubei, director of *Izvestia* and Khrushchev's son-in-law, came to Havana after making a tour of the United States. He carried an important message—namely, that the United States was preparing an invasion of Cuba and that all Soviet diplomatic attempts to stop it had failed. It was the contention of the Soviets that the Cubans had only one possibility left, which was to ask the Soviet Union for missiles. Now, what could Cuba do in such a situation? Wait for the invasion to take place and then react? And did the Cubans have any reason to doubt the word of the Soviet Union? Fidel had no doubts and sent a stream of military delegations to Moscow, those headed by Raúl Castro and Che Guevara among them. The result was a secret treaty about the installation of the missiles. What is not clear is why Khrushchev should have sent such an important message with his son-in-law instead of sending it through the usual diplomatic channels—through the ambassador, Andrei Gromyko, or some other Russian official. It seems that the missile business was one of Khrushchev's pet projects, one he worked out with the Soviet military, but one from which he excluded both the Party and the Soviet government.

This was all in Khrushchev's style. Perhaps surprise was the only way he could score any victories. It was the trick he had used at the Twentieth Congress of the Communist Party of the Soviet Union when he delivered his famous report on Stalin's crimes. Audacity was his favorite weapon, and it was most effective against Beria and others. It was a dangerous style, but one that proved effective in post-Stalinist Russia. This at least explains why Khrushchev would use his son-in-law as a messenger, but was the story of the U.S. invasion merely a Soviet assumption or did they have facts? Or was it both things? The CIA and the Pentagon certainly had plans worked out and a desire to put them into practice, but President Kennedy didn't seem to be going along. After all, if he kept U.S. troops out of the Bay of Pigs, why would he go ahead now? It seems that, in fact, the United States never wanted to get involved in a real conflict with the Russians, that all it wanted was to score a big political victory.

Khrushchev, on the other hand, seemed to have played the same trick on the Soviets that he played on the Cubans. He said that the Cubans had informed Adzubei that the United States was readying an invasion of Cuba and that Fidel Castro was asking for advice and "strategic defensive weapons," a euphemism for those famous missiles. I have no idea who made up that wonderful expression, but I do know who used it first: Fidel Castro. The USSR, practicing the kind of hypocrisy typical of a great power, demanded—as a matter of form, and you know how important form is—that the Cuban government formally request the

Soviet Union to install a few missiles in Cuba. Cuba made the request, and, wonder of wonders, it was accepted. But the greatest, most grotesque irony of this whole business is that according to the agreement signed by both countries—and here I challenge Fidel Castro to prove me wrong by publishing this agreement and all other documents relevant to the missile crisis, which are far from being military secrets by now, especially since Khrushchev himself is a mere Communist ghost—the Cuban land on which the missiles would be set up would be Russian property. Remember Guantánamo, anyone? Cuba would have no rights whatsoever with regard to that land, with those—what shall we call them, sister bases?—sister bases on them.

Nineteen sixty-two saw a rapid influx of thousands and thousands of Russians into Cuba, families included. We Cubans were surprised at more than one aspect of this friendly invasion. First, the way they dressed. They were years out of style; their clothes were ugly and badly cut; and their shoes! The man on the street began to wonder why, if socialism is in fact superior to capitalism, everything these Russians had was so shoddy. The women didn't even know how to walk in high heels. And there seemed to be great differences between various groups of Russians: the leaders, technicians, and officers had one style, and the soldiers and ordinary laborers had another—much inferior. People began to wonder about the question of equality under socialism. Later we noticed that the differences were also striking between city and country people, especially between the Moscow people and those from other cities.

The Russians were kept segregated from the Cubans, but when they were let out, they immediately went drinking. And when they ran out of money, they would trade—anything and everything—for a bottle of vodka or rum. But despite the disillusion they brought, the Russians as people seemed a sympathetic bunch, at least when they were sober. When they were drunk, they were wild. The Russians sent along a special police force, just like Marine MP's, who would beat to a pulp anyone who gave them trouble. Comandante Almeida, chief of Las Villas, said watching the Russians was like being in the old Plaza del Vapor when he was a kid: there was a huge clandestine barter industry. Drunken Russians would give anything for a bottle, from tools to the clothes on their back—which led to some great jokes about primitive communism by our budding Marxist humorists.

But if the Russians could come out to see the Cubans, the Cubans could not go in to see the Russians, not even the comandantes. The territory—the "sister bases"—where the installations were being constructed was off limits to all Cubans. There, everything except the soil itself was imported from Russia. It was all very hush-hush, but you'd have to be an idiot not to know what was going on. They closed the ports and set up curfews for port cities and then sent through to the bases long caravans of trucks covered over with tarpaulins. "Must be importing palm trees, judging by the shape," was what you heard in the street. They also thought maybe Khrushchev had gone crazy and was actually going to fire his missiles at the imperialists from Cuba.

But that wasn't the point of the missiles at all. Over the course of my talks with him in 1960, I began to understand Khrushchev's parabolic way of speaking. The USSR felt itself surrounded by U.S. bases, so it wanted to have its own bases on territory as near to the United States as some of the U.S. bases were to the Soviet Union. That would be a way of opening negotiations for a reduction in bases and, by the way, a means to keep the United States out of Cuba. As a plan it had its logic; as a fact it was infantile. Did anyone really think all that stuff could be brought all the way from Russia in secret? Only a bureaucratic mind on the Russian or Chinese model, used to doing everything in secret— within its own frontiers—could have dreamed up a scheme like that. But what about Fidel? He seemed to have a blind belief in the Soviet military machine and shrugged off any doubts by saying that it was the Russians who were calling the tune. He felt like one of the powerful, as if he were involved in world-changing events. In any case, he didn't think there would be a real conflict between the United States and the Soviet Union. And if there was an invasion, it wouldn't be his fault. Don't forget, Fidel gets his kicks from war and high tension. He can't stand not being front-page news. A Kádár he could never be.

The second error in this missile business was the rectification of the Soviet-Cuban military communiqué published by the Moscow press and *Prensa Latina*. President Dorticós made a hasty public correction of the communiqué, but all he actually proved to anyone who cared to notice was that there had been a change in quality and quantity in the military relationship between the USSR and Cuba. The error was Khrushchev's, and it was colossal.

All during this phase of the missile crisis I was first in Algeria, with Ben Bella, then in Milan, Rome, and Greece. I did more of the touring, especially among left-wing Europeans, I so desperately needed. I got back to Havana on October 20, two days before Kennedy's speech. The missiles were a kind of public secret—no one spoke about them, but all knew. According to Fidel, only five people were in on the secret: Fidel himself, Raúl, Che, Ramiro Valdés, and Dorticós. The army, the comandantes, the government, the people, no one else knew anything certain, but they did imagine what was going on. Those living near the bases, of course, knew everything. Rumors were flying all over—even to Miami with the Cubans who were fleeing. But not even the CIA believed the missile story. Finally the U-2 flights confirmed it.

I had been delayed in my return because I had had to go to Prague, and there were no seats available for the Havana flights. Ben Bella had indeed visited Cuba, but he left just before I got back. He knew nothing about the missiles. October 20 was a Saturday, and *Revolución* did not come out on Sunday, so I went over to the office just to say hello. The place was ringing with press releases from the United States. President Kennedy canceled his weekend vacation and returned to Washington; all U.S. troops in Florida were on full alert, and there was a general mobilization. Something was up. At *Revolución* we were lucky in that we had a lot of experienced reporters, some of whom had worked for the Associated Press and United Press International as well as for U.S. newspapers. We had to do something spectacular with the Monday issue to inform the people of what was happening in the United States.

But of course you just can't say certain things without confirming them with the government. I called Celia Sánchez and Fidel, but no one knew where they were. President Dorticós was not answering the phone, either at the palace or at home. Che, we were told, was in Pinar del Río. I was not in the habit of talking to Raúl under any circumstances, so he was out of the question, as was Escalante. So once again it fell to me to bring out an issue that would cause an uproar. That was my value as a journalist, and it was no minor talent, if I do say so myself. Well, the headline read: U.S. PREPARES INVASION OF CUBA, and when it hit the streets the phone started ringing off the hook.

A NERVOUS MONDAY

It wasn't yet 9:00 A.M., and President Dorticós was calling me down to his office—in a voice full of disgust. After a cold greeting he launched into a diatribe: "Another one of your irresponsible, alarmist headlines! How could you announce an invasion without at least consulting with the government? You make us look ridiculous." Escalante, standing next to Dorticós, chimed in: "For a long time now *Revolución* has just done what it damn well pleases." Dorticós: "This is serious, Franqui, very serious." Dorticós's telephones never stopped ringing, because people all over the island were clamoring for information. Mixed in with those calls were angry protests against me by Raúl Castro, Ramiro Valdés, Carlos Rafael Rodríguez, Blas Roca, Manuel Piñeyro, and others. But those who believed what *Revolución* said, the majority, were requesting instructions. All Dorticós would say was: "This is more of *Revolución*'s alarmism." The only two voices we didn't hear that morning were those of Fidel and Che.

Then Dorticós demanded concrete proof of the imminent invasion. He also spoke about an official denunciation of the headline and perhaps calling a halt to both my and *Revolución*'s irresponsibility. My only arguments were Kennedy's canceled weekend trip and the military mobilization in Florida, together with the tension evident in the press and in Washington. This was mere alarmism, according to Dorticós. I replied by pointing out that out in the Sierra I had often taken onto myself the responsibility for broadcasting important matters over Radio Rebelde, that since Fidel and the others were often far away I had no other choice. That includes the news about the withdrawal of the American troops that had entered Yateristas, the fall of Batista, and the instructions concerning the general strike and the takeover of barracks and police stations by rebels and militiamen. I said it was the same in peacetime, that if I were unable to find anyone with whom to consult, I would follow my instincts. I thought this autonomy was only proper for a revolutionary journalist, whose major obligation was to inform the people. I added that if they liked they could find a substitute for me.

The hours passed and more "alarmist" news (according to Dorticós) came in—this time from the U.S. press. Escalante said they were nothing but alarmists, but I pointed out that the U.S. press was usually quite well informed and had often scooped governments. They said I overestimated capitalism, and I said they not only underestimated it, but turned it into a monolith. (But what I didn't understand was why neither Fidel nor Che had called. Did they already know what was happening? To this day I'm not sure.) Then the news announced that Kennedy was about to address the nation and the world. Dorticós said he would speak about the conflict between China and India, and I took his bet, saying if Kennedy didn't talk about Cuba and the missiles, I would step down as director of *Revolución*.

At 5:00 P.M. Kennedy spoke, and the missile crisis, as announced by *Revolución*, became public. Kennedy announced the naval blockade, and the world got ready for trouble. At about 8:00 P.M., Fidel Castro, accompanied, oddly enough, by Dorticós and the palace guard, burst into *Revolución*, laughed, and said that the palace boys had made a mistake. I laughed, too, and said I wished this time we had been wrong. In any case, this was Fidel's way of praising the perspicacity of the whole newspaper. Right on the spot, as in the old times, Fidel dictated the first Cuban statement on the crisis. He then corrected the manuscript—again, as he had done during the war—and told us to send it out to *Hoy*, the Communist paper, *Prensa Latina*, and the international news services. He was saying that for the moment *Revolución* was his paper.

Fidel's visits to *Revolución* always coincided with political changes, critical moments when he felt it necessary to arouse anti-American, anti-Russian Cuban feelings. Then and only then did he visit us; otherwise it was impossible to see him or speak to him. Now we were in almost constant communication, and the pitch of the crisis began to rise. We began to hear about how this would be the end of Cuba, about how there would be a nuclear war. The Cubans took it all with a grain of salt, saying that if the Yankees invaded, they would fight to the death. Then the drums came out and a festive atmosphere came into being, the usual Cuban method for dealing with danger, tension, and war. Fidel was thinking of missiles, but I wasn't. I just couldn't get Khrushchev's figurative use of language out of my mind. To me those missiles were never real. It was like the history of the Soviet Union, from the peace of Brest-Litovsk to the treaty between Hitler and Stalin—fictions.

I talked to Fidel about the Russians, saying that to them we were mere pawns, which they would more than willingly sacrifice to get at the United States. He was furious and accused me of pessimism and anti-Soviet prejudice. Fidel then went on to project scenarios. He thought he was in Moscow, showing Khrushchev how things should be done, analyzing Dean Rusk and Kennedy, saying that we shouldn't worry about the Yankees, that they were the ones who should be worrying. He went on to say that if he were in Moscow, he would send the government to the subway, which was supposed to be safe during nuclear attack, that this would be a kind of psychological attack on the Yankees. The palace guard oohed and aahed and told him he was brilliant. I suggested that, if Khrushchev were to do such a thing, all of Russia would panic, and that the whole idea seemed far-fetched because the Russians didn't really hate the Americans. I went on to point out that the Russians were good at defense, but not really famous as fighters on the offensive. Fidel laughed and made fun of my assessment. Someone tried to add fuel to the fire and really get me, but Fidel stopped him short: "You're wrong. If the invasion comes, Franqui will point out to me as we head to the front that a lot of you so-called tough guys are really assholes who fold in the first breeze." Then he added that anyone who might try to turn tail in a fight would find the entire people pushing him forward. Everyone said, "Sure thing, Fidel," and that's where the conversation ended.

Tension kept mounting, but nothing concrete happened—and this was something Fidel didn't like. One day, with a look of astuteness on his face I remembered from the guerrilla days, he said, "Now I'm going to find out if they'll invade or not, if this is for real or not." He said nothing more and drove his jeep to Pinar del Río. Not a few palace guards looked mighty pale then—which drew a good laugh from Amejeiras. Fidel went to one of the Russian rocket bases, where the Soviet generals took him on a tour of their installation. Just at that moment an American U-2 appeared on a radar screen, flying low over the island. Fidel asked how the Soviets would protect themselves in war if that had been an attack plane instead of a reconnaissance plane. The Russians showed him the ground-to-air missiles and said that all they would have to do would be to push a button and the plane would be blown out of the sky. "Which button?" "This one." Fidel pushed it and the rocket brought down the U-2. Robert Anderson, the American pilot, would be the only fatality in that war. The Russians were flabbergasted, but Fidel simply said, "Well, now we'll see if there's a war or not." But nothing happened.

It was curious, by the way, to see how many revolutionary tourists either went home or decided to postpone their trip to Cuba at those moments. The real friends, people like Juan Goytisolo, came no matter what and offered their services. The people were the real index of what was happening; they were calm and ready for anything.

MISSILES WITHDRAWN!

It was Sunday, October 28, and we were setting up the Monday edition of *Revolución*. The Associated Press teletype began to chatter, and I read the flash: "Khrushchev orders the withdrawal of missiles from Cuba." I turned pale. I had imagined it, but that's not the same as reading it. I picked up the phone and called over to Once Street. Celia answered and put Fidel on.

"Fidel, what should we do about this news?"

"What news?"

I fell silent, and Fidel began to wonder if the line was dead. I just said, "The news that just came over the wire." He then made me read the flash.

"Son of a bitch! Bastard! Asshole!" Fidel went on in that vein for quite some time. The Russians had abandoned us, made a deal with the Americans, and never even bothered to inform us. Fidel had no idea. He went on cursing, beating even his own record for curses—he would warm up for speeches by walking around cursing for a while before beginning his speech.

I wanted to laugh, but I kept my mouth shut—as the saying goes: "When de white man talking, nigger, keep you mout' shut." When he finally calmed down, he told me to set up a special edition and that he would send the text to me and to *Hoy*. Everybody in the editorial offices was dumfounded: the missiles were leaving, and Fidel had known nothing about it. This would be Fidel's famous five-point statement (five is one of his favorite numbers, by the way). In the preamble, he referred to "strategic nonoffensive weapons," which was quite ambiguous, so vague that only someone in the know could figure out what he meant. At no time did he refer to the withdrawal of the missiles. In fact, the preamble never appeared in the Russian or socialist press and finally disappeared from the Cuban version as well. I called Fidel, and he asked me what I thought. I said the statement was fine, that we would keep printing new editions throughout the night (he wanted a million copies printed), but what should we say about the withdrawal? Fidel simply said, "Franqui, you take care of it tomorrow." I should have guessed. He knew I would publish the news about the withdrawal of the missiles, but he refused to take responsibility for it. He wanted to suggest that it was okay to publish the news, but that he was not responsible. The one responsible would, of course, be yours truly.

This was going to be a dangerous business. What Fidel would do would be this: make a deal with the Russians, but at the same time tell the people about the missile withdrawal and also rile the people up against the Yankees. To publish the news about the missile withdrawal would mean the end of the paper and of me as well. But it was a good story.

A NEW HEADLINE ON THE WITHDRAWAL

That Monday, *Revolución*'s headline read: SOVIETS WITHDRAW MISSILES. That was the end. People poured out into the streets, and then the comic songs began.

> Nikita, Nikita, Indian giver,
> You don't take back what you once deliver.
> Fidel, go ahead:
> Bop the Yankees on the head.

The Party boys went crazy, from Raúl Castro, to the Party, to the Soviet embassy. I was accused of being anti-Soviet and anti-Communist. When people called to tell me I was playing too rough, I told them they ought to go down to the Russian embassy and talk to them about it, that *Revolución* wasn't withdrawing the missiles, the Russians were. Fidel never called, and neither did Che. They knew that the counterblow by the Soviets and their Cuban allies would not hit them but me. It was the end, but it was an end I rather liked.

INSPECTION OF THE ISLAND

Khrushchev's haste left Cuba in a bad position because not only did the Russians withdraw their missiles, but they also agreed to allow the Americans to inspect the island, just as Kennedy demanded—this without informing or consulting the Cuban government, without the approval of the prime minister. To accept inspection would be the end of everything, as the Congo demonstrated. The people were outraged and dead opposed to any inspection. Fidel felt his power threatened and identified with the people, just as Che says in his farewell letter, his last great moment. For an entire week *Revolución* published a series of articles that emphasized our differences with the Russians and heightened our sense of Cuban nationalism. We also exalted Fidel's role as symbol of our differences with the Soviets. I take responsibility for all of this, and I have no reason to invent justifications. What I hoped to do was to erase from the historic memory of the Cuban people any vestige of the sentimental sympathy the Soviet Union might inspire—for example, any memory of the Soviets as benefactors during the U.S. blockade. That sympathy was genuine, and even appeared in a little song.

> Fidel, Khrushchev,
> We love 'em both.
> Climb another rung:
> Long live Mao Tse-tung.

The feeling was sincere, but the people were now singing the one that began: "Nikita, Nikita, Indian giver . . ."

That tremendous year of 1962 taught the people many things. From the moment the revolution declared itself Communist, everything went to hell. There was chaos, rationing, Party politicking, imprisonment, persecution, fear of the military, the sense that you were always being watched. The people associated all that with the Soviet Union, and it was important for me that they realize what the origins of that oppressive "Russian-Cuban" reality were. Fidel always managed to come out of every difficult situation looking better than when he went in, and this despite the fact that the responsibility for all of it was his. Every nation must learn its own limitations. We had reached ours, and I saw no way out of our situation. The people were saying they saw no reason to fight against one oppressor so that they could have another, and that in itself seemed important to me. They no longer believed in the Soviet Union because of what they had seen for themselves: Party politics at work and then being left to hang in the wind. And this was precisely where *Revolución* came in, this was our historical justification: for people to know how to read and write is a fundamental first step, but to be informed and to be able to think for themselves is just as important as a second step.

One day Fidel called me up and said, "Lay off the Soviets, okay? Eleven articles against them is more than enough." Of course, Joaquín Ordoquí and a few others who assumed the defense of the USSR would be punished later on, supposedly for being CIA agents.

WHY DOESN'T JACKIE DO THE INSPECTING?

After the withdrawal of the missiles, an episode occurred between Fidel and the Federation of Cuban Women. Fidel impulsively rejected the inspection agreed on by the United States and the Soviet Union and answered Kennedy on television. Off camera, he said, "What do you think about this: how about my telling Kennedy to send Jackie down to do the inspecting?" "Terrific, Fidel," Vilma Espín answered. And then came the women's chorus: "Terrific, Fidel, terrific." They were splitting their sides with laughter, but I didn't crack a smile. Fidel looked me up and down and asked me if I didn't agree. I told him I didn't like the joke. "But it's fantastic!" (Women's chorus.) Then Fidel asked me why I didn't like it, and I told him that if he wanted to insult Kennedy at a personal level, the joke might be effective, but that Cubans in fact didn't like attacks on women. "You're backward!" (Women's chorus.) I reminded him of an event that took place during the Ortodoxia days, one in which Eduardo (Eddy) Chibás lost a polemic precisely because he alluded to a woman. "You're right," said Fidel, "I like the idea, but I won't use it." The women's chorus looked down in the mouth. Some of them probably thought I had Fidel's ear, but no one did, then or ever. Once in a while he would throw an idea around if he wasn't sure about it—as in the case of the slur on Jackie Kennedy—but usually Fidel asked questions just to find out how other people thought.

I knew Fidel well. If he honored you by calling you by name or by patting you on the back, your days were numbered, brother. Usually he uses only vague, imprecise expressions in conversation, and he always treats people as objects. And when he's angry, he cuts you dead. This not only happens to people but to places as well. If he gets mad in a certain place, he not only never visits it again but sees to it that no one can mention the place by name in his presence. A real spoiled brat, who can only be manipulated by reverse psychology. If you want him to do something, suggest the opposite. Then he would do what you wanted. So campaigns against someone or something just wouldn't work with Fidel. That's how *Revolución* and I survived as long as we did—there were so many against us that Fidel reacted in a contrary fashion. Not that he liked me or the paper, but when he feels he's being pressured, he postpones taking action—even if he really wants to.

Leaving Fidel's ill will aside, the pressures against *Revolución* were becoming intolerable. The Party boys wanted another *Pravda*, so they started saying that *Hoy* would be Cuba's *Pravda*— that is, the Party's newspaper—while *Revolución* would be Cuba's *Izvestia*, the government paper, controlled by the government. I figured it would be better all around to go down swinging, but I had a few low blows held back for grand occasions. So one day I said to Fidel, "Wouldn't one new paper be better than two old ones? We'd waste much less paper." He perked up, so I added, "And why should you just copy the Russians?" That did it.

MIKOYAN

When Anastas Mikoyan came to Havana, no one, but no one, wanted to see him. He went all over Cuba desperately trying to track Fidel down, without any luck. Khrushchev had passed him the Cuban hot potato, and now the old Stalinist (anti-Stalinist, in those days), the only Bolshevik to survive the Stalin era, was exploring Cuba in search of Fidel Castro. But Mikoyan recognized the illness as soon as he arrived. He immediately saw that he was being watched, that he was under absolute surveillance. If by chance he did get to talk to some minister or other, the conversation was always held in a room with Cuban popular music blaring out to cover any indiscretions. The Soviet embassy was, naturally, in disgrace and regarded as a center of conspiracy.

They might have suspected me or accused me of anything, but certainly not of being pro-Soviet. So I went down and looked him up. Naturally, we could not discuss the missile crisis, but we could and did discuss Stalin. Mikoyan was obsessed with Stalin and really poured his heart out. He calculated twenty million dead by Stalin's decree, above and beyond the slaughter of all the old Bolsheviks. He talked a great deal about the all-pervading fear of that period in Russia and, without saying it directly, implied that he had noted the same thing in Cuba.

He said they were trying to rectify things in the Soviet Union, that Bukharin, Kamenev, and Zinoviev were going to be exonerated, that even Trotsky's case was going to be reviewed. He spoke sympathetically about Solzhenitsyn, especially about *One Day in the Life of Ivan Denisovich* and the GULag books. He said there was a strong resistance movement against the Party apparatus, which would tolerate only certain changes, and which wanted above all to continue to enjoy what it had won for itself. Khrushchev, he said, was fighting like mad to reform the system, but he concluded sadly, saying, "What a life!" I couldn't figure out if he was talking about life under Stalin, life now, his life, or our life. It looked to me as if we Cubans were entering the same pattern the Russians hoped they were leaving behind. He went on to say that they had abolished the police force under the direct orders of the Central Committee. (I wondered to myself about the other police forces.) Years later, fallen from power, Khrushchev would confess to his friends that the dumbest thing he ever did was to abolish that police force, that that was the reason he was kicked out. Mikoyan, of course, was important in that removal.

Fidel never wanted to break with the Soviets because it was against his nature. His power was linked to the Soviet structure. But he could never accept the idea of an inspection of any kind by any agency of the island because that would have finished him off. Finally Kennedy and Khrushchev came to an accord: what the Americans were concerned about were the missiles and the nuclear warheads. The U-2s had already brought proof that the bases were dismantled, so now all that was left was to see the missiles. That was done at sea in a kind of striptease, where the Russians would show what was discreetly under wraps. This done, the Russians promised not to do such a thing again, and the Yankees promised not to invade Cuba. Fidel asked Mikoyan if the Russians would at least leave the MIG-23s behind. Mikoyan said yes, Khrushchev said yes, Kennedy said no. Then it was Fidel who had to track down Mikoyan to find out what was happening with the MIGs—but he figured it out beforehand.

There was an episode at the Soviet embassy that typified the Russian situation. Old man Mikoyan was seen running through the embassy with a paper in his hand chasing another Russian who just would not stop. Finally, Mikoyan cornered the guy, who said, "Please pardon me, Mr. Vice–Prime Minister. Do whatever you want with me, put me in jail even. But I cannot send that cable without an order from Security." "But I'm ordering you—I, the Vice–Prime Minister!" The man wouldn't do it. Mikoyan turned to the people around him and said, "This is what Stalinism has done for us. If you haven't lived through it, you can't believe it."

MIKOYAN AND THE CROCODILES

Mikoyan and Fidel finally settled their differences and together made a visit down to the Zapatas swamps, the scene of the Bay of Pigs war. Fidel had always loved the swamp for some reason or other and kept his picturesque crocodiles well fed. A photo in the family album shows Fidel, Mikoyan, and the crocodiles. It has no caption, but a version of it was circulated by Fidel himself. It's called "The Crocodile and the Sardine" and the story goes like this: Mikoyan examines the crocodiles for a while and then notices some little fish swimming in the same water. "Comandante, why are these little fish here?" "Mr. Vice–Prime Minister, those little fish are there so the crocodiles can eat them." And that is exactly what the missile crisis was: two great powers fooling around at the expense of a small one. The Cuban people realized they were alone in the world. Only Fidel saved his skin—and in fact he came off in better shape after the crisis than he had been in before it. It was the beginning of the end for Khrushchev, an end marked by differences of opinion between *Izvestia*—edited by Khrushchev's son-in-law—and *Pravda*, the Party's paper. The real joke is that the nuclear warheads had never been installed in the missiles: they never got to Cuba because the Russians never tried to pass through the U.S. blockade.

A FAMOUS INTERVIEW

At year's end, Fidel was surrounded by reporters who were all trying to get him to speak about the conflict with the Soviets and about the remnants of the October crisis that had not yet been settled. Among these reporters was Claude Julien of *Le Monde*, who during the underground days had committed the unintentional indiscretion of reporting the declared position of the Cuban Communist Party with regard to the rebels—namely, that it was opposed to both the urban insurrection and the fighters in the Sierra. Julien was accused, by Carlos Rafael Rodríguez and the correspondent from *L'Humanité*, during the mildly self-critical congress of the PSP (in 1944, the Cuban Communists had changed the name of their party from Unión Revolucionaria Comunista to Partido Socialista Popular), of "anti-Communist prejudice." But what he really did was to report what he saw: the 26 July Movement and the Directorio were fighting against Batista. Julien began to hang around *Revolución* and wait—forever, it seemed—for the chance to interview Fidel. He had begun to despair when suddenly a call came through in January 1963. Fidel told me to have Julien over at my place and that he would speak to him that night.

This was not Fidel's usual method, so I figured he was trying to pull a fast one (on me). If something somehow went wrong with this interview, it would be my fault. In fact, I had little to lose, because I knew that after the missile crisis *Revolución* was finished, and so, for that matter, was I. I was just waiting for the Comandante to push the button. I suspected that what Fidel wanted to do was to make his disgust with the Russians such a public matter that the Soviets would have no choice but to invite him to Moscow and make up with him. Some people thought there was no chance for a reconciliation, but that was because they listened to what Fidel said without thinking of the larger context. They heard him damn Khrushchev and the abandonment of Cuba by the Russians, but they didn't remember how he had once damned Che, Raúl, and the Communists back in 1959. This was Fidel's habitual method: he would use rhetoric to find out what other people were really thinking—then he'd have them where he wanted them. As for me, well, I just wanted to get out of Fidel's line of fire, out of *Revolución*. I couldn't quit, because no one quits on Fidel—Huber Matos, who had done so, was beginning his fourth year of imprisonment on Isla de Pinos. But it seemed that Raúl, Ramiro Valdés, Carlos Rafael Rodríguez, and others just wanted to see me rot along with *Revolución*. I was hoping I could set up a photographic history of the Cuban Revolution—in Paris, Algeria, Edinburgh, anywhere.

A LONG NIGHT WITH FIDEL

Waiting for Fidel is a lot like waiting for Godot, so that night I arranged a real old-fashioned party, complete with entertainment by Elena Bourke, Florián Gómez, Miriam Acevedo, and Celeste Mendoza. There was roast pig, with the right sauce, and a continuous supply of daiquiris. Juan Arcocha and Edith Gombos translated. I had lots of goodies around the house because at Christmas and New Year's the Comandante had the habit of sending gift baskets around to comandantes and friends. These baskets held fruit, wine, Spanish *turrón*, cognac, and other delicacies that could help take the edge off a year of rationing. They were also a good sign; it meant that the Comandante had not forgotten you, even if you were in disgrace. They even reached some prisoners, but those were the Comandante's "poisoned" baskets.

(This largesse extended to wedding gifts as well. When a certain comandante-minister got married, he was given a house in the Miramar district, a new car, assorted whiskies, dishes, and perfume for the blushing bride [she was a Catholic-Communist who had asked Monsignor Sachi, the fidelista papal nuncio, to perform the ceremony]. As an old veteran of Prague and Moscow remarked, "Only the best for the proletariat." We were all more or less caught up in that cynical sentence. There were three solutions to the problem: become cynical oneself, actually believe that one deserved the privileges and objects one enjoyed, or become neurotic and invent all kinds of justifications. A woman I knew from the underground days was given a huge house all for herself, so she took in some orphan children to fill it up. "I couldn't very well say no to Fidel. Besides, he'd like us all to live like this." But, of course, there just aren't enough houses or lovely things for everyone; that's supposed to come with time, and with the reforms from above, if they ever materialize. Not everyone fell for all this stuff, not everyone was corrupted by the system. A lot of us tried to do our best, without being counterrevolutionaries, until we had to bail out.)

At midnight Claude Julien and his wife were nervously eying their watches. Would he come or not? At 1:00 A.M., the singers were finishing the refrain of a song by Matamoros: "It's time for the singers to go." They were a bit put out because they had hoped to see the Comandante, but it was getting late. Just at that moment, Fidel made his entrance, saying to those same singers: "Okay, now it's my turn to be the Cuban artist." He started talking, and it was a veritable verbal flood. There was still some music being played, but since Fidel doesn't really like party music, he turned to the musicians and cut them right off: "You guys take a rest and let me take over for a while."

Fidel had always been a good drinker, even with the Russians, who are real pros. But even they turned green when they saw Fidel take out those cigars of his. But that night it looked as if Fidel was going to get really drunk. I thought maybe it had something to do with what he was going to say to Julien, and it did. Fidel was going to imply things and yet not say them outright, cause a fuss, and get invited to Moscow. Fidel really felt that he had come out a winner in the missile crisis. After all, he had rejected the demands of the United States, the Russians, and the United Nations—there was no inspection. And Cuban nationalism was at fever pitch. Cuba would not be invaded—Khrushchev and Kennedy had agreed on that. But what Fidel wanted was to cut a new deal with the Russians, in Moscow. So this wouldn't be a formal interview; it would be informal, in a friend's house, at a party. And if something did go wrong, I would take the rap.

Fidel began to tell all about the missiles and the crisis—old stuff, but in a really bitter tone, really anti-Russian. Fidel stopped once in a while and noted, watching Julien, who was watching me: "You're getting a journalist's banquet out of this party. But you're the friend here, not the journalist." Then off he went on the Russians again. I wondered why a chief of state would say all these things to a foreign journalist and in my house, and then I realized that Fidel wanted all this to come out in *Le Monde* so the Russians would make up with him. And if something "out of character" were to appear—well, it was my fault; after all, the Comandante was tipsy, it was a party, there was the translation problem—he could get out of any indiscretion. By 3:00 A.M. my wife, Margot, was sleeping, and this annoyed Fidel because he hated anyone to doze off during his sermons, even though half the country went to sleep when he talked on TV. Anyway, Margot had gone to sleep listening to more than one VIP spout off; it was self-defense, pure and simple. Finally, dawn arrived, and Fidel decided to go home. He dropped Julien and his wife off at the Habana-Libre—a gentleman through and through.

LE MONDE'S BOMB

Claude Julien went home to Paris, and time began to pass. Fidel started calling me to ask why my journalist friend had not yet produced a line about that evening. I think poor Julien had some real problems: he was a left-wing Catholic, an honest and good newspaperman. He was pressured by Marta Frayde, the Cuban representative at UNESCO, a friend (later a prisoner) of Fidel. Finally Julien published his piece* and brought the house down. UPI and AP reproduced his article but in more strident tones.

---

* In *Le Monde*, March 22, 1963.

Fidel was by now knocking Nikita all over the place. The Soviets called Raúl and Ramiro Valdés to mobilize them. The article would be interpreted as a CIA plot, but the whipping boy would be Franqui. Fidel told me he would deny everything, say it was all a lie, an enemy plot; that he had met this friend of mine at a party at my house, and this stuff was the result. He even told me I should deny everything. I told him I couldn't do that, that undoubtedly the Yankees had mistranslated him, but that if Julien published even a tenth of what he (Fidel) had said that night, the Russians would be fuming.

"Well, then, stop him. I'll deny everything."

"But Fidel, you remember what you said that night. I tried to stop you, but you told me to shut up. And besides, anyone can recognize your voice."

"What are you talking about?"

"Well, Julien had a tape recorder with him and recorded everything you said."

I was sure he hadn't recorded anything, but I wanted to see how Fidel would react. I then told Fidel to wait for our translations of the *Le Monde* articles, and to stop paying attention to the U.S. versions. Fidel began to calm down and then asked me to tell Edith Gombos to have Julien tone down the other articles. I wondered (out loud) if it wouldn't be better if our ambassador talked to him, but Fidel wanted to keep the matter out of official circles. I went on to say that things would work out for the best, that the Russians would be inviting him to Moscow in no time. I even made the same bet I made about the U.S. invasion plans back on October 22. Fidel was eventually invited and made a Hero of the Soviet Union. But before he left, I took off for Paris.

6

BACK IN EUROPE

Fidel was the measure of all things. The country, resentful of friends and enemies alike, had turned in on itself. It wasn't absolutely alone in the world. World opinion was with Cuba, and Cuba had the support of the democratic nations of the Americas. Inside Cuba, tensions relaxed and repression also diminished during those first days of 1963. It was clear that something new had to be done; the old communism, Russian- or Cuban-style, just did not work. Under the old capitalism, the economy had worked, but no one wanted to go back to capitalism. It wasn't possible. We would have to develop our own solutions to our problems, and we could if Fidel returned to the people. Fidel was our last hope, and 1963 was a year of reflection, nationalism, and strife.

The socialist romance with the USSR had lasted two years. It was born with the U.S. economic blockade and ended with the maritime blockade. We had learned that ideals and realities are quite different things, like words and acts. The USSR had used us and then abandoned us. Our revolution had worked until Fidel had proclaimed Cuba to be socialist—after that, nothing worked. People were thinking that Fidel got us into this fix, but only because of the danger from the United States. But he also got us free of the Communists and wouldn't let anyone inspect our island. Others thought it was all nothing but illusion, that Fidel had tangled us up with the Communists because that was exactly what he had wanted to do in the first place. They had guaranteed his power, and now there was no turning back.

I knew where I stood. As a socialist who believed in democracy and human dignity, I was the declared enemy of the Cuban Communists and the Soviet Union. All my actions and the policies of *Revolución* at least had the virtue of clarity: we were antimilitarist, proculture, proart, in favor of free labor unions, tolerant of homosexuals, and totally opposed to terrorism of any kind. My enemies accused me of trying to divide the revolution from within and of being the evil genius behind every conspiracy that reared its head. In the early months of 1963, I sensed that a historical period was closing, and it seemed appropriate that *Revolución* should die with it. But it wasn't going to go out with a whimper.

I did not have many options at the moment. I could not resign from *Revolución* because no one resigns under Fidel. I despised Miami and the counterrevolutionaries, and I could not take up the position of Raúl Chibás, living in exile as a professor, independent of both the extreme right and the extreme left, a permanent critic of both and, therefore, despised by both. I could see that Che himself was running into problems, in part because he thought in terms of Latin-American revolution on a grand scale instead of revolution in Cuba alone. My only chance was Europe, so I went, only to return when my substitute as director of *Revolución* had been named. I had a perfectly good excuse for going to Europe (aside from the real reasons)—to work on the projected book by Fidel, other books that were in the planning stage, and the traveling photography show that would tour Paris, Africa, and the Soviet Union. I could count on Ben Bella's help, and the show was also scheduled to go to Algiers after its Paris debut.

I left for Paris just before Fidel left for Moscow. It was spring, and I set up the show in a hall on Saint-Germain-des-Prés. Sartre gave a lecture, as did Jacques Duclos, a French Communist leader; he had been strongly recommended by the Franco-Cuban Society, a Party-dominated organization that monitored Cuban affairs in France. I still had some friends among the left-wing intellectuals, so things were not all that bad. We organized a Cuban festival to close the show, and several film makers helped me out. Alain Resnais got permission to close the Place Saint-Germain by saying he was going to do some filming there, and Agnes Varda, Roman Polanski, and Robert Klein turned out with cameras to give the show an air of legitimacy. The Cuban embassy promised me a Cuban orchestra that was very popular in Europe at the time, the Matecocos. There would be a conga, which would snake around the square and pass through the hall, the church, and the café. For some reason or other, the Matecocos never showed up, and embassy support was so weak that Ben Bella ended up paying for the catalogue as well as for all other expenses.

So we improvised. Oscar López got things rolling with his music, as did José Dolores Quiñones, whose electric guitar kept coming unplugged as the conga wound around corners. Edith Gombos was our star rumba dancer. She may have been born in Hungary, but her rhythm was pure Caribbean. The French are not well versed in Cuban music and dancing, but those present had a good time. At least they said they did. I really suffered, thinking back on my Paper and Ink shows, because this puny offering made me ashamed. But we did what we could, and no one was really disappointed.

The photography show made the rounds—London, Edinburgh, Warsaw, Moscow; then on to China, Vietnam, and Korea. In Korea, Kim Il Sung ordered the bikinis the mulatto militia girls had on covered over. Meanwhile, the bureaucracy kept finding reasons not to let my wife, Margot, and our children out of Cuba. Finally I sent a telegram directly to Fidel, and the business was taken care of. I went back to Milan, spoke to my friend Valerio Riva, editor at Feltrinelli, and began to work on the Fidel book and my own *Book of the Twelve.* With my advance I rented a tiny apartment in Albissola Marina, where Wifredo Lam—my friend at the time—was living. "Out of sight, out of mind," the saying goes, but soon both friends and enemies began to comment on my absence from Cuba. This European sojourn was quite different from my 1961 and 1962 trips. Those had been filled with interviews and talk; this time there was nothing but silence.

Because of the photography show I made two trips to Algeria. On the first I went through Paris and had a disagreeable encounter.

The Cuban delegation that had accompanied Fidel to Moscow had decided to take a detour away from that socialist paradise to see Paris, the hell of capitalism. Among the VIPs were Emilio Aragonés and Jorge (Papito) Serguera, nicknamed the Napoleons because at the Military Academy they claimed they could have won the battle of Waterloo and beaten Wellington, although they had both yet to fire a shot in real war. Osmaní Cienfuegos was there, capitalizing on his brother's name, as was Juan Abrahantes, who had also inherited the fame of his dead brother. Escalona was there, too, along with Papito Serguera, one of Raúl's boys.

The delegates wanted action—parties, French girls, *la dolce vita*. They were bored by having spent too much time in Moscow. A Belgian woman who happened to be in the embassy was astounded at these happy warriors (only Escalona had seen action) and their way of treating any and all women as sexual objects. Security made sure they had a good time, although some of their antics provoked more than one scandal.

Serguera told me about how tough things had been for Khrushchev when he found himself in a minority on the Politburo during the missile crisis. I almost wept. Then he told me about the new sugar agreement between Cuba and the Soviet Union and how it was going to save the Cuban economy.

Our dislike was mutual, mine for the delegates and theirs for me. They went back to Moscow and I went on to Algiers, where Ben Bella received me with his usual cordiality, and we opened the exposition that he had underwritten.

We spoke at length about both of our situations, and he invited me to stay and help organize the Algerian press. He even wanted to create a *Revolución* with the weekly then directed by our friend Jacques Verges. (Verges was a Franco-Algerian I had met through Ben Bella. He was editing a magazine—also named *Revolución*, at the suggestion of Ben Bella, after ours—in Paris.) I asked him to consult with Havana.

I also ran into Che Guevara in Algeria. He was beginning to make now, in 1963, a series of trips, as he had done in the early months of 1959. In Cuba, traveling meant disgrace, a kind of forward retreat. We talked about China. Che knew my opinion of the Soviet Union because we had argued about it so often, but now even he was changing, taking on a more critical point of view. He had discovered several truths about socialism in the real world and had come to sympathize with the Chinese Revolution. He severely castigated the Soviets and their bureaucracy and fervently desired a new revolution in the Third World. He believed guerrilla war was a genuine possibility in parts of Africa. His "one, two, three Vietnams" were his constant dreams. He told me that in China he had learned an important lesson: use your own two feet. The people, he said, were the wealth of China, not heavy industry. And the Chinese were independent of the Soviet Union, kept out of other countries, and hadn't even left troops in North Korea after the war.

I tried to argue that the Chinese had yet to free themselves of the Soviet system—the root, as I saw it, of all our problems. He said the Chinese Communist Party was not like the Soviet Party because it was not split by factionalism, that Mao was not like Stalin, but really more like Lenin. I expressed my doubts about Mao and about the notion of the Party-state as owner of all property, but I admitted that I did admire the Chinese sense of self-reliance, its desire to remain independent of both capitalism and the Soviet Union. I felt closer to Che than ever, despite his dogmatism. He had begun to see socialist reality and was now using Chinese dogma to combat Soviet dogma. His intervention in Cuba's economy, his notion of centralization and nationalization, had caused serious damage to the economy. This all came out in his polemic with Charles Bettelheim and the others. But he had learned from his experience.

We were both looking for a way of accommodating ourselves to our situations, but we both knew there was no way to do this. "With Fidel, there is neither marriage nor divorce" was the way Che summed it all up. He could never be a bureaucrat, and, probably because he underestimated his popularity in Cuba because he was an Argentine, he never saw himself as a Trotsky to Fidel's Stalin. But the Cuban people did love him. He believed in history, whereas I had become something of a nihilist.

I went back to Albissola to wait. Armando Hart and Haydée

Santamaría, stopping over in Paris, had wanted to see me. They gave Lisandro Otero a note telling me where they were. But Otero, furious because my friend Guillermo Cabrera Infante had won the Biblioteca Breve Prize of the Seix Barral publishing company for his extraordinary novel *Three Trapped Tigers*—Otero's own *Pasión de Urbino*, a poor piece of work, had gone nowhere— and secretly trying to squeeze me out at Feltrinelli for the Fidel book, never told me a thing. He really did me a favor, because I got back to Albissola Marina more quickly, and in October I received a cable from Havana telling me I had been relieved of my duties as editor of *Revolución*. As usual, the cable reached me after the notice had been published in the papers. There was a protest by the *Revolución* staff, and Fidel changed the wording of the official statement. Instead of saying, "Carlos Franqui has been relieved of his duties," it now said, "Comrade Carlos Franqui has been relieved of duties as editor of *Revolución*." Now I began to get ready for my return to Havana.

A ROUGH NIGHT

Because I like to do the unexpected, I returned to Havana in December—alone. My family stayed behind in Albissola Marina. Valerio Riva, Heberto Padilla, and I all decided to meet in Havana, but we made sure we came by different routes. For some reason, I was the last to arrive, so I wasn't at home when Valerio looked me up. There was only a guard who made an insulting remark about me, an act that thoroughly upset Valerio. I came in the next day, December 31.

On January 2, 1964, Celia Sánchez invited me to a reception in the Palace of the Revolution to commemorate the fifth anniversary of our victory over Batista. My entrance created a mild sensation. Some stared at me in shock, others with disdain, others with ironic grins. They knew I was alone, the ex-director of *Revolución*. I stared right back at them, because I could never take these palace-guard types too seriously. My first overtly hostile exchange was with Nicolás Guillén, "the bad guy," as Neruda called him.

"You here, Franqui?"

"Why, Nicolás, I thought you'd be in Moscow!" (Guillén's only act as cultural ambassador was to pick up his paycheck once a month at the Ministry of Foreign Relations. People said he was the most expensive ambassador in the world.) I left him and moved on to Carlos Olivares, our ambassador to the USSR, ex-Vice-Minister of Foreign Affairs during the days of heavy Party activity. He had been President Urrutia's secretary, but in fact all he did was spy on Urrutia and spread rumors, among them the one about Urrutia's intention to resign in 1959. Olivares held his hand out to me right in front of everyone, but I told him to stick it where it might do him some good.

I have never been fond of receptions. I've seen a lot, and the only ones that seemed amusing, at a theatrical level, were those in Buckingham Palace, because of the gardens, the sentimentality of the English with regard to their queen, and the prancing left-wing politicos marching in step with a monarch. We Cubans are good at parties, but our attempts at court ritual are somehow pathetic. Then I saw Che. He was sober, ironic, aloof. He was criticizing Dorticós's elegant suit and some of Fidel's wasteful expenditures. Fidel and Dorticós constituted the receiving line and had to shake hands with thousands of guests—more than one of whom wouldn't wash his right hand for days after squeezing the flesh of the Comandante. Finally Fidel gave up, saying in his phony folksy way that it was easier to spend a day cutting cane than a night shaking hands at the palace.

Che asked me what I thought of a piece he had recently published about the underground war. I told him point-blank that he was limited by the fact that he had lived only through the Sierra fighting and had no idea of the city war. I went on to say that the Sierra people thought that the city fighters were responsible for all our failures and disdained them for it.

"Well, that April strike was a failure wasn't it? Didn't it put the whole revolution in danger?"

"Sure it did, Che, but what about the *Granma* landing; wasn't it a disaster? And what about Alegría de Pío? Who saved the revolution after that rout? The underground militias in Santiago, that's who, those run by Frank País, who took over the whole city."

Che chalked Alegría de Pío up to inexperience and pointed out that those who survived, helped by a few peasants, launched the first guerrilla campaign. I reminded him that those peasants he mentioned had been organized by Crescencio Pérez, Luis and Manuel Fajardo, and others who were stationed with trucks to provide transportation for the landing party.

I mentioned that the Directorio had executed Colonel Blanco Rico, Batista's head of intelligence, as well as Salas Canizares, Batista's chief of police—one of the most hated men in Cuba. Che kept listing the victories by the Sierra troops, from the La Plata outpost to the Uvero barracks. I tried to convince him that the so-called failures of the Directorio—the assault on the palace, for example—were essential to the final victory because they demonstrated that no place in Cuba was safe. It was that that stirred the middle classes and the older generation to move against Batista. I tried to tell him that we were involved in a false argument, that I was not trying to diminish the importance of the Sierra in the slightest, but that, by the same token, he should admit the importance of the urban fighting.

"The guerrilla war was the motor force of the revolution."

"No, Che, neither the guerrilla war, nor the urban war; it was the 26 July Movement that encompassed both. And let's not forget Civic Resistance, with its professional people and middle-class supporters. To say nothing of the trade unions, with their strikes and work stoppages. Even you, Che, will have to admit that the Directorio under Chomón and Cubelas helped you enormously in Las Villas."

"Yes, but you won't deny that the guerrilla war was much more radical ideologically than were the city fighters, who were always vacillating. We always came up on the short side when it came to arms and supplies."

I said the guerrillas were no more radical than the city fighters, but that in fact this was not a real issue because the revolution was not inspired by Communists of any stripe but by a spontaneous desire to be free.

"And who really led the revolution?"

"We never for a moment denied that the leader of the revolution, from Moncada on, was Fidel, as leader of the 26 July Movement. But I insist we add Frank País, José Antonio Echevarría, and Daniel [René Ramos Latour] to any list of leaders."

Che's points, basically, were that I consistently underestimated the importance of the guerrilla war and that I underestimated the significance of peasant support for the guerrilla war. To this I could only say that he had lived through the experience of the Sierra in greater depth than I. I, on the other hand, had seen the underground war and had been in prison, in exile, in addition to having experienced the Sierra. I tried to suggest that credit could not be given exclusively to one group, that where he saw peasants spontaneously coming to the aid of the guerrilla war, I saw peasants—Crescencio Pérez's clan, for example—who had been organized by Frank País and Celia Sánchez into the 26 July Movement. My experience from these different perspectives taught me that the guerrilla war developed as a result of a process that had begun before Moncada, when Fidel was a leader among the Ortodoxos and the students.

We were standing on a corner arguing like that under the eyes of the palace guard. Che told me to write my version of the revolution; he thought that each of us should write down our own experiences. Then he asked me about the book I was supposed to do with Fidel, to which I could only reply that I sincerely hoped that the book would someday exist—that I was writing it, but without much hope of ever being able to publish it. That's when we went our separate ways. In any case, I knew that Fidel's mythmaking would eradicate the memory of the key role the city fighters had had in the revolution, that there would be only one history—that of the leader and his twelve followers. One story, one leader.

A RUN-IN WITH RAÚL

The reception went on and on. The drinks flowed, and there was anything you could think of to eat. And cigars—the palace was filled with smoke. At about 11:00 P.M. Fidel left. His right hand was swollen from so much handshaking, his beady eyes were shining; he had enjoyed himself because he was surrounded by ass-kissers. Then an assistant to President Dorticós politely—all too politely—asked me to step into the presidential office. Dorticós was Fidel's thermometer. If you were in Fidel's good graces, you would know it because Dorticós would treat you well; if not, he wouldn't know you. I suspected something was up, and when I went in, I found quite a rogues' gallery: Dorticós, Che Guevara, Faure Chomón, Vilma Espín, Aleida March de Guevara, Oscar López; Flavio Bravo, Alfredo Guevara, Raúl Castro (the Prague group); and a mixed bag of comandantes, ministers, captains, and doctors.

Raúl, more than a little drunk, greeted me: "Whadya say, Accattone?"—an allusion to Pasolini's film about a pimp. I simply asked Raúl if he had bothered to look at his own face in a mirror lately, at which he became livid. Che tried to calm us down by passing from Pasolini to Fellini—Italian movies were all the rage at the time—and Dorticós picked up his lead.

(To me:) "You must like Italian films."

"Sure, especially *La Dolce Vita*," added Raúl (also to me).

"Yeah, I like *La Dolce Vita*, but Fellini's, not the one you see hanging around palaces."

Raúl jumped in with: "We know you're working for the Chinese, that you're pro-Chinese. You're running that magazine the Chinese finance in Paris." (This was the magazine, *Revolucíon*, that Verges was editing. I hadn't seen either Verges or his magazine, so I could say nothing.)

"Look, Raúl, I admire the Chinese Revolution for lots of reasons, one of them being that the Chinese have tried to get clear of the Russian model."

Then Raúl really surprised me. "Che works on that magazine, too," he said. "He's pro-Chinese. And you're anti-Soviet. You've said as much right here." He was accusing me, and I had the feeling that this was some kind of trial. But was Che also on trial?

Che and Raúl were good friends in the early days of the war, but they drifted apart during the times of heavy Party politics, when Che began to criticize the Soviet system and the Czechs, who had sold us the junk they couldn't use. Che said nothing; he only stood there grinning ironically. I kept wondering what they wanted from me—I was nothing—until I realized that my physical presence was what bothered them. They wanted me gone.

"You're an anti-Soviet," Raúl repeated.

"Look, Raúl, if the Russians really were Soviets, I would be with them. The Party liquidated the Soviets right off the bat. Your problem is that you think that bureaucracy and Soviet mean the same thing. The other thing is that you love Stalin, the man who was the enemy of the people, the new czar who killed thousands of Bolsheviks and millions of innocent people."

Raúl shouted me down: "Nobody offends Stalin when I'm around!"

"Really? Listen, Raúl, when I was in Moscow the first time I called him a motherfucker right in his mausoleum in front of the Russians themselves. I'll do it again for you, right here, if you like." Now he went crazy, foaming at the mouth, shouting his head off.

Dorticós, ever the clever lawyer, stepped in. "This gentleman is a Trotskyite," he said. I denied it, but added that he could call me an anti-Stalinist anytime he liked. I went on to say that

I never kept my feelings secret, as did some persons I could mention, and that I had told Fidel himself how I felt about Stalin, power, bureaucracy, and repression in the Miguel Schultz Prison. I would be glad, I said, to talk about the invasion and occupation of Poland, Budapest, and Prague if they cared to.

"Well, suppose we put you up against the wall? History would absolve us," said Raúl.

"History absolved us when we rose up against Batista, but now that you're in power and can kill like a Batista, you'll find that you'll be condemning yourself, just as Batista did. So save your threats," I answered.

"I'll shoot you right here and now!"

I ripped open my shirt and shouted, "Start shooting if you know how!" (Don't think I didn't see the comic side of all this histrionic bullshit. But I was having fun.)

Then Raúl calmed down and asked me what I thought of the attack on the presidential palace. Now Faure Chomón, the leader of that attack, was right there, so I figured this one was going against him, too.

"I think, Raúl, that was an act of extraordinary bravery, the most revolutionary act in the history of Havana. From a Marxist point of view"—this I said in an ironic tone—"it was the act that stirred the consciousness of the masses in the capital and shook the dictatorship right down to its very foundation." Then I told Raúl that on that March 13 I was being tortured in the Bureau of Investigations and that Mariano Faget, one of Batista's assassins, had asked me the very same question. He thought I had been in on the attack—which I hadn't; it had been the Directorio, not the 26 July Movement, that had mounted the assault. The only reason Faget hadn't killed me was that when the colonel in charge of killing prisoners at the Bureau called the palace for instructions, Luis Gómez Wangüemert had answered the phone and told him that Batista was dead and that the Directorio had taken over.

Poor Chomón was as silent as a mouse; the same man who had had the guts to attack Batista's palace couldn't say a word now. He wasn't going to fall for one of Raúl's provocations. Now I began to feel ridiculous. Then Aleida March said she was leaving because she didn't like to see people ganged up on like that. Dorticós tried his Trotsky ploy one more time, so I turned to him and said, "This isn't my first violent argument with Raúl, but I have no intention of arguing with people like you, who were not even in on the revolution." His jowls began to tremble, and that reminded me of Camilo Cienfuegos's laughter when he talked about people like Dorticós or Augusto Martínez Sánchez and their trembling jowls when they were afraid.

Dorticós, white with rage, fell into rhetoric. "You, sir, are offending the office of the presidency."

"The only person being offended here is me" was my answer.

I finally left. A car pulled up alongside me, and I figured I would be arrested. But no, they gave me a ride to L and Twenty-third streets. I went to the Habana-Libre and ran into some foreign writers and journalists.

I was nervous and needed a walk. I went down to the old tropical market, but it didn't exist any more. No more fish. No more fruit. No more flowers. Where was it all? The socialist market was empty, bureaucratic, and ugly. The whole city was becoming Haitianized. You now saw chickens and turkeys in coops on balconies; there were vegetable gardens wherever there was some open land. Once upon a time only the Chinese had these minigardens; now everyone did. The salt in the air was destroying the walls of the houses because no one bothered to paint any more. It was early in the day, and the first lines had already formed, people looking for bread or for the cup of coffee they would never find. No neon signs, no lights, fewer cars than I had remembered. Buses were now a rarity, and taxis were impossible to find. Women came carrying pails of water.

As day dawned, it dawned on me that I was in real danger. In my mind's eye, I could see the past like a film. I reviewed it all and found no way out of what I had done, no way out of where I was. I should have thought things over when we came down from the mountains into Santiago at the beginning of January in 1959. Fidel said he would miss the war. I knew I wouldn't, but I knew I would miss something else—the future I had fought for. Everything was different, but nothing had changed. Only the power had changed hands. The people still had to work and obey.

SUGAR ACCORD: MADE IN USSR

The story of my run-in with Raúl got around quite quickly. Fidel left for Moscow, and soon after Celia Sánchez called me to say that Fidel was not pleased with the way Raúl and Dorticós had attacked me in the palace, but that I shouldn't have argued back as I had. Fidel would speak with me on his return. Raúl didn't want Fidel to publish his book with Feltrinelli because it was Pasternak's publisher and Pasternak was anathema to the Russians. Raúl, who really seemed to be in charge of everything, was quite concerned with history. He and his Party cronies issued a decree that enabled them to gather all the documents relevant to the revolution in an archive that would be run by Geisa, a Communist married to Leonel Soto, one of the Prague group. They even got all of Celia's papers. I was the only person who refused to give his Sierra papers. My collection was the best, because it had everything in it about Radio Rebelde; the underground actions in which I participated; *Revolución*; propaganda; the archive Camilo Cienfuegos gave me when he left the Sierra; and statements and letters by Fidel, Che, Daniel, and virtually everyone else. Camilo and Che had told me that, whatever happened, I was to be responsible for publishing a documentary history of the revolution.

Raúl had done me a favor. Fidel could not be pushed into things, so now I had breathing room. I thought that I was morally obligated to inform Latin America about what had happened in the Cuban Revolution and that our revolution was not going to be the wellspring of future revolutions. I had to tell how the Communists had opposed the revolutionary activity that included all classes of Cuban society and both the cities and the country. I had fallen afoul of power and was about to enter the worst part of my life, and yet I felt happy. I returned to the people, to the interior of Cuba—in fact, to the interior of Havana, which I hadn't really seen since 1961. I walked, took buses, visited all sorts of places. I had no salary, but friends lent me money. I thought I would call Margot and have her and the children come back; after all, we had always shared a common fate in the past. I went along Route 30. The people were somber, silent, devoid of the humor they once had. I went to the movies; there were lots of seats for the Russian films no one wanted to see and huge lines of people waiting to get in to see the Italian films. People went crazy if they had a chance to see an old Hollywood film.

The attitude of the people was fascinating. Watching the ICAIC news, they remained silent. They would clap sometimes, but very little, even for Fidel. It was hard to tell if they were tired or just bored with the long speeches they'd been made to suffer through over the past few years. Even at mass meetings people kept quiet. Fidel noted it and explained that "enthusiasm has been turned into awareness." All those crowds with their songs and mottoes, their joy and passion, had disappeared. Che wondered if the people would ever be brought around, if they would ever get over the errors caused by Party politics. In any case, Party pressure was coming back on, Security was back in action, and the Defense Committees were keeping their eyes peeled. This was because of Fidel's trip to Moscow.

New collective persecution began. There were reeducation camps set up for intellectuals and artists. On the way to my house in Miramar, I passed in front of the house in which Comandante Manuel Piñeyro lived, the famous and dangerous Redbeard, second in command of Security, the man in charge of revolution in Latin America. He had a huge house surrounded by a huge piece of land, a farm right in the city. And it was a real farm, with all kinds of chickens, pigs, ducks—all taken care of by army personnel. It was a kind of conspicuous consumption by a new class. It was incredible that in a city where everything was rationed, where scarcity was the order of the day, where the socialist police had forbidden citizens to keep pigs or chickens in their houses, a chief of police was doing it right out in the open. I remembered that Fidel had denounced Batista's officers for using soldiers as farm laborers, and now both the army and the police were doing the same thing. It was a kind of sickening joke.

Everything had changed, yet nothing was different. I waited for the bus. Regis Debray went by in a limousine and asked if I wanted a ride, as did one or two comandantes or ministers. I stayed at the bus stop. It was really funny to watch the comandantes who lived in those huge houses come tearing out after the kids who would climb over their walls to steal mangoes. Was I seeing the past, the present, or the future? I chose to be with the people.

THE MOSCOW ACCORD

The sugar agreement signed in Moscow on January 23, 1964, was announced in Havana with great fanfare. There were pictures of the reconciliation between Fidel and Khrushchev in all the papers. One remark Khrushchev made to Fidel struck me as important: "Who's fooling whom here?" The Russians were buying Cuban sugar at a higher-than-world-market price. Cuba would be the sugar bowl of the socialist world. Khrushchev said the Russians would invent a machine for cutting cane and would present it to Fidel. It never came. In the old days, the difference between the market price and the price the United States paid for sugar was called the differential, and what that did was to guarantee a market for our product. Now we were doing the same thing; we were tied to the same monoculture and the same single market, only this time with the Russians. The morning the agreement was announced was, for me—in the words of my friend Guillermo Cabrera Infante—a real "view of dawn in the tropics."

APPENDIX

1. COMMUNISM

A. PUBLIC DOCUMENTS

(These documents were written and published between May 1957 and March 1962.)

INTERVIEW BY JULES DUBOIS OF FIDEL CASTRO, CARACAS, VENEZUELA, MAY 1958

Q. Because you were in Bogotá, Colombia, in 1948 at the Anti-imperialist Student Congress and participated in the events of the ninth of April of that year in Bogotá [the "Bogotazo"], people have called you a Communist or a Communist sympathizer. Are you now or have you ever been a Communist?

A. There is no logical reason why I should be called a Communist or a Communist sympathizer simply because I attended the Congress. I was one of the organizers of the Congress, whose main

The quotations in this appendix have been taken from *Diario de la revolución cubana* (Barcelona: Ediciones R. Torres, 1976), hereafter cited as *DRC*, and from *Revolución*, hereafter cited as *R*.

focus was to fight against dictatorships in the Americas. On the ninth of April I joined a crowd marching on a police station. These people were not Communists but followers of Jorge Eliecer Gaitán, head of the Liberal Opposition Party, who was assassinated that same afternoon for political reasons. I did what every student in Colombia did: I joined the people. As far as my real participation is concerned, I tried, insofar as it was possible, to avoid the fire-bombings and vandalism that caused that rebellion to fail. But my actions didn't amount to a drop in the bucket. I could have died there, as did so many anonymous fighters, and perhaps now no one would even remember me. My conduct could not have been more disinterested or altruistic, and I do not regret having behaved as I did, because I feel honored by my actions. Is that a good reason for thinking me a possible Communist? I have never been, nor am I now a Communist. If I were, I would be brave enough to say it publicly. I don't recognize any judge in this world to whom anyone has to render an account of his ideas. Every man has a right to think in absolute liberty. I have often told how I think, but I understand that you, as a U.S. journalist, have to ask about Communists.

Q.: People accuse the movement you lead of being Communist. What is the political ideology of your movement?

A.: The only person who wants to accuse our movement of being Communist is the dictator Batista, so that he can continue to receive weapons from the United States, weapons that are covered with the blood of murdered Cubans, weapons that are inspiring the hatred and the hostility of a people who are among the most freedom-loving, the most desirous of human rights, in the Americas. That our movement is democratic may be seen by its heroic struggle against tyranny. What is shameful is that a government that proclaims itself a defender of democracy before the world should be supplying military aid to one of the bloodiest dictatorships in the world, and the irony is that even with the help of the United States, and of Somoza and Trujillo, Batista cannot defeat us. He'll have to wipe out the entire nation before he'll be able to plant in its ashes the idea of "democracy" espoused by Trujillo, Somoza, and the U.S. State Department. The people of the United States should be told that the policies of its government are discrediting it. Is any other explanation necessary for the growing hostility of all of Latin America?

Q.: People say you favor the socialization or nationalization of privately owned industry in Cuba, especially those owned by Americans. What is your opinion of free enterprise and what guarantees do you offer for U.S. capital invested in Cuba?

A.: The 26 July Movement has never spoken about socializing or nationalizing any industry. That's just a stupid fear people have about our revolution. From the first day of our struggle, we have declared that we favor the full application of the Constitution of 1940, whose bylaws establish guarantees, rights, and obligations for all elements that participate in production. This includes free enterprise and invested capital, as well as many other economic, civil, and political rights. There are certain people who are very concerned that economic rights not be violated, but these same people don't care at all if other rights of citizens and the nation are violated. So as long as the dictator guarantees their economic rights, they support him and don't care that he kills scores of citizens every day. The 26 July Movement is fighting for our rights and for the Constitution, and it considers that freedom and life, not wealth, are the supreme human values. . . . We do not in any way deviate from our idea of civilian rule. The dictatorship should be replaced by a provisional, entirely civilian government that will restore normalcy and hold general elections within a year. (*DRC*, pp. 443–45)

INTERVIEW BY JULES DUBOIS OF RAÚL CASTRO
SECOND FRONT, JULY 1958

I ask Raúl Castro about his trip to Vienna to attend a Communist Youth Congress and about his subsequent travels behind the Iron Curtain when he was a student at the University of Havana. This is his answer: "The Communists asked me for a contribution to send a delegate to the World Youth Congress in Vienna, in 1953. I wanted to travel and I thought that would be a good opportunity. I offered to pay my own passage if they would let me go, and they accepted. So off I went. At the Congress I got into a discussion with a Rumanian delegate, and the head of the delegation subsequently invited me to visit his country. I also visited Budapest on the trip. I would go to China if I had the chance, because I like to travel and I want to see the world. But this doesn't mean I'm a Communist."

That night Raúl Castro slept in a bed opposite mine in the hospital. Before he left I gave him a typewritten list of the following questions I had asked him and the answers he had given. After our conversation, he sent written orders that the rest of the captured sailors be set free, and he sent a messenger to Puriales with the order. The jeep trip took thirteen and one-half hours.

Q.: Why did the Frank País column of the *Segundo Frente* kidnap the Americans and take some people from Moa and Nicaro?

A.: We had to arrest the U.S. citizens for the following reasons: (1) To attract world attention, specifically that of the United States, to the crimes being committed against our people with weapons supplied by the United States to Batista. These are weapons for continental defense, and in one of the sections of the agreement the use of those arms in internal matters is specifically prohibited. These U.S. citizens are international witnesses. (2) To stop the criminal bombings—with fire bombs, rockets, and even napalm— the enemy was carrying out at that time against our forces and, above all, against the defenseless peasants. These bombings had absolutely no military objective. (*DRC*, p. 532)

Camilo Cienfuegos: Among all the rebel troops, I knew only three soldiers whose ideology was Communist. (Columbia, *R*, January 10, 1959)

Fidel Castro: I think this is one of the lands with the greatest natural wealth. The thing is that at the present time the sugar mills have certain advantages. Within five months we will have those advantages. They [the foreign owners] think that we are a small nation and perhaps a cowardly one. They think that, faced with the enormous power of the country from which they come, we will have to give in to their whims and insolence; they think we are fools and that we are going to do foolish things. A few have all the privileges, while the others, the vast majority, have all the misery. The worker is the main creator of wealth, not the capitalist sitting in a comfortable office on Wall Street. The revolution will end all that. Our revolution has Cuban roots. Some people prefer not to recognize that and try to invent absurd comparisons. Our revolution is thoroughly Cuban and will figure among humanity's great events. It seeks justice through liberty. ("The Sugar Harvest, Vital for the Revolution," Meeting of the CTC, February 10, 1959, *R*, p. 2)

Amidst ideologies that struggle for power, the Cuban Revolution rises up with its new ideas and new events. They [our enemies] are not going to confuse the people by calling us Communists. (Appearance at the Civic Institutions, Havana, *R*, March 17, 1959)

Our Revolution is olive-green, just like the mountains in Oriente Province. (*R*, May 23)

"Extremist agitators." Raúl Quintana, Radio Rebelde: Are they Communists? Fidel: Perhaps they have a great deal in common. (May 23)

FIDEL CASTRO IN CENTRAL PARK, NEW YORK CITY, APRIL 29, 1959

This is the doctrine of our revolution; that it is a revolution of the majority, that it united public opinion in a great national desire, and it hopes also that the peoples of the Americas will join together in a great American desire. Our revolution practices this democratic principle and is in favor of a humanist democracy. Humanism means that in order to satisfy the material needs of many it is not necessary to sacrifice man's dearest desires, which are his freedoms, and that the most essential freedoms of man mean nothing if his material needs are not satisfied as well. Humanism means social justice with liberty and human rights; humanism means what is usually meant by democracy, but not theoretical democracy—real democracy, human rights with the satisfaction of the needs of man. Because with hunger and misery you can only create an oligarchy, but never a true democracy; with hunger and misery you can create a tyranny, but never a true democracy. We are democratic [in that we favor] the right of all to work, to eat; [we are] sincerely democratic, because a democracy that only talks about theoretical rights and forgets human needs is not a sincere democracy; not a true democracy. No bread without liberty, no liberty without bread; no dictatorship by one man, no dictatorships by classes, groups, castes. Government by the people without dictatorship or oligarchies; freedom with bread, bread without terror: that's what humanism is all about. (*R,* April 25, 1959)

FIDEL CASTRO AT THE CONGRESS OF THE CONFEDERATION OF CUBAN WORKERS, HAVANA, NOVEMBER 18, 1959 (CTC)

I

I was invited to this final meeting of the Workers' Congress. As the hour approached in which we were to attend this closing session, we began to hear rather disheartening news—that many jobs had been left undone, that there was an atmosphere of tension at the Congress. All the comrades who spoke to me said that this was not right. They said even more, that I shouldn't have come to the Congress because there was a risk in attending such a restless assembly, that there was a real risk—the risk of seeing this shameful spectacle you are putting on here tonight. [*Shouts and applause.*] Comrades, I have not come here to practice demagoguery.

It's hard to accept the very idea that it might be dangerous to attend a congress of workers for whom we have done so much. The 26 July Movement: that name is closely linked to us, and if there is in this Congress a majority also linked to it, how is it possible to explain why there should be any fear related to the presence of the Prime Minister at the Congress? . . . [There were] union meetings in which it seemed to me that everyone had gone crazy . . . and there was even a moment in which I thought people were going to stop speaking, because I could hear shouts here and there between divided groups. I had the impression that you were playing with a revolution you held in your hands; I had the sensation—a hard, disagreeable sensation—as of a mass of men, of leaders, in fact, who were not behaving in a responsible way . . . if, in fact, the working class or its representatives know what they are doing.

I can only feel truly dissatisfied when I see that the working class is being invalidated in self-defense and in defense of the revolution, because what I saw here tonight was not the kind of action that a working class to which one could issue arms could take.

We have said: the revolution demands that the workers be organized like an army. . . . Even if the revolutionary government found itself in a minority situation in the Congress, with an executive and a counterrevolutionary CTC, don't think the revolution is going to start shaking with fear.

II

I'll say it again: I am not going to allow the revolutionary government to be held up by the maneuvers of reactionaries who will turn up tomorrow at the revolutionary government defending their positions with all the bad faith in the world.

May the propositions be accepted by the assembly to determine who will be secretary-general. [*Applause. Shouts of "David! David!"*] Those in favor of Comrade David Salvador . . . [*Shouts of approval.*] I want to know if this is a unanimous vote or a majority vote. . . . [*The vote of confidence is approved unanimously.*]

Abstention of the Communists: After David Salvador Manso was designated leader, the worker-director of the PSP [Partido

Socialista Popular], Faustino Calcines, read a declaration in the name of his party expressing his party's abstention. The Executive Committee of the Central Union was made up of the following leaders: Secretary-General, David Salvador; First Vice-Secretary-General, Noelio Morell; Second Vice-Secretary-General, Armando Cordero; Secretary of Organization, Jesús Soto Díaz; Vice-Secretary of Organization, Hector Carbonell, Finance Secretary, José Pellón; Finance Vice-Secretary, José Gómez; Recording and Corresponding Secretary, Alfredo Díaz, with Gerardo Núñez Miranda as Vice-Secretary; Secretary of Public Relations, Eladio Carranza, with Migdilio Machado as Vice-Secretary; Secretary of Foreign Relations, Odón Álvarez de la Campa, with Manuel Guerrero as Vice-Secretary; Secretaries of Union Culture and Education, Rafael Monea and Jorge Estevánez; Secretary of Agrarian Affairs, Pedro Perdomo, with Raimundo Anal Pérez as Vice-Secretary; Secretary of Youth and Sports, Luis Felipe Guerra, with Felipe Ayala Cano as Vice-Secretary; Secretary for Statistics and Economic Affairs, Constantino Hermida, with José García García as Vice-Secretary; Delegate to Official and Owner Organizations, Octavio Louit, with Alberto Vera as Vice-Delegate.

A Motion for Raising the Minimum Wage to 100 Pesos per Month

The plenum meeting of the Tenth National Congress of the Revolutionary CTC rejected a motion for raising the minimum wage to 100 pesos per month. This raise would not be in accord with the economic policy of the revolutionary government, whose goal is full employment but not more wages for those already employed (except in truly justifiable cases). (*R*, November 23, 1959)

Fidel Castro: I am a Marxist-Leninist. ("Universidad Popular," a Communist TV program)

Fidel Castro: In the university, we began to learn about the *Communist Manifesto*, about the writings of Marx, Engels, and Lenin, and that this began a process. I can say openly, confess it honorably, that many of the things we have done in the revolution were not invented by us, not by a long shot.

People have asked me if I thought at the time of the Moncada assault as I think today. I have replied to them that I thought then much in the way I think today. That is the truth. That was the path our revolution had to take: the path of the anti-imperialist struggle, the path of socialism—that is, of the nationalization of all large industries and businesses, the nationalization of the basic means of production and the planned development of our economy at the fastest rate possible.

And what kind of socialism should we have adopted? Utopian socialism? We had, in point of fact, to adopt scientific socialism. That's why I began by saying with all frankness that we believed in Marxism, that we believed that it is the most correct, the most scientific—in fact, the only truly revolutionary—theory. I say it with pride and confidence: I am a Marxist-Leninist and I shall be a Marxist-Leninist until the day I die. (*R,* December 1, 1961)

PARTY POLITICS: FIDEL CASTRO ON NATIONAL RADIO AND TELEVISION, MARCH 26, 1962

. . . The tendency to distrust everyone, anyone who is not an old militant revolutionary, not an old militant Marxist.

. . . workers, peasants, students, the poor, important sectors of the middle classes, intellectuals—all embraced Marxism-Leninism, all embraced the struggle against imperialism, all fought for the socialist revolution.

. . . The path the revolution would take, the path the people would take, could be seen in a series of laws passed to benefit the people: those that lowered telephone bills; those that nullified the rapacious contracts negotiated under Batista and backed by him; those related to urban reform; those that deal with lowering rent; those related to agrarian reform, the nationalization of foreign-owned companies, and later the nationalization of all large corporations.

Of what party politics am I speaking? The party politics that believes that the only comrades who can be trusted, the only ones who can run a farm, a cooperative, the state itself or anything else, must be old militant Marxists.

. . . Where is the root of this party politics, which is implacable, indefatigable, systematic, and ubiquitous? Where are the causes of this party politics? It was difficult to understand that this spirit is engendered only under certain circumstances.

At times you might think, well, this is the policy of a single group, this is the policy of a party; there are many people behind this. The fact is, we are all responsible to a greater or lesser degree.

. . . This revolution was straying from its course and heading for a thicket. . . . It was making a straitjacket for itself, a yoke, comrades; we were not promoting a free association of revolution-aries, but an army of domesticated, well-trained revolutionaries.

At times a series of coincidences occur that allow individuals to foul up the function of an organization, to distort its functions, to waste its best opportunities—to destroy them or use them in the worst way. And this, simply put, was what was happening. . . .

And when we came to see just how things were, we found a hell of a mess—excuse my language. . . . Aníbal Escalante, a Communist, made serious errors. The fact is that Communists do make mistakes; they are men like the rest of us! Aníbal Esca-lante, abusing the confidence we all had in him, followed, in his position as Secretary of Organization, a policy that was not Marx-ist, a policy that departed from Leninist norms of organization for a vanguard party of the working class, and tried to create an instrument that would enable him to pursue personal goals. We think that Aníbal Escalante did not act in a mistaken and unconscious way, but that he acted in a deliberate and conscious way. He allowed himself to be swept away by personal ambition, and the result was that he created a series of problems—in fact, he made a chaos of the country. . . . It was very easy, given the nation's total acceptance of conditions, to turn that apparatus, already accepted by the people, into an instrument for attaining personal goals. The prestige of the ORI [Organizaciones Revoluci-onarias Integradas] was immense.

. . . He used this situation to set about creating a system of controls that were all in his hands. . . . A policy of privilege: he was creating conditions and imparting instructions that tended to transform that apparatus, not into an apparatus of the vanguard of the working class, but into a nest of privileges, of tolerance, of benefits—into a system of favors of all kinds. He was totally distorting the role of the apparatus. Of course, it is logical that this would create a horrible situation of party politics; this explains why this party politics came into being, why this insatiable, implacable, incessant party politics appeared everywhere, from one end of Cuba to another.

. . . The Communists had numbered a few thousand—the old Communists, that is: The nation that had embraced the Marxist-Leninist cause was made up of millions of citizens.

. . . He [Escalante] had appointed members to the National Directory with a Nazi "Gauleiter" mentality instead of a Marxist mentality, since there were gentlemen taking on the airs of Gauleiters instead of [acting like] Marxist militants. . . . Didn't he know anyone else? No, because when the people here were fighting, he was hiding under his bed. This man was creating havoc in the Cauto River area, one day's march from the Sierra Maestra; it wouldn't have been any problem for him to have put on his pack [and go to join the rebels] when Cowley [Col. Fermín Cowley Gallegos] was murdering workers and peasants [in reprisal for 26 July Movement attacks]—when Cowley murdered Loynaz Echevarría and so many other militant revolutionaries—in a cowardly way, all in one night. Or when the workers, peasants, and students were murdered by soldiers—and he wouldn't have had to walk for more than a day to join the ranks of the revolutionary forces.

By the same line of reasoning, it could be said that the Montecristi Manifesto [an anti-Batista statement] was a reactionary document, that the [French] Declaration of the Rights of Man of the year 1789 was a reactionary document. What kind of junk does a person have to have in his head to think that way?

And someone else said the Moncada assault was an error and that the *Granma* landing was an error. . . . What we are talking about with regard to Moncada and the *Granma* landing is not the event itself but the route it took—the correct, revolutionary route, the route of armed struggle; not the politicking route, the electoral route, but the route of armed struggle against Batista, the route that history has declared to have been correct. . . . One day we went to a certain place and found there more than one hundred officers we had seen fight in other battles. "What are you doing? Aren't you in charge of troops?" "No." "What had happened to these comrades?" "Well, because their political level was low, they were not permitted to command troops." . . . How could anyone take an officer's command away because of his low political level and put some young graduate in charge because he could recite a Marxist catechism from memory even if it had nothing to do with fighting? So we conclude that any graduate, even one who has never fought or had any inclination to fight, has a higher political level and should therefore command troops. Is that what you call Marxism or Leninism?

The masses were not integrated into the political process. And yet they were talking about Integrated Revolutionary Organizations [ORI], but what were those organizations? They were made into an organization by the militancy of the Partido Socialista Popular. The other organizations, the Directorio and the 26 July Movement, what were they? Were they organizations backed by an old militant group? No, they were organizations that had great mass sympathy; they were [supported by] a torrent of mass sympathy.

. . . How were these nuclei formed? I'll tell you: in every province, the Secretary-General of the PSP was named Secretary-General of the ORI; in all municipalities, the Secretary-General of the PSP was named Secretary-General of the ORI; in all the nuclei . . . the member of the of PSP was made Secretary-General of the nucleus. Do you call that integration? The person responsible for this policy is Comrade Aníbal.

. . . Some people began to wonder: but is this communism, Marxism, or socialism? This high-handedness, these abuses, these privileges, all this, is it really communism? They would answer their own questions the way the Indian Hatuey answered the priest who asked him if he wanted to go to heaven (the Spaniards were about to burn him at the stake): Hatuey said, "Not if these guys are going to be there." They got out the old militants and made them members of the directorate—those, that is, who were left, because some had been placed in other positions, such as Chief of Personnel, Administrator. . . .

Naturally, the masses do not elect the nucleus. The Party does not use elections; it selects through the process known as democratic centralism. (*R,* March 27, 1962)

CHE GUEVARA ON PARTY POLITICS

. . . Shall I say that you also have a part in this? The Defense Committees, an institution that sprang up in the heat of the people's vigilance, which represented the people's fervent desire to defend their revolution, started to turn into a catchall, into a den of opportunism. It started to turn into an organization the people disliked . . . full of people eager for power, opportunists of all sorts, who never stopped to think of the damage they were doing to the revolution. . . . All that is a lesson we have to learn and a truth we have to recognize: any security force of any kind must be under the control of the people. . . . Out in Matanzas, the chiefs of the revolution went around with ropes through the town saying that the INRA would supply the rope if the people would supply the victim. Well, no one was turned in—at least I never read of anyone—and I never heard of anyone's doing his job, not even to inform the security forces that such things were going on. That was like the example of the so-called red terror people wanted to establish in Matanzas against the white terror, although they never realized that the white terror existed in the minds of a few weirdos; we unleashed the white terror with our absurd actions and later we added the red terror. . . . A counter-revolutionary is someone who fights against the revolution, but someone is equally counterrevolutionary if he uses his influence to get a house and then two cars, and then violates the rationing system—the guy who ends up having everything the people lack. (*Conversaciones del Ministro del Interior* [Lectures of the Minister of the Interior], Ediciones Revolucionarias, 1976)

B. ARCHIVE OF THE CUBAN REVOLUTION

(INTERNAL DOCUMENTS OF THE 26 JULY MOVEMENT DURING THE UNDERGROUND DAYS, DURING IMPRISONMENT, AND DURING THE WAR, 1952–58; PUBLISHED FOR THE FIRST TIME IN 1976, IN *Diario de la Revolución cubana*)

Melba Hernández: I remember well when he [Abel Santamariá] began to read Marxist materials, which he did at Fidel's suggestion. I don't know exactly how, but I do remember that one day after reading Machiavelli, his reading Cuban history—because he always loved Cuba—one day Abel turned up reading another type of literature. (P. 65)

Jesús Montané: Raúl participated in the movement in a slightly improvised manner at first. He had visited the socialist countries, and when he returned, he joined the Movement. He was arrested when he returned from Europe, and the police kept one of his diaries. I went to see him while he was in jail and he told me all his experiences on his trip. He was very enthusiastic about things.

Melba Hernández: Antolín Falcón, the chief of the Bureau, to convince me that all that was crazy, would refer to Raúl's madness in his diary. Falcón would say, "But can you believe this stuff? Look what this diary says about the socialist world as paradise."

Jesús Montané: The specific watchword we would shout was "Revolution! Revolution!" The Communists would shout "Unity! Unity!" (P. 68)

Juan Almeida: It was my first contact with Fidel. He went around with one of Lenin's books under his arm where everyone could see it. The very book that turned up at the Moncada assault. (P. 71)

1953: FIDEL AND THE PROSECUTOR (THE MONCADA TRIAL)

A Lawyer: Who was the intellectual author of this insurrection?
The Accused: The intellectual author was José Martí.
Another Lawyer: Was Abel Santamaría studying any of Lenin's books?
The Accused: Possibly. We were reading Lenin and other socialist writers. Anyone who doesn't is an ignoramus. (P. 77)

FIDEL CASTRO: PRISON LETTERS

December 18, 1953

Over the past few days I've read some interesting books: William Thackeray's *Vanity Fair*, Turgenev's *A Nest of Gentlefolk*, *The Life of Luis Carlos Prestes*, Jorge Amado's *The Knight of Hope*, the Dean of Canterbury's *The Secret of the Soviet Fortress*, Eric Knight's *Fugitives of Love*, Nikolai Ostrovski's *Thus We Temper Iron*—a modern Russian novel, the moving autobiography of the author who participated in the revolution as a young man—A. J. Cronin's *The Citadel*. From the life of Prestes to the last title I mention, I'm not sorry for having read a single one: they all have enormous social value. (P. 87)

January 27, 1954

You ask me if Rolland would have been equally great if he had been born in the seventeenth century. Human thought is undoubtedly conditioned by the circumstances of an age. Thinking about a political genius now, I would dare to assert that he depends exclusively on his age. Lenin in the age of Catherine the Great, when the aristocracy was the dominating class, would have been a bold defender of the bourgeoisie, which was then the revolutionary class, or he would have been swallowed up in history; Martí, if he had lived when the English took Havana, would have fought alongside his father in defense of the Spanish flag; Napoleon, Mirabeau, Danton, and Robespierre—what would they have been in the time of Charlemagne but humble serfs or unknown inhabitants of some feudal castle? Julius Caesar would never have crossed the Rubicon in the first years of the Republic, before the class struggle that shook Rome had intensified and the great plebeian party had developed and made both necessary and possible Caesar's rise to power. Julius Caesar was a true revolutionary, as was Cataline, while Cicero, so highly honored by history, incarnated the genuine Roman aristocrat. This did not prevent the French revolutionaries from anathemetizing Caesar and deifying Brutus, the man who thrust the dagger of the aristocracy into Caesar's heart. This just shows that the republic in Rome was the equivalent of the monarchy in France. . . .

Even the greatest ideas are conditioned by the historical moment in which they appear. Aristotle's philosophy is the culmination of the work of the philosophers who precede him (Parmenides, Socrates, Plato) and would have been impossible without those precursors. In the same way, Marx's doctrines are the culmination in the social area of the efforts of the utopian socialists and synthesize, in philosophy, German idealism and materialism. Marx, of course, was more than a philosopher: he was a political genius, and his role as such depended entirely on the epoch, the scene in which he lived. . . .

Literary, philosophic, or artistic genius has a considerably wider area in time and history than the world of action and reality, which is the only stage that political geniuses possess. (Pp. 90–91)

March [1954]

. . . I can't tell you how moved I was by Victor Hugo's *Les Misérables*. Of course, as time passes, I am tiring of his excessive romanticism, his rhetoric, and the heavy weight of his erudition, which is at times tedious and exaggerated. Karl Marx wrote a great book on the same theme, Napoleon III, called *The 18th Brumaire of Louis Bonaparte*. If you compare the two books, you can really see the huge difference between a scientific, realistic concept of history and a purely romantic interpretation. Where Hugo doesn't see anything but a lucky adventurer, Marx sees the inevitable results of the social contradictions and the struggle of interests prevalent at the time. For the one, history is chance, while for the other it is a process controlled by laws. Hugo's writing recalls our own political speeches; [it is] full of poetic faith in liberty, righteous indignation against the outrages he suffers, and confident hope in his miraculous return. (P. 92)

April 4 [1954]

It's 11:00 P.M. Since 6:00 [P.M.] I have been reading Lenin's *The State and Revolution* after finishing two works by Marx, *The 18th Brumaire of Louis Bonaparte* and *The Civil Wars in France*. All three books have a great deal in common and are of inestimable worth.

. . . After breaking my head on Kant for a good while, Marx seems easier than saying an Our Father to me. He, like Lenin, had a terrific appetite for polemic, and I really enjoy myself and laugh as I read them. They were implacable and terrifying to their enemies. Two real revolutionary prototypes.

Now I'm going to eat: spaghetti with squid, Italian bonbons for dessert, fresh coffee—and then an H Upmann 4. Don't you envy me? They all take care of me . . . They never listen, and I'm always fighting with them so they won't send me anything. When I take a sun bath in my shorts in the morning and I feel the sea air, it's as if I'm on a beach, then in a small restaurant. People are going to think I'm on vacation. What would Marx think of such a revolutionary? (P. 97)

April 15 [1954]

The great resemblance the great social reforms since antiquity until today have to each other is curious indeed. Many of the measures taken by the Paris Commune in 1870 are, I think, similar to Julius Caesar's laws. The problems of land, living space, debts, and unemployment have reappeared in all societies since remote times. I am excited by the grand spectacle offered by the great revolutions of history, because they have always meant the triumph of projects that incarnate the well-being and happiness of the great majority compared with the tiny special-interest groups. . . . How little importance is given to the fact that African slaves in revolt created a free republic by defeating Napoleon's best generals! It's true that Haiti has not progressed much since then, but has the fortune of other Latin American nations been better? I'm always thinking about these things because I would sincerely like to create a revolution in this country from one end to the other. I would be willing to earn the hatred and ill-will of a few thousand, among them a few relatives, half the people I know, two thirds of my professional colleagues, and four fifths of my prep-school classmates. (Pp. 98–99)

April 17 [1954]: Letter to Melba Hernández and Haydée Santamaría

Third, lots of smiles and glad-handing for everyone. Let's use the same tactic we used during the trial: we defend our point of view without raising a ruckus. There will be time enough to smash these roaches all at the same time. (Pp. 99–100)

CARLOS FRANQUI: LETTER TO FRANK PAÍS FROM THE PRÍNCIPE PRISON

April 1957

The Communists don't believe in the insurrection. They criticize both the sabotage and the guerrilla attacks. They say we are playing the game of the regime's terrorists. They say the 26 July Movement is "Putschist," adventurist, and lower-middle-class. They cling to their hypothetical "mobilization of the masses" and their classic "unity, unity," the same theses we see in *Carta Semanal*. In the discussions here Ursinio Rojas, from the Central Committee, Villalonga and Armas, both Communist worker leaders, take part. On our side we have Armando [Hart], Enrique [Oltuski], Faustino [Pérez], and me. The Communists don't understand the nature of the tyranny and they don't believe in the possibility of revolution, of which they believe they are the only representatives. The Communists evidently believe Batista will return to legality and elections, as happened in 1939. They are the very Communists Batista was killing in 1935 and who allied with and voted for Batista in 1940. They are a bureaucratized, reformist, and politicking party that cannot overcome its own limitations. (P. 240)

FIDEL CASTRO: LETTER TO FRANK PAÍS FROM THE SIERRA

July 1957, "True Revolution"

I am very happy and I congratulate you for having seen clearly the need to elaborate plans for national works, without regard to the time they may require. We are in no hurry. We shall fight here for however long it takes. We shall end this struggle with either death or the triumph of the *true revolution*. We can now say that expression out loud. Old fears are fading. (P. 266)

CHE GUEVARA: LETTER TO DANIEL [RENÉ RAMOS LATOUR] FROM THE SIERRA

December 14, 1957

I belong, because of my ideological background, to that group which believes that the solution to the world's problems lies behind the Iron Curtain, and I understand this movement as one of the many provoked by the desire of the bourgeoisie to free itself from the economic chains of imperialism. I shall always think of Fidel as an authentic left-wing bourgeois leader, although his figure is glorified by personal qualities of extraordinary brilliance that set him far above his class. I began the struggle in that spirit: honorably, with no hope of going beyond the liberation of the nation, intending to go when the post-revolt situation would turn toward the right (toward what you and your associates represent). What I never imagined was the extremely radical change that Fidel brought about in his own platform with the Miami Manifesto. What I learned later seemed impossible—namely, that the will of the man who is the authentic leader and motor force of the

Movement was so misrepresented that I am ashamed to have thought as I did. Fortunately, Fidel's letter arrived during the time we were waiting for bullets, and it cleared up what could be called a betrayal. Besides, Fidel says, he has received no money, bad bullets, and men who are insufficiently armed. If things are in this state, why renounce contacts that give me the chance to get something that will move our cause forward, in honor of a false unity that crumbles at its very base, when the Directorio Nacional betrays the agreements it has with the man I recognize as our supreme leader? Piferrer may be a crook, but the person who orchestrated the Miami Plan is a criminal; and I think I'm the right man to deal with him because I never sacrifice anything even though I get only a little. In Miami, we sacrificed everything and got nothing: we've handed over our asses in the most detestable act of faggotry in all of Cuban history. My historic name (which I feel I will earn with my actions) cannot be linked to that crime, and I want to declare that right here.

I do this, naturally, so I can leave the testimony that will substantiate my impunity, but the common task that unites us and my sense of obligation have combined to cause this letter to be limited to our respective persons. I am disposed to participate, to the degree I am capable, in achieving the common goal. If you are hurt by this letter because you think it unjust or because you consider yourself innocent of the crime and you want to tell me so, fine. If it hurts you to the point that you want to terminate contact with this part of the revolutionary forces, all the worse for you: in one way or another, we shall go forward, because the people cannot be defeated. (P. 362)

DANIEL [RENÉ RAMOS LATOUR]:
LETTER TO CHE, SANTIAGO

December 18: The Washington-Moscow Polemic

. . . If I am answering your letter I do it out of the respect, admiration, and high opinion I have of you—which has not diminished in the slightest despite your words. Be that as it may, like you I would like to leave a written statement concerning my honor as a revolutionary, which is in no way inferior to yours or Fidel's or that of anyone else who has participated in this cruel struggle to liberate a people and orient it on its evolutionary path to a greater future.

I would like you to know also that anything that comes to us we consider addressed to the national directorate of the Movement, which is made up of a reduced number of comrades who strive for unity so there will be no autocratic decisions. For that reason your letter has also been read to the other members of the directorate and my answer is that of all the others.

With regard to the disdainful manner with which the material we sent was received, we must tell you that everything there is the result of the efforts of a large number of Cubans who have worked enthusiastically, facing great danger in order to get (first) money, and (later) the materials, and (still later) the transportation to move them to the Sierra. Our people moved that material right under the noses of hundreds and hundreds of soldiers, knowing all the time that if they were caught they would be murdered: we wouldn't have the luck to fall in combat in a heroic way because we don't have enough weapons for our own men. It's a shame, but many comrades have even given the bullets for their sidearms, weapons absolutely essential for them, weapons that would at least let them die fighting. It's painful to deprive these revolutionary and militant comrades of the 26 July Movement of their weapons, because they are in no way less revolutionary or militant than their colleagues in the Sierra. These weapons were only acquired through sacrifice and disciplined action—for example, our comrades at Mayarí, who overcame thousands of obstacles to get fourteen or fifteen rifles (some from an assault on an outpost, others from the *Corynthia* expedition), then gave them all to the Sierra. These same men then found themselves without weapons when they went to burn cane fields, having to face a vastly superior army. But this does not matter, because we stay here, against our own wishes, because we think it necessary. . . .

"The Salvation of the World"

I have known about your ideological background ever since I first met you and I have never had occasion to mention it. This is not the moment to argue about where "the salvation of the world" lies. I only want to leave testimony of my opinion, which, of course, is entirely different from yours. I don't think anyone on the directorate of the Movement can be called "right-wing." These are all men who want to free Cuba, to move forward the revolution that began in José Martí's political thought and that was frustrated by the intervention of the United States. Our basic differences lie in the fact that we are trying to put the governments of the tyrannized people of "our America" into the hands of those people. Once formed, those governments will band together and make themselves respected by the great powers.

Yankee Domination and Soviet Domination

We want a strong [Central] America, mistress of her own destiny, an America that can face the United States, Russia, China, or any other power that tries to attack its economic and political independence. On the other hand, people with your kind of ideological background think that the answer to our problems is to free ourselves from evil Yankee domination by means of a no less evil Soviet domination.

We believe that with the overthrow of the dictatorship of Fulgencio Batista *by means of the action of the people*, we shall be taking a step along the path we have marked out.

As far as I am concerned. I can tell you that I think of myself as a worker; I worked as a laborer until I gave up my living in order to join the revolutionary forces of the Sierra, abandoning at the same time my studies in social sciences and political law, which I had begun in order to prepare myself the better to serve my nation. I am a worker, but not one of those kind who fight in the Communist Party and who are greatly concerned with the problems of Hungary or Egypt, which they cannot solve, and are incapable of giving up their jobs in order to join a revolutionary process that has as its immediate goal the overthrow of this opprobrious dictatorship.

A Caudillo for All That

Let's talk about *unity*. Before the appearance of the 26 July Movement, I never fought in the ranks of any party or political organization. I renounced the Auténtico governments as immoral and I doubted the ability of the Ortodoxia to further the desires and aspirations of the Cuban people. I viewed the Ortodoxos as a group of men around a more or less well-intentioned caudillo— but a caudillo for all that—who had no well-defined program, no set doctrine.

I think that the dreadful coup of March 10 had as its only positive effect the elimination from Cuban public life of the cheap politicos who were in those parties.

The Pact between Fidel and Prío

Since I believed as I did, I could never be sympathetic to the pact between Fidel and Prío before November 30 and much less to the one that Felipe Pazos has attempted to make recently— which is much more negative, because he attempted to forge it precisely in the moments in which the 26 July Movement had rallied public opinion and had presented itself as the means for achieving all possible gains. This was also the moment in which the Batista government, forced by an increase in revolutionary activity, had to put into practice its most barbarous measures and to inaugurate the harshest press censorship in the history of Cuba, a clear proof of the weakness of the regime.

FIDEL CASTRO: LETTER TO CELIA SÁNCHEZ, FROM THE SIERRA

June 5, 1958

. . . When I saw the rockets they fired at Mario's house, I swore that the Americans would pay dearly for what they are doing here. When this war is over I shall begin a longer and greater war: the war I'll wage against them. I realize that this is my true destiny. (Pp. 471–73)

2. TERROR

FIDEL CASTRO: LETTER TO NATI REVUELTA, MARCH 23, 1954

. . . Robespierre was an idealist and an honorable man until his death. With the revolution in danger, the frontiers surrounded by enemies, traitors with daggers poised to stab him in the back, vacillators gumming up the works, it was necessary to be hard, inflexible, and severe. He had to sin on the side of excess, never on the side of moderation, because he might be the cause of total loss. A few months of terror were necessary to end a terror that had lasted centuries. Cuba needs many Robespierres. (*DRC,* p. 94)

FIDEL CASTRO ON EXECUTIONS, JUNE 1957

We executed very few people, very few indeed, throughout the course of the war. We didn't execute more than ten guys in twenty-five months. Out in the Escambray, Carreras executed thirty-three all by himself, and without fighting any war. For us to execute someone, it had to be a case of betrayal—a spy, for example. Carreras didn't execute people, he murdered them.

We really only shot traitors, and a couple of cases of people who committed rape. There was one man, a teacher, who carried off a peasant's wife. Then he went to the Jigüe zone, and he passed himself off as Che, so he could examine women. Then Che himself went to Jigüe and caught the teacher. At that time there was an outbreak of banditry; some people had extorted money and done other things, thirty men who had run into some prostitutes and had raped them. It turned out that the teacher was brought in at the same instant we were shooting the rapists. He came in and I just told him to get out. There was no trial: he was just pardoned, forgiven. (*DRC,* p. 245)

OFFICERS IMPRISONED AND SENTENCED
ALONG WITH HUBER MATOS

Captains: Miguel Ruiz Maceiras, Rosendo Lugo, Napoleón Bécquer, Roberto Cruz Zamora, Carlos Cabrera, José López Lago, Edgardo Bonet Rosell, José Martí Ballester, Vicente Rodríguez Camejo, Alberto Covas Álvarez, Miguel Crespo García, Rodosbaldo Llaurado Ramos, Elvio Rivera Limonta, Jesús A. Calunga, José Pérez Álamo, William Lobaina Galdós, Carlos Álvarez Ramírez, Dionisio Suárez Esquivel, M. Esquivel Ramos, Manuel Nieto y Nietos, Mario Santana Basulto, E. Cossío y Barandela.

JEAN-PAUL SARTRE

When the lights went on in that instant, they brought half a million faces out of the darkness. . . . In the darkness, under the lights of the Yankee electric company, Castro addressed the Yankees, declared them responsible for the sabotage, and challenged them: "You will not break us either through hunger or war. And if you attack us, you know we shall win." . . . That day something appeared in the glare of daylight: hatred. When *La Coubre* blew up, I discovered the hidden face of all revolutions, its dark face; the foreign threat felt *in anguish*. And I discovered Cuban anguish, because I suddenly shared it.

One has to have seen the ever alert joy of building and the anguish, the permanent fear that a stupid violence will break it all down. One has to have lived on the island and have loved it in order to understand that every Cuban at every moment feels two passions at the same time, and that one is increased by the other. . . .

After the sabotage, the Carnival festivals were suppressed, and there was a national fund-raising to buy arms and planes.

A few days before, the applause and shouts of the mass had revealed to me the revolutionary joy of renewing the festival of a national holiday. After the tragedy, the big cars still had their gaudy decorations, their exterior joy, but they passed through the dark streets with the slowness of a funeral cortège, and their loud music exploded amidst an anxious silence. ("Hurricane over Sugar," Havana, 1960)

3. THE 26 JULY MOVEMENT

FIDEL CASTRO: LETTER TO LUIS CONTE AGUERO, AUGUST 14, 1954, ON THE CULT OF PERSONALITY AND AMBITION

The greatest obstacles to the integration of such a movement are: cult of personality, group ambition, and caudillos. It is so difficult to have each man of value and prestige put his person at the service of a cause, a vehicle, an ideology, and a discipline, shedding his vanity and personal aspirations. First, I ought to organize the men of the 26 July Movement and turn the fighting men, those in exile, in prison, and on the street—more than eighty young men bound up in the same action of changing history and making sacrifices—into a compact, unbreakable unit. The importance of such a perfectly disciplined human nucleus constitutes an incalculable value in the process of creating fighting cadres for the rebel or civil organization. Of course, a great civil-political movement should count on the necessary force to conquer power, be it through peaceful or revolutionary means, or it runs the risk of being co-opted, as happened to the Ortodoxia, just two months before the election. . . . The conditions indispensable for the integration of a true civic movement are: ideology, discipline, and leadership. The three are essential, but leadership is absolutely necessary. I don't know if it was Napoleon who said that one bad general in war is worth twenty good ones. (*DRC,* pp. 106–7)

FIDEL CASTRO: LETTER TO CELIA SÁNCHEZ, FROM THE SIERRA

August 1957: "Everything for the Sierra"

Our motto from now on should be: *All rifles, all bullets, all supplies for the Sierra!*

When, after Uvero, in your presence I suggested to David [Salvador] that it was the right moment to open the Second Front, the process in this front had not developed as it has now. Then it seemed doubtful that a larger force could sustain itself here; today enormous perspectives are opening. We must fill the breach we have opened before we think about other possibilities. Perhaps in the future the opportunity for other fronts will present itself. (*DRC,* p. 298)

FIDEL CASTRO, MAY 26, 1958, ON A REBEL COMANDANTE IN HAVANA

Even though the Movement has numerous brave revolutionaries with battle experience, the naming of a comandante from our forces—which for us is a sacrifice from the military point of view— follows our intention of using the experience of our military campaigns in the development of a new battle strategy in Cuba. We are also striving to achieve the goal of an absolute identification between the comrades of the militia forces and the forces in operations of the 26 July Movement, coinciding with the establishment of a common general staff to plan and direct the action of all our military forces. (*Signed*) Fidel. [Fidel named Comandante Delio Gómez Ochoa principal leader of the 26 July Movement and ordered him to reorganize the Movement and to suspend underground activities. In fact, the military intervention liquidated the autonomy of the Movement.] (*DRC,* p. 446)

4. DIRECTORIO

Fidel's order to Che, Maffo, December 26: "Advance only with 26 July Movement Forces."

Che: I haven't got either the time to write you a long letter or facilities to do it—the only light I have comes from a lantern.

ON HAVING WON THE WAR

We have won the war: the enemy is crumbling everywhere: in Oriente we have ten thousand soldiers trapped. Those in Camagüey cannot escape. This is all the result of one single thing: our effort. You have to take this political aspect of the struggle into account in Las Villas as a fundamental matter.

For now, it is of the greatest importance that the advance toward Matanzas and Havana be carried out by the forces of the 26 July Movement. Camilo's column should be the vanguard and take over Havana when the dictatorship falls if we wish to avoid having the arms in the Columbia base given out to all the groups, which would create future problems for us. At this moment the situation in Las Villas is my main concern. I cannot understand why we should fall into the folly that was the principal reason why we sent you and Camilo to that province. It turns out now that when we could have taken it definitively, we are only making things worse. (*Signed*) Fidel Castro R. (*DRC,* p. 667)

FIDEL CASTRO, SANTIAGO DE CUBA, JANUARY 2, 1959, ON THE 26 JULY MOVEMENT

There is moreover another matter. The 26 July Movement is a majority movement, isn't that so? And how did the struggle end? When the tyranny fell, we had taken all of Oriente, Camagüey, almost all of Las Villas, Matanzas, and Pinar del Río. The struggle ended with the forces that had arrived at Las Villas, because we rebels had Comandante Camilo Cienfuegos and Comandante Guevara in Las Villas on January 1 because of the treason of Cantillo. Camilo Cienfuegos had the order to advance on Havana and to attack the Columbia base; Comandante Ernesto Guevara was in Las Villas also, with the order to advance on Havana and to take over La Cabaña and any other military installation of any importance. In the last analysis, we won because of our effort, experience, and organization. Does that mean that the others did not fight? No! Because we have all fought, just as the people have fought. There was no Sierra in Havana and yet the general strike was decisive for the complete triumph of the revolution. This is the only revolution in the world that has produced no generals. Not one, because the rank that I took and that my comrades gave me was that of comandante, and I have not changed it despite the fact that we have won lots of battles. I want to go on being a comandante. The first thing we—we who have brought about the revolution—have to ask ourselves is what our intentions were in doing it, if in any of us there lurks a secret ambition, an ignoble intention.

When people talk to me about columns, fronts, troops, I always start to think that our strongest column, our best troops, the only troops capable of winning the war on their own, were the people. A general can't do more than the people. An army can't do more than the people. People ask me which troops I prefer to command and I always answer that I prefer to command with the people. Because the people are invincible, and it was the people who won this war. We had no army.

The history of these two years of war is the history of a series of errors committed by our enemies: they consistently underestimated us. They thought they could fool the people, but they soon found that the revolution was stronger because of their betrayal than it would have been without it. I don't know if this man [Batista] thought we would stand around and do nothing. As soon as the situation materialized for overcoming him, it was over in ten hours. An extraordinary event has taken place in Cuba. (*DRC*, pp. 697, 709)

INTERVIEW WITH FIDEL CASTRO, TELEVISION STATION CMQ, JANUARY 1959

Luis Gómez Wangüemert: Last night, at the Columbia base, you said someone had stolen 500 rifles from a barracks. Do you think that problem has been resolved with the declarations made by the Directorio?

Fidel Castro: I don't think the problem can be resolved so easily, because words don't solve problems. I know many of the Directorio's fighters, who fought tooth and nail against the dictatorship. But today's declarations seem ambiguous and ill-intentioned. I don't attribute that attitude to the Directorio as a whole but to Mr. Faure Chomón, because he is profoundly hostile to the 26 July Movement.

Eduardo Alonso: These frictions between groups, could they be the result of a bad interpretation of the agreements among them?

Fidel: We have been remiss about the agreements precisely to avoid certain problems. I have always thought the revolution should be carried on by a single movement. If people talk now about a single party, why didn't they talk before about a single army? Isn't it true that you need unity more in war than in peace? (*R,* January 10, 1959)

Camilo Cienfuegos: Captain Chinea is going to talk with the Directorio comandantes Chomón and Cubelas about the San Antonio arms matter. There is a confusion here but no real friction.

5. GUERRILLA WARFARE

ERNESTO (CHE) GUEVARA: WHAT IS A GUERRILLA FIGHTER?

. . . Guerrilla war, you see, is not, as is commonly thought, a mini-war, a war by a minority group against a powerful army. No, guerrilla war is the war of the entire people against the dominant oppression. The guerrilla fighter is the people's armed vanguard, and the guerrilla army is made up of all the inhabitants of a region or a country. That is the basis of its power and its triumph, why, in the long or short run, it wins out over any power that tries to oppress it—that is, the base, the foundation, of the guerrilla war is the people.

It's impossible for small, armed groups—no matter how mobile they are, no matter how well they know the terrain—to survive the organized pursuit of a well-supplied army without that auxiliary help. (*R,* February 19, 1959)

6. ECONOMICS

Fidel Castro: We have demonstrated in a whole series of stories how a revolution against a modern army is impossible unless there is an economic crisis. (*R,* January 23, 1959, p. 13)

Che Guevara: A lack of industry in a country is a reason for calling that country underdeveloped, and there is no doubt that Cuba fits that description.

Now, we have to ask ourselves how it was that Cuba, an underdeveloped country, enjoyed in the past a flourishing situation—at least outwardly. This was the result of the climate and of the development of a single industry: sugar. Because of climate and the sugar industry, Cuba had some prosperity. The sugar industry reached the level of development it did because of U.S. investment, and in investing so much money, the Americans broke the very laws they gave to Cuba. (*R,* March 3, 1959)

Here is a partial list of the "owners" of Cuba:

Persons, Companies, Groups	PROPERTY IN CABALLERÍAS (1 CABALLERÍA = 13.42 HECTARES)
1. Cía. Atlantica del Golfo	19,251.6
2. Julio Lobo	14,894.4
3. Cuban Trading Co.	12,499.2
4. Cuban American Sugar Mill	10,822.2
5. Central Cunagua, S.A.	10,174.7
6. Sucesión Falla Gutiérrez	6,988.8
7. Nueva Cía. Azucarera Gómez Mena	6,950.3
8. Compañía Cubana	5,020.2
9. Miranda Sugar States	3,976.0
10. García Díaz y Cía.	3,976.0
11. Central Violeta Sugar Co.	3,679.5
12. Punta Alegre Sales Co.	3,470.4
13. Cía. Central Altagracia, S.A.	3,238.5
14. Santa Lucía Co., S.A.	3,062.3
15. Fernando de la Riva y Domínguez	2,962.4
16. Compañía Central Cuba, S.A.	2,926.9
17. Central Senado, S.A.	2,832.1
18. Agroindustrial de Quemados de Guines	2,548.0
19. Manuel Aspuru	2,489.2
20. Mamerto Luzarraga	2,096.3
21. Belona Sugar Co.	2,090.8
22. Central Australia (Bandes)	1,987.0
23. Cía. Azucarera Central Ramona	1,848.0
24. Central La Francia, S.A.	1,088.0
25. The remaining mills (70) of fewer than 1,000 each	57,288.5

TOTAL: 188,161.3

FIDEL CASTRO: SPEECH TO THE TWENTY-ONE
[LATIN-AMERICAN NATIONS], BUENOS AIRES

Latin America's economic development requires a financing of thirty thousand million dollars over a period of ten years. Only from the United States can we get such a sum and only through government financing. Political instability—tyranny—is not the result of underdevelopment but the cause of underdevelopment. The origin of our problems is economic in nature. (*R*, May 2)

MONTEVIDEO SPEECH

It has been demonstrated in Cuba that it is possible to have a revolution not inspired by hunger, without the army, and against the army. (*R*, May 6)

Cuba imports from the U.S.A. more than one hundred million dollars' worth of food products: fats, 26 million; cured meats, 8.5; milk products, 5; dried fruits, 8; other: fish, eggs, rice, wheat, chocolate, flour. INRA [Institute of Agrarian Reform]: We must import fewer food and consumer products and more machinery for production, such as tractors, factories (Oscar Pino Santos). Cuba loses one thousand million dollars in its import-export relationship with the U.S.A. (Fidel, *R*, May 15)

1958: Cuba exported to the U.S.A. $528 million but imported from the U.S.A. $546 million. Latin America's exports to the U.S.A. equal $3,768 million. Imports from the U.S.A. equal $4,467 million. The deficits of 1957 and 1958 are $450 million.

Antonio Núñez Jiménez (INRA): Cattle ranching takes up 70 percent of the surface of the national land, 3,000,000 caballerías, more than five million head of cattle. Only five thousand caballerías are under intensive cultivation. The ranchers: small cattle ranchers owning one or two caballerías come to about 70,000. There are also breeders, feeders, overseers, and agents. The sale of cattle is paralyzed for two months. There are more cattle out to pasture but less grass and drought. Half the cattle than before are sold. (*R,* September 23, 1959)

USSR OFFERS TO BUY 2,700,000 TONS OF SUGAR

Both parties discussed the problems created for the Cuban economy by the economic aggression of the United States. The Soviet Union agreed to take any possible measures to assure the supply of items of vital importance for the Cuban economy that cannot be obtained from other countries and also expressed its willingness to acquire two million seven hundred thousand tons of Cuban sugar in case the United States carries out its threat not to buy any more Cuban sugar. If the United States does buy any Cuban sugar, the Soviet Union would reduce its purchase by an identical amount, always taking into account the existing agreement it has with Cuba that obliges it to buy a million tons of Cuban sugar annually and to sell certain export products such as oil. (*R,* December 20, 1960)

DECLARATION OF THE MINISTRY OF COMMERCE OF THE GOVERNMENT OF CUBA

I

The information offered by the Embassy of the United States on the Cuban-Soviet Exchange Agreement has elicited the following observations: First: It is natural that the price the Soviet Union pays for Cuban sugar be that of the world market and not that paid by the United States, because the Soviet Union is part of the world market, not the U.S. market. All countries that buy Cuban sugar pay the world price, except the United States, which constitutes a market apart, with a different price, not arrived at through international agreements but by means of a separate law. Second: It is true that Cuba has on several occasions sold sugar to the Soviet Union at a price lower than the world price. But these discounts are privileges given not to the USSR, but to those countries that have bought in one lot a large quantity of sugar. . . . Fourth: It is true that Cuba receives more income from its exportation of sugar to the United States than it does from the world market. If the United States had bought at the world price, "Cuba would have received"—in the words of the U.S. embassy—"150 million dollars less in 1959." But the embassy should also have pointed out what would have been the effect, as much for U.S. producers of sugar as for the Cuban sugar industry, if the government of the United States were to break the quota system and pay the world price for sugar. Free trade and competition would eliminate domestic production in the United States, a production that today receives a high subsidy, and Cuba would be selling the United States not 3 million tons but 7 million tons, and the world price would not be what it currently is—3 cents—but much higher, because the world supply of sugar would decrease because of the elimination of inefficient and expensive producers. . . .

II

Sixth: The embassy of the United States is right when it affirms that "under the Cuban-Soviet Agreement the bulk of the income derived from sales to the Soviet Union must be spent on Soviet products." Cuba will possess a favorable amount of dollars in its balance of payments with the USSR in the amount of 20 percent of the total value of its exports to that country. Nevertheless, the embassy omitted this extremely important fact: Cuba spends on the purchase of U.S. products not only all its income derived from sales to the United States but also 20 percent more. In the last ten years, the balance of payments with the United States shows a negative figure on Cuba's side of $1,000 million. The balance with the Soviet Union would not be a deficit, but with the United States it is.

Cuba sells about 50 percent of its annual sugar production to the United States. Sales of Cuban sugar to the United States are limited by a quota, which is reduced from time to time. If Cuba wants to have harvests greater than 2,800,000 tons (the amount of the U.S. quota), it must seek other markets. Our sales to the world market also suffer from the limitations caused by self-supply programs in the buying nations.

Why lament the fact that Cuba has succeeded in opening a permanent market of a million tons of sugar with the Soviet Union? Those million tons are not taken away from the quota of the United States, but are derived from the production that exceeds the quantity sold to the United States. Cuba does not produce exclusively for the United States. (*R,* February 15, 1960)

SUGAR AGREEMENT

Fidel on Soviet Television

Khrushchev on the agreement on the price of sugar: The Soviet government and the government of the Republic of Cuba have arrived at a long-term commercial agreement. This agreement guarantees the security of the Cuban economy from the unfavorable consequences of the fluctuations of the price of sugar on the world market and from the economic sabotage of U.S. monopolies. It also broadens the possibility for planned, long-term development of the national economy of the Republic of Cuba and for the constant raising of the material well-being of the Cuban people. (*R,* January 22, 1964)

7. MISSILES

RUSSIAN MISSILES

Nikita Khrushchev [said that] "The imperialists are seriously mistaken if they think that the nations taking the path of independence are alone . . . the government of the USSR expresses its willingness to buy from Cuba, for delivery in 1960, the 700,000 tons of sugar the United States has refused to purchase." This was the first declaration of solidarity in the course of a week dedicated to a vigorous offering of friendship. Earlier, Khrushchev had asserted that if the United States attempted to intervene in Cuba it would have to deal with Soviet missiles. He affirmed that he was not interested in having bases in Cuba, as was being claimed in the United States, because Soviet missiles can hit a target at 13,000 kilometers' distance. (*R*, July 18, 1960)

8. RATIONING

NATIONAL MEETING ON PRODUCTION

Carlos Rafael Rodríguez: But in order for these things to come about, the national economy must run a profit, must earn, because if the basic branches of the economy are not cost-efficient, and the branches depend on the cost-efficiency of the profit of each business, then the national economy not only cannot finance those non-cost-efficient branches, but it itself cannot grow, develop, or advance.

Che Guevara: Now we are quickly going to review the work of the Ministry of Industries, in particular its weak elements.

We must emphasize errors, find them, and show them in the light of day in order to correct them as quickly as possible. And naturally, there are errors and great weaknesses in production. Some may be justified, but the important thing is not to justify the error but to keep it from being repeated.

In [the Ministry of] Industries, errors have been committed that have resulted in considerable scarcity in supplying the basic necessities of the people.

. . . But there are businesses and many comrades—and the Ministry has been weak in this—that identify quality with counter-revolution, that consider quality a capitalist vice and [feel] that in this socialist era it is not necessary to be concerned with quality. . . .

But the fact is, the people don't like certain things that do occur, and it is for that reason we are gathered here today: so they don't happen again. It is not a good thing, for example, that there be soap in Havana if there is no soap out in the country: if there is no soap in the country, there should be no soap in Havana . . . because some comrades think at times that you can just give anything to the people, that if you give them something no good, or just not good enough, or in insufficient quantities, or that if you don't keep up supplies and the people protest, then the people are counterrevolutionary. And that's just not true, not true at all. (Applause.)

Fidel Castro: . . . you can say that as far as national order is concerned, that in general we are right much more often than we are wrong.

. . . we have supply problems; this is due to the fact that our people increase their consumer capacity at the rate of 500 million pesos each year. . . .

People have forgotten *malanga*! This despite the fact that we have said that if there is nothing left to eat we will eat *malanga*. [*Malanga* is a farinaceous root widely consumed in Cuba; it sustained the rebels in the Sierra—Trans.]

[T]he scarcity of *malanga* caused an immediate pressure on sweet potatoes, and they began to run out. And then, with no *malanga* or sweet potatoes, and with enough potatoes left for normal consumption, potatoes too began to grow scarce. . . .

We have in our hands virtually all of the nation's resources.

Che: We said that we just can't blame everything on the increase in consumption. We have had problems in the areas where there has been a lack of production, a decrease in production . . . the increase in consumption has not been of such magnitude as to distort production totally. There have been, naturally, greater pressures because of the increase in consumption, but the reality is that there have been considerable and rapid decreases in production.

Santos Río, Chief of Production of the INRA (Institute of Agrarian Reform): It would be a good thing to point out that we think we are close to doubling the income of those agricultural workers involved in sugar cane who are working in cooperatives. Before, the estimated annual income of such a worker was $300.00. . . .

But in meat production we have gone to extremes. We find ourselves obliged every day to send thousands of fatted steers just for national consumption to the first twenty-five slaughterhouses. . . .

If the consumption of cattle in Cuba runs to a million head, and we don't have more than 781 thousand, we can march to disaster and in seven or eight years (or fewer, because the people are eating more and more) consume our entire stock.

9. FROM THE CHINESE SIDE

Che Guevara: What is all this about revisionism or even Trotskyism? Well, when we began to ask ourselves about these things— I don't know if there is any survivor of that era here now—well, they said: "He's a revisionist; we have to ask the Party about it, because it's a bad thing." That's where the problem began, and it was a violent matter. The Bible, which is the Manual, because unfortunately the Bible is not Marx's *Capital* here but the Manual instead . . . So people ask me: do you know this system? Really, I was already a little, let's see, I said to them: "I don't know that system here in the Soviet Union, but I do know it very well. In Cuba there was lots of it and in capitalist societies there is lots of it, because it's pure capitalism. . . . And in lots of other things I have expressed opinions that may be closer to the Chinese side: guerrilla warfare, the people's war, the development of all those things, voluntary labor, being opposed to material reward as a stimulus, all that series of things that the Chinese take up, and since they identify me with the budgetary system, all that stuff about Trotskyism gets mixed in. They say the Chinese, too, are nationalistic and Trotskyites, and I've been tarred with the same brush. (Look, I had some heated arguments of a scientific type over in Moscow . . .) (*Revolutionary Works*)

ABOUT THE AUTHOR

CARLOS FRANQUI was born in 1921 in Cuba to a peasant family on a sugar-cane plantation. As a teenager, he joined a group of working-class Communists in Cuba's Oriente Province and worked on *Hoy*, the Communist newspaper. He later broke with the Communists and joined Castro's rebellion against Batista. He lives in Italy with his wife.

ABOUT THE TRANSLATOR

ALFRED J. MACADAM lives in New York and teaches Latin-American literature at Barnard College and Columbia University. He is the author of *Modern Latin American Narratives: The Dream of Reason*. He has translated works by Jorge Luis Borges, Adolfo Bioy Casares, Severo Sarduy, and other contemporary Latin-American writers.